ven thinking the words *stage school* sent a
excitement rippling down her spine.

And it wasn't just *any* stage school. The
rick School of the Performing Arts in central
idon was only the most famous, the oldest, the
ierally-all-round-coolest-and-best stage school
the country, if not in the known universe. No
inder people called it . . . Superstar High. The
rrick had produced enough stars to fill a whole
w galaxy!

'This book was amazing! There is
not really much more that I can say about
it except WOW!'
Beth, 13

'I read it all in one weekend because
I enjoyed it so much'
Georgia, 10

Special thanks to Helen Moss

Superstar High

Star Friends

Isabella Cass

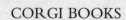

CORGI BOOKS

SUPERSTAR HIGH STORIES: STAR FRIENDS
A CORGI BOOK 978 0 552 56236 2

First published in Great Britain by Corgi Books,
an imprint of Random House Children's Books
A Random House Group Company

Series created and developed by Amber Caravéo
Copyright © Random House Children's Books, 2010

1 3 5 7 9 10 8 6 4 2

NOBODY'S ANGELS
First published in Great Britain by Corgi books, 2009
Copyright © Random House Children's Books, 2009

THE TIME OF YOUR LIFE
First published in Great Britain by Corgi books, 2009
Copyright © Random House Children's Books, 2009

The Random House Group Limited supports the Forest Stewardship Council (FSC), the leading international forest certification organization. All our titles that are printed on Greenpeace-approved FSC-certified paper carry the FSC logo. Our paper procurement policy can be found at www.rbooks.co.uk/environment.

Set in Bembo

Corgi Books are published by Random House Children's Books,
61–63 Uxbridge Road, London W5 5SA

www.**kids**at**randomhouse**.co.uk
www.**rbooks**.co.uk

Addresses for companies within The Random House Group Limited can be found at:
www.randomhouse.co.uk/offices.htm

THE RANDOM HOUSE GROUP Limited Reg. No. 954009

A CIP catalogue record for this book is available from the British Library.

Printed and bound in Great Britain by
CPI Bookmarque, Croydon, CR0 4TD

Nobody's Angels

Isabella Cass

For Grandma

CHAPTER ONE

Holly: Dreams, Puddles and Louis Vuitton

Holly Devenish had dreamed of this moment all her life.

Well, perhaps not this *precise* moment — she was wrestling her backpack out of the boot of the taxi — but for twelve years, four months and seventeen days she had dreamed of arriving to start her first term at stage school.

Even thinking the words *stage school* sent a thrill of excitement rippling down her spine.

And it wasn't just *any* stage school. The Garrick School of the Performing Arts in central London was only the most famous, the oldest, the generally-all-round-coolest-and-best stage school in the country, if not in the known universe. No wonder people called it . . . Superstar High. The Garrick had produced enough stars to fill a whole new galaxy!

As she gazed up at the grand school building, the rose-coloured brickwork glowing softly in the

September sunshine, Holly could still hardly believe her luck. If Miss Toft, her dance coach since she was a toddler in a tutu, hadn't secretly entered her for the 'Steps to the Stars' competition, this would never have been possible. The judging panel had included two dance teachers from the Garrick, and the prize was a scholarship to the famous school. The Garrick didn't admit students until Year Eight; so today Holly was just one of eighty twelve- and thirteen-year-old students arriving to begin their first year – and their new life – at Superstar High.

The backpack was wedged firmly against a holdall full of dance shoes and was refusing to budge. Mum had disappeared through the imposing double front doors of the school to let them know that Holly had arrived, and the taxi driver was nowhere to be seen. It was an enormous backpack – the kind a family of four might take for a month-long camping trip to Outer Mongolia. At a pinch, they'd probably be able to camp *in* the backpack.

Summoning up every ounce of strength in her petite, fine-boned frame, Holly grabbed the shoulder strap with both hands and gave an enormous heave.

'*Yes!*' she shouted as the backpack shot out of the boot and over her shoulder.

And crash–landed in a puddle the size of a small lake. *SPLASH!*

'*Eeeuuu-arggghhhh!*'

The sound was a cross between the dying squawk of a strangled parrot and the mating cry of a howler monkey. Hardly daring to look, Holly turned round.

On the far side of the puddle stood a matching set of luggage in soft beige leather: three suitcases, a vanity case and two hat-boxes. Muddy water was polka-dotted across every single one of them.

Not to mention the cream suede boots of their owner.

Very slowly Holly lifted her eyes from the boots to the face of the girl wearing them: a tall girl with ruler-straight blonde hair cut into a sharp bob. Her eyes were the cold blue of a gas flame. There was only one word to describe her expression: furious.

'I – I'm so sorry. It – it just came off in my hand . . .' Holly stammered, staring at the torn strip of canvas still clenched in her fist. She couldn't believe it! She'd been determined to leave her clumsiness behind when she started at the Garrick, and here she was, in the running for the Klutz of the Year award before she'd even got in the door!

'Sorry? Oh, you *will* be,' Furious Girl spat. 'That's *Louis Vuitton*!'

'Oh no! Where?' Holly gasped, looking round to see who else she had managed to drench. Then she realized the girl was referring to her designer suitcases. She felt a blush begin to creep across her face; although her skin was a dark caramel shade, she knew it wouldn't hide the fact that she was entering tomato territory.

'I don't suppose you have *any* idea how much this luggage *costs*,' Furious Girl snapped, 'but I'll be sending you the cleaning bill, you stupid, clumsy little—'

An even taller girl suddenly stepped out of a gleaming black Mercedes. She had golden hair in two long plaits under a black beret that was perfectly plain but somehow had *style* written all over it. She removed her designer sunglasses, took a sip from her bottle of mineral water and sized up the situation. 'Hey, girl, lucky they're only last year's design!' Style Girl spoke with the kind of punchy New York accent Holly recognized from American TV shows. 'Now, if it was *this* season's collection, I can see how you might be a *teensy* bit mad about it!'

'Yeah, *right*! Like you'd know what this season's Louis Vuitton looks like!' Furious Girl snarled. 'It's not even in the shops yet!'

Style Girl smiled and swept a perfectly manicured hand towards the tiny vanity case she was towing behind her. She stepped aside to reveal a set of matching luggage being stacked into a teetering mountain by a uniformed chauffeur and a large man in a brown cord suit and a turban. *So that's where my taxi driver got to*, Holly thought.

Holly wouldn't honestly have known the difference between this season's Louis Vuitton and last season's Topshop, but the look on Furious Girl's face left her in no doubt: the luggage mountain was the genuine article.

Raising one eyebrow a fraction, Style Girl smiled at Holly. 'Hello, how're you? I'm Belle Madison,' she said with a friendly, if slightly formal, handshake. Turning graciously towards Furious Girl, she held out her hand again. 'And you are . . .'

But the owner of last season's luggage had vanished.

'. . . really quite annoyed!' Holly answered on her behalf.

Belle grinned. She turned to the taxi driver and waved a ten-pound tip in front of his nose. He and the Mercedes' chauffeur scooped up the suitcases and staggered after her.

Holly watched in hushed admiration.

'Bianca Hayford,' said a voice.

'Er, sorry?' Holly muttered, suddenly noticing a

pretty red-haired girl, who was trying to lift Holly's marooned backpack out of the puddle.

'The drama-queen you just showered with muddy water,' the girl said. 'Her name's Bianca Hayford.'

'Er, is she a friend of yours?' Holly asked.

'Oh, now, do I look like I'd have a friend who only uses *last year's* Louis Vuitton?' the girl replied. Then she threw back her head, catching sparks of sunshine in her flame-red curls, and laughed a bubbling, throaty laugh. 'Just kidding!' she said. 'I saw the name tags on those fancy designer bags of hers.'

This girl is seriously glamorous, Holly thought, gazing at her new friend, who was wearing a figure-hugging black 1950s dress, a fake-fur wrap and leather biker boots. *What's more, she actually has a figure for the dress to hug!* Holly thought enviously. She couldn't help glancing down at her own slim frame in its white T-shirt and skinny jeans. It was far from curvy!

'Well, come on then. Let's get your bag out of this puddle. Oh – my name's Cat. Catrin Wickham, if you want to be posh!' Cat spoke in a soft Irish accent. As she heaved at the backpack, drops of water flicked from it onto her dress and she broke out into that dangerously infectious laugh again. '*Eau de Puddle!* Everyone's wearing it this season!' she said.

Holly couldn't help laughing as she held out her hand politely and introduced herself. But Cat leaped across the puddle and engulfed her in a great big hug. Holly hugged her back. Usually she felt a little shy and awkward when she met new people, but somehow shyness didn't seem to be an option with Cat!

'Great to see you're making friends already!' Holly's mum called as she emerged from the school building.

And enemies! Holly thought, thinking of Furious Girl and hoping she wouldn't be running into her again for a very long time.

Somehow she didn't think she'd made it onto Bianca Hayford's Christmas card list.

CHAPTER TWO

Holly: Welcome to Superstar High!

'This is Lucy Cheng,' Holly's mother said, smiling as she introduced a slim Chinese girl in a tracksuit who'd followed her down the steps. 'She's in Year Ten here — she's going to look after you.'

Then, with a quick hug and a mumbled 'Love you,' she turned away to hide her tears and hurried back to the taxi. For a moment Holly longed to run after her — she'd never been away from home for more than a week before, let alone to boarding school, and she felt a little scared. But then she glanced at the flight of steps leading up to the front door. Each one was flanked by a pair of tiny trees in clay pots, expertly pruned into star shapes. *The Steps to the Stars!* Holly thought. She had worked so hard to get here. Dancing was her life!

The excitement was like a swarm of bees trying to burst out of her ribcage, and all thoughts of going home with her mum vanished. She knew she was right where she wanted to be.

'Ooh, can I come with you and see your room?' Cat asked. 'I've been here since the crack of dawn!' She chatted non-stop as they dragged Holly's bags up the steps. 'I can't wait to meet my roommate; she hasn't arrived yet. I wonder who you'll be sharing with . . .'

Holly followed Lucy and Cat into a huge, elegant entrance hall. The rich tones of the oak-panelled walls were highlighted by shafts of golden sunlight flooding through the high windows, which followed the curve of a grand, sweeping staircase to the floors above. Armchairs were clustered around coffee tables strewn with magazines. A group of students in Victorian costumes were sitting talking about a film shoot, while others poured themselves drinks from a watercooler in the corner. On the other side of the hallway there was a reception area, with pigeonholes, notice boards and a big old-fashioned desk.

And everywhere Holly looked, people were bustling purposefully from place to place, up and down the stairs, in and out of corridors, some carrying instrument cases, others with spotlights or micro-phones. The soundtrack was the *clatter-chatter-buzz* of shared activity.

Two girls in sweats and legwarmers were leaning on the banister doing quad-stretches while a third was talking into a mobile phone. Holly caught the spine-tingling words *audition* and *casting* and she couldn't wait to be part of it! She was crazy about all forms of dance – from classical ballet to Irish folk dancing – and she loved singing too. Her dream was to play starring roles in big West End and Broadway musicals – Roxy Hart in *Chicago*, Sandy in *Grease*, Baby in *Dirty Dancing* and this place, Superstar High, was her big chance!

Holly snapped out of her daydream as Lucy led her over to the reception desk, which was manned by a plump lady with a helmet of tightly curled white hair. She was sitting in a large, important-looking black leather swivel chair, and the name-badge on the lapel of her red-and-mauve-checked trouser suit announced that she was MRS N. A. BUTTERWORTH, SCHOOL SECRETARY.

'Hello, dear, welcome to the Garrick.' Mrs Butterworth smiled at Holly, patting her ample tartan-armoured chest with both hands as she reached for the glasses hanging on a gold chain around her neck. She settled the glasses on the tip of her powdered nose and peered over them at the computer screen. 'Devenish . . . Devenish . . . Ah yes, here we are. Room twenty-five!'

'Brilliant! That's next door to me,' Cat declared.

Before Holly could say anything, Mrs Butterworth suddenly swivelled her chair out from behind the desk and, with a quick shove, scooted halfway across the hall. 'Felix Baddeley! Ethan Reed!' she bellowed. 'Get over here, you big lardy lumps! Help this little lass upstairs with her bags!'

Two of the Victorian students hurried across to the desk, where Mrs Butterworth had returned to her position of command. She was obviously not a woman to be disobeyed. The boys grinned as they stood to attention and saluted.

The one Mrs Butterworth had addressed as Felix was sporting a Sherlock-Holmes-style cape, and a deer-stalker hat over a tangle of dreadlocks. The other, Ethan, was wearing breeches and a waistcoat. He reached up and peeled a bushy old-fashioned beard from his jaw. A *very* attractive jaw, Holly couldn't help noticing, in spite of the red marks left by the beard-glue. He had short dark hair, sea-green eyes, and a slightly lopsided smile.

'Ooh, he *smiled* at you, Holly,' Cat whispered, nudging Holly's elbow as they followed Lucy and the boys up several flights of stairs.

'Sshh! He'll hear you,' Holly told her. 'Anyway, he was just being polite. He smiled at everyone equally!'

'Some of us,' Cat said with a grin, 'more *equally* than others!'

'Here we are,' Lucy announced. '*Home sweet home!* Complete with Shreddie, the school cat,' she added, pointing to a colossal marmalade cat sitting like a security guard outside room twenty-five.

Holly stooped to tickle Shreddie's soft golden ears and then pushed open the door.

The light, cosy room was decorated in white and primrose, with cheerful yellow and orange accessories. The two beds were covered with cushions and throws, and beside each one was a study area with a bookshelf and desk, complete with an angle-poise lamp and a pile of fat new textbooks. The centre of the room contained a collection of beanbags, a sheepskin rug and a round coffee table topped by a vase of sunflowers.

Light flooded into the room from one large window, and sitting in the window seat, a tall girl in a white dressing gown was towel-drying her blonde hair, her feet resting on a small beige suitcase.

'Hey, *Belle!*' Holly called out, delighted that her roommate was someone she'd already met.

But the girl who looked up was not the ultra-cool and friendly American who'd rescued her from the unfortunate puddle-bomb incident. There was no mistaking those glacier-blue eyes.

Holly was sharing a room with . . .

Bianca Hayford.

CHAPTER THREE

Cat: A Lucky Escape

Cat watched in horror as Bianca fixed Holly with her icy stare.

'Oh, no, not Little Miss Clumsy!' Bianca said.

There was one of those long silences where everyone exchanges *significant* looks. At least, they do in films. In reality, Cat noticed, people usually just stared at their feet. Holly was *totally* mesmerized by her shoes right now! Just when it was starting to get really uncomfortable, Holly lifted her chin and stepped forward with a brave smile. 'Bianca, I'm sorry about your bags,' she said quietly, 'but it was an accident. Could you just get over it so that we can be friends?'

Wow! Holly is tougher than she looks, Cat thought. *She's like Maria in* The Sound of Music. Cat knew she would've *died* if she'd had to share with Bianca. Or thrown a hissy fit and demanded to switch rooms.

Confusion flickered across Bianca's face. She clearly wasn't used to people standing up to her. 'Well . . . just make sure it doesn't happen again. Oh, and two more things,' she added. 'First thing: *my* side – *your* side.' She gestured at the two halves of the room like an air stewardess indicating the emergency exits. 'Don't cross the line!'

Cat felt anger sizzling up inside her. Who did Bianca think she was, talking to Holly like that? She opened her mouth to protest.

'And the second thing?' Holly asked calmly, before Cat could get a word out.

'Don't let that cat in here!' Bianca hissed.

For a moment Cat thought that Bianca had singled her out for special attack. Then she realized that the other girl was pointing at Shreddie, who had nosed his way into the room.

'I have *allergies*!' Bianca explained.

Cat scooped Shreddie up and snuggled her chin into his fur. 'Come on, mate. Some people just don't appreciate us . . . See you later!' she mouthed to Holly, stepping gratefully out of the room. It seemed that Holly was more than capable of dealing with Bianca by herself!

When Cat pushed open the door of her own room next door a moment later, she did a double-take – and almost dropped Shreddie. It was the blonde-girl-plus-Vuitton-luggage combo all over again — except *this* blonde girl was standing on her head. 'Er, what are you doing?' Cat asked.

'*Sirsha-asana*,' the upside-down girl said.

Uh-oh, Cat thought. *Holly got the mean one, but I got the crazy one!*

'Yoga,' said the girl, lowering her legs. 'It's very relaxing.'

Cat recognized Belle Madison, the just-stepped-out-of-American-*Vogue* girl who'd saved Holly from the Wrath of Bianca.

Belle smiled warmly. 'Hey, roomy. Great to meet you!'

Cat grinned back and glanced around the room. Belle had already unpacked a shiny new laptop, a small electric keyboard, a mini-fridge and, most importantly, an enormous box of Belgian chocolates which was sitting on the coffee table.

'Welcome to room twenty-four.' Cat laughed with relief. Thinking of Holly, she felt she'd had a *very* lucky escape.

CHAPTER FOUR

Belle: Belgian Chocolates and True Confessions

'Shall we open those chocolates?' Belle asked as she settled down on the beanbags with Cat and Holly later that evening. 'They were on offer in Duty Free on the way over from New York and I couldn't resist them.'

'Hmm . . .' murmured Cat, pretending to think hard. 'Should we open the big box of Belgian chocolates or not? That's a difficult one! Oh, go on then, seeing as you're twisting my arm!'

'It'd be rude not to,' Holly agreed, grinning.

Cat reached over and started tearing off the cellophane.

Belle glanced happily around her room. It was smaller than she was used to, but bright and comfortable and prettily decorated in blues and turquoises. Her roommate, Cat, had already put up posters of glamorous 1950s movie stars like Marilyn Monroe and James Dean. And now Belle had her clothes hanging in the wardrobe, and her things arranged as she liked them.

It's all just perfect! she thought. *My first night at Superstar High! Sitting in my room chatting with new friends . . .*

They'd talked all through dinner already – but there was so much to talk *about*!

'We moved over to England from Dublin last year,' Cat was saying. 'My dad's a professor of ancient Irish history at Cambridge University. And my mum did a bit of film work years ago, so she was really keen for me to come here. I want to be a serious theatre actress, you know – the stage, the lights, the greasepaint. I can't believe I'm really here – at Superstar High!' She threw her hands in the air in celebration.

Holly smiled shyly. 'I'm just an ordinary girl from north London – my mum's a teacher and my stepdad's a gas-fitter,' she said. 'But I want to be a star! This is a dream come true for me!'

'Me too!' Belle agreed. 'I don't want much – just to be the greatest singer the world has ever seen!'

Holly and Cat both laughed. 'Whereabouts in America are you from?' Cat asked, unwrapping another chocolate.

Belle shrugged. 'Nowhere in particular. My parents

are both in show business and they're always travelling.' *Although not together*, she thought privately. Since her mom and dad separated when she was six, they had avoided even being in the same time zone. Belle had been shuffled between expensive apartments in New York and LA and luxury hotels in Europe. But she didn't want to talk about her celebrity parents. She hated to admit that her father was a famous film director and her mother a super-model. She didn't want anyone to think she was showing off.

'So I'm a bit of a nomad,' Belle continued. 'I don't have any siblings and I've always had private tutors and coaches – I've never even been to school before.'

'Wow!' Cat exclaimed. 'No school! How cool is that?'

'Not very!' Belle said wryly. 'It's just kind of *lonely*. I've never had any friends my own age.'

'That would be tough,' Holly said thoughtfully. 'I couldn't survive without my friends.'

'Yeah, me neither!' Cat agreed. 'Though the Garrick isn't like *normal* school. No uniform for a start. Whoever designed the uniform at my last school obviously didn't have red hair because it was pale grey and yellow! It made me look like the Corpse Bride . . .'

Belle sank back into her cushions, laughing. She was

having a such a great time! She was on the first rung of the magic ladder to singing stardom, *and* she had two amazing friends already! Cat was so funny and Holly was really sweet. Suddenly she felt the time was right to reveal her parents' identities – and get it over with. 'Er, I've got a confession to make . . .' she muttered.

'Ooh – you're a vampire?' Holly asked with a grin.

'Worse than that! It's my parents – they're—'

'Dirk Madison and Zoe Fairweather!' Cat finished for her matter-of-factly. 'I know! I overheard Bianca gossiping about it at dinner. She was telling everyone on her table what a "stuck-up cow" you are – and how her designer luggage wasn't good enough for you.'

A sick feeling churned in Belle's stomach. This was exactly what she had dreaded. Everyone would hate her before they even knew her! 'But I only said that thing about her luggage because she was being so mean to Holly,' she groaned. 'I'd never judge somebody by their luggage.'

'Phew!' Cat said. 'So I can bring my battered old cases out of hiding then.'

Holly threw a cushion at Cat. 'Don't worry, Belle. We're not going to let Bianca Hayford spoil Superstar High for us. Who cares what she says? We'll just rise above it!'

'R-i-i-i-i-s-e above it!' Cat echoed, standing on the bed and stretching out her arms like the wings of a soaring eagle.

'You're right.' Belle grinned, feeling her worries slip away, 'I am *so* rising above it!'

They were still chatting at nine o'clock, when Miss Candlemas, the housemistress, popped her head round the door, her broad frame swathed in bright printed fabrics and jangling with strings of beads. 'Hot chocolate delivery!' she announced, placing a tray on the coffee table. 'But don't expect room service every evening, gals! This is a first night only special! Own rooms by nine fifteen and lights out by ten please!'

Belle was asleep by 10.05!

CHAPTER FIVE

Cat: Mr Darcy and Star Quality

The next morning Cat heard Belle get out of bed. She forced open one eye and glimpsed her roommate slipping out of the door in co-ordinated pink running shorts and sports top. She glanced at her clock on the bedside table. It was 7 a.m. She *meant* to get up then too. She heard Belle come back in at 7.30. She *really, really* meant to get up then so that she'd have plenty of time to prepare for the tour of the school, which started at nine o'clock. In the end, of course, she leaped out of bed at 8.47, pulled on her trusty black mini-skirt and angora jumper and flew into the entrance hall, eye-liner in one hand, hairbrush in the other, with no breakfast and two minutes to spare.

Miss Candlemas was already handing out name-badges to the assembled students. 'Here,' Holly whispered, sneaking a piece of toast into Cat's hand. 'I was a bit late too. Do you want some of this?'

'Mm! Life-saver!' Cat mumbled through the

crumbs. *Holly's only known me a day and she can read my mind already!* she thought.

'Pop your name-badge on, dear,' Miss Candlemas chirped. 'Now, don't dilly-dally, people. Let's get this show on the road!'

'Move along now, campers,' a stocky, freckled boy with hair the colour of wet sand called out in a Scottish accent.

From the entrance hall 'at the heart of the original eighteenth-century building', they trooped into the dining room, with its ornately decorated ceiling and full-length windows. The serving area was tucked away at one end, and the long tables were covered in crisp white tablecloths. 'This was once the grand ballroom,' Miss Candlemas informed them.

Two ladies in hairnets and white aprons were tidying away after breakfast, but in Cat's imagination, Jane Austen heroines in ringlets and long dresses were dancing with handsome officers. Cat imagined herself there with them – she was Elizabeth Bennet in *Pride and Prejudice*. She had loved acting ever since she'd played Third Sheep in the school nativity play. Somehow she felt more real when she was in character than when she was being herself; even when she wasn't actually on stage, she was playing different roles in the virtual theatre in her head. 'Away with the fairies!' her dad called it.

Cat skipped a little step and held out her hand. 'Why, Mr Darcy, shall we dance?'

Oops, did I say that out loud? she wondered, hoping no one had noticed.

'How delightful to see you, Miss Bennet!'

Cat spun round to see who'd spoken. A skinny boy with wire-framed glasses and a floppy black fringe was grinning shyly back at her. She looked at his name-badge. It seemed that Nathan Almeida was a regular visitor to Fantasy World too! Cat smiled at him and winked – and then realized that the rest of the tour had moved on. She and Nathan grinned at each other and hurried after everyone else.

The tour snaked through the rest of the 'old school', taking in the common room, libraries, offices and function rooms, as well as the girls' accommodation upstairs. Then they followed Miss Candlemas through a door at the back of the hall into a pretty cobbled courtyard, making for the modern buildings arranged round the other three sides of the courtyard – through classrooms, state-of-the-art dance studios, recording studios and rehearsal rooms. 'Keep up!' Miss Candlemas called as she herded them round another shiny new block – this one housing the boys' rooms – and on to the sports centre.

'If you look to your right, campers, you'll see the Eiffel Tower,' the sandy-haired boy was saying, 'and to your left, the Taj Mahal . . .'

Cat peered across and read his name badge: NICK TAGGART.

Eventually they were ushered into the Redgrave, the school's purpose-built theatre. Cat loved all theatres, and the Redgrave was a beautiful one – she longed for the day when she could step out onto the elegant, curved stage and look out into a spellbound audience. The house lights were all on, illuminating the tiers of red plush seats. Cat breathed in the delicious theatre-smell of dust and nervous excitement, and sat down between Holly and Belle to watch the other new students file in for the welcome speeches.

Cat greeted Nathan Almeida with a friendly wave as he crept into the back row. Meanwhile Nick Taggart was goofing around with a bunch of other boys – Frankie Pellegrini, Zak Lomax and Mason Lee, according to their name-badges – pretending to be selling ice creams.

'Ice cream for you, miss?' Nick asked, plonking himself down in the seat next to Belle.

'Er, no, thank you,' Belle muttered politely.

'Ooh, go on,' Nick teased, imitating Belle's American accent and thrusting the imaginary tray of ice creams in her face. 'You know you want one! You're like totally drooooling for a Ben and Jerry's!'

'No, really I'm not!' Belle insisted, a little too loudly.

'Settle down, now!' warned one of the teachers, with a disapproving look at Belle and Nick.

'Uh-oh! Looks like we're on the Naughty Step already!' Nick grinned and tugged on one of Belle's long blonde plaits.

The boys all laughed, but Cat could see that Nick's in-your-face comedy routine was starting to freak Belle out. 'A white chocolate Magnum for me please,' she joked, to deflect his attention from her friend.

Belle looked relieved. 'What a dork!' she whispered.

Next, Bianca Hayford sashayed in, glancing around as if scanning for paparazzi. A serious-looking girl with wavy chestnut hair sat down next to her. 'That's Lettie Atkins,' Holly whispered. 'She called for Bianca this morning. They're friends from their old school.'

'*Lettie?*' Cat asked. 'Short for Lettuce?'

'Nicolette' – Holly grinned – 'but she said she got fed up with being called Knicker-ette. Some of the kids even called her Knickers!'

'Kids like Bianca probably! With friends like her, who'd need enemies?'

Everyone applauded as the principal strode onto the stage. James Fortune was still handsome – all crinkly blue eyes and white stubble – even though Cat thought he must be *ancient*. He'd been a famous actor-slash-heart-throb in the eighties. In fact, her mum had been downright *embarrassing* when they'd come for Cat's interview. She'd practically swooned when Mr Fortune arrived. She'd even started going on about how she'd been in a *Star Wars* movie.

'Oh, what part?' Mr Fortune had asked her, looking a little baffled. Cat's mum was only four feet some-thing, which obviously placed certain limits on the roles she could play.

'We filmed in California, of course . . .' Mum had muttered in response, suddenly keen to change the subject.

Mr Fortune had looked puzzled.

'Mum was an Ewok,' Cat had put in quietly, noticing the principal's stifled grin.

Her mother had glared at her. 'Of course, *some* people think the Ewoks were just glorified teddy bears!' she'd told him defensively. 'But there was a lot more to it than that, I'll have you know!'

Cat prayed silently that Mr Fortune had blanked the entire episode from his mind.

'Welcome to the Garrick School!' He took a moment to adjust the microphone. 'We study a balanced curriculum. Academic subjects in the mornings' – there was a groan from the audience at the word *academic* – 'and performing arts in the afternoons . . .' There was a loud cheer. 'As well as core lessons in singing, dancing and acting,' he continued, pacing up and down, hands clasped behind his back, 'each student has been enrolled in *advanced* classes according to their individual abilities. However' – he paused for dramatic effect – 'over the next few weeks, teachers will be observing lessons to identify students whose hidden talents we may have missed. If you work hard, you may be invited to join *additional* advanced classes after half-term.'

Cat felt her heart race. Although acting was her Big Thing, and she'd already been selected for advanced acting classes, she'd love to earn a place in advanced Latin American dance too!

'Finally' – Mr Fortune beamed – 'as you all know, the Garrick School is nicknamed Superstar High. But being a star is about more that just sparkling on the outside. True superstars shine on the *inside* too. You've all proved you have star potential. Our mission now is to help you develop into well-rounded people – who also happen to be performing arts professionals with that all-important *star quality*!'

CHAPTER SIX

Cat: First Impressions

It was Wednesday afternoon. Cat was on her way to the first dance class of term, trailing behind Holly and Belle. 'I wish we were starting with Latin dance,' she grumbled. 'I love salsa and cha-cha-cha! Anything with a bit of passion!' She paused to stomp out a series of flamboyant flamenco steps.

'Sorry, but the timetable clearly says, *Girls – ballet – all levels – Miss Morgan*,' Belle told her.

'Miss Morgan was a judge at the Steps to the Stars competition,' Holly added. 'She's great but she's really fierce!'

'Just what I need.' Cat grimaced. 'I did ballet when I was a kid, but I wasn't much good. I just don't like it really.'

'I love it,' Holly said. 'It's got everything – strength . . . grace . . . control . . .'

Miss Drusilla Morgan, head of the Dance Department, was waiting for them in the dance studio – a tiny wizened gnome of a woman in an old-fashioned black leotard, her white hair pulled back in a bun under a wide elastic hairband.

'Off with them!' she screeched, banging her stick on the floor as the girls stepped out from the changing room. 'No hiding under those dreadful T-shirts! I want a good look at you all today, before I split you up into ability groups – advanced, intermediate and . . .'

Complete no-hopers, Cat thought as she pulled her baggy black T-shirt over her head. She felt *way* out of her comfort-zone in her new navy leotard. She'd never felt particularly boob-heavy before, but now she was surrounded by girls the size of toothbrushes. She suddenly felt like a Yorkshire pudding in a pancake house.

'Hair up!' Miss Morgan yelled.

Cat had tethered her hair into a loose knot, but this obviously wasn't 'up' enough. Miss Morgan snatched a handful of curls and scraped them back, anchoring them to Cat's head with sharp little hair-grips which she plucked from her own hairband.

This must be what it feels like to have a face-lift, Cat thought.

As they started the barre exercises, Cat couldn't help comparing herself to the other girls as she worked through her *pliés* and *tendus*. She hated to admit it, but

Bianca Hayford was very good. Belle was all elegance and poise, of course. Gemma Dalrymple, a tall bronzed athletic-looking Australian girl, and Serena Quereshi, a petite Pakistani girl from Manchester, were also excellent ballerinas. But it was Holly who really stood out! Especially when they moved on to the faster *allegro* section; she was as graceful as a butterfly.

'*Magnifica*, Holly. *Che bellezza!*' Miss Morgan cried, clapping her hands as Holly executed another perfect *grand jeté*.

Cat wasn't entirely sure *why* her exclamations were in Italian. As far as she could tell, Drusilla Morgan was no more Italian than a tin of spaghetti hoops. But, whatever the reason, Cat definitely didn't bring out the Italian in her.

'Pull up! Bottom in! Shoulders down!' Miss Morgan told her as Cat took up her position on the back row for the *enchaînements*. 'You are not without talent, Catrin, but you must work! I want to see sweat!'

If I sweat any more I'll dissolve, Cat thought, exchanging a pained grin with Belle.

Cat remembered Holly's words – *strength, grace, control. That just about sums up everything I'm not!* she thought. She decided she'd just have to *act* the part of a dancer! She'd be Darcey Bussell in *Swan Lake*. No, she would be Holly! She imagined her body losing its curves, and her muscles becoming toned and lithe . . .

'That's much better, Catrin!' Miss Morgan shouted, smiling at her for the first time.

It was all going so well. She could be a butterfly too!

'*Bene!* Catrin' – Miss Morgan beamed – 'come to the front row! Now, tell me, what are the key qualities in a ballerina?'

Cat grinned. 'Ooh, I know this. *Strength, grace, control* . . .' she said.

There was a long silence. She looked up. Everyone was staring at her. What had she said? OK, she wasn't exactly the Einstein of the ballet world, but they were Holly's words and she was fairly sure Holly knew her stuff.

Next to her, Belle was desperately trying to communicate something with her eyebrows. Then Cat realized it wasn't *what* she'd said, it was the *way* she'd said it. She'd plunged so far into character that she'd accidentally answered in Holly's north London accent.

'Instead of *mocking* those with more talent than yourself, Catrin,' Miss Morgan shouted, banging her stick, 'you would do better to try and *learn* something from them.'

'I wasn't mock—' Cat started, but Miss Morgan had already moved on to the next sequence.

Behind her, she heard Bianca barely suppressing her sniggers. Suddenly she felt more like a big hairy caterpillar than a butterfly!

Thank the Lord the lesson isn't mixed, she thought; at least none of the boys were there to witness her public humiliation.

Cat glanced towards Holly at the end of the row, hoping her new friend hadn't been offended. Holly's shoulders were trembling. *Oh, no – she wasn't crying, was she?* Cat spent the rest of the lesson trying to catch Holly's eye. Finally they passed in a rapid *glissade* sequence across the studio. 'Sorry, I didn't mean to—' Cat mouthed.

'I know!' Holly whispered back, fighting to keep her composure as a snort of giggles escaped her.

'*Silenzio!*' screeched Miss Morgan. 'Ballet class is no place for idle chit-chat!'

'That went well then!' Cat sighed, grinning ruefully at Holly and Belle as they changed out of their dance clothes at the end of the class. 'It's so-o-o important to make a good first impression on the teachers, I always think!'

CHAPTER SEVEN

Holly: Butterflies and Cinderella

The only butterflies Holly felt as she entered Mr Grampian's acting class the next afternoon were the ones fluttering around in her stomach. Acting was her weakest link. She could get up on stage and dance any time. And singing was no problem either. But when it came to straight acting, she felt like a fish out of water. It was as if she were lost without a soundtrack. But she was determined to conquer her doubts and improve – she knew that to succeed in the competitive world of musical theatre she would need all three strings to her bow.

Leslie Grampian – or Hawk-man, as Holly thought of him – had a mane of flowing white hair and an alarmingly hooked beak-like nose. He also had a strange just-swallowed-the-dictionary style of speaking that meant that she wasn't always *entirely* sure what he was talking about. All of which just added to her anxiety. So when he asked them to get into groups of three and enact their own version of a 'five-minute fairy tale', Holly's butterflies went into overdrive.

'Ten minutes' brainstorming to formulate your scenario!' Mr Grampian called out.

'What's up, Hols?' Cat asked. 'You look as if you're about to be sick!'

'Just a bit nervous . . .' Holly muttered.

'OK then, you be Cinderella,' Belle said briskly. 'Nervous will be *perfect* for that part. Cat and I will be the Ugly Sisters. Cat, you be loud and I'll be—'

'Very, very bossy?' Cat suggested with a grin.

Belle's eyebrows quivered uncertainly.

'Cat was just kidding!' Holly explained. She'd noticed that in spite of her style and sophistication, Belle hadn't quite got to grips with some of the more basic everyday concepts of friendship – like *teasing*, for example. It was probably something to do with not having been to school; after all, being teased was one of the first lessons you learned there – along with tying your shoelaces and putting your hand up to go to the loo.

'Sorry, I'll wave a flag next time,' said Cat. 'Oh, and that was more kidding!' she added, holding her hands up in surrender.

Belle grinned and looked relieved.

Cat turned to Holly. 'Come on, then, Cinders. Let's get to work.'

'So, here's what we should do—' Belle began.

'Ooh, Belle thinks she's a big-shot director, *just like Daddy*!' Holly heard Bianca say loudly to her group. Cat and Belle had not missed the snide comment either.

'*R-i-i-i-sing* . . .' Holly started to whisper, and the other two joined in with a chorus of, '*R-i-i-i-sing above it!*' Cat added a discreet aeroplane-taking-off gesture with one hand.

'As I was saying . . .' Belle continued with a smile.

When it was their turn to perform to the class, Holly took her position and concentrated on sweeping ashes from a make-believe fire. When Belle marched into the imaginary kitchen and ordered her to iron her new Christian Lacroix dress, she jumped up and stammered her apologies for not having done it earlier. Then Cat flounced in, hair speedily back-combed into a bird's-nest tangle, a giant wart crafted from Blu-Tack in the middle of her nose. 'Cinders, what have you done with my goat-urine-and-thistle beauty cream?' she screamed, so loudly that Holly actually jumped, even though she knew that was what Cat was going to say.

'I haven't touched it!' Holly trembled. Ugly Sister

Cat took a sly glance at Holly's pretty face, then reached out a hand, as if unable to resist touching the soft skin. Then she ran her fingers over her own face. The class was silent as they watched the Ugly Sister sadly comparing her own grotesque complexion with Cinderella's natural beauty. Then they laughed again as Cat 'accidentally' kicked over the dustpan and told Holly to sweep it all up again.

Holly grinned with relief as the class applauded and Mr Grampian beamed. 'Excellent! Superlative characterization, all of you!'

But he singled Cat out for special praise. 'Splendid! That hint of poignant sadness in the middle of the comic performance was inspired!'

He's right, Holly thought. *Cat really is a brilliant actress.*

'Isn't Mr Grampian just the loveliest teacher in the entire Solar System?' Cat enthused as they left the class a little later.

'Maybe,' Holly said. She didn't feel *quite* as terrified of Hawk-man as she had at the start of the class, but she wasn't sure she'd stretch to *lovely*! She'd rather have Miss Morgan any day. 'Thanks for helping me out back there,' she added.

'You did fine, Hols.' Cat smiled and gave her a hug.

'You'll be winning Oscars before you know it!' Belle added.

'No, I think that'll be Cat's job.'

As they entered the main corridor, Holly paused to read a poster on the Drama Department notice board. 'Hey, Cat,' she said, 'you have got to try for this!'

Cat studied the poster: beneath a blood-soaked dagger were the words, MACBETH AUDITIONS NOW OPEN: YEARS 8–10.

'Yes, Catrin, your friend is indubitably correct. That would be a most auspicious decision!' Mr Grampian announced as he strode past, balancing an enormous tray of coffees.

Holly and Cat exchanged puzzled looks. 'Erm, *auspicious . . .*' Cat murmured. 'Does that mean it would be a good idea or a bad idea?'

Belle laughed. 'It means *You go for it, girl.*'

CHAPTER EIGHT

Cat: Algebra and Other Problems

It wasn't until Friday evening that Cat had a moment to herself. She snuggled down on her bed, laptop on her knee, to write an e-mail to her sister. *This place is amazing!* she typed. *It's like Disneyland and High School Musical rolled into one!*

Cat had never actually been to Disneyland. But neither had her eight-year-old sister, Fiona, so she allowed herself a little artistic licence. They'd both seen all the *High School Musical* films, of course – again and again.

My roommate is called Belle, Cat continued. *She's American and she wants to be a famous singer. And my other best friend, Holly, is a brilliant dancer . . .*

Cat stretched. Since Wednesday's ballet class she had felt as if she'd been in the scrum for the Irish rugby team. She stroked Shreddie, who – with blatant disregard for school rules – was curled up on her bed, kneading her maths book with his velvet paws. Which reminded Cat – she was *meant* to be doing homework. It was so unfair! The Garrick was a stage school – why did they have to study all these boring school subjects? It was Super*star* High, wasn't it? Not Super*nerd* High!

English was OK, but maths and science gave her brain pins and needles. Cat prised the book from Shreddie's claws and frowned at the algebra symbols. *She was Hermione Granger poring over a book of spells in Hogwarts' library: 'If X is equal to two Y squared . . .'* she chanted in an ultra-brainy voice, waving her pencil in the air like a wand.

It didn't help.

Cat sighed and gazed around the room. Her eyes lingered on the jumble of family photographs she'd pinned on her corkboard. A warm evening breeze ruffled the curtains at the open window. Voices drifted up from the courtyard far below. Someone somewhere was practising the violin.

Belle and Holly had gone off to the sports centre for a swim.

So here she was.

In her room.

By herself.

All alone.

Cat had thought it would be great fun living at

the Garrick, away from her batty mum, her dad – who was more at home in twelfth-century Ireland than twenty-first-century Cambridge – her noisy twin brothers and even Fiona. She adored her sister, but she could be hard work at times. And it *was* fun. She loved it. But she'd had no idea she'd miss her family so much!

The lump in Cat's throat suddenly bull-frogged into a sob.

And then another.

Belle and Holly would be back soon, she realized. She couldn't let them see her like this. *She was good old Cat – the life and soul of the party!*

Chin up, old bean! Let's have none of this blubbing, she chided herself in her best *Malory Towers* voice. But it was no use. She was *seriously* homesick. And now an image popped into her head of her little dog, Duffy, sitting waiting at the back door for her to come in from school.

Tears flowed down her cheeks and dropped onto Shreddie's fur. She loved life at Superstar High. But she *really* wanted to go home – just for a visit. If she left now, she could get a train and be there in a couple of hours . . .

CHAPTER NINE

Belle: Chlorine and Karaoke

At that moment Belle was climbing out of the swimming pool.

'Wow! That's what I call *class*!' came a boy's voice from the top of the steps.

Belle looked up to see a drop-dead-gorgeous boy with short dark hair and green eyes, chatting to the lifeguard.

She smiled, pleased at the compliment. It was the first time she'd worn her new white Versace bikini and she hadn't been sure it suited her.

'Smooth leg action,' the boy continued, 'nice strong arms . . .'

Hel-lo! Getting way too personal here! Belle thought.

'She breathes really well too,' the lifeguard agreed.

Belle had never considered breathing to be a particular skill – except in singing class, of course . . . That's when she realized they weren't even looking at her. They were watching Holly slicing through the water like a miniature torpedo in Speedo goggles.

Belle sighed as she blow-dried her hair in the changing room. Holly really was a good swimmer. And a great dancer too. And Cat was so lively and fun and such a talented actress. And their families sounded so nice and *normal*. She couldn't help feeling just a little bit jealous . . .

Wouldn't it be great to be noticed for something other than your designer clothes and your famous parents? she thought to herself.

Ever since she could remember, all Belle had wanted was to be a singer. And if there was anywhere that dream could come true, then it was here at Superstar High! Belle loved everything about the Garrick. OK, *almost* everything. Having to share a bathroom was proving a little hard to get used to. And then there was Bianca, of course . . .

One day, Belle thought, grinning at her reflection as the smell of scorched hair snapped her out of her reverie and made her turn off the hairdryer, *one day, people will look at me and they won't say, 'Isn't she Dirk Madison's daughter?' or 'Hey, her mom's Zoe Fairweather!' They'll say, 'Wow, that's Belle Madison, international singing superstar – La Diva!'*

Returning to her room, Belle put her bottle of

water and her purse down on the coffee table. Holly followed her in, and knocked them off with her swimming bag as she dived onto a beanbag, scattering drops of pool water from her soggy braids.

'I think I'll stick to yoga in future,' Belle said, hanging her towel neatly on the radiator.

Cat was sitting on her bed, wearing a satin bathrobe over a sparkly mini-dress. Her laptop was lying open next to her.

What's wrong with this picture? Belle wondered.

Cat was silent. Cat wasn't laughing . . . but Cat was always laughing!

Holly must have noticed it too. 'Hey, Cat?' she asked gently. 'Have you been crying?'

Cat swallowed hard and cracked a grin. 'Oh, no, of course not! It's just that I, erm . . . er . . . poked myself in the eye with my wand – erm, I mean *pencil*—'

'With your *wand*?' Belle asked incredulously.

But Cat was already acting out an over-the-top pantomime of stabbing herself in the eye – much to Shreddie's irritation. He jumped down from the bed and padded out of the room.

That wouldn't make both *eyes red, would it?* Belle thought. She followed Holly's glance towards the floor – a small holdall was spilling out its contents of underwear and make-up. 'Are you going somewh—?' Belle started to ask, but Holly stopped her with a don't-go-there kind of look. Then Belle noticed the family photograph that Cat was stuffing under her pillow. *Poor Cat! She must be homesick!* Belle realized. She'd never experienced homesickness but she could see that her friend was really suffering.

'Well, I know those algebra problems really suck, but blinding yourself to get out of doing them seems a little *drastic*!' Holly teased.

Belle was surprised for a moment that Holly – who was always so kind – was making a joke when Cat was clearly upset. But then she saw that it had worked perfectly. Cat grinned and started to look like her old self again.

'Yeah, come to the library with me before breakfast tomorrow and we'll work on them together,' Belle added, following Holly's lead and sitting down on the bed next to Cat.

Cat smiled gratefully. 'What is this *be-fore break-fast* of which you speak?' she asked, pretending to be puzzled. 'Unknown concept – cannot compute!'

Soon they were all rolling on the bed laughing; Belle could almost *see* her old vocal coach, Daphne, shaking her head in horror, 'All that cackling – you'll damage your larynx!' Daphne would have said. But, for now, Belle was prepared to live dangerously. Sometimes friends were more important than vocal cords.

'Right, I'm off to my room to get changed,' Holly announced a little while later. As she opened the door to leave, Belle heard a commotion in the corridor.

'That creature's lurking outside my room *again*!' Bianca yelled. 'Lettie, get rid of it!'

Belle peeped out of the door and smiled when she saw Shreddie curled up outside Bianca and Holly's room. Shreddie liked Cat because she allowed him on her bed. But for some unfathomable feline reason, he absolutely *adored* Bianca Hayford.

'Oh, look,' Bianca snorted, pointing at Belle and Holly, and then holding her nose. 'It's the Chlorine Doreens! They must have found a *puddle* to swim in! Or maybe Daddy's bought little Belle her own pool! Euurghh! The chlorine fumes are making me sick! Come on, Lettie, we need to start getting ready!'

Rise above it, Belle told herself. *Rise above it!*

Lettie giggled awkwardly, then picked Shreddie up and handed him to Holly, before following Bianca into her room.

'Get ready for what?' Holly murmured, hovering in the doorway.

'Personality of the Year awards?' Cat suggested from behind her.

'*Rise above it!*' Belle reminded her.

'Of course! It's the party! Tonight in the common room!' Cat exclaimed. 'I can't believe we forgot about it!' She ushered Holly back into the room, slamming the door shut behind her.

Belle felt a sudden tingle of anticipation – she'd attended hundreds of film premieres, fashion shows and receptions, but she'd never been to a school party before. She couldn't wait!

'I'm not really dressed for a party' – Holly hesitated – 'and I can't go back to my room and change now. Bianca'll start going on about the chlorine again. She calls it "chemical warfare"!'

Holly's so petite and pretty that she always looks great, Belle thought. But she could see that the damp-tracksuit-and-slipper-socks combo was probably not her *best* look. 'No problem!' She handed Holly a pink Abercrombie & Fitch T-shirt and some cropped jeans from her wardrobe. 'Try these!'

'And the best thing is,' Cat added, 'they've got a karaoke machine!'

'*Auspicious!*' Holly grinned as she pulled on the clothes. The jeans were full-length on her, and slipping off her hips.

'Here, use this . . .' Belle gave her a leather belt with a big silver buckle.

'And these would look great on you!' Cat added, throwing Holly a pair of chunky silver bangles.

Belle picked out her favourite jeans and a simple white Stella McCartney top for herself. Then she smoothed her hair with straightening irons. Meanwhile Cat was accessorizing her black mini-dress with black tights and zebra-print stilettos. Belle pretended not to notice as she retrieved her make-up bag from the half-packed holdall, before kicking it out of sight under the bed.

'Well, what are we waiting for?' Cat cried, gathering her hair into a messy up-do and applying a final slick of lip gloss. 'It's Friday night! Let's *par*-tay!' She threw her arms around Belle and Holly and conga-danced them out of the door. 'Forget Girls Aloud! Never mind The Sugababes! Make way for the Chlorine Doreens!'

Holly laughed. 'That must be the worst name for a girl band I've ever heard!'

And this, Belle thought, *is the best Friday night I've ever had. And the party hasn't even started yet!*

★　★　★

The end-of-first-week party was a Garrick tradition. The older students organized it every year to welcome the new intake. They'd transformed the common room with disco lights and mirror balls and provided food and drinks. Belle helped herself to a mineral water while Cat grabbed a Fanta and a handful of peanuts. Holly was already on the dance floor.

Belle wasn't surprised to see Nick Taggart and his friends already up at the karaoke machine, belting out *Bohemian Rhapsody*. She cringed as Nick winked at her a few minutes later. 'This is for our American *belle* of the ball!' he shouted, launching into Bruce Springsteen's *Born in the USA*.

'Not sure about this music!' Holly grimaced, tripping over Belle's foot as she stepped off the dance floor and helped herself to Cat's Fanta.

'Come on, we've got to do *something* to stop these guys hogging the karaoke all night.' Cat pulled Holly and Belle along with her. 'Belle, you choose!'

Belle studied the song choices on the screen of the karaoke machine. She'd never sung with Cat and Holly before, so she picked something everyone would know. Abba was always a good bet.

She needn't have worried. The girls complemented

each other perfectly. Cat's voice was husky and powerful, while Holly had the sweet tone of a choir girl. They absolutely nailed *Dancing Queen*. Belle saw all the students flood onto the dance floor – except for Nathan Almeida and Lettie Atkins, who watched quietly from the back.

There was wild applause, then shouts for more. 'OK!' Cat laughed as they launched into an energetic version of *It's Raining Men*.

As the music faded out, Bianca Hayford marched up to the karaoke machine.

Holly smiled and handed her the microphone. 'Here, Bianca, you have a go!'

'About time too!' Bianca snapped.

As Bianca started singing *My Heart Will Go On*, Belle listened in stunned silence. *Wow! Bianca can* really *sing!* she thought. *How can such a bitter person have such a sweet voice?*

Belle was listening so intently that it was a moment before she tuned in to the mumble of discontent around her. The students were all standing around the edges of the empty dance floor.

'Her heart's going on . . . and on . . . and on . . .' Zak muttered to Frankie, Mason and Nick.

Belle turned to look at the boys standing behind

her. 'What's the problem?' she asked. 'Bianca has an *awesome* voice . . .'

'It's a time-and-a-place thing!' Frankie explained. 'It's *way* too early for a slow ballad!'

'Yeah, we're *Stokaboka*, man!' Zak wailed. 'We've got our dancing pants on!'

Belle glanced down. Zak was wearing a pair of baggy Bermuda shorts. With his long sun-streaked hair and deep tan, Zak Lomax looked – and sounded – like a surf-dude waiting for the next big wave.

'Yeah, come on, girls. Let's get this party back on track.' Nick flung his arms round Belle, Cat and Holly and marched them towards the karaoke machine.

Belle protested – but she had to admit, if only to herself, that in fact she was *dying* to get back to the karaoke machine with Holly and Cat. This time they sang *Girls Just Wanna Have Fun*. Belle watched in delight as the dance floor filled up again and Nick gave her a big thumbs-up sign.

Was he laughing at her? Belle wondered. It was hard to tell. But one thing was for sure: he really was a bit of a dork!

When the track ended, Belle high-fived triumphantly with her two friends.

Cat laughed. 'Wow! That was fun!'

'Brilliant!' Holly agreed.

Their eyes were sparkling with exhilaration; Belle couldn't remember ever feeling this alive! Singing with Holly and Cat was amazing! It was as if someone had just turned the volume control on her life up to maximum.

'Awesome!' she gasped through the grip of Cat's bear hug. So awesome, in fact, that it had given her a truly *awesome* idea . . .

CHAPTER TEN

Belle: Harmony and the Class Clown

Over the weekend Belle was so busy, she decided she'd better keep her truly awesome idea to herself. At least for now.

They'd already been given piles of homework, and she stayed up late on Sunday night finishing a science report on electrical circuits.

Now it was Monday afternoon and Mr Garcia's singing class was drawing to a close. They'd been working on vocal harmony. Belle had enjoyed the lesson, but as they sat in a circle in the warm studio, with the rain drumming rhythmically on the windows, she started to feel v-e-r-y, v-e-r-y s-l-e-e-p-y . . .

'So you'll need to work with a partner for this assignment . . .' Mr Garcia's deep voice rumbled.

Belle shook herself and sat up straight. *Where am I? Assignment? What assignment?*

'Belle, will you be my partner?' Nick Taggart had thrown himself at her feet, landing on bended knee as if proposing marriage. 'Say you will or my heart will break in two!' he begged.

'Fabulous idea!' Mr Garcia boomed, rubbing his gleaming bald mahogany-brown head as if to polish it further. 'Nick and Belle, you should be able to come up with something really interesting!'

'Oh, yeah, *really* interesting!' Bianca Hayford muttered.

'I'm a little shaky on the details of this assignment,' Belle whispered to Holly and Cat as they stacked away the chairs. She was *not* going to admit, even to her closest friends, that she'd fallen asleep in class.

Holly grinned. 'Yeah, I noticed you were *resting your eyes* for a moment there! Each pair has to pick a pop or rock song – then work out two-part harmonies and record them on a CD . . .'

'*By next week!*' Cat mouthed, her grey eyes wide with indignation.

'Howdy, pardner,' Nick drawled in an American accent, catching up with Belle as they left the studio. 'Let's mosey on down to the ole music library and pick ourselves out one helluva song.'

Belle nodded reluctantly, grimacing at Nick's Texan cowboy impression. In fact, she thought as she followed him to the music library, Nick's natural lilting Scottish accent was pretty much the only thing about him she liked. Belle took her singing very seriously, and she was quite sure that Nick did not. He was a loud-mouth and a show-off who spent all his time doing dumb voices and acting the class clown. And now she was stuck with him for an entire week.

'After you, ma'am!' Nick steered Belle through the door of the music library, where floor-to-ceiling shelves were crammed with CDs and musical scores. Several students were sitting at the computer stations in the centre of the room. Others were browsing along the shelves or listening to music through headphones in booths arranged along one side. Settling down at a free computer, Nick raked back his hair – so thick and straw-like, it reminded Belle of the thatched roofs of cottages she'd seen when she'd visited the English countryside – then jabbed expertly at the keyboard and pulled the library catalogue up on the screen. 'What'll it be, m'lady? Metallica? Kiss? Ice-T?'

An hour later Belle found Holly in the common room, eating toast and Marmite and chatting about ballet with a group of Year Ten girls, including Lucy Cheng. The common room, now restored to normal operation after the karaoke party, was furnished with big squashy easy chairs. There was a widescreen TV at one end and a kitchen area at the other. There was even a huge open fire for winter. The walls were covered with signed photographs of old Garrick students – who were now international superstars.

Belle joined Holly and started to fix herself a peanut butter and jelly sandwich. The older girls drifted off to the other end of the common room to watch TV.

'So, did you and Nick find a "helluva" song?' Holly asked her.

'No way! He's into all kinds of wacko heavy metal stuff. I just don't get it! Why was he so keen to work with me?'

'Duh!' Holly laughed. 'Maybe it's the fact that you're the best singer in the class *by miles*. And, oh yeah, perhaps because he fancies you!'

'*Fancies* me?' Belle asked.

'You know, has a crush on you . . . wants to go out with you . . . ?'

'I know what it means! But Nick Taggart? He's such a . . . clown!'

'Well, clowns have feelings too,' Holly replied.

'Anyway' – Belle frowned – 'Bianca is just as good a singer as I am. Why didn't he want to work with her?'

'Hel-lo!' Holly said, giggling. 'Nick may be a clown but he's not completely *insane!*'

'Oh, look, here's Cat.' Belle changed the subject from the deeply unpleasant notion of Nick Taggart *fancying* her. Her idea of the perfect guy was a tall dark handsome Johnny Depp look-alike: cool, sophisticated – and with a singing voice to die for, of course. Nick Taggart most certainly did not fit the bill!

Cat was with Nathan Almeida. They were both carrying piles of books and laughing, but Nathan stopped short when he saw the other girls and immediately started sidling towards the door. Belle smiled; Nathan was from Mexico, but he was a million miles away from her carnival-and-fiesta-party-animal image of a Latin American guy. To say that Nathan was *shy* would be like saying that Mariah Carey was an *OK* singer. The only person who'd broken through his shell was Cat.

'Nathan's going to help me with my electric circuits!' Cat said, helping herself to toast. 'Mrs Salmon threatened me with a detention or instant death or something if I don't hand that report in tomorrow!'

'And I'm sure The Fish won't let you off the hook!' Holly joked.

Those circuits have a lot to answer for, Belle thought.

If she'd not stayed up working on them until midnight she wouldn't have fallen asleep in the singing class and could have escaped being paired with Nick on the harmony assignment!

'We're off to the study room!' Cat waved as she shimmied out of the room, Nathan hot on her heels.

'He's supposed to be a very gifted actor,' Belle whispered, 'but I've never even heard him speak, let alone act.'

'Maybe he's a mime artist?' Holly said, performing a brief attempting-to-escape-from-a-glass-box mime.

Belle grinned. 'Boys! Are they *all* weird or is it just the ones *we* know?'

CHAPTER ELEVEN

Holly: Pirouettes and the Kiss of Life

Later on Monday afternoon Holly was leaving her room with her dance bag over her shoulder. She'd booked one of the small studios to practise her *pirouettes* with some of the other keen ballerinas. Miss Morgan had made it clear that all dancers should be putting in several hours' practice a week outside of lesson time, especially the 'elite' group, and Holly was determined to live up to expectations.

Holly had invited Belle and Cat to come along, of course, but Belle was busy working on her maths homework and Cat had also declined. In fact, her exact words were: 'I'd rather flush my head down the toilet . . .' Ballet was not flavour of the month with Cat!

Suddenly Bianca appeared in the corridor with Lettie and Mayu Tanaka. Mayu was Bianca's new best friend. With dark almond-shaped eyes and long black hair in ribbon-tied bunches, she looked as cute as one of those little Japanese Kimmi Dolls. But she had a lot in common with Bianca – a mean streak as wide as the M25, for one thing.

Holly's first instinct was to hide, but she forced herself to stand her ground. She'd seen bullies in action at her old school, and from the moment she'd realized she was sharing a room with one she'd made a conscious decision not to be intimidated. She deployed the Shield of Full-on Friendliness as her main defence.

'Anyone like to join me for some ballet practice?' she asked.

Lettie put down her cello case and looked as if she was about to accept. Although Lettie's speciality was music, Holly had noticed that she was also an excellent dancer. But Bianca spoke for all of them: 'Er, I don't *think* so!'

'Like we even need the extra practice!' Mayu sneered in her little-girl voice that should have been sweet but somehow always managed to sound bitchy.

'Yeah!' Lettie mumbled rather unconvincingly.

'OK, but if you change your mind, Lettie, I'll be in studio seven,' Holly called over her shoulder as she hurried off down the corridor.

Some time later, Holly glanced at the clock and nearly jumped out of her skin – which would have been tricky, as she was standing on one leg with the other foot tucked in behind her knee.

It was twenty-five past seven! Everyone else had left, but Holly was still in the dance studio. After almost two hours she was snapping her *pirouettes* round so fast that she was in danger of getting whiplash. Something magical always happened when she was dancing: she shook off the clumsy-klutz Holly of the everyday world and shifted into a completely different dimension.

And she always lost track of time.

Holly gazed into the mirror-wall behind the barre. It was not a pretty sight: face shining with sweat, her hairband fighting a losing battle with her braids. And people thought that ballet was such a ladylike pursuit!

If you don't get to the dining hall in the next five minutes, you'll miss dinner, she told her reflection.

And Monday was pizza-and-salad-bar night. Her favourite!

Figuring that a rush to the dining room would be as good as a warm-down, she tore off her ballet shoes, pulled on sweat pants and stuffed her feet into trainers. It was now 7.26. She helter-skeltered down the stairs, elbowing her way through a group of students and instrument cases. Taking the last five steps in a single bound, Holly propelled herself through the double doors into the courtyard. She banked sharply round the corner and sprinted towards the back door of the entrance hall.

Suddenly she was burying her head in a football shirt.

She was flying backwards through the air.

She was landing on the path on her derrière.

Holly cracked open one eye and saw a flurry of pages drifting down around her, followed by a muddy football, which landed – *smack* – in the middle of her forehead.

Ow! That really hurt! Holly thought, but she was too winded even to groan.

'Great block tackle!' a boy's voice was saying somewhere. 'We could do with her in our back four!'

'Yeah, she'd do better than you!' someone laughed, as if from a great distance.

Holly struggled to sit up and focus on a face that was now only inches away. Short dark hair. Sea-green eyes. Square jaw. Hang on, she recognized that jaw. It was the one that had once worn the Victorian beard. It belonged to Ethan Reed. She'd noticed him at the swimming pool a few times too. Not just *noticed* him, in fact, but really *noticed* him . . .

He was absolutely stop-whatever-you're-doing-and-stare-till-your-eyes-pop-out gorgeous.

And, she'd heard – Ethan Reed being the kind of person people talked about *a lot* – that not only was he a brilliant actor; he was also a freestyle swimming champion *and* captain of the school football team – which explained the ball.

'Are you OK?' he asked.

And now he was gently touching her neck. *He must be feeling for a pulse*, Holly thought. *Oh, no! He'll try the kiss of life next if I'm not careful!*

'Don't kiss me, I'm alive!' she squeaked.

Ethan laughed. 'Yeah, I usually only kiss dead girls!' he said.

Oh, brilliant! Holly berated herself. *Congratulations, Miss Holly Devenish, Idiot of the Year.* Not content with head-butting Ethan Reed in the chest, she had now addressed him with the single most stupid sentence ever to be uttered in the entire history of mankind: *Don't kiss me, I'm alive.*

If she lived to be a hundred, she knew that sentence would haunt her for the rest of her life.

'I'm really sorry,' Ethan was saying, putting his arm around her shoulders to help her up. 'I didn't see you flying round the corner at the speed of light. I didn't *mean* to bombard you with footballs . . .'

'I only had four minutes—' Holly stopped. She was babbling again.

'Hey, I remember you!' Ethan said. 'It's Holly, isn't it? We carried your bags upstairs on the first day of term.'

'Yes, that's right,' Holly mumbled. 'With your beard . . .' *Argh!* she screamed to herself. When exactly had she lost the ability to speak normally?

There was a pause while Ethan processed the *beard* part. 'Right!' He laughed. 'The Victorian costumes! We'd been doing a film shoot; a Christmas Special for CBBC.'

'Oh yeah!' said the other boy, who Holly now realized was Felix Baddeley. 'What on earth did you have in that backpack by the way? I was soaking by the time we got to your room.'

Could this encounter get any more humiliating? Holly wondered.

It could. And it did.

'And I've seen you in the pool too,' Ethan said. 'I didn't recognize you with your clothes on for a minute.'

Felix guffawed and Ethan paused, embarrassed. 'Sorry,' he said with a sheepish grin. 'That didn't come

out right! I haven't seen you with *no* clothes on –
obviously. I don't hang around spying through the
keyholes in the girls' changing room or anything like
that. I meant, I've seen you in your swimming costume
– I love your breathing—'

Am I hearing this right? Holly wondered. *Is Ethan
really talking complete and utter gibberish – just like me?
That's so sweet!*

'Er, guys,' Felix interrupted. 'I hate to break up the
party, but we need to get to the gym. Circuit training,
remember?'

'And I've got to get to dinner,' Holly mumbled.

'You'll have missed it now,' Ethan said, pulling her to
her feet. 'Here, take this,' he added, tugging a yellow-
napkin-wrapped item from his pocket. 'Piece of
pepperoni and anchovy pizza. I was saving it for
later.'

'Oh, no, I couldn't,' Holly gasped, eyeing the greasy
wedge of paper suspiciously.

'I insist!'

Very gingerly, Holly took the pizza and started
heading towards the double doors into the hall.

'Hope I bump into you again soon!' Ethan called
after her.

Holly opened the first door she came to. And

walked into a rack of cabbages. This wasn't the hall! She was in some kind of storeroom. After a few moments among the vegetables she stumbled across a door at the other end of the room.

To her relief, it opened into the entrance hall.

She felt wobbly and light-headed – especially when she remembered Ethan's sea-green eyes.

Must have really overdone it on the pirouettes, she thought.

CHAPTER TWELVE

Belle: Girls Just Wanna Have Fun

'It's not like Holly to miss dinner,' Belle mused as she and Cat left the dining room.

Cat sank into one of the big leather sofas in the entrance hall and propped her feet up on the table. 'Let's wait and see if she turns up. She probably just got carried away with her ballet!'

Belle could hear the stack of homework on her desk calling her name, but she was curious to know what Holly was up to – and she'd saved her a piece of pizza.

'OK, just for a moment then,' she agreed, perching on the sofa. After years of singing lessons and yoga, she'd got into the habit of sitting up straight. *Correct posture is essential for good singing technique*, her old singing teacher always said.

Suddenly Belle spotted Holly emerging from a door next to the dining room. She looked dazed and dishevelled, as if she'd been caught in a storm.

'Over here, Hols!' Cat yelled.

'What happened to you?' Belle asked.

'Oh, er, nothing . . . bit of a dizzy spell, that's all . . .' Holly murmured.

'Hmm,' said Cat suspiciously. 'So what were you doing in the kitchen storeroom, anyway?'

Holly flopped down in the middle of the sofa and put her trainer-clad feet up next to Cat's favourite zebra-print stilettos. 'Er . . . short cut!' she said.

There was definitely something odd about Holly this evening, Belle thought. She was usually so sensible and *grounded*. And what was that big splat of mud on her forehead?

'Are you feeling OK?' Belle asked, handing her the pizza she'd saved.

'Yeah, fine,' Holly replied absent-mindedly.

Belle noticed that she was already clutching a napkin-wrapped piece of pizza in her other hand. 'How did you get that?' she asked, but Holly wasn't listening.

'Feels like we've been here for ever, doesn't it?' she murmured dreamily. 'I can't believe it's only a week since we walked in through those doors – I thought the students sitting in here looked *so cool*. Now it's us!'

Cat laughed. 'Hey, *we're* cool!'

'Yeah, you bet!' Belle said. 'In fact, so cool, it's given me an idea . . .'

Belle's *awesome* idea had been burning a hole in her brain ever since the karaoke party. It had been so much fun, singing together with Cat and Holly. And judging by the cheers and calls for more, they had sounded pretty good too. So it was really an obvious move – *they should form a band*.

There was only one thing that had prevented Belle from sharing her idea with the other two before now: if she didn't score top marks in all her academic subjects, she would have to leave Superstar High!

Although Belle's father was a film director, he was dead set against her following him into showbiz. He said he'd *seen what the pressures of celebrity could do to people*, and he wanted Belle to train as a doctor or a lawyer. It had taken her months to persuade him to let her go to stage school rather than to a traditional boarding school. He had finally given in – on condition that Belle's grades at the end of the first term were all straight As.

Belle knew her friends thought she studied so hard because she was a natural-born egghead. They didn't know that her future at Superstar High depended on it. And that was why she couldn't afford to take time out to sing in a band.

But Belle had been *born to sing*! And they all wanted to be *performers*, didn't they? Surely they should get as much practice as possible. And Belle had always dreamed of forming her own girl group . . .

'Let's form a band!' she blurted out, unable to contain the thrill of the idea any longer. She would just have to set her alarm clock an hour earlier and *make* extra time.

'What? Us three?' Cat asked in amazement.

'Well, unless Victoria Beckham and Cheryl Cole just popped in . . .' Holly joked.

'Way-hay!' Cat shouted, stamping her feet up and down on the table.

Belle looked at her friends. They hadn't actually agreed. Perhaps they didn't want to be in a band. 'So, do you want to?' she asked nervously.

Cat and Holly exchanged looks. 'Of course we do!' Cat exclaimed. 'You didn't really think we'd say no, did you?'

Belle leaned back, suddenly feeling outrageously happy. She had two of the best friends in the world and they were all going to form a band!

Noticing that her gold Jimmy Choo sandals had somehow joined the other feet on the table, Belle started singing *Girls Just Wanna Have Fun*. Cat and Holly joined in, the three of them swaying from side to side in perfect time. As they finished the chorus, the girls clapped hands in a jubilant three-pronged high-five.

Belle was fizzing with joy. *We're really going to be a band!* she said to herself.

Then a fourth hand joined the high-five from behind the sofa.

A big, knuckly boy's hand.

Nick Taggart started trilling along in a high-pitched falsetto that even Belle had to admit was actually pretty impressive.

'So can I join the band?' he asked.

Belle looked at her friends for help. Surely they didn't want *boys* muscling their way into the band? Especially not Nick Taggart. He'd turn it into a comedy act!

Luckily Cat came to the rescue. 'It's – a – girl – band!' She spoke the words slowly, as if talking to a two-year-old.

'You know. For *girls*,' Holly added. 'The clue's in the name.'

'What do you mean, *girls*?' Nick pouted.

Cat giggled. 'Erm, d'you think there's maybe a

couple of things that your parents forgot to explain to you?'

Nick roared with laughter at that. Belle couldn't help joining in. Maybe he wasn't *quite* as annoying as she'd first thought. But she was still relieved he wasn't going to be joining the band!

She looked up and suddenly noticed that Bianca had come into the hall with Lettie and Mayu. They were leaning against the water-cooler, pretending to examine something fascinating on an iPod screen. It was obvious they were eavesdropping. Now Bianca looked up and grinned nastily.

'Ooh, look, Miss America is planning to start a band!' she taunted, fixing Belle with her laser-beam glare. 'It's the new Spice Girls – Spoiled Spice—'

'Spoiled Spice?' Bianca's words stabbed like a knife. Belle had almost got past worrying that everyone hated her because of her glamorous parents, but now the wound was re-opened. *Rise above it,* she told herself, but it wasn't working: *what if everyone really does think I'm spoiled?*

'Clumsy Spice,' Bianca went on, 'and Chubby Spice!'

Belle felt Cat flinch and momentarily forgot her own wounded feelings. Cat wasn't chubby! She just had a few more curves than most of the other girls. But that was a *good* thing – unless you wanted to be a high-fashion model! In fact, Belle knew from her mom that even super-models were getting fed up with the size-zero thing . . .

'Yeah,' smirked Mayu, pointing at Nick. 'And *Confused* Spice!'

'Young lady! How many times do I have to tell you?' The blood-curdling yell was accompanied by the unmistakable rattle of Mrs Butterworth, scooting across the hall in her swivel chair.

Belle, Cat and Holly guiltily snatched their feet off the coffee table. But, to their huge relief, neither they nor their feet were the target of Mrs B's wrath.

'Bianca Hayford! Yes, *you*, madam!'

Bianca's face switched from Snow-Queen white to glowing red.

'Park your backside on a chair if it needs a rest,' Mrs Butterworth scolded, skidding to a halt next to Nick Taggart. 'You'll break that water-cooler if you keep leaning on it like that!'

Bianca turned on her heel and flounced off.

'Ah, Miss Madison!' Mrs Butterworth exclaimed as she caught sight of Belle. 'I've just taken a phone message for you – from your father's personal assistant, dear. He'll be in London at the weekend. He'll meet you for tea at The Ritz on Sunday. How lovely!'

Cat and Holly were both smiling, looking slightly envious and very pleased for her, but all Belle felt was a wave of panic. There was only one reason she could think of why her dad would come to visit during term time. *He's changed his mind and decided to pull me out of Superstar High!* she panicked. Her dream of forming a band had been so close, she could almost touch it.

Now she was horribly afraid that it was over before it had even begun.

CHAPTER THIRTEEN

Cat: *Macbeth* and Original Material

Cat was in Mrs Salmon's Wednesday morning science class. Nathan – who'd appointed himself as her personal scientific adviser – had insisted they sit at the front. Belle was on her other side, frantically taking notes. The Fish (Holly's name for Mrs Salmon had stuck) was droning on: '. . . electric circuits, blah, homework must be in by tomorrow, resistors, volts, blah . . .'

Cat was busy arguing with herself about signing up for the *Macbeth* audition. She'd been thinking about it ever since they'd seen the poster in the Drama Department, and today was the deadline. *How can a newcomer like me hope to compete against all the older students?* she wondered. *But I so want to be part of it . . .*

At last the bell rang.

Right, Cat said to herself. *I've made up my mind.* She clapped shut her textbook and scraped back her chair.

'*One, two, three, eyes on me!*' Mrs Salmon slammed her

hands down on the desk. 'Did I *say* anyone could go yet?' The Fish's plump face had flushed from its usual shade of, well, *salmon-pink*, to a deep fuchsia.

One, two, three, eyes on me! Cat thought. *What was this, nursery school?*

'Catrin Wickham? Are you in a hurry to get somewhere more important?'

Cat decided that it was probably best not to answer that question truthfully. 'Er, no, miss. Sorry.'

Cat hurried to the Drama Department and found the *Macbeth* sign-up sheet. She imagined she was Keira Knightley signing autographs on the red carpet after another glittering premiere and began to sign with a flourish . . .

Kei— she wrote. Oops! She glanced over her shoulder to make sure no one had noticed, scribbled out ~~*Kei*~~ and wrote *Catrin Wickham*.

'Hello, Cat!'

Cat jumped as if she'd been caught with both hands in the biscuit jar. She whirled round to find herself nose to nose with Nathan. His hair was even more pudding-basin-like than usual today – like the detachable plastic hair of a PlayMobil figure. The way she described Nathan to herself, Cat thought, he sounded like a total geek-monster, but there was something oddly likeable about him.

'May I borrow your pen? I will sign up too.' Nathan had one of those soft voices you had to lean closer to hear, with just a trace of his native Spanish accent.

'Ah! Most commendable! Two exemplary students hitching their respective wagons to Mr Shakespeare's illustrious star,' Mr Grampian remarked, striding past with another huge tray of coffees.

Either he has a lot of friends or he has a serious caffeine habit, Cat thought. 'Don't ask me,' she laughed in reply to Nathan's blank look. 'I've no idea what he's on about either!'

Cat grabbed a cottage-cheese–and–celery sandwich from the dining room – since Bianca's Chubby Spice comment she'd switched from her usual cheese and salami – and joined Holly and Belle in one of the rehearsal studios in the new block, which they had booked for their first ever band practice.

Belle sat down at the piano in the corner and started to play the introduction to *Girls Just Wanna Have Fun*. The three of them improvised harmonies together while Cat picked at her sandwich (*Yuck! She hated cottage cheese and celery!*) and Holly figured out the controls on the state-of-the-art sound system.

Cat laughed. 'Whoa! You could fly a spaceship with all these flashing lights and buttons!' The world of technology was a total mystery to her, but luckily Holly seemed to know what she was doing and had soon hooked their MP3 players up to the speakers via the mixing desk.

'OK,' Belle said. 'Let's start by picking a variety of songs to sing along to – so we can get a feel for what works for us and what doesn't.'

Cat grinned at Holly, resisting the temptation to say *Aye-aye, Cap'n.* Belle could be a bit touchy on the whole bossiness issue – especially since Bianca's stupid Spoiled Spice comment. 'OK, as long as we start with *my* music collection!' she insisted. 'I've got some great stuff in here – Blondie, The Killers, the Foo Fighters . . .'

Holly pressed a button to start the first track and they began to sing.

Their voices sounded fantastic together, even though they were very different. Cat's voice wasn't perfect, she'd be the first to admit, and she couldn't always hit the high notes, but she captured the emotion in a song with a raw, bluesy sound. Holly had a sweet voice and a faultless sense of rhythm, which kept them in perfect time.

And Belle's voice? Well, Belle's voice was just un-be-liev-able! It was warm, powerful and subtle, with perfect pitch and the widest vocal range Cat had ever heard; it was hard not to be jealous!

After half an hour of rock, they moved on to Holly's selection of show tunes. 'Can we start with something from *Joseph*?' she pleaded. 'That was the first musical I ever saw. I was six!'

Cat smiled. 'Take it away, Hols!'

'How about *Any Dream Will Do*?' Belle suggested. 'I love that one!'

It wasn't the kind of music that Cat usually listened to, but she had to admit the songs were great fun to sing. And Belle gave her and Holly so many tips on how to get the most out of their voices that they were soon starting to sound really professional.

Cat laughed breathlessly. 'Wow! This is brilliant. We're going be the best band ever!'

'We *could* be a great band,' Belle said, her face suddenly clouding over, 'if we get the chance.'

'What do you mean?' Holly asked. 'This *is* our chance!'

'Oh, nothing,' Belle mumbled, sipping from her bottle of water.

Cat wasn't sure what she'd meant either, but Belle

wouldn't say any more. She was keen to keep practising, so Cat picked up Belle's iPod and started scrolling through the menu.

'Let's see what you've got on here,' she said. 'What shall we sing next?'

But before they could start, the bell rang for afternoon classes.

'Come on,' Holly urged. 'It's ballet. We don't want to be late for Miss Morgan – do we, Cat?'

Miss Morgan was waiting for them in the dance studio with the boys' ballet group in tow. But to Cat's delight, they weren't going to be doing ballet and Miss Morgan was only there to observe and to introduce a new, young and enthusiastic dance teacher. Sarah LeClair, she explained, had starred in several West End shows – until a badly broken ankle had ended her career as a professional dancer. *Hooray*, Cat thought. Not about the broken ankle, of course, but no ballet, no Miss Morgan and no butterfly-from-hell experience. Even better, they were working on jive – one of Cat's all-time favourite dances.

'OK, class!' Miss LeClair called. 'Finish your warm-ups and find a partner! Let's see how much jive you already know.'

Cat noticed Belle doing some very fancy footwork before the music even started – trying to position herself as far away from Nick Taggart as possible. Cat caught Holly's eye and grinned. They both thought Nick was hilarious, but Belle seemed to find his class-joker act confusing. She hadn't figured out yet that boys-doing-random-weird-stuff was just part of everyday school life – like lost property and detention.

Cat decided to help out: if Belle had to partner Nick on the dance floor as well as in the singing class, it could just drive her over the edge. 'Cat Wickham to the rescue!' she whispered to Holly as she charged across the room and grabbed Nick's arm.

As soon as *Rock Around the Clock* fired up, Cat realized that she and Nick were a great match – on the dance floor, that is! They jumped through catapults, yo-yos and pretzels with wild abandon.

Miss LeClair laughed. 'A little *too* wild perhaps!'

Zak and Holly were dancing up a storm. As usual, Zak looked as if he should have a surfboard in his arms, not a dance partner – but he was clearly one of the best male dancers in the year. Lettie and Bianca were jiving expertly with Frankie and Mason.

Meanwhile Belle was doing her best with Nathan,

who wore the petrified look of someone attempting to do a swing step with a man-eating tigress.

Nathan's a sweet guy, Cat thought, *but he isn't exactly Billy Elliot!* She couldn't imagine anyone she'd *less* want to rock around the clock with!

Cat was still humming *Rock Around the Clock* as she, Belle and Holly stopped at Mrs Butterworth's desk to return the rehearsal studio key.

'Been practising for the competition, have you, girls?' Mrs Butterworth asked, peering over her glasses.

'Sorry?' Cat asked. 'What competition?'

Mrs Butterworth scooted out from behind her desk and pointed to a new poster on the notice board.

TALENT COMPETITION

OCTOBER 20TH

WINNERS TO PERFORM AT THE

GARRICK SCHOOL, GALA CHARITY SHOWCASE

ORIGINAL MATERIAL ONLY

Cat laughed. 'We're not *that* crazy! That's only a few weeks away.'

'Indeed!' Mrs Butterworth smiled at her. 'It's really for the older students. They started practising before the summer holidays.' Then she executed a swift 180-degree spin in her chair and freewheeled back to her desk.

'Anyway,' added Holly, 'it says *original material*. We haven't got any of our own songs.'

'But why not?' Belle exclaimed suddenly. 'It's fun doing all the old songs, but is it really stretching us creatively?'

Cat exchanged a reality-check look with Holly. 'Er, Belle, we're in a band to *sing*,' she pointed out. 'If we wanted to stretch ourselves we'd have joined your yoga class!'

'Well, I think writing our own original material would be an awesome idea!' Belle's eyes had taken on a determined glint that Cat hadn't seen before. 'And the Gala Charity Showcase is a huge event. They have casting agents there and everything—'

'Exactly,' said Cat. 'This competition is a mega-massive deal! It's not just some little school talent show with a couple of kids squeaking *Somewhere Over the Rainbow* and doing a few magic tricks.'

'But this could be our one big chance!' Belle sighed.

What's with the one-big-chance thing? Cat wondered. Was Belle planning to lose her voice at the end of term or elope with Nick Taggart?

'Well, I suppose there's no harm in *trying*,' Holly said diplomatically.

'*Thank* you, Holly,' Belle said. 'So, it's agreed? We'll each write a song and bring it to the next rehearsal.'

'Which is on . . . Saturday morning!' Holly gulped.

'Two days? To *write a song*?' Cat spluttered.

'How hard can it be?' Belle asked. '*If* you put your mind to it,' she added.

'Thinking about entering the talent competition, are we?' came Bianca's mocking voice from behind them.

Cat turned to see Bianca, Lettie and Mayu strutting past on their way to dinner.

'Looks like they're having *musical differences*,' Bianca went on, looking Cat, Belle and Holly up and down as if they were some form of insect-life.

'Sorry, I must have missed it, but did anyone actually *ask* for your input?' Cat snapped, feeling her temper spark. She knew she was meant to be *rising above it*, and saw the warning look in Holly's eye. But sometimes *rising above Bianca* was just too much of a challenge!

Bianca flicked her hair, but she was too taken aback by Cat's unexpected retaliation to come up with a response. Mayu wasn't, though. 'Ooh! Stress-yyyy!' she giggled in her little-girl voice. 'Come on, let's leave them to discuss their *artistic direction*!'

Mayu had cute little dimples in her cheeks and wore a pink mini-skirt with socks pulled up over her knees, but beneath the surface she was as sharp as a razor – *like a toxic Dolly Mixture*, Cat thought.

Bianca, Mayu and Lettie linked arms and continued to sashay towards the dining room.

'*Actually*,' Cat heard herself call after them, 'we've already got a brilliant song that'll blow the competition right out of the water!'

Holly and Belle opened their mouths, but both seemed to have lost the power of speech.

Bianca, Lettie and Mayu stopped and turned. Cat felt a delicious moment of satisfaction when she saw the astonished looks on their faces.

Then reality kicked in.

Oops! she thought. *I've really gone and done it now!*

CHAPTER FOURTEEN

Cat: Hot-water Bottles and Ninja Teachers

How hard can it be to write a song?

Well, think of the most impossible thing that you've ever done, Cat said to herself. *Or, more accurately, not done (because it's impossible, duh!). Then double it.*

It was Saturday morning, and Cat had been trying to get into the creative zone for two whole days. Belle had been spending hours working at the piano in the music room. Holly had been using some compose-o-rama computer program that she'd found when she was checking out the recording software for their harmony project. Cat was equally good at playing the piano and using computer programs – she couldn't do either.

To make things worse, she had planned to go home this weekend. She'd really been looking forward to it. Although she'd recovered from last Friday's attack of killer homesickness as soon as Belle and Holly had returned from the pool and cheered her up, she was still really missing her family. But she didn't want to let the band down, so she'd decided to stay at school and write her song.

She couldn't believe that she was the one who'd gone and told Bianca and her crew that they *already had a song*!

How smart was *that*!

Not for the first time, Cat wished she could learn to think things through before opening her mouth!

So here she was, sitting on a bench in the courtyard, looking for inspiration. She watched as Owen Mitchell and Tabitha Langley, two super-popular Year Eleven students, strolled past a bed of late roses, hand in hand, staring dreamily into each other's eyes. Yes, that was it: *a boy . . . a girl . . . flowers . . . young love* – what could be better? Cat was just beginning to feel musically inspired when Tabitha tripped and fell flat on her face.

Bianca and Mayu hurried past, both in heavy make-up and dress-to-impress outfits, talking loudly about a screen test for a TV advert they were attending. 'How's that amazing song of yours, then?' Bianca asked over her shoulder – narrowly avoiding stepping on Shreddie, who was right behind her as usual.

'*Peachy*,' Cat replied, flashing them a big cheesy smile. 'Just peachy, thanks . . . Give her up, Shreddie,' she whispered as the cat hopped up onto the bench next to her, staring longingly after Bianca. 'She's not worth it!'

OK, romance isn't working for me, Cat thought, turning back to her notebook. *What about a rebellious punk-style no-one-understands-me-because-I-am-young-and-tormented kind of song? I can really relate to that just now!* She scowled, thinking herself into the part of Angry Young Woman. She was Amy Winehouse with toothache. Fists clenched, brows furrowed . . . *I hate everybody in the world*, she scrawled, almost ripping the paper—

'Hi, Cat!' came a cheerful call.

Cat looked up, lips still curled in a ferocious snarl, to see Serena Quereshi and Gemma Dalrymple.

'We're going to Café Roma for lunch. Want to come with us?' Serena asked. Then she saw Cat's expression. 'Hey, are you OK?'

'Oh, erm, yeah, fine,' Cat mumbled, trying to arrange her face into a smile while holding onto her inner rage. 'Bit of stomach ache, that's all!'

'I've got this really great hot-water bottle you can borrow,' Gemma offered sympathetically. It was hard to imagine Gemma ever having aches or pains; she always looked as if she'd just stepped out of an advert for something ultra-healthy like pro-biotic yoghurt or muesli.

'Er, no thanks, it's probably just indigestion,' Cat replied. *Which probably isn't far from the truth*, she thought; all the celery she was eating these days was definitely not doing her stomach any favours.

'No worries!' Gemma smiled before heading off with Serena.

So much for anger, Cat mused. *It's hard to hate the world when the world comes up and offers you its favourite hot-water bottle!*

She suddenly noticed The Fish beetling across the courtyard in her white lab coat and her sensible shoes. *Oh, no!* Cat had been hoping to sneak last week's electric circuits homework into Mrs Salmon's pigeon-hole under a pile of papers so she'd find it on Monday morning and assume she'd overlooked it on Friday. What did teachers think they were *doing* coming into school at the weekend?

Mrs Salmon glanced down at her watch. Cat seized her chance. She leaped off the bench and bolted through a door at the back of the old school.

She found herself, heart pounding, in a small dark room that smelled of vegetables and old pasta. Ah-ha! This must be the short cut through the kitchen store-room that Holly had found. She just needed to find the door at the other end and she would come out next to the dining room. Cat took a step back, feeling her way along a rack of potatoes and . . .

Aaargh! Oomph!

. . . backed straight into a person.

Had The Fish somehow leaped, Ninja-like, into the storeroom ahead of her?

No, this was a tall, solid, man-shaped person.

A light flicked on.

The person was none other than James Fortune, retired heart-throb and principal of Superstar High.

'Oh, er, yes, h-hello!' he stammered, his hand on the light switch. 'Just checking the, er, *supplies*. You know . . .'

In the dark? Cat thought. She didn't say it though. He *was* the principal after all. He could lurk in a store cupboard whenever he liked.

Mr Fortune must have realized how feeble his excuse sounded, because he suddenly laughed. 'Actually, truth be told, I was avoiding someone,' he confessed.

'It wasn't Mrs Salmon by any chance, was it?' Cat asked.

'Er, yes, indeed it was.' Mr Fortune smiled wryly. 'She's been wanting me to look at a report recommending extra science tests every term, and I just haven't got round to it yet.'

'Snap!' admitted Cat. 'Science homework. *Tiny* bit late.'

Mr Fortune crinkled those famous blue eyes as he smiled at Cat across a shelf of cauliflowers. 'Ah, yes – Catrin, isn't it? Your mother's the Ewok? Well, coast should be clear now, I believe. After you!'

Cat stepped out of the cupboard, back into the courtyard, blinking in the sunlight, while Mr Fortune used the other door and disappeared into the entrance hall.

It was time for the band rehearsal and she was still no nearer to having written a song.

And she really was going to have to try and get her homework in on time in future!

CHAPTER FIFTEEN

Holly: *Twinkle, Twinkle, Little Star*

When Holly arrived at the rehearsal studio for band practice, Cat was already waiting. 'How did you get on with your song?' Holly asked.

'Rubbish!' Cat replied, holding up a dog-eared sheet of notepaper.

Holly laughed. 'Er, *I hate everybody*?'

Cat crumpled the page into a ball and drop-kicked it into the wastepaper bin.

'Me too,' Holly sighed, opening her laptop. 'I've got something, but I don't think it's going to be the next Number One!'

Holly pressed *play*. A few bars of synthetic-sounding piano and guitar tinkled out.

'Hmm, it reminds me of something . . .' Cat said, tilting her head thoughtfully to one side.

'*You're the One That I Want?*' Holly suggested hopefully. 'From *Grease*? That was the sound I was aiming for.'

'Erm, no. It's more . . . *Twinkle, Twinkle, Little Star*,' Cat replied.

Holly felt a twinge of disappointment. It had taken her ages to get to grips with the complicated song-composing program, and she hadn't thought her song was all *that* bad – although, listening to it now, actually it did sound a bit tinkly . . . Yes, Cat was absolutely right – *Up above the world so high* . . .

She burst out laughing. 'Yeah, but it *is* the disco re-mix!'

When Belle hurried into the room, Cat and Holly were singing a hip-hop version of '. . . *like a diamond in the sky*,' tears of laughter streaming down their faces.

'Sorry I'm late,' Belle puffed, pulling sheets of manuscript paper out of her leather portfolio. 'I was working on the harmony project with Nick. I know he's a total dingbat, but he's a genius with that recording software – and he's got much better vocal technique than I would have thought—'

'Woo-hoo! Sounds like you and Nick are really *harmonizing* these days!' Cat teased, still giggling.

'It's weird – he *does* have a really good voice when he stops goofing around long enough to use it,' Belle said vaguely.

Belle didn't even twig that Cat was teasing her,

Holly realized. In fact, Belle had seemed a little not-really-with-us for the last few days, and there was an anxious crease across her forehead. *She's working too hard*, Holly thought. *At least it's Sunday tomorrow. We'll have a nice lazy morning, and then she's seeing her dad at The Ritz for tea. That'll be a good break for her.*

Belle sat down at the piano, cleared her throat and began to play her song.

It started slowly. Then it suddenly went all jazzy, with lots of *doo-wah-diddly-bop-bops* up and down the scale. Then it turned into a ballad with a soaring gospel chorus and a disco beat . . .

The individual parts were cleverly written and beautifully sung. But, Holly thought, it was trying to be too many things at the same time. It was as if Belle had stuffed one of her beautiful Louis Vuitton suitcases so full of her designer clothes that she had to jump up and down on it to get it closed.

Belle ended on a glass-shatteringly high note.

There was a moment's silence.

'You didn't like it,' she sighed, her voice flat with disappointment.

'Er, you controlled that last note beautifully,' Holly said, trying to be tactful. 'Was it a high C?'

Belle looked expectantly at Cat.

Holly was trying to channel her thoughts into Cat's head. *Say something nice!*

Cat smiled. 'It was a bit over the top. In fact, that song was so far over the top that if it looked down with a telescope it wouldn't even be able to *see* the top!'

Oh, no! Holly thought. *Why does Cat have to be so honest all the time?*

Belle looked as if she was about to cry.

'What Cat meant—' Holly started, in an attempt to smooth things over.

'I *know* what Cat meant!' Belle said quietly. 'So let's hear Cat's song.'

'Er, I haven't written one,' Cat mumbled.

'Why not?' Belle asked.

'I got a bit distracted,' Cat replied. 'I had a secret liaison with Mr Fortune in a storeroom, for a start, and then—'

'You're just not taking this seriously,' Belle interrupted in a dangerously quiet voice.

'Just because I'm not tearing my hair out doesn't mean I'm not taking it seriously!' Cat spluttered.

Belle glared at her. 'You've *never* wanted us to do original material, have you? You didn't even *try* to write a song.'

'I *have* tried!' Cat shouted, looking as if she was

about to explode or burst into tears. 'I didn't even go home for the weekend because I was trying to write a *stupid* song for the *stupid* talent competition.'

Holly hated arguments. She had vivid memories of cowering in her bedroom while her mum and dad yelled at each other downstairs. That was years ago, and things were fine now that Dad had left and Mum had married Steve, but Holly still couldn't bear confrontations, especially between people she loved. She had to step in and stop it! She put her arm round Cat's shoulders and smiled at Belle. 'Hey, come on, you guys. Don't fight,' she said. 'Let's go and get some lunch.'

They marched in prickly silence to return the rehearsal room key to Mrs Butterworth.

Belle sighed pitifully as they passed the talent competition poster. '*Original material only*. I guess we won't be entering after all.'

'Bianca and her mates are going to just *love* this,' Cat groaned.

'You never know' – Holly smiled bravely – 'we *might* come up with something . . .'

'Don't hold your breath!' Cat muttered.

Belle turned on her heel and stalked off up the stairs.

'Oh, no!' Cat grimaced, clenching her fists to her

temples. 'I feel like a complete *maggot* now. I didn't mean to upset her. But that song *was* terrible.'

'I know,' Holly replied sadly. 'But there's something else bothering Belle at the moment. I just wish I knew what it was.'

CHAPTER SIXTEEN

Belle: Chocolate Macaroons and Lizard's Legs

Afternoon tea at The Ritz – Belle had been dreading it all week. She hadn't told Cat and Holly about her fear that she would be whisked away from Superstar High. Somehow she'd been fooling herself that if she avoided thinking or talking about it, the terrible threat might just go away. To leave the Garrick would be *unbearable*.

But as she stepped out through the front doors of the school, Belle felt as if a balloon was inflating in her chest, about to pop at any moment. She couldn't face it alone! She ran back upstairs and asked Holly and Cat to go to The Ritz with her. Cat was already on her way out and declined the invitation a little stiffly, but Holly jumped at the chance.

'Ooh, what shall I wear?' she cried. 'This is so-o-o exciting!'

'But you've lived your whole life in London,' Belle said in surprise. 'You must have been to The Ritz hundreds of times!'

Holly smiled. 'Walthamstow isn't really the bit of London that you see on the postcards. The nearest I've been to The Ritz is a packet of Ritz Crackers!'

As the taxi pulled away into Kingsgrove Square, Belle leaned back and closed her eyes. Her head was throbbing. On top of worrying about her dad, she was also feeling terrible about her argument with Cat yesterday. Would Cat ever forgive her for being so mean? 'I don't think Cat wants to be my friend any more,' she said softly to Holly.

'Of course she still wants to be your friend!' Holly exclaimed incredulously. 'It was just a silly disagreement. The only reason she's not coming with us is that she promised Nathan she'd practise for the *Macbeth* auditions with him.'

'But I said some really dumb stuff to her . . .' Belle went on.

'That's what friends are *for*,' Holly explained. 'They stick with you even when you do stupid stuff. *Especially* when you do stupid stuff, in fact!'

'Are you sure?' Belle asked doubtfully.

'I'm sure!' Holly said firmly, giving Belle's hand a quick squeeze. 'And you have to admit that none of us are exactly Andrew Lloyd Webber when it comes to songwriting.'

'I guess not' – Belle groaned – 'but I so wanted to enter that competition! It may just be my last chance—'

'What do you mean?' Holly asked.

Belle sighed and stared out of the rain-streaked window at the grey, crowded streets. She couldn't keep it bottled up any longer. 'I think my dad wants to take me out of the Garrick and send me to a "real school",' she said quickly, struggling to hold back her tears.

'What?' Holly gasped. 'But you only just got here!'

'I know, but he wants me to go to a proper school so I can be a brain surgeon or a nuclear physicist – anything as long as it's not a performer.'

'But why?' Holly asked.

'He's terrified I'll become some kind of drug-crazed, fame-hungry media-victim,' Belle explained.

'So we'll just have to convince your dad that the Garrick School is the Brainbox Academy for Studious Young Ladies.'

Belle smiled, but she wasn't at all sure her dad was going to be convinced by two members of the Garrick's newest girl band. *The band!* Belle made a mental note not to mention it.

When they arrived at The Ritz, Belle dragged her feet across the Palm Court restaurant in search of her dad's table as if she were on her way to the electric chair. She'd been here several times before, so she took little notice of the grand surroundings, but she couldn't help grinning when she turned to see Holly following in her slipstream, staring around at the domed glass ceiling, the gilded statues, the marble pillars . . .

'Oops, mind out!' Belle whispered, steering Holly away from a near-collision with a waiter carrying a tray of cakes.

Dad was sitting waiting. As always, his grey hair was immaculately groomed and he was wearing sunglasses and a beautifully cut grey wool Armani suit. He stood to greet Belle with a hug and a kiss.

'Dad, this is my friend, Holly Devenish,' Belle said.

'And what do you do, Holly?' he asked as they sat down.

'I'm a dancer,' Holly told him immediately.

Belle's heart sank as Dad made a 'Mmm' noise in his throat.

'But I'm also very interested in science and maths,' Holly piped up quickly. 'My mother's a teacher, so she really wanted me to get the best education possible.'

'But she's happy for you to go to a stage school?' Dad asked with a sceptical frown.

'Not just *any* stage school,' Holly reassured him. 'The Garrick has some of the best SATS results in the country – and it was rated Outstanding in its last inspection.'

Belle watched in awe as her father smiled and nodded and questioned Holly further. Now Holly was telling him about some 'Teacher of the Year' award that Dr Norris, their maths teacher, had recently won. This was going better than Belle could possibly have hoped! She'd had no idea that Holly would turn out to be her secret weapon in the campaign to prove that Superstar High was Brainiac Central.

'Well, you girls must be hungry,' her dad said eventually.

As Belle glanced down at the menu, she heard Holly gasp with delight. '*Chocolate* afternoon tea! That sounds like heaven on a plate!'

Dad signalled for a waiter and ordered chocolate afternoon teas all round.

As Belle kissed her father goodbye outside The Ritz, she was holding her breath. He'd still said nothing about wanting her to leave Superstar High; maybe she'd been worrying about nothing all along. But at the last second, as the taxi pulled up, Dad touched her arm and drew her to one side.

Belle swallowed nervously.

'Sounds like the Garrick's doing a fine job,' her father said, smiling. 'Work hard and have fun!'

Belle was so relieved she couldn't say anything, so she simply nodded instead.

Her father turned to Holly. 'Well, good to have met you,' he said warmly.

'Thank you for tea, Mr Madison,' Holly replied politely as she climbed into the taxi. 'And thanks for inviting me,' she added to Belle once they were both settled inside. 'I had the best time.'

'You earned it, Holly,' Belle told her with a grin. 'You *really* earned it!' She leaned across and gave Holly a Cat-style bear hug.

Holly laughed. 'You're welcome. I knew having a teacher for a mum would come in handy one day!'

Belle closed her eyes and leaned back against the leather seat. What a difference an hour could make! If she hadn't been held down by the seat belt, she felt as if she could float away on a cloud of happiness. The relief was almost overwhelming.

Her future at Superstar High was safe! At least for now.

'I'm not sure that last chocolate éclair was such a good idea!' Holly groaned, holding her stomach as they walked back to their rooms.

'Or maybe it was the five chocolate macaroons and the hot chocolate with chantilly cream and marshmallows that preceded it.' Belle stopped outside her room as she heard voices coming from the other side of the door:

'*Eye of newt and toe of frog, Wool of bat and tongue of dog . . .*'

Although Belle knew that the spooky voice belonged to Cat, it still sent an icy chill down her spine.

'*Macbeth*,' Holly told her. 'Second Witch.'

'*Lizard's head and owlet's wing—*'

'*Leg!*' said a boy's voice. 'It's lizard's *leg*, not lizard's head.'

'Grr! I'm *never* going to get this right!' Cat snapped.

'Don't worry, Cat. You will be the finest old hag in all the school.'

'Wow!' Holly whispered. 'I don't know who that is, but his voice sounds gorgeous.'

Belle knew exactly what Holly meant: the boy's voice was soft and earnest. Somehow he made being an old hag sound like a twenty-four-carat compliment.

'*By the pricking of my thumbs*' – Cat cackled – '*Something wicked this way comes. Open, locks, Whoever knocks!*'

'I think that's our cue,' Holly said, pushing open the door to see Cat standing in the middle of the room brandishing a celery stick.

Sitting opposite on a bean bag, holding a copy of *Macbeth*, was Nathan Almeida. He looked up at Holly and Belle and addressed them in the deep, stagy tones of an Elizabethan Scottish nobleman. '*How now, you secret, black, and midnight hags!*'

'Well, excuse *me*.' Holly put her hands on her hips, pretending to be mortally offended. 'And who exactly are you calling *hags*?'

Cat laughed. 'Don't blame Nate, blame William Shakespeare. It's the next line of the play.'

Belle smiled, but then she hesitated. She'd been so elated about her dad letting her stay at the Garrick that she'd forgotten about her disagreement with Cat. 'You're an awesome witch,' she said, hoping that Holly was right, and Cat really *was* still her friend.

'Thank you *very* much.' Cat said indignantly.

'Sorry, I meant that was awesome *acting*!' Belle explained.

'I know!' Cat grinned, jumping up and smothering Belle with one of her high-impact hugs. 'Look, I'm sorry about yesterday.'

'Me too.' Belle gulped. 'I had something on my mind – but, thanks to Holly, it's all OK now.'

'Have to go now! Things to do!' Nathan mumbled, suddenly bashful again, now that they had returned to twenty-first-century dramas. He hurriedly gathered his books together and slipped out.

As she closed the door behind him, Holly's foot brushed against something lying on the floor.

It was a large brown envelope bearing a printed label:

FOR BELLE, CAT AND HOLLY

CHAPTER SEVENTEEN

Cat: *Opposites Attract*

'Ooh, what's that envelope?' Cat croaked, her voice hoarse from cackling her Second Witch lines all afternoon. She was dying to hear all about The Ritz and what Holly had done to save the day, but that would keep for later. The envelope was too intriguing!

Holly passed it to Cat and collapsed onto the bean bag next to her. 'Can't . . . breathe . . .' she groaned. 'All internal organs replaced by chocolate!'

'Go on, Cat, open it,' Belle urged.

'Maybe it's a love letter!' Holly giggled. 'From a secret admirer—'

'Addressed to all three of us?' Cat said as she tore open the envelope and tipped out the contents. 'A really *greedy* secret admirer?'

A CD and a single sheet of paper slid onto the coffee table.

Cat turned the CD over; it was unmarked. The page,

however, was printed with music. 'It looks like a . . . song!' she breathed.

'Who's it from?' Belle asked, kneeling down for a closer look.

Holly shook the envelope and peered inside. 'There's no note.'

'Look,' Belle said, pointing to the corner of the page. 'I thought those letters were part of the music at first, but they must be the composer's initials.'

Cat looked. Belle was right. Two letters were printed at the end of the song: N.A.

'Well, we know who that is, don't we?' said Holly.

'We do?' Cat asked.

'N.A. – Nathan Almeida. It's obvious that he really fancies you, Cat—'

'Yeah, right!' Cat scoffed. 'I doubt Nate's even noticed we've *got* a band!'

'Well, let's see what the song's like,' Belle said, picking up the music and sliding the CD into her laptop. It was a backing track – a simple guitar arrangement with a drum beat underneath. She studied the musical score and picked out the harmony parts on her electric keyboard. After the first few bars she started to sing the words of the chorus:

'If opposites attract,
Why aren't you here with me?
And it's breaking my heart
That we're still poles apart.'

As Belle finished singing, Holly and Cat both burst into loud applause.

'That's an amazing song!' Cat said, looking really impressed.

'It's so romantic,' Holly agreed. 'And it shows your voice off perfectly, Belle . . .'

'. . . without going over the top,' Cat added.

'And the lyrics are great,' Belle commented. 'They sound as if they come straight from the heart . . .'

'. . . without being pass-the-barf-bag soppy!' finished Holly.

Cat played the CD again.

'Look – there's a high section here that suits Holly's voice,' Belle pointed out. 'And this part would be great for you, Cat . . .'

Bubbling over with excitement, they played the CD again and again, taking turns to work on their different parts.

'We are chalk and cheese,

The skies and the seas
Like bitter and sweet,
A trick or a treat . . .'

Cat looked at Belle and Holly. Their eyes were shining. They were back on track, the way they'd been before she'd had that stupid quarrel with Belle. It felt great! 'So I don't suppose anyone still feels like entering that talent competition?' she asked, putting on her doomiest, gloomiest voice.

Belle let out a delighted shriek and snatched up the music score in both hands. 'Thank you, N.A! Whoever you are!' she cried, planting a huge kiss in the middle of the page.

'Auspicious!' they all shouted in unison.

Just then, the door banged and Bianca stormed into the room. Lettie and Mayu were not far behind – not to mention Shreddie.

Now, what was it that Macbeth called the three witches? Cat asked herself. *Oh, yes, 'the black, and midnight hags'.*

'If you don't stop playing at pop stars in here,' Bianca spat, 'we'll report you to Miss Candlemas!'

'Yeah!' added Lettie lamely. 'We'll report you!'

Cat laughed. 'Ooh, I'm so-o-o scared!' Their housemistress was strict about some things – like boys having to be out of the girls' accommodation by nine p.m. and not letting the bath overflow – but she never stopped them having fun. In fact, she often joined in with any 'high jinks', as she called them.

Cat looked at Belle and Holly, who were both smiling and mouthing the words, *R-i-i-i-se above!*

'Well, some of us have been *trying* to revise for a maths test,' Mayu simpered.

And that, thought Cat as she climbed onto her bed and did her special *rise-above-it* soaring-eagle impression, *was highly unlikely*. The maths test tomorrow was on something even *she* found easy. And they'd obviously just been having an extreme makeover session next door: they were each wearing an entire Boots-counter worth of make-up and their hair was crimped to a crisp.

'Well, it's giving me a migraine,' Bianca complained, rubbing her temples and looking at Cat suspiciously. 'What *is* that music you keep playing anyway?'

'Oh, nothing you'd know,' Belle muttered, slipping the song-sheet under a book.

'Just some old, er, Ukrainian folk song,' Cat added quickly.

'Old Ukrainian folk song!' Lettie snorted with a disbelieving look.

'*Old Ukrainian folk song?*' Holly echoed after the Midnight Hags had set off down the corridor.

Cat giggled. 'I know, I know! It was the first thing that came into my head.'

'That's worrying,' Holly told her. 'Very worrying!'

'Come on, let's go to dinner,' Cat said. 'I'm starving. *Some* of us haven't been stuffing ourselves with cakes all afternoon!'

'And you never know,' Belle added. 'We might discover the identity of the mysterious N.A. while we're there!'

CHAPTER EIGHTEEN

Holly: Wild Flowers and Gangsta Rap

The mysterious N.A.?

About as mysterious as this tube of toothpaste! Holly thought as she got ready for bed later that evening – having hastily cleared up the mess that Bianca and her friends had left all over the floor after their makeover session, including several items of her own make-up that they'd pillaged from her drawer. Bianca's imaginary line down the middle of their room obviously didn't apply to Bianca herself!

Holly was convinced that the songwriter was Nathan Almeida!

One, Nathan's initials were N.A.; two, he adored Cat; and three, he was in the room just before the envelope appeared. The only mystery was why he hadn't just signed his full name in the first place.

Lucky Cat – she had a secret admirer. Even better, she had a secret admirer with a secret identity.

Nathan's just like Spider-Man, Holly reflected as she

climbed into bed. Not the running-up-tall-buildings-and-shooting-webs-out-of-his-wrists part, obviously. But, like Peter Parker, Nathan was the mild-mannered, geeky guy who transformed into a superhero. Nathan was Songwriter-Man!

Holly was strolling through a wildflower meadow. The setting sun was streaking the sky with peach and gold. The boy walking next to her slipped his hand into hers. It was Ethan Reed. 'Holly, I love your breathing!' he whispered.

She gazed into his limpid green eyes. 'Don't kiss me,' she murmured. 'I'm alive.'

A giant otter came scampering across the path. '*Eurgggh!*' it screamed. 'That is the grossest thing I have ever seen in my life!'

The otter sounded just like Furious Girl—

Holly sat bolt upright. She was in bed. It was Monday morning. It had only been a dream.

Only?

It was *only* the most embarrassing dream she'd ever had.

'Oh! My! God! It's revolting!' Now there was no mistaking Bianca's furious voice.

Holly opened her eyes, steeling herself for the worst.

A cockroach? A rat? Or had Shreddie mistaken Bianca's bed for his litter tray?

Bianca was standing in the middle of the room, clutching her industrial-sized make-up bag. Dangling from her fingers was a crumpled yellow napkin.

Not just *any* crumpled yellow napkin.

It was the crumpled yellow napkin from the pepperoni and anchovy pizza that Ethan Reed had given Holly after their collision.

Yes, she *had* kept it.

But, no, she *hadn't* kept it in Bianca's make-up bag.

She'd put the napkin in the bottom drawer of her bedside cabinet, along with her make-up and other odds and ends.

'Oh, er, yeah, that's mine,' Holly mumbled.

'So how did it get into *my* make-up bag? This is so-o-o not acceptable! There's gunk all over my Bobbi Brown shimmer blush! I do have allergies, you know!'

Allergies to paper napkins? Holly thought.

But she could guess how the napkin had found its way into Bianca's bag. Bianca and Lettie and Mayu had obviously thrown it aside when they were rooting through Holly's make-up yesterday afternoon. Holly must have scooped it up with Bianca's make-up when she was clearing up last night.

'Don't *ever* touch my stuff again!' Bianca bellowed. And before Holly could even begin to point out how hypocritical that was, she stomped off to the bathroom, slamming the door behind her.

Welcome to another fun-packed morning in room twenty-five, Holly sighed, flopping back down on her bed.

I think I'll go for another swim this morning, she thought. *And no, it's not just because Ethan is usually at the pool first thing! Everyone knows swimming is good for your core strength!*

In spite of her core strength, Holly's heart skipped a beat when she found that Ethan *was* at the pool, swimming backstroke lengths.

Holly couldn't help remembering her dream and blushing furiously when he came over to chat to her about tumble-turns and arm-extension. She nodded and shook her head, hardly uttering a word in case something ridiculous slipped out – *Don't kiss me, I'm alive*, for example . . .

Later, after a morning of geography and science, Holly grabbed a plate of pasta and pesto and sat down to lunch with Cat and Belle. Cat was checking her eyeliner using the back of a spoon as a mirror; Belle was studying her timetable. 'I'm going to book a rehearsal room this evening so we can work on the new song,' she said.

'Sorry,' Cat apologized. 'I'm going through Nathan's audition speech with him tonight. His Macduff still needs work.'

'What about we get together for half an hour and make a start?' Holly suggested quickly. Ever since the Great Original Material Dispute, she was getting good at picking up the trouble-ahead warning signs: a slight eyebrow-twitch from Belle; a defiant twinkle in Cat's eyes when Belle was planning her life for her. Time for Holly Devenish's International Peacekeeping Force to step in.

'Hey! Whassup, home-girls?' Nick Taggart shouted in an American street-gangsta voice, flipping a chair out from their table and draping himself over the back of it. 'MC Snoop Nicky Nick done wrote you ladies one buzzin' song!'

'*You* wrote us the song?' Cat gasped with a gob-smacked expression that Holly could read like a book; a book with very large print that opened with the sentence, *Could Nick 'Court Jester' Taggart be the secret song-writer who delivered* Opposites Attract *to our door last night?*

'So-o, how did you know that we needed a song?' Cat asked slowly.

'Belle told me,' Nick replied, forgetting for a moment that he was a hardcore gangsta from the mean streets of The Bronx, 'when we were working in the music library.'

Belle was very quiet.

Nick hollered across the dining room, 'Hey, my good bros, come help me out here!' Frankie, Zak and Mason swaggered over. 'We gonna lay down some sweet vibes for my ladies!' Nick told them once they'd finished exchanging convoluted handshakes.

'Wicked!' Mason whistled. Mason Lee, a tall Hong Kong Chinese boy with hair gelled into impressive porcupine spikes, was a talented percussionist. He picked up the rap beat with his palms on the back of a chair. Zak and Frankie joined in, screwing up their faces and making record-scratching sounds.

Nick pulled a piece of paper out his pocket with a flourish.

Cat grabbed it, and when she could stop giggling, started to chant the rap that Nick had written for her:

'They call me Cat 'cos I knows where it's at,
Non-stop, round-the clock, don't mock this rock chick
'Cos she's ready to paaaar-tay . . .'

Cat finished her verse and handed the paper to Holly.

Holly glanced at the words. It certainly wasn't *Opposites Attract*! Feeling a little self-conscious at first, she started the rap. After a few lines she was having so much fun she started throwing in some hip-hop dance moves. Zak joined her with a spectacular break-dance routine.

> '*Holly's the name, but I ain't so prickly,*
> *You want my love, better get here quickly.*
> *Check my smooooooth moves, in the groove, I ain't*
> *sickly . . .*'

As her verse ended, Holly suddenly became aware that all the other students in the dining room had gathered round to see what the commotion was about. She sat down quickly and handed the paper to Belle. Belle started to back away with an expression almost identical to Bianca's greasy-paper-napkin-in-the-make-up-bag face, but everyone was now clapping along in time with MC Nick and the Crew – so, reluctantly, Belle took the paper and began to chant:

'*Belle of the ball, fairest of all, she so tall,*
Ding, baby, ding, you got that ring-a-ding thing,
Gotta believe her, she my diva, this girl can sing . . .'

As Belle finished, the three friends fell about laughing at themselves while the boys high-fived and the spectators gradually drifted back to their food.

That was fun, Holly thought as they filtered out of the dining room. Not exactly a masterpiece of song-writing, though. In fact, it had to rate as ten-year-old Gorgonzola on the Cheese-O-Meter. Surely a boy who rhymed *I ain't sickly* with *Ain't so prickly* couldn't have written *Opposites Attract.*

And anyway, Nick's surname was Taggart. His initials were N.T., not N.A.

Unless the A stood for—

'Hey, Nick,' Cat yelled back across the room to where he was now entertaining his 'fans' with Ali G impressions. 'What's your middle name?'

Cat's thought processes had obviously taken the same direction as Holly's.

Nick looked up and a deep blush flamed across his freckled face. 'What's it to you?' he shouted, gruffly pushing back his chair and heading for the door.

'Oo-ooh!' Cat grinned. 'I think we're on to something here!'

'No way.' Belle shook her head. 'No way is that buffoon our N.A.! *Ding, baby, ding? Ring-a-ding thing?* I rest my case!'

'Maybe that's what he *wants* us to think,' Cat suggested. 'That cheesy rap song could be a clever bluff. You know, to put us off the scent?'

'Baloney!' Belle retorted, coming to an abrupt stop in order to avoid bumping into Bianca, who had just come racing into the dining room. 'We're going to have to keep looking for our mystery songwriter,' she went on, stepping carefully round Bianca, who shot her an evil look. 'Whoever's secretly supplying us with songs, it isn't Nick. He's just not that smart!'

'Are you sure?' Holly asked. Then she noticed that Bianca was looking curiously at them, so she lowered her voice. 'After all, you did say he was a genius with the recording software . . .'

'Of course I'm sure,' Belle insisted, but a shadow of uncertainty passed across her face. 'Well, *pretty* sure,' she added.

Holly caught Cat's eye. Was it possible that Belle was starting to change her mind about Nick Taggart?

CHAPTER NINETEEN

Cat: *Twist and Shout*

Nick Taggart's a lot smarter than Belle gives him credit for, Cat thought as they left the dining room. And he was *way* more likely to be the Phantom Songwriter than Nathan was. Nathan didn't seem to like music, for a start. He'd even asked her to turn off The Killers when they were working on the electricity report! And he was really struggling with the harmony project—

Oh, no! The harmony project!

It was Monday! And Monday meant Mr Garcia's singing class. The singing class where they had to give in the CDs with the harmonies they'd recorded.

Cat and Holly had chosen their song. They'd learned how to record their voices onto the backing track. They'd worked out their harmonies.

There was just one minor problem – they hadn't actually *recorded* anything. That was supposed to have happened this lunch time. The one they'd just frittered away entertaining the entire school with an impromptu rap show.

Cat glanced at the clock in the entrance hall. They had ten minutes. If they ran straight to the recording suite and recorded both their voices simultaneously, they *might* just do it.

'Holly Devenish,' she said, 'I've got three words to say to you!'

Holly looked at her blankly. She'd clearly forgotten all about the assignment too.

'Twist! And! Shout!' Cat yelled.

'*Aarggghhhh!*' Holly screamed, clutching Cat's arm. Together they raced out of the hall, across the courtyard and into the recording suite – where Mayu was just closing her files on one of the computers, ready to head for the class.

'Mayu! Leave it switched on!' Holly panted. 'We'll lock up!'

'Oops! Sorry,' Mayu, said, curling her lip in a Cruella de Vil smile as she pressed the power button. 'Too late!'

'Grr!' Cat growled, stuffing their CD into the drive. Holly switched the computer back on, clicked frantically on the mouse and opened up their *Twist and Shout* audio file. Pulling on their headphones as the introduction started, they leaned into the microphone.

It was a Beatles concert and the fans were screaming . . . Cat pictured herself as John Lennon and Holly as Paul McCartney as they launched into the song . . .

'Sorry we're late,' Cat puffed as they barrelled into Mr Garcia's class at 1.35.

'Never mind, you're here now!' Mr Garcia rumbled. 'We're about to play the first CD. We're going to give each pair a mark out of ten for technical merit and originality. Let's get the ball rolling with . . . Bianca Hayford and Mayu Tanaka. Ah yes, *If I Were a Boy* by Beyoncé.

'I thought *you* were working with Bianca,' Cat whispered to Lettie.

'I was,' Lettie whispered back, 'but Bianca asked me to switch. Mayu's voice is much better than mine.' Her mouth drooped for a moment, but then she hurriedly added, 'But it's OK, I'm working with Mason Lee instead, and he's really musical.'

'Knickers, shush, will you?' Bianca hissed. 'I can't hear my song!'

'Please don't call me that,' Lettie whispered.

'OK, *Lettie*. Whatever,' Bianca replied hurriedly.

Over the next hour they listened to all the students' recordings. Frankie Pellegrini – who had an angelic singing voice, although he had the beat-up face of a junior boxing champion – had recorded a great version of a Westlife song with Zak Lomax, but Bianca and Mayu's *If I Were a Boy* was still easily the best. Mr Garcia picked up the last CD in the pile. 'Ah yes, Nick Taggart and Belle Madison – *Tragedy*, the old Bee Gees classic.'

Holly and Cat exchanged intrigued glances. Belle had kept this project Top Secret. But as soon as the song started, it was clear it was something very special. Nick sang the high parts in a perfect falsetto, blending skilfully with Belle's superb vocals in the lower range.

Mr Garcia led the class in a round of enthusiastic applause. Then he studied his clipboard. 'Hmm, there is one pair who have failed to submit anything: Holly Devenish and Catrin Wickham.'

Bianca turned and smirked triumphantly.

'Here it is, sir,' Cat said sweetly. 'We were just adding the finishing touches!'

Bianca's face fell.

Twist and Shout thundered out of the speakers. Cat looked across at Holly. Holly grinned back at her. It wasn't *quite* up to The Beatles standard, of course, but it really didn't sound bad at all. Although the tempo was a little too fast and there was an interesting *breathless* quality, it had drive and raw energy.

The class clapped and whooped as the track galloped to the finish.

'Mm! Nice *immediate* sound,' Mr Garcia murmured, 'and a great sense of *urgency*. Technically, though – let's just say the harmonies need some *refinement*!'

Mr Garcia examined his notes. 'It appears there's a tie for top score,' he said, 'between *If I Were a Boy* and *Tragedy*. I suggest we put it to a class vote.'

The result was overwhelming. Nick and Belle's *Tragedy* was the clear winner.

Nick threw his arms around Belle and planted a big sloppy kiss on her cheek. Cat waited for Belle to shove him away, but it seemed that in all the excitement she had forgotten that this was *Nick Taggart* kissing her! Only for a moment though. Soon she grimaced and rubbed her cheek. Cat caught Holly's eye and grinned.

'Hmmph! If I hadn't had that throat infection,' Bianca fumed, 'and all that trouble having to re-work the arrangement when Lettie let me down . . .'

'So-o-o-o,' Nick pleaded, turning to Cat and Holly, 'can I join your band now?'

'No way!' Cat laughed. 'Singing in a high-pitched voice still doesn't make you a girl!'

CHAPTER TWENTY

Belle: *Done Looking!*

Belle was still buzzing from the success of *Tragedy* almost a week later. What's more, band rehearsals were going fabulously and they now had a stellar song to perform for the talent competition.

She was still having to get up early every morning to fit in extra study time to make sure she got the A grades her dad expected, but she could live with that.

It doesn't get any better than this! Belle thought as she rolled up her yoga mat on Sunday afternoon, sipped her herbal tea with heather honey to protect her throat, and pulled on her favourite Manolo Blahnik boots before skipping off to a special invitation-only singing workshop with Larry Shapiro.

Yes, *the* Larry Shapiro! The world-famous vocal coach was running a series of workshops with a hand-picked group of Garrick students while he was in London working on a new musical. Larry Shapiro was only one of Belle's greatest heroes! He'd worked with everyone from Mariah Carey to Plácido Domingo!

Belle entered the studio and took a seat next to Frankie Pellegrini. Even Bianca's psycho death-stare couldn't spoil her mood today. *Although if looks could kill,* Belle thought, *I'd be a chalk outline by now and Bianca would be up for first-degree murder.*

When Larry Shapiro, tall and slightly stooping in a light blue suit, and wearing his trademark badly-fitting hairpiece, called for the first volunteer to demonstrate vocal control techniques, Belle's hand shot up. She was ready to sing her heart out!

Belle danced back up the grand staircase towards her room. She couldn't wait to tell Cat and Holly all about the workshop. Larry Shapiro said she had the makings of a world-class voice! There was Cat now, on her way across the entrance hall. 'Hey, Cat!' Belle called over the banister. 'Up here!'

Belle was still regaling Cat with her Larry Shapiro experience as they pushed open the door of their room. 'Wow!' Cat said, giving Belle a hug. 'That's brilliant— Ooh, what's this?'

A brown envelope lay on the carpet.

Cat picked it up, tore it open and pulled out a sheet of paper and a CD. 'Another song!'

The waft of chlorine that was becoming Holly's signature fragrance preceded her into the room. *She's been going swimming an awful lot lately*, Belle thought as she quickly moved the irises off the coffee table before they could be knocked flying by Holly's kit bag.

'Look, the Song Fairy's been again, Hols!' Cat laughed, waving the CD in the air.

'And it's signed N.A. again!' Belle added.

'*Auspicious!*' Holly and Cat chorused.

Belle studied the song carefully and played the CD track on her laptop. It was completely different to the last one. While *Opposites Attract* was a romantic ballad, *Done Looking!* was a lively song with a Latin American mambo sound:

> '*We're done looking! Now we're leaping!*
> *We won't stay in the shallows,*
> *Won't hide in the shadows,*
> *We'll take our friends by the hands,*
> *Take a chance, catch the wave, live our dream . . .*'

'Awesome!' Belle gasped when the three of them had sung the song – while dancing around the room to the infectious beat – for the fifth time.

'Having a little bop in here, are we, gals?' chuckled

Miss Candlemas as she called in to hand over a pile of clean sheets. All the girls had to strip their beds on Sunday mornings and make them up with clean bed-linen in the evening. Belle had never had to make her bed before coming to the Garrick, but she really enjoyed the novelty of doing all her own chores. Unlike Cat – whose side of the room always looked like a war zone!

'Just doing our Sunday laundry dance!' Cat grabbed a pillowcase and started improvising a little routine. Holly and Belle joined in.

'Wish I could stop and boogie with you myself – but, no rest for the wicked, eh?' Miss Candlemas laughed, shaking her head as she bustled off.

'So, now our mystery songwriter has struck twice and we still don't know who it is!' Holly said, dropping her pillowcase and frowning over the musical score.

'You know, this song describes exactly how we feel about this competition!' Cat said, flopping down on the pile of clean sheets. '*Take our chance! Live our dream!* Which means this N.A. guy must be someone who knows us really well! Like Nick Taggart!'

'No way!' Belle almost choked on her mineral water. 'It's definitely Nathan Almeida! Hel-*lo!* Latin

American song – Latin American guy! Anyone see the connection?'

Cat laughed. 'This is *Nathan* we're talking about! He's not exactly Ricky Martin, is he?'

'True,' Belle admitted, trying to pull her sheets from underneath Cat. 'But *Opposites Attract*? That's obviously about you and Nathan – you're outgoing, he's shy—'

'Right back at you!' Cat argued. 'You're cool, Nick's a screwball. Or at least he *pretends* to be. You're chalk and cheese, just like the song says.'

No way! Belle thought. She couldn't deny that she and Nick were opposites. And she had definitely started to get on with him a lot better since the success of the harmony project. But as for being attracted? *Never going to happen!*

'What makes you so sure the writer is even a boy?' Holly said thoughtfully.

Belle stared at her. She'd never considered that N.A. could be a girl.

'Nah!' Cat said, after giving it a moment's thought. 'Why would a girl want to be anonymous? There'd be no reason to be embarrassed about it, like a boy would be . . .'

That was a good point, Belle thought. 'And I can't

think of any girls with the initials N.A., can you?' she added.

'No,' Holly admitted. 'Cat's probably right. But we need some hard evidence before jumping to conclusions that it's Nick – or Nathan . . .'

Holly is so sensible and fair-minded, Belle thought admiringly. *If she wasn't going to be a dancer, she'd make a great lawyer.*

'Yeah! Let's raid their rooms and look for clues,' Cat suggested excitedly. 'Like *The Famous Five*.'

'Or maybe not,' Holly said. 'What about trying to find out what Nick's middle name is first!'

Cat grinned. 'Remember how embarrassed he looked when I asked him? I bet it's because it begins with A and he doesn't want us to work out that *he's* N.A.!'

'N.A. is so *not* Nick Taggart, but just to be sure, I'll find out what his middle name is,' Belle offered. *It'll be easy enough*, she thought. *All I have to do is sneak a peek at the mail in his pigeonhole. One of the envelopes is bound to have Nick's middle name on it – or at least his initial.* She was quite sure it would start with something other than A.

'And *you* could work on Nathan, Cat,' Holly suggested.

'How? I can't just beat a confession out of him,' Cat protested.

'No beating required. Just use your feminine charms!' Belle told her. 'It's pretty obvious he fancies you.'

'Hmm. I'm not so sure, but I suppose I could try and, you know, flirt with him a bit or something,' Cat said thoughtfully.

'Awesome idea! You work it, girl!' said Belle.

'So, Belle, are you going flirt with Nick to find out his middle name then?' Cat asked, with a mischievous look.

Belle laughed. 'Wait and see. I have my ways!'

'OK, it's a plan!' Holly clapped her hands. 'Cat's on Advanced Flirting Duty with Nathan. Belle's on Undercover Reconnaissance with Nick — and I've got a funny feeling I've seen the initials N.A. somewhere else as well, so I'm going to try and track down where.'

'We'll have the Mystery of the Secret Songwriter wrapped up in no time!' Belle predicted.

'But let's go down to dinner first,' Cat suggested. 'It's dangerous to flirt on an empty stomach, you know!'

CHAPTER TWENTY-ONE

Cat: Magnetism and Mambo

After dinner Cat hurried back to her room to change into her best flirting outfit. She pulled off the baggy jumper she'd taken to wearing a lot since Bianca's Chubby Spice comment. *The one advantage to all this dancing and celery,* she thought, looking at herself critically in the mirror, *is that I'm definitely losing weight.*

Feeling buoyed by this, she rummaged through her wardrobe and selected a slinky black mini-dress, black tights and her favourite zebra-print high heels. Then she applied extra eyeliner, pinned her hair into a romantic tangle with a few artistically arranged trailing curls, and set off for Nathan's room in a cloud of Obsession.

She reached the end of the corridor, then ran back, grabbed a couple of random science books from her desk, and set off again.

The boys' rooms were in the new block next to the pool and the sports centre. Cat had ventured along these corridors only once or twice before. She wrinkled her nose at the odour of slightly stale boy. The girls' corridors didn't exactly smell of sugar and spice and all things nice – more a mixture of shampoo, talcum powder and chocolate – but at least it wasn't crisps (assorted flavours), old sweat and weapons-grade deodorant. She passed the room that Nick Taggart shared with Zak Lomax. Rock music thudded out from behind the closed door.

Cat knocked at Nathan's door just as his roommate, Frankie Pellegrini, was heading out for the gym. Frankie whistled softly as his eyes drifted across her low-cut dress. Nathan looked up from the laptop screen on his desk. 'I've found some excellent websites on the fundamental principles of magnetism,' he said, seemingly oblivious to Cat's *femme fatale* look. 'It *was* magnetic fields you wanted to revise, wasn't it?'

'Oh yes,' Cat purred. 'You know, magnetic attraction . . .'

She was a glamorous Russian secret agent seducing James Bond into revealing the location of the nuclear missile . . . She sat down on the edge of Nathan's chair, wriggled a little closer and—

'Here, I'll get Frankie's chair for you,' Nathan offered, jumping up and almost knocking Cat off her perch. Once he'd installed her next to him on another chair, he settled down in front of the computer again.

Cat leaned across and placed her hand over Nathan's on the mouse. 'So,' she said, 'the thing about magnets is that *opposites attract* . . . ?'

'That's correct,' Nathan agreed, nudging Cat's hand gently aside and clicking with the mouse. 'If you study this diagram here, you'll see that there are two poles—'

'We're a bit like that, aren't we, Nate?' Cat said, smiling coyly. '*You and I* . . .'

'Like what?'

'Opposites! You're all *shy* and *thoughtful* and *deep*, and I'm . . . not . . .'

Nathan nodded. 'Well, yes, that's probably why we're such good friends.'

'*Very* good friends!' Cat simpered. 'The kind of friends who might want to help each other, you know . . . secretly?'

'No, it's OK,' Nathan replied, looking slightly puzzled. 'I'm happy to help you with homework any time, and I don't mind *who* knows about it.'

This is Mission Impossible, Cat thought. *He hasn't got a clue what I'm talking about.* In a last-ditch attempt, she changed tack. '*Done looking, now we're leaping!*' she announced. She gazed into his eyes for a spark of recognition – eyes which, she noticed for the first time, were dark brown with gold flecks . . .

Nathan frowned and pulled off his glasses. 'Have I got something stuck on the lens?' he asked, squinting at them.

Phew, that's a relief! Cat thought. *I thought he was going to kiss me for a moment.* Not that there was anything *wrong* with Nathan, of course. He was a great mate. Just not boyfriend material!

'So, Nate, do the letters N.A. mean anything to you?' she asked, giving up on the flirting and going for the direct approach.

Nathan frowned as he replaced his glasses. 'Well, they're my initials, but—'

'What about anything else or any*one* else?' Cat demanded.

Nathan scrunched his brows up in thought. 'Let's see, N.A. . . . Oh, yes!'

'What?' Cat asked excitedly. Maybe she was wrong. Perhaps he was about to crumble and confess to being the Phantom Songwriter . . .

'Na is the symbol for the chemical element sodium.'

My work here is done, Cat said to herself in her best Russian-agent accent.

Although it wasn't, because she really *did* need help with understanding those magnets. 'Sorry, can you just explain that thing about the poles again?' she asked.

'Of course,' Nathan said, smiling happily. 'It's quite simple really. If you look at this chart . . .'

The next band practice was on Tuesday evening. Holly had spent the last few days working out a mambo-style dance routine for *Done Looking!* Bands were only allowed to perform one song in the talent competition and, after some argument, Cat and Holly had persuaded Belle that they should choose the lively, energetic Latin American number rather than the slow, romantic *Opposites Attract*.

Holly started up the *Done Looking!* backing track on the sound system in the rehearsal room and walked her friends through the steps – which involved lots of hip-swinging and quick-stepping, with cute little jumps on the *Now we're leaping!* hook-line.

'Holly Devenish! You are brilliant!' Cat collapsed on the floor, panting with exhaustion after the third run-through. Singing while dancing such an energetic routine wasn't going to be easy, but Cat was sure that it would really wow the judges if they could pull it off.

Belle was a little hesitant at first. Cat could see that

the extravagant Latin American style wasn't her natural habitat. But Holly was a patient teacher, and she simplified some of Belle's moves. 'After all, Belle's singing the lead vocals,' she said tactfully, 'so it's not fair to expect her to do as much on the dance side!'

By the end of the rehearsal, Cat was leg-achingly exhausted. But it was a good feeling. Things were really starting to slot into place. And they were all beginning to feel the excitement.

The talent competition was only a few weeks away!

'So,' Belle said as they walked back across the courtyard after the rehearsal, 'we've got another big decision to make. We need a *name* for our band!'

'I've been thinking about that,' Cat said. 'What about something beginning with N.A. – you know, in honour of our secret songwriter?'

She waited for Belle to argue, but to her surprise, she agreed immediately. 'Hey, great idea!'

'Hmm. What about . . . er . . . Next Answer?' Holly suggested.

'Too boring!' Belle said. 'Naturally Auspicious?'

Cat laughed. 'Too long! How about . . . Nervous Attack?'

'Too scary!' said Belle.

'Nibbling Anteaters?' Holly ventured. 'Noisy Alligators?'

'Too weird!' Cat and Belle said together.

'*Aarggh!* We'll be stuck with the Chlorine Doreens if we don't think of something soon,' Holly groaned.

'Hey, girls, need some help?'

Cat turned to see Nick walking behind them, with Zak. 'We need a name for our band,' she said. 'And it's got to start with the initials N.A.'

'Er, why?' Nick asked.

'Because we say so,' Cat retorted with a grin. 'So no arguments!'

'Whoa! That's rad, man!' Zak exclaimed. 'No Argument!'

'Mm, not bad . . .' Holly said.

'I've got it!' Nick shouted, punching the air. 'Nick's Angels!'

'*Nick's Angels?*' Cat laughed as Belle emitted a very uncool, un-Belle-like snorting sound that was somewhere between horror and amusement.

'You know, like *Charlie's Angels*,' Nick explained. 'That was three gorgeous girls. Charlie was their boss. I could be, like, your *manager*.'

'Ha ha! Very funny!' Belle scoffed, not even remotely

close to amusement now. 'We don't need a manager. And we are certainly not *your* angels!'

'Yeah. We're *nobody's* angels, thank you very much!' Cat laughed, poking Nick in the ribs.

Then she suddenly stopped laughing, replaying what she had just said in her head.

She looked at Holly and Holly looked at Belle. There was a long freeze-frame pause and then . . .

'That's it!' Holly said.

'We're Nobody's Angels!' all three girls shouted in unison.

CHAPTER TWENTY-TWO

Holly: *Dirty Dancing* and Stormin' Norma

The following Sunday morning Holly was singing to herself and dancing a few steps as she crossed the entrance hall. She'd gone with Miss LeClair and a group of other students on a trip to see *Dirty Dancing* in the West End last night – and she couldn't get the music out of her head. *One day*, she daydreamed, *that will be me up there on stage, singing and dancing . . .*

She stepped out through the front doors and blinked in the bright sunlight. A group of boys in football strip were standing around at the bottom of the wide stone steps.

One of them was Ethan Reed.

Holly paused on the top step. She immediately forgot all about West End musicals. *This* was her big chance to prove to Ethan that she was not a total dimwit. She would walk down the stairs calmly and sanely; no head-butting or spouting gobbledygook this time. Luckily she was on her way out to meet Belle and

Cat at the Café Roma on the other side of Kingsgrove Square for brunch, so after her swim she'd changed into her favourite jeans and even slicked on some lip gloss.

Well, here goes. Step down, two, three . . .

Ethan looked up and flashed his high-voltage smile. 'Hi, Hol—' he began

'About flippin' time too, Baddeley!' yelled one of the boys. 'We'll be late for the match!'

Holly turned, just in time to see Felix Baddeley hurtling out of the door behind her . . .

. . . and tripping on his boot-lace. He teetered for a moment before tumbling in a tangle of limbs and shin pads . . .

. . . and crashing into Holly.

In that split second Holly realized that if she fell down all six steps, she would probably break her ankle at the very least. *You can't dance with a broken ankle. Just look at what happened to Miss LeClair!* There was only one option.

As her legs started to crumple, Holly bent her knees, pushed off and jumped, launching herself in a sideways dive.

This could go one of two ways, she thought as she watched the terracotta pots with their little star-shaped trees speed past. *Either Ethan will reach out and catch me . . .*

. . . or I'll crack my head open on the pavement.

At the top of her trajectory, Holly's brain cut out and her body switched to Dance–Mode Override. Her legs extended and her toes pointed. Her arms swept up elegantly into fifth position. Her face arranged itself into the big smile that dancers always wear to mask the pain.

And she landed in Ethan's arms.

Her momentum took him by surprise and he almost dropped her. But just as her braids brushed the ground, he summoned up his strength and swept her up again. Holly twisted round in his arms and sprang away with a half-turn to land perfectly at his side. She stretched out her arms like a gymnast dismounting from the beam.

Felix, who was now lying at her feet, winded but apparently uninjured, held his hand up for a knee-high high-five. 'Way cool!' he whistled. 'That was like *Swan Lake* meets *The Matrix*!'

Ethan was grinning at her. The rest of the footballers were staring, open-mouthed.

Holly felt as if she were back in one of her dreams. She had just jumped into Ethan's arms! She felt as if she were still soaring through the air.

'Sorry I'm late, Ethan,' Felix groaned. 'I got waylaid by Stormin' Norma about some stupid permission slip for the away match—'

'*Stormin' Norma?*' Holly couldn't help asking.

Ethan laughed. 'Mrs Butterworth. We've always called her that since we found out her name's Norma.'

'Yeah, either that or The Chairminator!' Felix added.

But Holly wasn't listening. She was picturing Mrs Butterworth sitting behind her desk on the first day of term with a name-badge stuck on the lapel of her bristly tartan jacket: MRS N. A. BUTTERWORTH, SCHOOL SECRETARY.

At last she remembered where she'd seen the initials N.A. before!

Holly ordered a large cappuccino and a chocolate brioche and took a seat next to Cat and Belle at the back of Café Roma. They were poring over an official-looking form.

'Looks boring!' Holly said, still smiling. She hadn't really come back down to earth yet, but decided she'd tell Cat and Belle about the Ethan stair-jump *later*; she wanted to keep it as her own treasured secret for just a little longer.

'Entry form for the talent competition. We've got to

hand it in to Mr Garcia tomorrow,' Belle explained. 'Along with a copy of the musical score for the backing band.'

Holly examined the form. Cat and Belle had filled out most of it already.

NAME OF BAND/GROUP/ PERFORMER:	*Nobody's Angels*
MEMBERS OF BAND/GROUP:	*Belle Madison, Cat Wickham, Holly Devenish*
NAME OF SONG:	*Done Looking!*
NAME OF SONGWRITER:	

'Name of songwriter?' Holly said. 'But we still don't know who N.A. is!'

'No,' said Cat, 'but it's not Nathan Almeida! I turned the Flirt-O-Matic up to Maximum, and all I got was the chemical symbol for sodium.'

'I haven't found out about Nick's middle name yet,' Belle sighed. 'I've asked his buddies and looked at his mail, but no luck.'

'At least we can rule out the N.A. I was trying to remember,' Holly said. 'Turns out it's Norma A. Butterworth!'

Cat howled with laughter. 'I can't see Mrs B as our secret songwriter! She'd have to get out of her chair to come up to our room for a start!'

Croissant crumbs scattered across the table. Holly was pleased to see that Cat seemed to have given up on the strict cottage-cheese-and-celery diet she'd been following since Bianca called her *chubby*.

'Well, we'll just have to leave the form blank for "songwriter" and hope the organizers accept it, I guess,' Belle said. 'Unless . . .' she added thoughtfully.

'Unless what?'

'I've had an idea.'

'Uh-oh!' Cat grinned and held her head in her hands. 'Not another of Belle Madison's Legendary Awesome Ideas. I seem to remember that it was one of your awesome ideas that got us into all this in the first place!'

'Well, the last two songs have been delivered under our door on Sunday evenings,' Belle continued, ignoring Cat's remark. 'Today's Sunday. We could hide in our room and—'

'Keep watch in case we get another visit,' Cat interrupted. 'Genius!'

'It's awesome!' Holly agreed, feeling a thrill of excitement. 'Operation Song-catcher is *go*!'

CHAPTER TWENTY-THREE

Holly: Operation Song-catcher

Operation Song-catcher commenced at seventeen hundred hours precisely; after Belle had checked they'd all made a 'bathroom visit'. There was no keyhole but the crack between the door and the frame was just wide enough to glimpse a narrow strip of anyone outside in the corridor.

They turned off the lights and got into position. Holly took first shift, kneeling with her eye pressed to the crack, while Cat lounged on a beanbag and Belle did yoga exercises to pass the time.

Now all they had to do was wait . . .

. . . and wait

. . . and w a i t . . .

Holly checked her watch. It had only been ten minutes!

'What if they're wearing a disguise?' Belle whispered from her lizard pose.

'Ooh yeah! Like Zorro,' Cat said, 'or Batman—'

'Sshh!' Holly hissed. 'I can hear something!'

She held her breath. Footsteps were coming along the corridor. The light coming through the crack was blocked by a leg. Holly could hear scary-shark *Jaws* music in her head.

There was a knock at the door.

Checking there's no one here! Holly thought.

Then an envelope appeared under the door. Holly felt her heart thump against her ribcage. The envelope-slider stepped back and she caught a glimpse of black jeans and trainers. *It was Nathan Almeida!*

Holly turned slowly, her eyes wide with amazement. 'I saw him!' she squeaked. 'It's—'

'Nathan. I know.' Cat grinned, holding up the sheet of paper she'd already ripped out of the envelope. '*Dear Cat,*' she read aloud. '*Here's a list of some magnetism websites you might find useful—*'

'Sshh!' Belle whispered, taking up position for the next shift at the door. 'The real songwriter could come along at any minute—'

Suddenly Holly jumped. What was that scratching noise at the door?

'Cat!' Belle whispered, her eye still glued to the door.

'What?' Cat whispered back.

'No, it's *the cat,*' Belle breathed, quickly opening the

door and scooping Shreddie inside. He glared at them all disapprovingly before curling up on Cat's bed to wash his paws.

Cat took her turn, then Holly again. She was starting to think the Phantom Songwriter was never going to turn up when she heard footsteps approaching. Could this be it?

'False alarm!' Holly sighed a moment later. 'It's only Bianca with Mayu and Lettie. They've just gone into our room.'

Shreddie must have heard Bianca's voice too. He jumped down from the bed and started miaowing at the door, desperate to see his True Love.

Cat picked him up and cuddled him. 'Shreddie, you are one mad cat,' she whispered into his fur.

Holly stood up and stretched her legs. 'Your turn, Belle,' she said.

But Belle – now in downward-facing dog pose, with her eyes only centimetres from the carpet – was staring, transfixed, at the gap under the door. Holly followed her gaze. The corner of a brown envelope was sliding slowly towards them. As quickly as she could, Holly crouched down again in lookout position—

But at that moment Shreddie scrabbled frantically out of Cat's arms.

Cat screamed. Holly jumped and banged her head on the doorknob. Shreddie leaped onto the coffee table, knocked over the irises and pounced on the envelope.

But it had already been snatched back from the other side of the door.

Feeling slightly dizzy, Holly opened the door. The corridor was empty. And silent.

'Oh, no! We've scared them away!' she groaned.

'So we still don't know who it is – and even worse, they'll probably never write us another song after this!' Cat grumbled, kicking a bean bag. 'Whose brilliant – or should I say *awesome* – idea was this?'

'I'm really sorry,' Belle said sadly. 'I thought it would work.'

'It's not *your* fault!' Holly sighed, disappointment descending on her like a cold wet blanket. 'We *all* thought it would work.'

'Yeah, Holly's right. I'm sorry,' Cat said. 'It *did* seem like a good idea at the time!' Then she broke into a smile. 'What are you like, Hols, hitting your head on the doorknob? Are you OK?'

Holly laughed, rubbing the bruise. 'Yeah . . . It *was* pretty funny when Shreddie knocked over the vase of flowers. He's even clumsier than I am!'

'Maybe he's secretly in league with Bianca,' Belle said as she started mopping water from the table, 'and he did it deliberately to mess up our plan!'

Holly made a heroic attempt to look on the bright side. 'Well, no good crying over spilled water! At least we tried. We'll just have to put the initials N.A. on our form and hope that it's enough.'

As Belle was carefully putting the entry form for Nobody's Angels into Mr Garcia's pigeonhole, Holly had an idea. She took a pen and notebook from her bag and wrote a message:

Dear N.A., We are very sorry for trying to catch you out earlier. We won't do it again. Thank you for everything.
Love from Holly, Cat and Belle

She folded the note over, wrote *N.A.* on the front and placed it in the pigeonhole for students with surnames beginning with A.

Maybe, just *maybe*, the songwriter would find it, forgive them and come back again.

CHAPTER TWENTY-FOUR

Belle: Laundry Lists and Middle Names

Belle was worried.

It was a blustery Thursday morning and she was finishing her early morning run around the school grounds. She had an English essay on her desk waiting to be finished, but that wasn't the problem. She checked the integrated stop-watch-and-heart-monitor gadget on her wrist; she'd been a little slow, but *that* wasn't the problem either.

Belle was worried about the talent competition. Would Mr Garcia accept their entry, even though they'd not filled in the full name of the songwriter on the form? Or would Nobody's Angels be disqualified before they'd even started?

Belle slowed as she passed the back of the sports centre. Miss Candlemas was taking delivery of clean sheets and tablecloths from a laundry van. 'Ooh, Belle!' she called. 'Be a love, and' – Belle removed the earpiece of her iPod and strained to hear over the squally breeze

– 'pop along to Mrs B's office and bring me the laundry list off her desk. She's late this morning – here's the master key.'

Belle caught the key and jogged around the new buildings, across the courtyard and into the entrance hall. Mrs Butterworth's office or 'inner sanctum', as she called it, was behind the big desk in the reception area, next to the pigeonholes – so she could easily scoot between the two. But now the black leather swivel chair sat empty behind the reception desk.

Belle knocked and then turned the key in the lock. She soon spied the laundry list on the desk in a tray marked OUT. She picked it up, but as she was turning to leave, she glimpsed something out of the corner of her eye. Between the out-tray and a spider plant was a pile of papers.

The top page was headed, *Almeida: Nathan Alejandro*. Below the name were typed the words: *Science Test*.

Ooh, Belle sighed, *what I wouldn't give to see* my *test result. Maybe just one little peek*, she thought, inching towards the papers, but then she paused. Mrs Butterworth could turn up at any moment and if she was caught snooping, she was pretty sure it would be game over for her at the Garrick.

She forced herself to leave the test papers

untouched, but just as she was about to go, she realized something that set her pulse racing so fast she thought her heartbeat monitor might explode: Nathan's middle name was Alejandro! And if *Nathan's* middle name was on his test . . .

Swiftly Belle lifted the stack of papers about where she thought the Ts should be.

And that's when she heard the unmistakable sound of Mrs Butterworth's chair rattling towards her office.

She was going to be caught red-handed!

'Belle!' cried Mrs Butterworth. 'Whatever are you doing in my office?'

Belle didn't have time for finesse. With a swipe of the arm she knocked the spider plant and the stack of test papers cascading to the floor. 'Oh, no, I'm sorry!' she gasped. 'Miss Candlemas sent me to get the laundry list. You made me jump and—'

'Hm!' Mrs Butterworth frowned and peered at Belle over her glasses. 'This is really *not good enough . . .*'

'I'm so sorry. I'll pick everything up,' Belle said, throwing herself to the floor and beginning to scoop up the papers, all the while frantically trying to spot Nick's test and read his middle name without the school secretary noticing.

'No, leave them, dear,' said Mrs B, wheeling her

chair towards the desk. 'I'll be having *words* with Miss Candlemas. Giving my office key to a student when there could be all kinds of confidential documents in here . . .'

Belle backed out of the office, leaving Mrs Butterworth to tidy up. Once safely in the hall, she sank down onto the bottom stair to catch her breath and smiled for the first time since the dramatic failure of Operation Song-catcher last night. Because she'd caught sight of the name she was looking for: *Taggart: Nicholas Umberto*.

No wonder he'd been embarrassed about his middle name. And she'd been right all along. Nick Taggart was *not* the Song Fairy!

Belle skipped lunch to finish her English essay. Then she ran to Mrs Butterworth's desk to pick up the key for the rehearsal room she'd booked for a band practice. Belle expected the school secretary to scold her after this morning's Office Break-in Fiasco. But Mrs B only seemed concerned about her health. 'How are you feeling now, dear?' she asked.

'Er, fine, thanks,' Belle stammered, wondering if she looked pale.

Mrs B smiled. 'Oh, good. Well, one of the other girls

has taken the key.'

Holly or Cat must have picked it up already, Belle thought, racing over to the rehearsal rooms.

But when she opened the heavy sound-proofed door of the studio, it wasn't Holly and Cat adjusting the sound system and plugging in the microphones; it was Bianca Hayford and Mayu Tanaka.

CHAPTER TWENTY-FIVE

Holly: Warthogs and Weasels

When Holly arrived with Cat a few minutes later, she was surprised to find Belle in the rehearsal room with Bianca and Mayu.

'I just got here,' Belle grumbled, 'and found these two. Apparently they just felt like doing some singing practice!'

'No law against it, is there?' snapped Bianca. 'Or do we have to ask permission from your precious band if we want to sing now?'

'But we booked this room days ago,' Holly explained.

'Well, try telling your friend Mrs Butterworth that! She didn't seem to think it was booked when I spoke to her this morning.' Bianca's laugh was as cold as water dripping from an icicle.

Cat, on the other hand, looked as if she were about to erupt. She threw down her bag and stormed across the room. Holly opened her mouth to remind Cat to *rise above it*, but it was too late for that now. Far too late!

She could almost see the molten lava bubbling under Cat's flame-red hair.

'Bianca!' she yelled. 'You knew perfectly well we'd booked this room. You heard us talking about it this morning. You're a mean, selfish . . . *warthog*.'

Warthog? Holly thought. *Where did that come from?*

'Ooo-ooh! Temper, temper!' Mayu mocked in her sickly sweet voice.

'And you're just as bad, Mayu!' Belle said, striding over to stand shoulder to shoulder with Cat. Her voice was level but she was quivering with rage. 'You've done this deliberately to mess up our chances in the competition. You, you . . .'

'. . . *weasel!*' Cat shouted.

'OK,' Holly said, trying to calm the situation. 'Maybe there's another rehearsal room available . . .'

'No, this was the last one free when I booked it,' Belle seethed.

The door banged open and Holly turned to see Nick Taggart.

''Allo, 'allo, 'allo, what's going on 'ere then?' Nick barked in a comedy-policeman voice. He pretended to lick a pencil stub and write something down in a notebook. 'I was proceeding along the corridor in a northerly direction when I thought I 'eard a *disturbance* in rehearsal room two.'

Bianca and Mayu rolled their eyes.

'What seems to be the problem 'ere, then, madam?' Nick asked.

This is so not helping! Holly thought. She waited for Belle to put Nick in his place – or rather the place that Belle *thought* was his; like, maybe the recycling bins behind the kitchen. But to her astonishment, Belle looked at him as gratefully as if he really *were* a police officer arriving on the scene of a crime!

'Bianca and Mayu *say* they booked this room first,' she blurted out.

Nick grinned and nodded slowly. Holly could almost see the lightbulb flash on above his head as something clicked. 'Are you feeling any better now, Belle?' he asked, dropping the policeman act.

Belle frowned. 'Why does everyone keep asking me how I am today?'

'Why don't you ask Bianca?' Nick said pointedly.

Bianca's mouth was trying to move in several different directions at once, but no words came out. She jabbed at random buttons on the sound desk.

'OK, *I'll* tell you, Belle!' Nick said, grinning. 'I happened to be in Mrs B's office this morning when she got a phone call. Not that I'm *nosy* of course, but – the caller said that Belle was ill and could they book rehearsal room two instead. I assumed it was Holly or Cat, but just maybe it was someone else . . .'

Everyone stared at Bianca. Her mouth was now firmly stuck in gulping-goldfish mode. 'Whatever!' she spat finally. Then she stood up, grabbed her bag and flounced off, 'accidentally' barging into both Belle and Cat as she passed. Mayu sidled out after her.

'Grr!' Cat growled. 'Those two! Mean, devious, treacherous little . . .'

'. . . *warthogs?*' Holly suggested.

Belle giggled. 'But did you see the look on Bianca's face when Nick caught her out?'

Holly leaned back against the wall and sank to the floor. Within a few moments all four of them were helpless with laughter.

'That was brilliant, Nick!' said Cat. 'You're a star!'

Nick grinned at her. 'All in a day's work! Hey, can I stay and see how you're getting on?'

'Er, I don't know . . .' Holly stalled. She didn't mind, but she was sure Belle wouldn't want Nick sitting in on their rehearsal.

But, 'Sure,' Belle told him. 'If it's OK with you two?

Nick could give us some useful feedback. You know, on the technical side . . .'

Holly looked at Belle in amazement. If she didn't know better, she'd *almost* think that Belle was growing quite fond of Nick!

'We'll take all the help we can get!' Cat said gratefully.

'I would be honoured to give you the benefit of my valuable opinion!' Nick settled himself into a chair by the sound desk. 'When you're ready, girls. From the top!' he said, clapping his hands.

'I'm beginning to regret this,' Belle muttered.

When Holly, Cat and Belle finished performing *Done Looking!* Nick applauded enthusiastically. 'Great song! It's so feel-good, and the dance routine really works.'

'Thanks,' Holly said, delighted with this reaction to her work.

'Cat's energy was great,' he added. 'And Belle, you were amazing. Your voice was perfect.'

Belle smiled broadly and pulled up a chair next to him. 'We were wondering about putting an extra chorus in the middle . . .'

Nick nodded. 'Good idea. I can edit the backing CD for you. And you know what I think might really work? How about doing one verse in Spanish for a real Latin flavour?'

'That'd be great,' Holly said, 'but does anyone speak Spanish? I don't.'

'Nor me, but I could ask Nathan to do a translation and then teach us how to pronounce it?' Cat offered, her eyes twinkling with excitement.

'Awesome!' exclaimed Belle.

Holly smiled. It seemed they were becoming Nick's Angels after all! But he was being so mega-helpful that no one was objecting now.

'Which one of you is the songwriter, anyway?' Nick asked. 'Or is it a joint effort?'

Holly exchanged *should-we-tell-him?* glances with Cat and Belle. 'Oh, why not?' Belle said, speaking for all of them.

So, as they packed their stuff away, the girls gave Nick an abridged version of the Mystery of the Secret Songwriter, leaving out a few minor details – like the fact that Nick himself had been one of their prime suspects. 'But we still have *no idea* who N.A. is!' Belle concluded.

'Hm . . . N.A. . . .' Nick murmured thoughtfully. 'Maybe they're not the writer's initials at all. N.A. stands for Not Applicable – you know, like when a form asks how many times you've been married or had the bubonic plague or something.'

'So, if the letters N.A. *aren't* initials, the writer could be *absolutely anyone* . . .' Cat said slowly.

'*Oh, no!*' Holly gasped, suddenly realizing that this was a *catastrophe*. 'We've only gone and filled in *Songwriter: Not Applicable* on our entry form!'

'Mr Garcia's going to think we're total head cases!' Cat groaned.

'What are we going to do?' Belle said despairingly. 'They'll definitely disqualify us from the talent competition now!'

Holly stared at Belle and Cat, seeing her own rising panic reflected in their eyes.

'Not necessarily,' Nick said in a reassuring tone. 'Wait and see. People probably make mistakes on their forms all the time. They'll get in touch with you if there's a problem.'

Holly looked gratefully at Nick. She really wanted to believe him.

'OK,' Cat said. 'We'll just have to hope for the best.'

Holly jumped as the bell suddenly rang for afternoon lessons. As she picked up her bag, her emotions were whirling around like a kaleidoscope. They just *couldn't* be thrown out of the talent competition now, could they?

CHAPTER TWENTY-SIX

Holly: Burning Ears and Smiling Eyes

A few minutes later, Holly trooped into Mr Grampian's acting class with Nick, Cat and Belle. They were in one of the larger performance spaces, but the room still seemed more crowded than usual.

'Welcome, fellow thespians!' Hawk-man proclaimed. 'Today, my esteemed Year Eight students, we are joining forces with the *crème de la crème* of Year Ten in a combined exploration of the dramatic arts . . .'

As he spoke, Holly was still worrying about the talent competition. Her attention wandered to the group of older students sitting at the back. She recognized several faces – Lucy Cheng, Felix Baddeley and . . .

. . . Ethan Reed!

Holly instantly felt a blaze of heat engulf her ears. She shuffled her chair so that she was out of sight behind Cat. *Holly Jasmine Devenish*, she reprimanded herself, *just grow up!*

This thing with the burning ears happened every time she saw Ethan. Which was quite often since she'd started going swimming several times a week. She knew that Ethan liked her. He always smiled and chatted about his training schedule. But he obviously only liked her as a friend.

And I like him as a friend too, Holly told herself.

She peeped out. Ethan was leaning over to talk to someone. The corners of his eyes did a kind of smiling-thing that made her heart do a little dance – even though he wasn't even smiling at *her*.

OK, I like him as more than a friend! Holly finally admitted it to herself. But what chance did she have? He was Mr Super-Popular-Good-Looking-Year-Ten-Guy, and she was . . . well, she was just Holly. She would be a laughing-stock if she told anyone about it. *Just keep quiet and get over it*, she told herself.

'Can you see all right back there, Hols?' Cat asked.

'Oh, er, yeah, fine, thanks,' Holly mumbled, tuning back in to the class.

The Year Ten students, Mr Grampian explained, had written one-act plays, and were now going to work on their directing skills by acting them out with the help of the Year Eight students. They would spend the first hour rehearsing the plays. They would then perform them to the class so they could all evaluate each other's acting and directing. He started to read through the groups of students that would be working together. Ethan Reed was the first name called out.

'Ah yes, Ethan – you're working with Nathan Almeida, Serena Quereshi and Holly Devenish.'

Holly's ears burned once again.

CHAPTER TWENTY-SEVEN

Cat: Secret Love and Other Mysteries

'Next, Duncan Gillespie,' Mr Grampian continued. 'And your chosen few are Nick Taggart, Mason Lee and Catrin Wickham.'

Cat and the rest of her group pulled up a circle of chairs. Duncan was a tall gangly boy with thick dark hair swept forward as if he were standing in a wind tunnel. He talked the group through his play as he handed out scripts. 'It's about a sweet old lady called Mrs Stanley,' he said. 'That's you, Cat. But she leads a secret double-life as a blackmailer.'

Cat soon forgot all her worries about the talent competition as she immersed herself in her character. Mildred Stanley was a complex part, and she loved the challenge. She was blissfully happy as she worked, discussing the dialogue and the best way to bring out the tensions between her character and her husband and her grandson – played by Mason and Nick.

Cat's group was first to get up on the stage. The play

went brilliantly: she delivered her final line, '*I'm off to Las Vegas on the next plane!*' to rapturous applause.

'Magnificent!' Mr Grampian declared as the actors took their bows.

'Thanks, Cat.' Duncan grinned. 'You really brought Mildred to life for me.'

Cat smiled back. 'No problem! She's a great character – although I wouldn't like to meet her!'

Elated, she settled down to watch the other groups. Lucy Cheng, Bianca, Lettie and Zak were next, performing Lucy's play about a group of friends at an audition for a quiz show—

Audition!

Hearing that word, Cat's brain suddenly skidded off-track into a tailspin of worry. She'd been trying to put the *Macbeth* audition out of her mind and concentrate on the talent competition, but now both were only a few days away. She was used to pre-audition nerves, of course; she'd done hundreds of auditions before. But she hadn't been able to spend nearly enough time rehearsing her Second Witch. Time! It seemed to be in short supply these days. Except in Mrs Salmon's science lessons, where every minute seemed to last longer than the one before—

Suddenly Cat was aware that something was going

on. While she'd been contemplating the deep philosophical concept of Time, the next play had started. Ethan Reed was on stage with Holly, Nathan and Serena. The play was a wartime romance. A prisoner of war, played by Ethan himself, seemed to be falling in love with the prison commandant's daughter, played by Holly. Nathan and Serena were excellent as the cruel commandant and his down-trodden wife. Cat nibbled her fingernails, nervous on Holly's behalf. She knew how insecure Holly was about acting.

But her concern was soon replaced with amazement. *Holly was brilliant!* Each time Ethan glanced at her, she blushed and turned away, but then looked back with a sad, yearning expression. She perfectly captured the anguish of secret love. Ethan and Holly portrayed the doomed relationship so beautifully that when Ethan's character was transferred to another prison camp, Cat felt tears running down her face.

Mr Grampian blew his hawkish nose into a silk handkerchief. 'Profoundly moving!' he sniffled. 'Captivating!'

When did Holly turn into a spellbinding actress? Cat marvelled. *Has she secretly mind-morphed with Kate Winslet?*

'I never knew Holly could act like that!' Belle whispered.

'Nor did I!' Cat mouthed back.

But then she remembered how often Holly had been going swimming lately. And of course she'd heard about the diving-into-Ethan's-arms-on-the-steps incident. The whole school had heard about that! And it made her wonder . . . *Maybe Holly hadn't been acting at all.*

After the acting class, Cat felt restless and unable to face settling down to her mountain of homework. She suggested to Holly and Belle that they play some tennis to take their minds off the talent competition.

'So why the big secret, Hols?' Cat asked as they strolled towards the school tennis courts in the mellow late-afternoon sunshine.

'What do you mean?' Holly asked, dropping the tennis ball she was trying to balance on her racket.

'You and Ethan!' Belle smiled. ''Fess up!'

'There's nothing to confess,' Holly said quietly.

'Oh, fine, so you won't be interested to know then . . .' Cat said slowly.

'Know what?' Holly asked.

'Just that Ethan obviously really fancies you!' she replied. 'The way he kept looking at you, it was so sweet!'

'Really? Do you think so?' Holly asked eagerly. Then she stopped herself and blushed.

Cat smiled to herself. *How easy was that?*

'Oh, so you *do* like him then?' Belle asked.

'Well, maybe a bit, I suppose,' Holly admitted reluctantly. 'Oh, OK, I *really* like him. But it's pointless – he's way out of my league.'

'Don't put yourself down, Holly,' Belle said seriously. 'Cat's right, he *was* looking at you. If you asked him out, I'm sure he'd say yes.'

'Ask him out?' Holly squawked. 'Are you *insane*? I can't even *talk* to him without turning into a jellyfish! Oh, look, there's Gemma,' she added, changing the subject. 'Let's ask her if she wants to come and play doubles.'

Cat waved Gemma over.

'Don't say anything about Ethan, will you?' Holly whispered as Gemma trotted over to join them. 'I'm really glad I've told you guys, but that's enough True Confessions for one day!'

'We promise!' Cat said with a grin.

CHAPTER TWENTY-EIGHT

Belle: Shopping, But Not As We Know It

If shopping were a martial art, Belle would be a black belt. She'd shopped for Christian Dior jackets in Beverley Hills, Versace boots in Milan and bought her Louis Vuitton luggage in Paris.

So, on Saturday morning – the day before the talent competition – when Cat and Holly suggested they go shopping for outfits for their performance, Belle *assumed* they'd be hopping into a taxi and heading for Knightsbridge. She *loved* Harrods and Harvey Nicks.

She didn't expect to be sitting on a double-decker bus that was crawling through the bustling London streets towards Camden Market. Markets were places for buying fruit and vegetables, weren't they?

But she was so happy she didn't mind where they were going! All week the girls had lived in dread of hearing news that they'd been disqualified from the talent competition because they hadn't provided the songwriter's name on their entry form. But when the letter from Mr Garcia had finally arrived, it was simply a confirmation of their place in the competition. Belle, Cat and Holly had practically fainted with relief!

They hadn't been disqualified! At last it was really happening!

'You can get *anything* in Camden Market,' Holly was saying. 'I'm sure we'll find something with a Latin American look to go with the song.'

'But not like that frilly frou-frou stuff they wear for ballroom dancing,' Cat insisted. 'We want something a bit edgy.'

Belle looked down at her white Italian-cut jeans and Chanel coat-dress. Then she glanced at Holly, who was wearing a Billabong hoodie and a short checked skirt, and at Cat, in her black leather jacket and glittery silver mini-dress. They all looked so different – would they ever find anything they agreed on?

'Here we are. Come on!' Holly shouted, jumping up excitedly.

'I love this place!' Cat grinned as she clattered down the stairs after her.

Belle followed Cat and Holly along Chalk Farm Road into the Stables Market. They elbowed their way through crowds of shoppers and tourists, all rummaging through the goods piled on the stalls: crafts, jewellery, hot dogs, piercings, saris, CDs – and lots and lots of clothes. It was fun, in a manic kind of a way, Belle thought. *But there are no proper changing rooms! No assistants to bring you different sizes!*

'Come on,' Cat said, darting towards a huge stall of vintage clothing. She burrowed in and pulled out a spangled red flamenco dress with two layers of ruffles. 'Perfect!' she cried. 'And look – with these shoes—'

'Hang on, what about this one?' Holly said, pulling a pink puffball skirt off a rack.

'I am *not* wearing that!' Belle winced as Cat held out a floaty blue and purple dress with a feather trim. 'I'd look like a demented peacock!'

'Oops, this skirt's way too big.' Holly giggled as she pulled it on over her jeans and it immediately dropped round her ankles.

'Oh, no, this dress has a stain all down the front.' Cat sighed. 'It looks like engine oil.'

Belle stared, trying to imagine *who* would work on their car engine in a red flamenco dress.

This wasn't shopping as she knew it!

Two hours later, they still hadn't purchased a thing.

'Anyway,' Belle sighed as they sank down at a table

outside a small café and ordered frappuccinos. '*Matching* outfits would be better. Then we'd really look like a band.'

'That's true,' Cat agreed.

'Maybe we should go to Oxford Street instead,' Holly suggested.

'But it would cost a fortune,' Cat moaned.

'I've got it!' Belle announced, suddenly thinking of a fabulous plan. She whipped her mobile phone out of her handbag. 'Desperate times call for desperate measures!'

'What are you doing?' Holly asked.

'Something I vowed I would never do,' Belle answered with a grin. 'Using my parents' contacts to further my career!'

Cat and Holly gazed, wide-eyed with curiosity and admiration, as Belle got through to her mother. Zoe Fairweather was about to step out onto a catwalk in Rome, but she had time to give Belle the number she asked for: 'Yes, call Pixie Ormolu, darling. She's the best fashion stylist in London; works with *all* the top magazines – tell her I sent you . . . Oh, and good luck with the competition. Got to go, I'm being called!'

One more call and Belle had arranged an

appointment with Pixie Ormolu at her warehouse in Covent Garden. 'OK, we're doing this *my* way now!' she insisted. '*Taxi!*' she yelled, stepping out into the street and waving her Prada handbag in the air.

Pixie Ormolu worked miracles. The tiny woman with spiky bleached blonde hair, pillar-box-red lipstick and oversized black-framed glasses greeted the girls with hugs and kisses.

'Zoe Fairweather is one of my absolute *favourite* clients!' she trilled. She showed the girls into a spacious changing room with wall-to-wall mirrors. Then she flitted around like a humming bird, fetching garments from the miles of racks that ran the length of the building. Within an hour Belle was wearing an elegant silver dress with three narrow frills of black velvet across the skirt. Cat had a fitted black velvet dress with silver ruffles round a plunging neckline that showed off her curves, while Holly wore a short geometric-print silver and black dress. Belle admired their reflections in the mirror.

They looked like superstars!

They held hands and jumped up in the asymmetric leap that ended each chorus of *Done Looking!*

'Just, er, checking that there's enough room for

movement in these dresses!' Belle explained, seeing Pixie's puzzled look.

'Got to fly, girls!' Pixie called back as she darted out of the changing room. 'Can't keep my super-models waiting! Just bring the dresses back when you're finished with them. Oh, and good luck!'

Belle felt unbelievably happy as she Cat and Holly walked up the stone steps of the Garrick School and into the entrance hall. They were laden with bags full of their stunning new outfits and accessories. They had the band, they had the song, and now they had the look – it was all lining up perfectly for the competition tomorrow.

'I can't wait!' Holly breathed, as if reading Belle's mind.

'I know,' Cat agreed. 'I bet I won't be able to get to sleep tonight!'

Belle crossed the hall to check the pigeonholes for messages. She pulled out a letter and tore open the envelope with her teeth as she caught up with Holly and Cat on the way upstairs. She was really looking forward to a soak in the bath and a camomile tea . . .

It took her a moment to register what the words on the page were saying. She stopped dead in her tracks.

Her bag fell and slid down the stairs. Feeling as if she might collapse at any moment, Belle read the note out in a small shaky voice:

'*Dear Miss Madison, Miss Devenish and Miss Wickham,*
Please come to my office at 9.30 tomorrow morning with respect to an urgent matter concerning your entry for the Garrick talent competition.
Yours sincerely, James Fortune (Principal).'

CHAPTER TWENTY-NINE

Cat: Girl-size Tears and Man-size Tissues

At 9.25 the next morning Cat stood outside the principal's office with Belle and Holly.

It was competition day! None of them had slept much, but it was out of worry, not excitement.

We can't prove that our song is original material.

They'll think we were trying to cheat.

We're going to be thrown out of the competition . . .

These thoughts had been revolving around Cat's head all night, like abandoned suitcases on a baggage-reclaim conveyor belt.

Belle was pale, with violet rings under her eyes, and even Holly's beautiful brown skin was more cold tea than caramel this morning. Cat could feel an angry mob of spots threatening to break out on her chin.

'Ready?' she asked. Belle and Holly nodded grimly. With a weight in her stomach like a sack of wet cement, Cat knocked.

'Come in!'

Cat pushed open the door. Originally the old library, the principal's office was carpeted with oriental rugs and lined with burnished oak shelves of leather-bound books. Mr Fortune sat behind an antique desk with Mr Garcia standing beside him.

'Ah, excellent – sit down, sit down,' Mr Fortune said, indicating a row of three chairs.

'Now, Mr Garcia,' Mr Fortune said. 'If you would be good enough to explain the situation to our young friends . . .'

Light flooded in through the sash window and bounced off the polished desk and Mr Garcia's head. 'Yes, certainly, Principal,' he replied. 'As you know, it is a rule of the talent competition that all entrants must perform *original material*, and must list the writer or composer on the entry form. Naturally we assumed that the initials N.A. on your form' – he paused and tapped the piece of paper in his hand – 'were an abbreviation of Nobody's Angels; indicating that your song was jointly written by members of the band—'

'However,' Mr Fortune interrupted, 'yesterday we received information that this was not the case – that you are *not* the writers of the song and, more importantly, that *you do not know who the writer is* . . .'

No prizes for guessing where that information came from!

Cat thought. *Someone with the initial B, no doubt.* And she wasn't talking about Beyoncé.

Cat couldn't bear it any longer. She had to explain that they weren't cheats. 'It's true! We don't know who wrote our song,' she blurted, 'but we weren't trying to pretend it was written by Nobody's Angels.'

'No,' Holly added. 'And we didn't mean *Not Applicable* either.'

'The song was given to us secretly by someone who only signed themselves N.A.,' Belle said, her voice trembling. 'So that's what we put . . .'

Cat pulled the original song-sheets for *Opposites Attract* and *Done Looking!* out of her bag and slid them across the desk. 'Look – here in the corner. It just says N.A.'

Mr Garcia studied the pages. 'Yes, I see. But we don't believe that you were *deliberately* aiming to deceive us. We just have to know who the writer is, so we can ascertain that they have given permission for you to use their song and—'

So that's it then, Cat thought. *It's all over.*

There was a sobbing sound. She turned to see Belle's blue eyes welling with tears. She put her arm around Belle's shoulder and Holly reached across and took her hand.

'Now, now! No need to despair!' Mr Fortune beamed, passing Belle a box of man-size tissues. 'What Mr Garcia was just about to say was that a few moments ago we had a visit – from a certain songwriter with the initials N.A. – to hand in a signed letter giving permission for Nobody's Angels to perform these songs – although they still wish to remain anonymous.'

There was a long silence.

'So are you saying we *can* enter the competition?' Holly whispered.

'Yes, indeed.' Mr Fortune nodded. 'We simply wished to check that your version of events tallied with N.A.'s story.'

'Please go and arrange a time to rehearse with the backing band later this morning,' Mr Garcia told them with a smile. 'The competition will be starting at six thirty.'

'You could always take a short cut through the kitchen storeroom to save time,' Mr Fortune chuckled, doing his twinkly-eye thing in Cat's direction. 'And good luck!'

'Woo-hoo!' Cat shouted triumphantly as soon as they were out of the principal's office. She grabbed Holly and Belle in a group hug and they all jumped up and down, laughing away the tears.

'Can you believe Bianca sneaked on us like that?' Cat asked.

'Easily!' Holly and Belle giggled.

'Well, it didn't work,' she declared happily. '*Talent competition, here we come!*'

The rehearsal did not go well.

It wasn't the backing band's fault: this consisted of many of the Garrick's most musically gifted students, and the arrangement was excellent. The percussion section, with Mason Lee on drums, was lively and spirited – especially the all-important Latin American claves. The string section, including Lettie Atkins on cello, played with passion and verve.

But when the girls started to sing, their voices were lifeless. The sleepless night, followed by the roller-coaster morning, had sapped every last watt of Girl Power – and left them snappy and hyper-sensitive.

Cat accused Belle of coming in a beat early on the chorus. Belle complained that Cat was singing off-key. Holly was so tense that sometimes when she opened her mouth, nothing came out but a squeak.

And that was before they even tried adding the dance routine.

As they left the theatre, they hardly dared look at each other. It was Cat who finally put it into words. 'We're going to have to do *a whole lot better* than that tonight!' she moaned.

'I know – I'm sorry, I was rubbish,' Holly said, hanging her head sadly.

'It wasn't just you, Holly,' Belle said. 'I sucked too.'

'Hey, I'm sorry too,' Cat sighed. 'We're all just tired. Let's get some rest.'

'Yeah, we'll be amazing tonight,' Holly said bravely, linking arms.

'Awesome!' Belle grinned as she took Cat's other arm.

Cat laughed. '*Auspicious!*'

CHAPTER THIRTY

Belle: Living the Dream

The talent competition was finally underway.

Belle hovered in the wings. The waiting was killing her! She'd peeked out onto the stage several times and caught glimpses of the earlier acts, including Sammy Armitage, a comedian, Meredith Lutz playing jazz piano, and a group of male dancers called Move It! They were all awesome! And they were all older. Nobody's Angels were the only Year Eight act in the competition. For a moment Belle wondered whether this had all been a big mistake.

But they'd worked so hard. They had to give it everything!

Half the acts had already completed their performances. Owen Mitchell and Tabitha Langley were coming to the end of their romantic duet. It was a cute song, but Belle could hardly hear it for the blood pounding in her ears.

Nobody's Angels were up next.

Belle inhaled the dusty fragrance of the thick stage curtains and the heat from the spotlights. Tabitha and Owen were taking a bow. The audience – made up of Garrick staff and students – were clapping enthusiastically.

Belle turned to check that Cat and Holly were right behind her. Cat grinned back with a big thumbs-up sign. She'd recharged her batteries with an afternoon Cat-nap, while Holly had gone for a swim. They both looked spectacular in the outfits they'd selected from Pixie Ormolu's collection. Belle smoothed the front of her silver dress and reminded herself to breathe. She'd been doing yoga all afternoon to centre herself. *Work* with *your nerves*, she told herself. *Use them!*

Mr Fortune was walking up to the microphone. 'And the next act is the youngest in the competition . . .' he began.

Belle adjusted her radio-microphone headset and reached over to straighten Holly's wide satin hairband. She could feel the silver glitter Cat had applied to her cheekbones prickling her skin. She peeped out from behind the curtain and looked down at the panel of judges. She recognized the familiar faces of Mr Garcia, Miss Morgan and two other Garrick teachers. Then she noticed a fifth figure: a tall man in a blue suit and a ridiculous hairpiece.

It was Larry Shapiro, the world-famous vocal coach!

Belle felt as if the universe were holding its breath. Her fragile layer of calm was in danger of shattering. What if she messed up? *She would never be able to live it down.*

Then the world started turning again, aided by a firm push from Cat.

'OK, we're on!' Holly whispered.

'Please welcome . . . Nobody's Angels!' shouted Mr Fortune.

Applause ringing in her ears, Belle took her starting position at centre stage, Cat and Holly on either side of her. They were motionless, chins held high, looking out into the audience as the band began to play. Belle noticed Nathan Almeida and Nick Taggart sitting behind the judges. Then she saw Zak, Frankie, Mason, Gemma, Serena . . . Just about every Year Eight student had come to cheer them on!

The lights dimmed and Belle could now make out the words on the banners they were holding:

ANGELS ROCK
GO, ANGELS, GO!

She smiled. She had so many friends at Superstar High – and they were all rooting for her! Her moment of fear was behind her. Raw excitement took its place.

The music started.

Step, and sway to the left, step and sway to the right . . . Belle counted. *Left arm up, right arm up, spin round and . . . sing . . .*

> '*We're done looking! Now we're leaping!*
> *We won't stay in the shallows . . .*'

Belle felt as if she were flying on a magic carpet! Cat and Holly were right beside her, their voices soaring together, their steps in perfect unison.

At the end of the last chorus . . . '*catch the wave, live our dreams . . .*' they all jumped higher than they'd ever done before. Belle knew they'd given the performance of their lives. The audience was standing up, everyone whooping and waving their banners.

Mr Fortune almost had to *push* them off the stage to make way for the next act. They tumbled into the wings in a blur of laughter, hugs and whispered exclamations.

'I thought my heart was going to burst,' Holly gasped.

'And when I saw Larry Shapiro . . .' Belle added.

'And did you see all the banners?' Cat asked.

'Sshh!' hissed the stage manager. 'If you girls want to natter, go to the dressing room – there are still three acts to go.'

Belle came to her senses and looked around, noticing for the first time the other performers huddled anxiously in the wings.

Now all they could do was wait.

But had they done enough?

Breathe, centre, calm! Belle chanted to herself.

Every minute seemed like a lifetime!

At last the stage manager instructed them to go back on stage with the other acts: Mr Fortune was about to announce the winners.

Belle felt her legs trembling as she stood with her arms around Cat and Holly.

'In third place . . . Sammy Armitage.'

There was a cry of '*Yes!*' and applause as the comedian stepped up to collect his prize.

In second was the dance group, Move It!

'And first place . . .' Mr Fortune shouted.

Belle thought she would never breathe again!

'. . . goes to . . . Tabitha Langley and Owen Mitchell!'

Belle squeezed her eyes tight shut to hold back tears, struggling to keep a dignified smile glued to her face. She'd always known they were unlikely to come in the top three, but she had still *hoped*. She couldn't bear to look at Holly and Cat and see their disappointment. When the principal continued speaking, his words were just meaningless sounds – 'special prize . . . exceptional promise . . . Mr Garcia particularly enjoyed the Spanish verse . . .'

The words began to permeate Belle's brain. She opened her eyes and stared at Mr Fortune. Was he really saying what she thought he was saying?

'Highly Commended,' he continued, 'and a place in the Garrick Gala Charity Showcase goes to . . . Nobody's Angels.'

'*Yesssss!*' There was a blur of shrieking and crying and laughing. Belle couldn't believe it. 'Does he mean us?' she gulped.

'Yes, we've done it!' Cat screamed, squashing her in a giant embrace. Suddenly they were all jumping up and down on the spot and screaming.

'Come on,' Holly said, tugging the other two towards Mr Fortune as the audience applauded wildly.

Belle sniffed and wiped the tears from her eyes. This

was what she had worked for. She really *was* a singer. And it felt great!

She was catching her wave! She was living her dream!

As she hugged Holly goodnight in the corridor outside their rooms later, Belle thought she had never felt so tired in all her life.

Or so happy.

There was only one thing missing. 'I *wish* we knew who N.A. was so we could thank them,' she sighed. 'We couldn't have done it without that song!'

'Into your own rooms now, gals, lickety-split!' Miss Candlemas called as she steamed along the corridor. 'School in the morning – even superstars need their beauty sleep!'

Belle pushed open the door, and immediately noticed an envelope lying on the floor. *It must be another song*, she thought, picking it up and showing it to Cat.

'Hey, Hols,' Cat called as she and Belle stepped back out into the corridor. 'Look at this!'

Holly came out of her room, followed by Bianca, whose face was plastered with thick Shrek-green skin cream. 'I hear you lot somehow managed to scrape a place in the showcase,' she muttered ungraciously as she headed towards the bathroom.

Ignoring her, Belle tore open the envelope and pulled out a slip of paper. It wasn't a song, but it *was* from N.A. Cat and Holly stared at her, open-mouthed, as she read the note aloud.

'*To Belle, Cat and Holly. Congratulations!*
Will meet you at ten thirty tonight in C & B's room.
Love, N.A.'

Belle felt a jolt of excitement. But . . . *it was completely against the rules!*

'N.A.'s a *boy*,' she gasped. 'At least we think he is. We can't just invite a *boy* into our room after lights out. Miss Candlemas will go *ballistic*!'

'Well, *technically* we're not inviting him, are we?' Cat grinned. 'He's invited himself!'

'I'll sneak along at ten fifteen,' Holly whispered, ducking back into her room as Bianca reappeared from the bathroom.

CHAPTER THIRTY-ONE

Cat: She'll Be Wearing Pink Pyjamas!

Ten thirty?

That was *way* past lights out!

So it was risky enough that a dressing-gown-clad Holly was in their room, let alone that they were about to be visited by a Mysterious Stranger who was almost certainly a *boy*!

It's just like St Trinian's! Cat thought excitedly. *We could have a midnight feast next!*

Belle, on the other hand, was beside herself with worry: she insisted that she and Cat sit on their beds, ready to pretend to be asleep if Miss Candlemas should call in. She'd also arranged a pile of laundry in the corner as an emergency hidey-hole for N.A., assuming he actually showed up. Holly was curled up under a heap of cushions at the end of Cat's bed.

And, of course, the lights were all off.

At ten thirty precisely there was a very soft knock at the door.

Cat's heart did a back-flip. She looked at Belle . . .

There it was again.

'Er, I've got to get out of bed to open the door,' Cat whispered.

'Go on then,' Belle answered. 'But be quiet!'

Cat pulled the door open, trying not to let it creak, to find herself looking at . . . a pair of stripy pink pyjamas – which wasn't exactly what she'd been expecting. She lifted her eyes to the visitor's face and realized that it was only Lettie Atkins.

'Oh, hi, Lettie, it's you,' Cat said, feeling disappointed. 'We thought it was—'

'N.A., the songwriter,' Lettie whispered, slipping past her into the room and switching on a small torch. 'I know. It's me!'

'But your initials aren't N.A.!' Belle whispered from her bed.

'*Nicolette* Atkins,' Lettie whispered patiently. 'Lettie is a nickname.'

Cat was speechless. Could the songwriter really be the quiet, serious girl with the cello? She was friends with Bianca for a start! She'd always been part of the Mean Team. Although, now Cat came to think about it, Lettie had never really joined in with Bianca and Mayu's spiteful shenanigans. She just kind of tagged along.

'But why?' Holly asked. 'I mean, thank you so much, we *love* the songs, but why give them to us?' She moved over to make room for Lettie among the cushions on Cat's bed. Cat got back under her duvet and Belle came over to sit on the bed too.

'I've always loved writing songs,' Lettie explained, 'but I don't have a very good singing voice. And I'd rather be playing in the orchestra anyway. When I saw you guys at the karaoke party, you had such a great sound – and then I heard you saying you needed an original song for the talent competition, and I just *knew* I could write something perfect for you – but I also knew that if Bianca found out, she'd try to stop me helping . . . So I came up with the idea of delivering the songs secretly—'

'Hang on,' Belle interrupted. 'That's impossible! Last Sunday someone tried to deliver a song under our door. But you were in Bianca's room all the time. We saw you there!'

'Not *all* the time. I left Bianca's room to go to the loo – and started sliding the envelope under your door. Then, when I heard all the commotion, I just ran straight back into Bianca's room.'

Lettie was obviously telling the truth. Cat shook her

head. 'But, Lettie, why do you put up with Bianca bossing you around all the time?'

Lettie smiled. 'She's not so bad really. We've been friends since primary school. She's been much worse since we came to the Garrick though. I think she just feels threatened. She was used to being a big fish in a little pond at our old school. Here, *everyone* is super-talented and she's not Queen Bee any more.'

Cat laughed. 'No, she just acts like one!'

And then, suddenly, the door flew open and there was a blinding flash of light.

'Ha! Got you!' shouted Bianca, waving her digital camera triumphantly. 'A *boy* in the bedroom after lights out. Miss Candlemas will be *very* interested in this photo of . . .' Her voice trailed off as her eyes focused. 'Knickers?' she squeaked. 'Knickers! What are *you* doing in here?'

Lettie looked up from the laundry pile, where Belle had pushed her, and removed a sock from her head.

No wonder Lettie dropped 'Nicolette', Cat thought. *Who'd want to go through life being called Knickers?*

'Come in, Bianca,' Holly hissed, 'and join the pyjama party – quickly, before Miss Candlemas hears you.'

'I don't *think* we've left any boys lying around in here.' Cat pretended to check under her desk and behind the curtains. 'Is this a random spot-check, or did you select our room specially?'

'But . . . but . . .' Bianca was spluttering, 'I *heard* you! I know all about your so-called Mystery Songwriter. You got that note. You were planning to meet him in here tonight.' Then a sly smile stole across her face. 'Oh, so he's stood you up then, has he?'

There was a long pause as Cat exchanged glances with Holly and Belle in the light of the torch and the pale moonlight filtering through the curtains. None of them wanted to give Lettie away.

'I'm starting to think you've been making this whole secret songwriter thing up,' Bianca went on. 'Just to get attention.'

'It's me, actually. *I'm* the songwriter,' Lettie piped up nervously.

Bianca stared in disbelief. 'Knick . . . Lettie . . . What . . . ? How . . . ?'

'Look, Bianca,' Lettie said, 'we've known each other a long time. Ever since I had to hold your hand in reception class because you were scared of Father Christmas . . .' She paused, then continued in an increasingly confident voice, 'I like being your friend, but it doesn't mean I have to do everything you say. I wanted to write songs for Belle, Cat and Holly, so

I did. If you don't like it, fine, but don't make a fuss!'

All eyes were now fixed on Bianca. Everyone kept very still – as if she were a cornered pit bull that might attack at any moment. But Bianca suddenly caved in like a hot-air balloon when the burner is switched off. 'Well, you'll still be in loads of trouble,' she said, pouting, 'if Miss Candlemas finds out you're running around after lights out.' Then she seemed to perk up a little as the realization dawned. 'So you'd better do what I say if you don't want her to hear about it,' she concluded triumphantly.

'Like what?' Belle asked.

There was a long pause as Bianca thought about this. Her face contorted as if she were having an argument with herself. 'I want Lettie to be my room-mate,' she announced finally. 'Holly, you have to swap.'

And, with that, she marched out.

Cat, Holly, Belle and Lettie all looked at each other, then burst out laughing.

'So, would that be OK with you?' Lettie asked Holly. 'I share with Gemma Dalrymple at the moment.'

'It'll be my pleasure.' Holly grinned. 'How about we swap tomorrow?'

'Thanks,' Lettie said. 'Gemma's great, but Bianca and I – we go back such a long way. We're like sisters.

I'm really glad she wants me to be her room-mate.'

Cat laughed. 'This must be a first: Bianca has actually done something that's made everyone happy!'

'She must be sickening for something,' Belle said.

'See, I told you she wasn't *all* bad!' Lettie chuckled.

'Now you guys better go,' Cat said, 'before we really do get caught!'

CHAPTER THIRTY-TWO

Cat: In the Cauldron Boil and Bake

The next morning everyone was tired.

For the first time Cat could remember, Belle slept late and missed her morning run. Then there was a flurry of activity as Lettie and Holly got together with Gemma at breakfast to discuss The Big Swap. Gemma was perfectly happy with the arrangement and they all went off to clear it with Miss Candlemas, who gave them the go-ahead as long as they didn't get the idea that they could 'chop and change willy-nilly!'

At morning break Cat helped Holly to move her things into Gemma's room – fortunately it was only across the corridor. Then she found herself a quiet spot in one of the study rooms and ran through her Second Witch lines for the last time.

The *Macbeth* auditions were at lunch time today!

But, to her surprise, Cat found that she didn't feel panicky about it any more. She was actually looking forward to the audition. She was nervous, of course, but relaxed, somehow. The talent competition had taken her mind off worrying, and the success of Nobody's Angels had really boosted her confidence. She was in control. This multi-tasking business wasn't so hard, after all!

After an even-longer-than-usual science lesson, and then an hour of coastal erosion in geography, Cat and Nathan hurried to the Drama Department. SILENCE PLEASE: AUDITIONS IN PROGRESS said the large sign on the door of the main performance studio. Several other students were already loitering nervously in the corridor, reciting lines to themselves under their breath.

Cat put her ear to the door and heard a voice she recognized as Ethan Reed's, performing one of Banquo's speeches. She checked the schedule and saw that she was due to be called next.

The door opened and Ethan stepped out. He smiled at Cat and nodded for her to go in. Yep, she could see why Holly liked him. Those green eyes and long dark lashes . . .

'Good luck!' Nathan called after her.

Mr Grampian stood up and introduced the other members of the panel. 'Mr Steele is the Garrick's

Shakespeare expert and will be directing the play.' Cat recognized Mr Steele as one of the drama teachers; he returned her smile with a sharp nod and went back to fiddling with his pencil. 'And you have already met the estimable Duncan Gillespie, of course,' Mr Grampian went on. 'Duncan is the assistant director of this production . . .'

Duncan smiled warmly at Cat. She grinned back. This was her lucky day! Duncan had *loved* her portrayal of his character, Mrs Stanley, in the acting class. That *must* be a good sign.

'In your own time, please,' Mr Steele said, gesturing to where Cat should stand in an impatient manner, making it clear that she should, in fact, *get a move on* and certainly *not* in her own time.

Cat climbed up the steps and stood on the stage. She closed her eyes and cleared her mind of Cat Wickham thoughts (*dark eyelashes, the chocolate bar she'd promised herself as a reward*) and replaced them with Second Witch thoughts (*dark, malignant and twisted*).

Cat opened her eyes and stared up at the ceiling as if she were seeing a vision. Then she knelt down and felt around with claw-like hands, as if feeling for objects laid out on the ground. She began in a quiet, sinister voice, rising to a loud cackle as she added the ingredients of her spell.

'*Fillet of a fenny snake, In the cauldron boil and bake . . .*'

At the end of the spell Cat closed her eyes again. Then she fell forward from her kneeling position to lie face-down on the stage. She hadn't planned to end in this melodramatic way, but suddenly all the excitement and emotion of the last few days took its toll and her body just crumpled beneath her.

Slowly she looked up.

The members of the casting panel were all smiling at her.

'Really liked the way you collapsed at the end – like you were drained by the force of the spell,' Duncan said, nodding wisely.

'Thanks,' Cat mumbled, feeling a surge of relief as she stumbled offstage.

'We'll be contacting people about call-backs in a few days,' Mr Steele told her. 'Could you ask the next person to come in?'

Cat wandered out into the corridor in a daze.

'How did it go?' Nathan whispered.

'Really well!' She held up her hands to show her crossed fingers. 'Good luck, Nate!'

Now, where's that jumbo-sized Mars bar? she thought.

* ★ ★

In the afternoon, Mr Garcia's singing class was followed by an extra dance class – tap, with Miss LeClair. Miss Morgan was also there, observing again; the teachers were still trying to identify any extra students to include in the various advanced classes, which would all be starting after the half-term holiday.

Usually Cat enjoyed tap, but the combination of tiredness and Miss Morgan's beady glare meant that she stumbled her way through the lesson like a pantomime horse on automatic pilot.

As she and Holly headed out of the Dance Department, chatting about the audition, Cat realized that Belle had slipped away and gone on ahead. Entering the courtyard, Holly suddenly pulled her back into the doorway. 'Sshh! Look!' she whispered. 'What's Belle up to?'

Cat looked up and saw Belle sitting on one of the benches, still in her dance clothes, talking to Nick Taggart.

'So,' Belle was saying, in a hushed voice, 'you know how all the performers get two free tickets for the Gala Charity Showcase to give to guests?'

'Aye, I do indeed,' Nick answered, in the voice of a rather posh elderly lady from Edinburgh. 'And verrrry nice too. Those tickets are awful expensive to buy.'

'Anyway,' Belle hissed secretively, 'my parents are both overseas. So I wondered if you wanted one of my tickets – otherwise it'll just go to waste . . .'

Cat and Holly looked at each other.

'Aw! Sweet!' Holly exclaimed.

'*What a dork!*' Cat laughed, quoting Belle's first impression of Nick at the welcome speeches.

'I knew Belle was warming up to him *a bit*,' Holly whispered, 'but not this much!'

'It's probably best,' Cat said, 'if Belle never *ever* finds out that we overheard this conversation.'

CHAPTER THIRTY-THREE

Belle: Telling Lies and Matchmaking

Belle wasn't sure what had come over her.

She'd given a showcase ticket to Nick Taggart, of all people! But he *had* helped them with their song, and she knew that it was Nick, along with Nathan, who'd made all the banners and rounded up their fan club of supporters for the talent competition.

And that *still* left her with a spare ticket. Dad was in South Africa filming a new epic movie, and Mom was on a catwalk in Helsinki – or was it Hamburg? There was no chance either of them would interrupt their busy schedules just to come and see her sing. She was on her own. *Hey, girl*, she told herself. *Don't you start feeling sorry for yourself. Now, focus on these math problems.*

It was Wednesday evening. The weather had turned very cold and Belle shivered as she sat in the library with her homework. All the excitement of the talent competition had died down, but the Garrick Gala Charity Showcase was only two days away. They *should* be rehearsing *Opposites Attract* – they had to perform *two* songs in the showcase. But they were having a night off: Belle to catch up on her homework – half-term reports would be coming out any day and she had to make sure that hers was nothing short of perfection – Holly to do some ballet practice and go for a swim, and Cat to play table tennis with Nathan.

Cat and Holly had plenty of people to give their tickets to. Holly was inviting her mum and her old dance teacher, Miss Toft. Her stepdad had volunteered to stay home and babysit her little brother. Cat had a bus-load of family coming from Cambridge (so many that they had bought extra tickets) – Mum, Dad, two brothers, little sister. There was even a granny and an aunt coming over from Dublin.

I can't even find one person to give my last ticket to, Belle sighed. *How sad is that?*

'Hey, Belle, having fun?' Cat laughed as she breezed up behind Belle's desk. 'Thought I'd find you in here. Turns out table tennis is harder than it looks. I'm shattered.'

'Fun? Not really,' Belle replied gloomily.

'OK, I've got two things to cheer you up,' Cat announced. 'One, *Grease* is on telly in half an hour. I've just checked, and the fire's lit in the common room.

So put those books away, get your pyjamas on, and it's you and me for hot chocolates, a huge bowl of popcorn and a good sing-along. Holly's going to join us later.'

'It's a date.' Belle grinned. 'Pyjamas, here I come!' She was ninety per cent cheered up already, and Cat had mentioned *two* things. 'Where is Holly anyway?'

Cat laughed. 'That's the second Reason to Be Cheerful! I've just seen Holly in the sports centre. She was talking to Ethan Reed about backstroke technique or something. Except the way they were looking at each other was *nothing* to do with backstroke; it was all about luuuuurve!'

'Ooh, that's cute,' Belle said, smiling as she remembered how sweet Holly and Ethan had been together in the acting class. She felt ninety-five per cent cheered up now.

'Yeah, but you know how shy Holly is around Ethan,' Cat went on, shooing Belle out of the library as the other students were starting to glare at them. 'They'll probably never get past analysing each other's front-crawl kick!'

Suddenly Belle felt ninety-nine per cent cheered up. 'Hey, Cat, I've just thought of something! I've had a really—'

'Uh-oh, not another of your Awesome Ideas!' Cat said as they trotted downstairs on their way to the common room.

'Yeah! Why don't we send my spare showcase ticket to Ethan and pretend it's from Holly? You know, move things along a bit!'

'Belle Madison!' Cat exclaimed with a shocked expression. 'Are you suggesting we start *telling lies* and *matchmaking*?'

'Sorry, sorry. I just thought . . .' Belle stammered. She suddenly felt hideously embarrassed. Had she crossed some unwritten rule of friendship that she didn't know about? *Just when I thought I was getting the hang of it!* she scolded herself.

'It's the awesomest awesome idea you've ever had!' Cat grinned. '*Let's do it!*'

Belle laughed with relief.

'But don't you need your ticket?' Cat asked.

'No,' Belle said, her laughter suddenly fading. 'I don't have anyone to invite. Not like you – with all your family coming . . .'

Cat smiled. 'Yeah, I can't wait to see them. I've been really missing them. Especially at the beginning of term. I was so homesick.'

'Lucky you,' Belle said. 'I mean, lucky you to have a

home to be homesick *for*. My home is just hotels and stuff.'

'Hey, I've just had an awesome idea of my own!' Cat said. 'Why don't you come home with me for half-term next week instead of slumming it in some five-star luxury hotel?'

'Do you really mean it?' Belle asked.

'Duh! Of course I mean it!'

Belle couldn't believe her luck. She was meant to be staying in a hotel in Paris – where her mother had a fashion shoot – for the half-term week, with some boring old nanny her mum had dragged out of retirement to look after her. Hanging out with Cat and her family in Cambridge would be much more fun. 'I'd *love* to!' she said, returning Cat's bear hug with extra warmth.

She was now, officially, one hundred per cent cheered up.

'Half-term reports, girls, hot off the press!' Mrs Butterworth yelled, scooting across the hall to intercept them as they passed. 'I was just about to put them into pigeonholes.'

With trembling hands, Belle took the large envelope with her name on it. What if she hadn't got the straight As she needed for Dad to let her stay at Superstar

High? She held her breath and ripped open the envelope to get the moment of truth over with as quickly as possible.

She stared in disbelief at the table of results.

Some of them weren't As . . .

. . . at least half of them were A-stars!

Belle couldn't wait to phone her parents and tell them the good news!

'Oh, no!' Cat exclaimed, slapping her hand to her forehead. 'I can't believe it!'

Belle took Cat's report and quickly scanned the page. Cat had been expecting to do badly, but the results were mostly Cs and Bs with a sprinkling of As.

'What's the matter? This looks fine,' Belle asked. 'You got the As you wanted in English and history—'

'But look at this!' Cat groaned, pointing at the B for science. 'No escape from The Fish!'

Belle read the teacher's comment.

Catrin is a bright girl [Mrs Salmon had written] *and produces good work when she can be bothered to do it. I refuse to give her the excuse she wants to give up on science and so I'm placing her in the top set – which I will be teaching.*

Belle laughed. 'Well, you'll just have to work harder at being dim in future!'

Arm in arm, Belle and Cat danced up the main staircase to their room, singing at the tops of their voices.

Now Belle was a hundred and ten per cent cheered up.

Except, of course, as an A-star maths student, she knew there was no such thing as a hundred and ten per cent.

CHAPTER THIRTY-FOUR

Holly: That's What Friends Are For

The annual Garrick School Gala Charity Showcase was a star-studded, larger-than-life event. So large that it was held in the Gielgud Auditorium rather than the Redgrave Theatre. The Gielgud – shared by the Garrick School and one of London's universities – was twice the size. Hundreds of people had bought tickets to see the talented Garrick students, as well as special guest appearances by ex-pupils who were now world-famous superstars.

And today was the day!

With that familiar mixture of terror and excitement ricocheting around her body like balls in a pinball machine, Holly set off for the auditorium with Belle and Cat, taking the short cut across the school grounds. She and Cat were piled high with garment bags containing their outfits. Belle lugged a box stuffed full of make-up, hairbrushes and bottles of mineral water.

The girls hurried through the landscaped park, past

the tennis courts and sports fields, where a football match was about to start. Holly lingered there a moment, watching as Ethan led the Garrick All-Stars onto the pitch.

The dressing rooms were already abuzz with performers getting ready. Holly was starting to unload their garment bags when she heard a high voice warbling, 'Belle! Holly! Cat!' She turned to see Pixie Ormolu, the fashion stylist who'd lent them their outfits. She fluttered in, followed by a procession of three young men in designer jeans. 'My assistants!' she fluted in a flurry of air-kisses. 'Gary is an absolute *genius* with hair, Jean-Luc is my make-up *maestro* – and Terence, well, Terence is *very* good at carrying things.'

Pixie's team set to work, pinning up and straightening, glossing and powdering, while Pixie mostly just talked.

'Your mother asked me to come, Belle, as a personal favour. Zoe was simply *devastated* she couldn't be here, but Giorgio – that's Giorgio Armani, darling – couldn't spare her . . .'

Holly and Cat's reflections grinned back at each other in the mirror: *This was the life! Their own team of personal stylists!* The other Garrick students looked on in curiosity mixed with a dash of envy.

Holly's hair and make-up were the first to be finished and she wandered outside for some fresh air. She perched on a bollard in the car park, trying not to crease her dress. The light was fading from the October evening, and red and gold leaves were rustling in the trees. She could hear the distant shouts of the football match from across the sports field.

Holly took a deep breath as a jolt of adrenaline pulsed through her veins. *Not long now! This is it! Our chance to shine!*

The air was growing chilly and she hurried back to the steamy warmth of the dressing room. Cat and Belle were still sitting in front of the mirrors, chatting. Belle's hair had been pinned into an elaborate twist while Cat's glossy red curls cascaded around her shoulders as Gary, the hair genius, ran the hairdryer over them. The roar of the hairdryer suddenly stopped, leaving Belle's voice to ring out loud and clear: 'I sure hope Ethan got that ticket. He's going to be so happy when he thinks it's from Hol—' She stopped abruptly as she glanced in the mirror and saw Holly standing behind her.

Cat looked round to see why Belle had broken off; the smile died on her lips as she registered Holly's expression.

There was a long, long silence.

'You sent a ticket to Ethan Reed and pretended it was from me?' Holly asked in a low voice.

Belle gulped and nodded. 'We just thought—'

'How could you?' Holly sobbed. She was so distraught, she couldn't say another word. She turned and ran out of the dressing room.

'Holly, come back! The show's starting soon!' Cat called after her.

But Holly didn't stop running. She didn't know where she was going. Her head was a whirl of shock and confusion. All thoughts of the show had vanished. She just wanted to be alone, to disappear. She ran and ran until she stumbled into a small storage room in the basement of the theatre, full of wigs and hats on head-shaped stands. She slumped down in a corner and tried to make sense of what had happened.

How could *Belle and Cat have done this?* she wondered. *They're meant to be my friends! OK, so maybe they* thought *they were being helpful – but now I'm just going to be totally humiliated. Ethan will think I'm a stupid schoolgirl with a pathetic crush on him.*

The door of the storeroom swung open. 'Holly! Are you in here?'

Holly kept very still. There was no way she could

face talking to anyone yet, but a muffled sob escaped her. All at once, Belle and Cat were kneeling beside her, pleading for forgiveness.

'Pleeeeease, Holly,' Belle begged. 'We're so sorry, we didn't mean to hurt you – we knew you liked Ethan and we just wanted to, you know, help things along a bit . . .'

'Some help!' Holly sobbed. 'I'll never be able to face him again! I'll just die of embarrassment. He must think I'm such a sad case—'

'No way,' Cat said sternly. 'Ethan really likes you. I saw it with my own eyes, and my eyes are never wrong. I *know* he'll turn up tonight. You'll see.'

Holly sniffed. A small part of her was so angry she wanted to push Cat and Belle away. *It's too late to say sorry now*, this part said in a mean, whiny voice. She would never forgive them! And she certainly wasn't going to get up on stage and sing with them!

'Holly,' Belle pleaded, 'I know we did a really dumb thing. But remember what you told me in the cab to The Ritz? When I'd quarrelled with Cat?'

Holly shook her head.

'You said, *That's what friends are for – they stick with you even when you do stupid stuff*,' Belle reminded her.

'Stick with us, Hols,' Cat begged. 'We've got a show to do!'

Another part of Holly told her in a kind, firm voice that she would feel *so much better* if she just gave her friends a big hug and apologized for being so silly. This part – which was starting to sound very like her mum – also pointed out that she would regret it for the rest of her life if she threw away her chance of performing with Nobody's Angels tonight.

Luckily this part was much bigger and louder.

'Hurry up then,' Holly said with a weak smile. 'We're on in a few minutes!'

Cat and Belle helped her up and threw their arms around her.

As Holly hugged them back, a very small but quite excited part of her couldn't help wondering, *What if Cat and Belle are right? What if Ethan actually comes to watch me?*

By the time Holly, Belle and Cat had patched up their tear-smudged make-up and found their way backstage to the green room, the stage manager was having a panic-attack. 'Where the hell have you been?' he hyper-ventilated. 'No, don't tell me – you're on in' – he glanced at his watch – 'thirty seconds.' Thrusting wireless headsets in their direction, he frog-marched them to the wings stage right.

'Nobody's Angels!' the celebrity compère was shouting from centre stage. 'Take it away, girls!'

And, with that, Holly found herself dashing onto the stage as the band struck up the introduction to *Done Looking!* At least there was no time to be nervous. It was like diving off the top board. You just closed your eyes and plunged right in!

They were even better than in the talent competition! As she waited for the applause to die down and the music for their second song, *Opposites Attract*, to begin, Holly scanned the front rows of the audience, where the performers' guests were sitting. She spotted her mum, dressed up in her best purple evening dress, and her old dance teacher, Miss Toft, both clapping wildly. The tiny red-haired lady sitting next to her and the girl in the wheelchair must be Cat's mum and her sister, Fiona.

And it was then that Holly realized the face she was really searching for was Ethan Reed's . . .

She found Nick Taggart instead. Holly knew that Nick had one of Belle's tickets. So if Cat and Belle had sent the other ticket to Ethan, he should be in the seat next to Nick . . .

But the next seat was taken by a sun-tanned man in an expensive suit. Holly stared for a moment. To her astonishment, she realized it was Dirk Madison, Belle's father. No one had thought he was coming! Mr Madison caught Holly's eye and waved at her. She smiled back, then nudged Belle and subtly pointed to her father by moving her eyes in his direction. Belle looked shocked, and then delighted.

But Holly felt only a hollow sense of disappointment.

Ethan Reed hadn't shown up.

CHAPTER THIRTY-FIVE

Holly: Congratulations and Celebrations

Holly's heart plummeted.

Of course Ethan hadn't come to see her!

She pictured him throwing the ticket in the bin and then laughing about it with his mates. How could Cat and Belle ever have thought such a stupid idea would work? But it wasn't their fault – she just wasn't the kind of girl Ethan would notice . . .

Holly performed the second song, *Opposites Attract*, with extra feeling. Now she really knew what the song was about. Ethan was her opposite: he was cool and popular and smart and talented – and she was . . . just Holly Devenish. Tears ran down her face as she sang, '*It breaks my heart that we're still poles apart . . .*'

As the song ended, there was an emotionally charged moment of silence, followed by a tidal wave of applause. It was a standing ovation! In spite of her disappointment, Holly couldn't help grinning in amazement and jubilation as she held hands with Cat and Belle and bowed deeply. It was a fabulous moment, and nothing could ruin it for her. Everyone would assume that her tears were tears of joy.

Belle whispered something to the compère, who smiled and nodded. 'We'd like to thank Nicolette Atkins, our songwriter. Without her this would never have been possible,' Belle announced into the microphone, leading a round of applause for Lettie, who sat, blushing, behind her cello in the orchestra pit.

Then Holly ran offstage with Cat and Belle – who were so elated by their success that they chatted and giggled and hugged their way back to the green room, where the performers waited for the other acts to finish. Holly did her best to get caught up in the excitement, but her heart wasn't really in it.

'I can't believe it! My dad actually came to see me sing!' Belle exclaimed, grabbing a bottle of water from the dispenser.

'That's brilliant!' Holly said, as brightly as she could.

Not brightly enough, it seemed, because Cat suddenly noticed that something was wrong. 'What's the matter, Hols?' she asked.

'You were wrong,' Holly sighed, sinking down into a chair. 'Ethan didn't turn up.'

'Well, I'm sure there's a good reason,' Cat told her.

'Maybe he's ill,' Belle added.

'Yeah, right!' Holly snorted. 'He was well enough to play football a couple of hours ago.'

'Just came to say congratulations, girls!' a deep voice boomed. Holly looked up to see Mr Garcia, their singing teacher, striding towards them. 'You were fantastic. A triumph! I'm very proud to have you all in my class!'

And right behind him was Larry Shapiro. Holly watched Belle glowing with uncontained delight as the vocal coach congratulated them – and told Belle how much he admired her voice.

When the two men had left, Belle looked at Cat and Holly with shining eyes. 'This is the best night of my life!' she burst out. Then she clapped her hand over her mouth. 'Ooh! Sorry, Holly – I didn't mean to rub it in!'

Holly managed a smile. 'Hey, don't be silly. Let's enjoy our moment of glory!'

'That's the spirit, Hols!' Cat said, putting her arm round her friend's shoulders. 'Come on – the after-show party's bound to cheer you up!'

As they entered the lavishly decorated reception room, Holly, Cat and Belle were swept up in a whirlwind of congratulations. Holly embraced her mum and Miss

Toft, who were both brimming over with proud *that's-my-girl* smiles. Then she was introduced to Cat's extended family, and watched Fiona, dressed in her frilly party dress, gazing up adoringly as Cat tied balloons to the back of her wheelchair. Meanwhile Belle leaped into her father's arms. 'Dad! You're here!'

'Not every man has a daughter who can get straight As *and* knock 'em dead on stage!' he said, laughing. 'I was lucky there was an empty seat. I thought I was going to have to stand at the back.'

Holly sighed as she thought about who should have been sitting in that empty seat, and then noticed Nick Taggart making a bee-line for Belle.

'This your boyfriend?' Mr Madison asked Belle as Nick hovered at her elbow.

'Oh, no!' Belle laughed dismissively. 'Of course not! He's . . .' Then she paused, and finished, 'Nick's my friend, my *very good* friend.'

Nick beamed as if he'd been awarded the Nobel Prize.

Suddenly Holly noticed that there was music playing. Usually she would have been first out on the dance floor, but she didn't feel like dancing now. Even when Theodora Mackenzie, a senior agent from Star-Makers, the biggest entertainments agency in London, pushed her way through the crowd to congratulate the girls and give them her card, Holly smiled, but on the inside she felt empty. She chatted to Miss Toft for a while, then drifted to the buffet table and picked at a bowl of Twiglets. Cat noticed her alone and hurried over to join her.

Then they spotted Nathan Almeida running towards them brandishing a sheet of paper. *He must have gate-crashed the party*, Holly thought.

'Cat! Cat!' he yelled. 'The call-backs have come through for *Macbeth*. They want me back for Macduff!'

'Brilliant!' Cat said warmly. 'Well done, Nate.'

'But I'm afraid they don't want you back for Second Witch,' Nathan went on glumly.

Cat swallowed hard. Holly knew that she was devastated, even though she was trying to put on a brave face. She was about to give her friend a commiserating hug, when suddenly Nathan was shouting, 'They want you to try out for Lady Macbeth instead!'

For a moment Cat was silent. Then she screamed, 'But that's the *lead female role*!'

Nathan nodded. And then Cat seized him by the hands and hurtled round in a gravity-defying spin.

'Well done, Cat. Congratulations!' Holly and Belle

yelled as other guests stepped swiftly aside to avoid being bowled over by Cat's victory dance.

'Come here, you,' Cat said when they finally came to a stop. She eased Nathan's glasses off his nose. 'This is something I've wanted to do for a long time.'

'She's going to kiss him!' Holly heard Belle gasp. 'I don't believe it!'

But Cat simply swept Nathan's fringe out of his eyes. 'That looks better,' she said with a grin. 'And, Nate, don't ever do that to me again!' she added, swatting his shoulder.

Holly smiled, pleased by Cat's success but feeling a little flat. She knew she *should* be feeling great: her half-term report and grades had been really good, her two best friends were happy, and Nobody's Angels had just brought the house down – what more could she ask for?

She was half listening to Cat and Belle re-living the evening's performance when there was a commotion near the door. An enormous bouquet of white roses was stumbling into the room.

'I'm looking for Holly Devenish,' the roses panted.

Holly looked closer. Beneath the bouquet was Ethan Reed. He was wearing a tuxedo over a muddy football shirt. She stared, completely unable to speak or move.

'I think he means you,' Belle said quietly.

'Unless there's another Holly Devenish in the room,' Cat added, grinning and giving Holly a gentle shove.

In a zombie-like trance, she walked towards the roses.

'Holly, I'm so sorry I'm late,' Ethan said, hurrying over to her. 'I've come straight from the hospital – had to borrow the jacket from a doorman.'

'Hospital? Are you all right?' Holly asked, horrified.

'I'm fine. It's Felix! Broke his ankle in a flying tackle! I went with him in the ambulance to casualty. And I couldn't just leave him. He's a pain sometimes, but he's a mate – you know how it is . . .'

'Yeah, I know how it is,' Holly said, hoping the grin spreading across her face wasn't too blatantly idiotic.

'I wouldn't mind but he gave away a penalty!' Ethan grinned. 'Anyway, thanks for inviting me,' he added. 'You look beautiful . . . Oh, and these are for you.'

'Thank you!' Holly murmured as she took the flowers.

Surely Ethan must be able to hear my heart pounding like a pneumatic drill! she thought. But she didn't care. She just felt euphoric. *Ethan didn't throw the ticket away! He really did like me enough to come to the show!* And *bring me roses! And did he really say I was* beautiful? It was all too much to take in!

She was vaguely aware of Cat and Belle high-fiving somewhere close by.

Holly looked down at the note attached to the flowers. '*Get well soon?*' she asked.

Ethan bent over to look. 'Oops – hospital shop! Sorry!'

They were very close now. Holly could smell the sweet scent of the roses over a tang of hospital-strength disinfectant.

Ethan was gazing at her with an intense, searching expression. Holly looked back into those sea-green eyes and felt her insides turn to melted chocolate – in a good way, not a five-macaroon-tea-at-The-Ritz kind of way.

It was just like her dream. But without the talking otter.

Suddenly the words, *Don't kiss me, I'm alive!* were dancing in her head.

Ethan leaned closer. He was actually going to kiss her!

There's only one way to stop myself saying something stupid and spoiling this moment, Holly thought. She smiled, closed her eyes and returned Ethan's kiss.

Somewhere in the background, party poppers were exploding. Holly had never felt happier.

Now the celebrations could really begin.

TEN STEPS TO STARDOM!

How *you* can make it as a superstar . . .

There's an old saying: 'Reach for the stars' – and it's so true!

★ Step one – and the most important thing about becoming a superstar – is to aim high and believe in yourself. You'll get there eventually!

★ Watch and learn. From your teachers, your friends, professionals on stage – there's always something new to pick up.

★ Practice makes perfect. It really does! There are times when going through the same vocal exercises or rehearsing the same lines feels boring, but every superstar still does them!

★ Don't always focus on being great at just one thing. It's good to excel in your chosen field, but it helps to be a bit of an all-rounder too. Many of the biggest superstars can act, sing and dance!

★ Make sure you look after yourself – it's important to relax. Every superstar has a day off sometimes!

★ Whatever you're doing, make sure you warm up and down – you don't want to risk getting injured. If you do pick up an injury, even a sore throat, it's important to rest up or you could make something small much worse.

★ Sometimes it's easy to get swept up in superstardom: try and remember to keep your feet on the ground and not forget real, everyday life. Good friends are brilliant for keeping you grounded.

★ Try and keep as fit and healthy as you can. Part of being a superstar is looking as good as possible, so it's important to feel good too. Some lip gloss always helps!

★ Always remember that more than one person goes into making a superstar. Your teachers, parents, friends, wardrobe and lighting teams (to name just a few) are all really, really important. Remember to say thank you!

★ And finally, no matter how nervous you feel inside, don't let anybody see. Hold your head up, push your shoulders back and, most importantly – smile!

The Time of
Your Life

Isabella Cass

For Mac

CHAPTER ONE

Cat: Totally Under Control

Cat Wickham was walking on air!

OK, so she wasn't *exactly* defying the laws of gravity and bobbing around like a helium balloon. But she *was* fizzing with nervous excitement as she hurried to join her best friends, Holly Devenish and Belle Madison, on their favourite sofa in the elegant wood-panelled entrance hall.

It was the end of a long, busy afternoon at the end of a long, busy week – the first week back after the autumn half-term holiday – at London's world-famous Garrick School of the Performing Arts. And in just a few minutes Cat would be setting off to audition for a part in the end-of-term production of *Macbeth*.

And not just for any old part . . .

It was for the part of *Lady Macbeth*!

How brilliant was that? Cat marvelled for the millionth time. Only one of the best-known characters in a Shakespeare play – in fact, *any* play in the western world. Admittedly, not the *nicest* lady you could wish to meet – in fact, Lady Macbeth made the Wicked Witch of the West look like Snow White – but an actress's *dream*! First she bullies her husband into murdering the King so he can take the crown; *then* she places the blood-soaked dagger in the hands of the sleeping guards so it looks as if *they* did it.

What an amazing character!

Cat had never *dared* to hope that she might be up for a leading role in her very first term at Superstar High – as the Garrick was usually known. As a brand-new Year Eight student, she'd originally tried out for a smaller part as Second Witch – but the directors had called her back for The Big One.

What an amazing chance!

This was no ordinary production. The Garrick staged a variety of spectacular dance shows, concerts and plays throughout the year, and their annual Shakespeare production was renowned in the theatre world as a major showcase for upcoming talent. London's top casting agents and theatre reviewers were always invited, and could be spotted in the audience, on the lookout for the stage stars of the future.

And being a serious actress was all Cat had ever dreamed of. Playing Lady Macbeth could be the launch pad that would rocket her into the stratosphere, warp-speeding her on her way to leading roles at the

Globe and with the Royal Shakespeare Company in Stratford . . .

Back down to earth! Cat warned herself. She had to *get* the part of Lady Macbeth first! And right now she needed a moment to catch her breath after the high-energy salsa marathon – otherwise known as advanced Latin dance class with Miss LeClair – that she and Holly had just completed. Holly was still wearing sweats over her leotard, her braids tucked under a wide hairband and her flawless brown skin still glowing with exertion. But Cat had sprinted up to her room for a high-speed change into a slinky black dress and killer heels. She just couldn't see Lady Macbeth in a tracksuit, somehow.

'Don't let me get too comfortable!' Cat sighed, sinking back into the cushions and closing her eyes.

'Well, good luck,' Belle said, elbowing her in the ribs.

'Oof, what was that for?' Cat gasped.

Belle grinned. 'Getting too comfortable. You were practically *snoring*!' She looked effortlessly stylish as usual, in designer jeans and a simple but perfectly cut white T-shirt, her long blonde hair swept up in a loose knot. She'd spent her Friday afternoon in an advanced singing class rather than Latin dance – the flamboyant mambo and cha-cha-cha moves were not really Belle's cool, calm and collected style.

'I was clearing my mind, getting into character!' Cat countered.

Holly laughed. 'Not *too* much, I hope! Sharing sofa-space with a dagger-wielding psycho-lady? No, thank you!'

Cat looked up to see her good friend Nathan Almeida hurrying across the hall towards them.

'Cat, come quickly! We mustn't be late for the auditions!' he urged, sweeping his long black fringe off his forehead and adjusting his wire-framed glasses.

Nathan was followed, at a more leisurely saunter, by Nick Taggart – who grinned and threw his stocky frame down into the narrow gap in the middle of the sofa, bouncing Cat, Belle and Holly up into the air.

'Chill, Nate!' Cat told him as she landed back on the sofa. 'We've got two whole minutes!' Inside, her heart was pounding and her stomach was doing a Mexican wave, but she knew that the best way to deal with her nerves was to *act* laid-back and unruffled. If she could convince everyone else she was super-calm, she could sometimes even fool *herself*.

Nathan hovered uncertainly. He was a gifted actor, but offstage he was terminally shy. He was getting better, though – at least now he could actually *speak out loud* in public, which was a major breakthrough. He'd also struck up a friendship with Nick Taggart – a boy who didn't know the meaning of the word *shy*. Or the words *serious . . .* or *sensible* or *solemn . . . Maybe I should buy him a dictionary for Christmas!* Cat thought.

Noticing Nathan checking his watch *again*, she attempted to wriggle free from her position, jammed between Nick and Holly on the sofa.

'So, Nick, you're Scottish – didn't you want to audition for *Macbeth*?' Holly asked. 'After all, it is called *The Scottish Play*.'

'Och, no, ma wee lassie,' Nick replied, in an over-the-top Highlands accent. 'Far too much *doom* and *gloom* for me! Anyway,' he continued, 'I'm working on the sound desk. I've got this *wicked* sound-effect for when the dagger goes in under King Duncan's ribs – a sort of *scraping, squelching—*'

Belle laughed, holding up her hands. 'Eugh! Enough *squelching* already!' She was also trying to escape from the sofa, but was wedged firmly against the arm on the other side of Nick.

Cat smiled. Belle liked Nick a whole lot more now than she had at the start of the year – which wouldn't be difficult, since her first words on the subject of Nick Taggart had been: *What a dork!* – but she still didn't *always* get his non-stop comedy act. And she probably wasn't enjoying being pinned to the furniture by his left elbow much either.

Unable to wait any longer, Nathan grabbed Cat by the hand and tugged. She popped up from the sofa like a cork from a bottle.

Now that the all-important audition was getting closer and closer, she was so nervous her legs felt as if they'd been replaced by overcooked spaghetti – her knees almost buckled under her as she stood up. But she wasn't going to let anyone see. She disguised the wobble by pretending to check her tights for ladders.

Holly and Belle jumped up, hugged Cat and wished her luck. 'We'll follow you over to the Redgrave Theatre in a minute,' Belle said. 'It's great they're doing open auditions for the main parts. We can come and cheer you guys on.'

'Not literally, I hope!' Cat laughed, noticing Nathan's worried look. 'No yelling, *Go for it, Natey-boy!* as he comes on stage to do his Macduff speech, you two!'

'Spoilsport!' Holly replied, then turned to Nathan and hugged him too – so quickly he had no chance to sidestep the unexpected physical contact. He grinned shyly.

'I just hope you guys know what you're letting yourselves in for if you get these parts,' Nick said. 'There's only six weeks from audition to performance.

It's going to be *Biiii-Zeeee* – with a capital B . . . and a capital Zee!'

But Cat wasn't worried about the mountain of hard work ahead of her. This *was* Superstar High after all. And no one ever said being a superstar was easy! With a jaunty wave she turned and followed Nathan across the hall.

'Don't panic!' she told Nick over her shoulder. 'I've got it all *totally* under control.'

CHAPTER TWO

Holly: Icing on the Cake of Happiness

'I really hope Cat's right!' Holly sighed as Cat left.

'Aha! That's just what Lady Macbeth said,' Nick intoned in a mysterious *Lord-of-the-Rings*-prophecy kind of voice.

'What?' Belle scoffed. 'Lady Macbeth said, *I really hope Cat's right*? I don't remember that line!'

'Not that!' Nick laughed, batting her on the head with a cushion. 'The *don't panic, I've got it all totally under control* bit – Lady M said it when she was persuading Macbeth to stick the knife in. Or words to that effect, anyway! And look where it got *her* . . .' He mimed a throat-slitting action.

'Well, Cat's not exactly planning to *murder* anyone,' Belle said impatiently.

'No, but she's taking advanced drama,' Holly said, 'and advanced Latin dance. Plus, touch wood, she'll have the leading role in the play – there'll be hundreds of rehearsals.'

'And her school work, of course, and band practice,'

Nick added. Holly, Belle and Cat had formed a girl group, Nobody's Angels, shortly after arriving at Superstar High and had won a Highly Commended in the talent competition before half-term. Somehow, Nick had appointed himself as their unofficial band manager!

'Yeah – and time-management isn't exactly Cat's strong point,' Belle said.

That's true, Holly thought. Cat was always over-sleeping, putting things off to the last minute, and missing deadlines. It was part of what made Cat so lovably . . . well, Cat!

It hadn't been too disastrous so far, apart from a few near-miss detention situations in Mrs Salmon's science class. But things were going to get much tougher from now on.

For the first half-term all the new students had attended the same lessons: school subjects in the mornings, then core singing, dancing and acting classes in the afternoons. But now they'd been placed into their ability-sets for school subjects, and, on top of the core performance classes on Monday to Wednesday afternoons – which everyone still had to do – they were all taking specialist options, known as *advanced classes*, on Thursday and Friday afternoons.

Dance was Holly's passion, and she was taking the

advanced dance classes, which covered ballet, modern, jazz, tap and Latin. But although she had a good voice and loved singing in Nobody's Angels, she hadn't got into advanced singing yet; the standard was incredibly high. At least she was able to do an advanced musical theatre class, which included singing and which she loved – her dream was to star in West End and Broadway shows.

Belle was the musical one with the fabulous voice. She was in all the advanced singing classes and took piano and music theory lessons, *and* she was in the top set for every school subject! Belle's half-term report had been a glittering galaxy of A-stars. It wasn't *just* because she was smart, hard-working and organized; there was also the minor incentive that her dad had threatened to pull her out of the Garrick and send her to a 'normal' school if she didn't get perfect grades.

They were *all* going to be busy, but Holly knew that Cat would have to switch into high-octane turbo-drive if she was going to keep up with all her commitments.

'See you at the Redgrave in a few minutes!' Nick declared, leaping up from the sofa. 'I'm going to call for Zak on the way.'

Holly looked around contentedly as he disappeared through the back door into the courtyard. The entrance hall was a favourite meeting place. It was bustling with staff and students hurrying from classes to after-school activities, checking their pigeon holes for messages, or just stopping to chat with friends. Holly still couldn't believe that she was actually *part* of Superstar High.

It was the kind of place where *anything* could happen . . .

And usually did!

In fact, Holly thought, she was officially the luckiest girl in the world.

Great school, great friends – she even had a great room-mate, ever since Bianca 'Furious Girl' Hayford had thrown a strop and demanded she move out of their room and swap with Lettie Atkins.

Holly's new room-mate, Gemma Dalrymple, was a down-to-earth Australian girl who was almost as crazy about dancing as Holly was – and, most importantly, didn't go into nuclear meltdown if Holly stepped onto her side of the room.

Oh, and then, of course, ever since the gala showcase party just before half-term, she'd also had a great *boyfriend*!

Holly found her thoughts drifting. She was re-living the moment – the scent of roses, the sound of party poppers, Ethan's sea-green eyes . . . *her first kiss*. Holly's thoughts did a lot of drifting these days. She had to keep reminding herself that she hadn't dreamed the whole thing – that Ethan Cool-and-popular-captain-of-the-football-team-and-all-round-Year-Ten-superstar Reed was her real, live boyfriend! He was the icing on Holly's Cake of Happiness: thick, double-chocolate-fudge icing . . .

. . . with rainbow sprinkles on top!

'Ooh, sorry – what?' Holly asked, snapping herself back to reality.

Belle twitched her perfect eyebrows in a knowing smile. 'I was talking about Cat,' she said. 'It was lovely staying at her house for half-term, but her mum was on at her nonstop to try out for big West End musicals. She says it's the only way to break into the big time.'

'But how's Cat going to find time to trek round to professional auditions?' Holly asked.

'I don't know,' Belle sighed. 'She's going to be swamped. That's why I'm only going for a minor part in *Macbeth*. I want time to have a *life*!'

'And Cat doesn't even *want* to do musical theatre.' Holly shook her head. She knew Cat's dream was to be a classical actress – performing in Shakespearean tragedies and ultra-serious award-winning plays. 'Definitely not *The Lion King* or *The Sound of Music* –

I can't see Cat skipping around singing about whiskers on kittens and apple strudel . . .' she added. 'Shame, I love that song!'

'Me too,' Belle replied, grinning. Next moment they were singing harmonies on *My Favourite Things*.

Holly heard voices and turned to look over the back of the sofa. She stopped mid-note as she noticed an unfamiliar tall boy with shoulder-length brown hair slouching against the school secretary's desk on the other side of the hall. 'Hey, who's *that*?' she whispered.

Belle's beautiful singing voice trailed away and she joined Holly in spying over the back of the sofa as Miss Candlemas, the housemistress, hurried into the room, swathed in her multi-coloured scarves, beads and bangles.

Mrs Butterworth, the secretary, scooted out from behind her desk on her trusty swivel chair. 'Ah, there you are!' she grumbled, peering at Miss Candlemas over the gold frames of her glasses. 'Better late than never!'

Ignoring Mrs Butterworth's comment, Miss Candlemas beamed at the mystery boy. 'All aboard for the grand tour! Jump to it!'

The boy grinned, stood up straight and saluted cheekily.

'*The entrance hall lies at the heart of the original seventeenth-century building*,' Miss Candlemas recited as they crossed towards the dining room.

'. . . *which served as the grand ballroom in Regency times* . . .' Holly and Belle exchanged grins as they whispered the words in chorus. The speech was identical to the one Miss Candlemas had given when she showed them round the school at the beginning of September!

Holly laughed. 'Do you remember Nick Taggart doing his tour-guide act?'

'Yeah, it would be hard to forget!' Belle groaned.

'And how . . .' Holly's voice faded away as she realized that Belle was no longer listening. Her lavender-blue eyes had zoomed in towards the dining-room door.

Belle was *gawping* at the boy!

Holly hadn't realized that she was physically capable of doing anything as *uncool* as gawping, but that was the only word for the transfixed expression on her face. Holly looked at the boy more carefully.

His light brown hair was slightly dishevelled – but in a good I'm-too-cool-to-fuss-with-my-hair kind of way. He shook it back now and then to reveal hazel eyes and high, angular cheekbones. Not that Holly noticed such things, of course, now that she had a boyfriend. There was something pirate-like, something of the Johnny-Depp-as-Captain-Jack-Sparrow in his swagger and the rebellious glint in his eyes.

'Maybe he's thinking of applying here for next year,' Holly whispered. 'Not that you'd be *interested* or anything!' she added, grinning.

But Belle hadn't heard – or hadn't yet regained the power of speech. Holly couldn't be sure which.

It was time to set off to watch the auditions, and Holly and Belle followed the tour party out into the courtyard. Pirate Boy held the door open for them. He seemed to catch Belle's eye and stare at her for a brief moment before hurrying after Miss Candlemas and her call of 'No shilly-shallying now!'

Holly could hardly believe her eyes: Belle's perfect complexion – usually cream with a hint of peach – was slowly turning to raspberry with a hint of beetroot.

Belle was blushing!

But Belle didn't *do* blushing! Holly couldn't have been more surprised if her friend had started wearing jumble-sale dungarees and granny-knitted Bob the Builder tank tops. Gawping *and* blushing? Belle would be thrown out of the International Cool-as-a-Polar-Bear-with-Frostbite Club if she wasn't careful.

CHAPTER THREE

Belle: X-Ray Vision and Thought Waves

The *Macbeth* auditions were about to start.

Belle followed Holly into the Redgrave – Superstar High's beautiful theatre – and settled down in a red velvet seat. There was a buzz of expectant chatter among the audience of students who'd come along to support their friends. Belle couldn't wait to hear Cat's Lady Macbeth speech; she'd helped her practise all through the half-term holiday and knew that it was going to be something very special.

The warm, wood-polish-and-dust scent of the theatre sent a jolt of adrenaline coursing through Belle's veins. The last time she'd been here, she'd been on stage, singing in the talent show with Holly and Cat in Nobody's Angels. It had been an *awesome* experience, but she vividly remembered that split-second of blind terror when she'd spotted the famous vocal coach, Larry Shapiro, sitting with the other judges in the front row. Belle's ambition in life was to be an internationally acclaimed singer – the next Mariah Carey or Leona

17

Lewis. She'd never have forgiven herself if she'd stuffed up in front of such an illustrious judge in her very first term at Superstar High – and she had *almost* crumpled under the pressure! But luckily it had all gone fabulously well, and Larry Shapiro had even complimented her afterwards on her vocal technique.

But today the judges' seats were occupied by the casting panel, huddled importantly over their clipboards. Belle recognized Mr Grampian, the head of Drama. Next to him sat the play's assistant director, Duncan Gillespie, a Year Ten boy with thick dark hair, stiffly ridged like chocolate frosting, and then the director, a thin, wiry man who looked like a long-distance runner. Belle recognized him as Mr Simon Sharpe, the Garrick's Shakespeare expert.

She took a deep breath, letting the adrenaline ebb away. She was so relieved she wasn't auditioning today. The auditions for the minor parts – like the Messenger role Belle hoped for – would be taking place tomorrow.

'*And the award for best actress . . . goes to . . . Catrin Wickham . . .*' a dramatic Hollywood-celebrity voice boomed behind her.

Belle turned round. No surprise – it was Nick Taggart chortling with his friends Zak Lomax, Frankie Pellegrini and Mason Lee as they bundled into their seats.

'Shh!' Mr Sharpe hissed. 'Quiet, *please*!' He glared

in the direction of the disturbance, his small frameless glasses flashing like cats' eyes as they caught the light.

Belle cringed, but at that moment Lettie Atkins tiptoed in. She waved to Belle and Holly before sitting down next to Nick and engaging him in an intense conversation about sound-editing. Lettie, a softly spoken girl with long chestnut hair and serious brown eyes, was a super-talented musician, and was working on the musical arrangement for the play. 'We could fade in that creepy clarinet solo whenever the Three Witches appear,' she whispered, and – for once – Nick didn't answer with a wisecrack, but nodded thoughtfully.

'The commencement of auditions is imminent,' Mr Grampian announced.

Belle and Holly turned to each other and grinned. Mr Grampian always spoke like that. 'Why use one short word when ten long ones will do?' Holly whispered.

'Ethan Reed for the part of Banquo!' Duncan Gillespie announced.

It's so sweet how Holly's ears glow whenever Ethan's name is mentioned, Belle thought. *Luckily it's not as noticeable with her lovely caramel skin as it would be for me.*

Not that Belle made a habit of blushing, of course.

But then an uncomfortable image suddenly popped

into her mind. *That boy in the hall* . . . She'd felt her face burning then. It was the way he'd looked at her! As if he had x-ray vision and could read her innermost thoughts – the *really* deep-down ones she wasn't quite sure of herself.

And – this was ridiculous! – she could actually feel her face flushing and her stomach fluttering just at the *memory* of it. She wasn't sure whether she liked the feeling or hated it, but she was sure of one thing: she'd never felt like this before.

Anyway, she wasn't going to waste any more time thinking about some random boy who'd given her a funny look. She'd probably never see him again anyway.

'Nathan Almeida for the part of Macduff!' Mr Sharpe shouted.

Belle realized she'd missed Ethan's entire speech, but from the way Holly was smiling, it had obviously gone well.

She watched intently as Nathan gave a stellar performance as Macduff, reading the speech where he finds out that Macbeth has slain his entire family. He was so convincing, Belle sniffed back a tear as she joined in the round of enthusiastic applause.

'Bianca Hayford for Hecate, Goddess of the Witches!' Duncan called, flipping pages on his clipboard.

'Perfect casting!' Belle heard Nick chuckle behind her.

'Bianca as Queen Witch – she won't even have to try!'

Holly giggled and Belle couldn't help grinning. She'd first crossed swords with Bianca before they'd even got through the front door of Superstar High, in a heated exchange over their matching Louis Vuitton luggage collections.

And things had basically gone downhill ever since. Bianca seemed to have made it her Mission In Life to score points off Belle at every possible opportunity. Belle did her best to *rise above it*, but there was only so much rising a girl could do . . .

However she had to admit that Bianca's audition was excellent. She was wearing a white dress (from the new Versace winter collection, Belle noticed – Bianca must have been out spending her allowance over half-term; the Hayfords were a *very* wealthy family who'd made millions from their baby-food business, as Bianca was very keen to tell everyone – the millions part, that is, not the baby-food part). With her pale blonde hair pulled back from her face, she looked as cold and sinister as the Narnia Snow Queen – without the Turkish Delight.

'Two-minute break, then Catrin Wickham for the part of Lady M,' Duncan announced.

'Finally . . .' Belle breathed, grabbing Holly's hand in excitement.

'Did you notice he said *Lady M*?' Nick 'whispered' at high-decibel shouting volume in Belle's ear. 'It's bad luck to say the name in a theatre.'

'What name?' Belle asked.

'Well, duh! I'm not going to say it, am I?' Nick laughed. 'The name of this play . . .'

'What? You mean *Mac*—' Belle started, but he leaned forward and clamped his hand over her mouth.

'It's supposed to be like a curse or something!' Holly explained.

'Wicked!' Zak exclaimed.

'Oomph!' Belle muttered from behind Nick's sweaty palm.

There was another round of glowering and shushing from the casting panel.

Why did Nick always have to drag her into his crazy comic routines? Belle wondered as he finally peeled his hand off her face. She remembered how she'd thought Nick was a *total dork* when she first met him. And he definitely still had some dorkish tendencies, but over the weeks he'd proved to be a true and loyal friend and she'd secretly grown very fond of him. *Fond!* That made the poor boy sound like a pet guinea pig or something. In fact, now she thought about it, Nick *did* look a little like a guinea pig with his thatch of thick, sandy hair! Holly and Cat insisted that Nick teased and played jokes on Belle because he had a crush on her – it was a typical boy-thing, they said. Belle wasn't convinced . . .

She felt Holly grip her arm as Cat staggered onto the stage, paused and closed her eyes for a long moment. Then she lurched forward, raised her hands in front of her and stared sightlessly out into the audience. She'd teased her vibrant red curls into a wild tangle and looked totally deranged. Belle watched, enthralled, as Cat became the tormented, sleepwalking Lady Macbeth, frantically trying to wash her hands of the blood of the murdered King.

'*Out, damn spot! out I say!*' she cried.

The entire audience was spellbound, erupting with applause at the end of the speech.

'She *has* to get the part after that,' Belle breathed, rubbing her arm where Holly's nails had left crescent-shaped imprints.

But there was strong competition. Five other girls auditioned for Lady M, all of them older students in Years Nine and Ten, except for one: Mayu Tanaka – best friend and sidekick of Bianca Hayford – and possibly the only girl in their year with a meaner mean-streak. As Mayu spoke the words, '*Fill me from the crown to the toe top-full, Of direst cruelty . . .*' Belle shivered. Mayu looked so sweet with her bunches and doll-like face – and somehow that made the dastardly speech seem doubly evil. But then, all of a sudden, Mayu's voice faltered. She stared, saucer-eyed, into the audience. She'd forgotten her words! Belle couldn't help feeling sorry for her.

There was a long pause, broken only by muffled coughs from the audience, until finally Mr Grampian said kindly, 'Thank you, Mayu. I believe we have sufficient material to guide our deliberations.'

Mayu opened and closed her mouth, and then turned and shuffled slowly offstage.

That's the first time, Belle thought, *that I've ever seen Mayu at a loss for something nasty to say!*

She gazed at the casting panel as they conferred over their notes. She screwed up her eyes, straining to transmit her thoughts into the backs of their heads by means of telepathy: *Cat for Lady Macbeth, Cat for Lady Macbeth* . . .

Oops! she thought. *I hope the ban on saying the M-word in a theatre doesn't apply to* thought waves *as well as actual speech. Otherwise I've just put a double curse on Cat's chances.*

'Are you OK?' Holly asked. 'You look as if you've got a headache?'

Belle crossed her fingers.

Maybe that would be safer!

CHAPTER FOUR

Cat: The Shakespearean Miracle Diet

When the auditions were over, Cat slipped into one of the dressing rooms and stared at her face in the mirror. She needed a moment alone.

Her skin was pallid but her eyes glittered. She was panting as if she'd just run the London Marathon. Being Lady Macbeth was *exhausting*; all those dangerous emotions battling it out: ambition, guilt, fear – '*Here's the smell of the blood still . . .*' Cat replayed the words in her head; yes, she was pleased with how the speech had gone.

She'd done it. And it felt fantastic!

Now all she could do was wait.

But the waiting was such agony!

What if they gave the part to one of the Year Ten girls? Or even to Mayu Tanaka? She couldn't bear that! She'd have to run away to the Amazon rainforest and live in exile as a piranha farmer for the rest of her days.

She thought of the famous actresses who had played

Lady Macbeth: Judi Dench, Vivien Leigh, Ellen Terry, right back to Sarah Siddons in the eighteenth century . . .

This was the most important audition of her life!

'Cat! Are you in there?' Her reverie was shattered by the sound of Belle and Holly knocking impatiently at the door.

'Yes! Coming!' she yelled back. She rubbed her face as if to wipe away a mask. Lady Macbeth was disappearing. She applied a flick of eyeliner and a dab of lip gloss, then studied the result carefully for a moment and stuck out her tongue at her reflection. She was Cat Wickham again.

And Cat Wickham was starving!

After Belle and Holly had congratulated her on the audition, the girls hurried back across the courtyard, through the hall and into the dining room. Murder and madness were hungry work – and Cat had been too nervous to eat lunch or even breakfast. Perhaps she should market this as a new miracle diet: *Simply audition for a major Shakespearean role and watch the weight melt away!*

Or perhaps not, she thought, piling a double helping of lasagne onto her plate.

Last half-term she'd put herself on a celery-stick diet after Bianca had called her 'chubby', but she'd finally let Holly and Belle persuade her that she should stop trying to lose weight and be proud of her curves.

'Cat was brilliant, wasn't she?' Holly remarked, reaching for the water jug as they joined Nick and Nathan at their table in the spacious, high-ceilinged dining room. Everyone instinctively moved their plates out of the way. They'd all been friends long enough to know that, in spite of being a gifted, graceful dancer, hand–eye co-ordination was not Holly's strong point. If they weren't careful, their table would soon resemble the splash-zone at a dolphin show!

'A superlative performance,' Nick agreed, imitating Mr Grampian. 'And you were great as Macduff too!' he added, slapping Nathan on the back.

Cat nodded vigorously, her mouth too full for speech. Watching Nathan from the wings, she'd been so moved by his speech she'd been in danger of being too choked up to say her own lines.

Nathan smiled and mumbled something into his plate of salad.

The table filled up as Zak and Gemma sat down and started chatting with Holly about dance classes. 'Whoa! Yesterday's class – *way* gnarly, man!' Zak said, grinning as he poured ketchup all over his salad. 'Korsakoff was smashing us with a Momboosa workout!'

Cat smiled. You kind of had to *guess* most of what Zak was saying in his surfer-dude drawl. But he was an amazing dancer. Mr Korsakoff was the boys' ballet teacher — ballet was the only subject boys and girls did separately.

'Yeah, and Miss Morgan's giving us sheilas heaps of work too,' Gemma replied, exaggerating her Australian accent. 'Now we're working towards our Intermediate next year, ballet is our *numero uno* priority!'

They all laughed. Miss Morgan was well-known for peppering her speech with Italian phrases, although she wasn't the slightest bit Italian. Cat couldn't help liking Holly's new room-mate, Gemma, even though she looked far too healthy and wholesome to be true — bronzed, blonde and athletic, she looked as if she should be cycling along a country road in an advert for multi-vitamins. Even her laugh sounded well-balanced, unlike Cat's own unruly giggles.

'Ooh, Miss Morgan is *fierce*!' Cat laughed. 'I'm so relieved I'm not in advanced ballet — she's like a pit bull in a leota—'

'*Yeah, so we're going to be doing three extra practice sessions a week . . .*' Holly interrupted, in an unnecessarily loud voice.

Cat froze, instantly recognizing Holly's desperate *shut-up-danger-alert* look. Slowly she turned round. Miss Morgan was walking right behind her, with an Action Man lookalike – whom she recognized as Mr Korsakoff – towards the staff dining tables. 'Eek,' she whispered, praying Miss Morgan hadn't heard her. 'But don't you think Mr K looks like a sergeant in the Marines?'

'*I don't know but I've been told, ballet tights just leave me cold—*' Nick chanted, with a big grin.

'Shh!' Belle warned. 'He'll hear you!' Then a worried look flitted across her perfectly made-up face. 'You'll still have time for band rehearsals, won't you, Holly? With all your dance practice? We *have* to keep Nobody's Angels together.'

Holly smiled. 'Of course.'

'What about you, Cat?' Belle asked anxiously.

'Only if she's discovered the secret of human cloning over half-term!' Nick said. 'You'll need an extra ten copies of yourself if you get the Lady Macbeth part.'

'Sure, I'll still have time for the band,' Cat said airily, keeping up her girl-in-total-control-of-the-situation act. '*No problemo!*'

But secretly she was wondering whether, if she *did* get the part, she might have bitten off a teensy bit more than she could chew . . .

And she wasn't thinking about the super-heated cheese sauce she'd just burned her mouth on.

But Cat knew how much Nobody's Angels meant to Belle. The band was important to all of them, of course, and it was brilliant fun too – but for Belle it was more than important and it was more than fun. Singing was Belle's life: the Holy Grail and the treasure of Tutankhamun rolled into one. Cat wasn't going to let her friend down. 'I'll fit it all in somehow,' she breezed. 'I'll just have to get up earlier in the morning or something—'

There was a choking sound. 'Sorry,' Belle spluttered into a paper napkin. 'Carrot stick went down the wrong way.'

Cat guessed why Belle was choking and it was nothing to do with carrot sticks! As her room-mate, Belle knew better than anyone that Cat was *not* a Morning Person.

'Uh-oh . . .' Holly breathed, nodding towards Bianca, who was settling herself down at the next table and whispering secretively with Mayu and Lettie.

'Hm, I wonder what they're up to?' Cat mused, happy to change the subject from her crazy schedule.

'Oh, yes, I spent *ages* showing him round today,'

Bianca was saying importantly as she held her fork up to the light to make sure it was clean. 'Miss Candlemas asked me to take him under my wing . . .'

Cat had no idea who they were talking about, but whoever it was, she felt sorry for him. Being under Bianca's wing would be like being looked after by a large, very hungry vulture.

' . . . yeah, so anyway, his name's Jack Thorne, he's a Year Eight, and he's just starting here . . .' Bianca continued, flicking back her razor-sharp platinum-blonde bob.

'Why's he starting in the middle of term?' Lettie asked.

'His family has just moved back from Singapore. His dad's something big in banking. Jack's done *loads* of professional acting and singing already . . . '

'Ooh, I bet he's mega-rich,' Mayu simpered.

'And we already *know* he's mega-good-looking,' Lettie added.

Bianca smiled. 'And he's got mega-good taste too,' she said, with a sidelong glance to make sure that the occupants of Cat's table were listening, 'because he *totally* couldn't take his eyes off me!'

'That must be the boy we saw in the hall earlier,' Holly whispered, nudging Belle's elbow.

Cat noticed Belle trying to hide a slightly flustered

reaction, and . . . *was that just a trace of a blush?* 'Well, he obviously made quite an impression,' Cat remarked, shooting a quizzical look in Holly's direction.

'He did not make an *impression*!' Belle snorted. 'And anyway, he must be *demented* if he fancies Bianca.'

Cat grinned at Holly. 'Yeah, right! He sounds like a *total loser.*'

CHAPTER FIVE

Belle: Earthquakes, Gloating and Shepherds

On Monday morning Belle was woken by a crashing noise.

It must be an earthquake! She was about to *Drop, Cover and Hold On* when she remembered she wasn't in Los Angeles or San Francisco. She was in London. They didn't have earthquakes in London.

She opened one eye and peered at her alarm clock. It was almost six – time for her morning run. She opened the other eye. It wasn't an earthquake. It was Cat, banging drawers shut and stumbling out of the door, leaving a trail of pyjamas and bedclothes behind her.

Surely Cat hadn't started getting up early to do extra work *already*. Belle couldn't believe it! Cat usually bolted into the first lesson at eight thirty, still brushing toast crumbs from her sweater. And when they were at Cat's house in Cambridge at half-term, she'd stayed in bed until lunch time – while Belle would be up chatting to Cat's mum at the kitchen table, playing with Hannah

Montana dolls with her little sister, Fiona, or just listening to her brothers squabbling.

Cat was so lucky to have a lovely 'normal' family. Belle loved her own parents, but they weren't exactly Mr and Mrs Ideal Homemaker. Mom was a super-model and Dad was a film director; she caught glimpses of them as they jet-setted around the planet from one exotic location to the next.

Then Belle suddenly remembered: *Cat isn't getting up to do her homework! She's gone to check whether the* Macbeth *cast list has been posted on the notice board yet.*

Belle pulled on the running clothes she'd left neatly folded on the window seat, and raced along the corridor. She was dying to see the list too. Her audition for the Messenger role had gone well on Saturday.

It was still very quiet everywhere as Belle trotted down the sweeping staircase into the entrance hall, the polished wood of the banister cool under her palm. She spotted Cat at the notice board with the school secretary. Mrs B was sitting in her swivel chair, but had clearly just arrived – she was still wearing her tartan coat and a woolly hat was pulled down over her grey curls. As Belle approached, she saw that the cast list was on Mrs B's lap, along with the biscuit tin she kept her drawing pins in.

'Goodness me!' Mrs Butterworth laughed, shaking

her head. 'I came in extra early to put the list up, and you're already prowling around like a pack of hyenas! Here, you girls pin the list up. I can't do anything with you breathing down my neck like that.'

Cat almost ripped the piece of paper out of Mrs B's hand. There was a long silence as she scanned the page. Then her face crumpled. 'No-o-o,' she groaned. 'My name's not here!'

Shocked, Belle snatched the paper and ran her eyes down the list. It was true. Cat's name wasn't on it.

But nor was Lady Macbeth's.

'This can't be the full list!' Belle said, placing her hand soothingly on Cat's shoulder.

'No, it's not,' Mrs Butterworth called, scooting her chair back from her desk, brandishing a second page. 'That one's only the minor parts and ensemble.'

Cat looked up, her wide grey eyes brimming with tears. 'Oh!' she said weakly as Mrs B skidded to a halt and handed her the page and the drawing pins.

She read the list: '*Macbeth, Luke Morgan . . . Banquo, Ethan Reed,*' she murmured. Belle held her breath. Suddenly a huge smile spread across Cat's face. '*YESSSS! Lady Macbeth – Catrin Wickham!*' she shouted, throwing her arms up into the air.

'*You did it!*' Belle told her as they bounced around the hall in a victory jig.

There was a crash as the forgotten biscuit tin hit the floor. The lid popped off, spraying drawing pins across the tiles. Mrs B looked up from sorting the post at her desk and rolled her eyes.

'Oh dear, I'm worse than Holly!' Cat laughed as she crawled around on hands and knees, stopping every now and again to consult the list, still clutched in her hand, 'Brilliant! Nathan's got Macduff – and you got First Messenger, Belle. Well done!'

'My first big acting role,' Belle joked as she fished under the sofa for more pins. 'Five whole lines!' It *was* only a tiny part, but she was thrilled. Just being involved in the production was going to be great fun, and it was a chance to show that she could act as well as sing.

'Ooh, look' – Cat laughed – 'Bianca got Hecate.' Then she grasped Belle's arm as she crawled past. 'Oh, no, look at this: *Castle Servant and Understudy for Lady Macbeth – Mayu Tanaka!*'

'Mayu's going to *love* that,' Belle said. 'Being your understudy.'

Cat gave a wicked grin. 'Isn't she just.'

'Come on, I think we've got all the pins,' Belle said, attaching the lists to the notice board. 'Let's go and tell Holly the good news. We'll catch her before she goes off for her swim.'

They ran upstairs, passing Mayu, who was on her way down, and sped along the corridor. Cat ground to a halt outside the room next door to her own. 'I can't *wait* to tell Holly!' she said, throwing open the door.

'Cat, that's not—' Belle started.

But it was too late. Cat yelled triumphantly, 'Guess what – I got Lady Macbeth!'

'. . . Holly's room any more . . .' Belle murmured as she caught up with Cat, who was staring at Bianca.

Bianca was sitting on the edge of her bed in her dressing gown, with something that looked like a plastic gas mask stuck to her face. Lettie was still curled up in bed in her pink stripy pyjamas.

'I – I'm really sorry,' Cat was stammering. 'I forgot that Holly had swapped rooms . . . I'll . . . just be, erm, leaving . . . now . . . then,' she added, backing towards the door. 'You just go back to . . . er . . . whatever it is you were doing . . . er . . . What exactly *are* you doing, Bianca?'

'Steam inhaler,' Bianca snapped, fixing Cat and Belle with a stare of chilling disdain as she slowly removed the device from her face. 'For my allergies. And stress,' she added darkly. 'Which I get a *lot* of around here!'

At that moment there was a terrible howling noise in the corridor. Mayu pushed past Belle and Cat, who were still hovering in the doorway, and flung herself onto a beanbag. '*Under . . . s-s-study*,' she wailed. '*Her* understudy!' And she pointed a finger accusingly at Cat.

'Wha . . . ?' Lettie mumbled, sitting up sleepily.

'Oh, so that's *really* why you came in here shooting your mouth off,' Bianca said. '*Ooh, sorry, I forgot that Holly had swapped rooms!*' she mocked, imitating Cat's soft Irish accent. 'As if! Major league *gloating*, more like!'

'Yeah,' Mayu snarled, her despair quickly turning to rage. 'And you should have seen them laughing at me on the stairs just now—'

'We weren't laughing,' Belle objected.

'Let's get out of here,' Cat whispered. 'I'm going to tell Holly – then I'm going straight back to bed.'

'And take that revolting animal with you!' Bianca shrieked, throwing a sock in the direction of Shreddie, the school cat, who had sneaked in behind them.

A little later, Belle was jogging round the sports fields, listening to Basement Jaxx on her iPod and watching the sun rise in a blood-red sky. She remembered a scrap of an old rhyme – *Red sky in the morning, shepherds' warning!*

Belle was a city girl. She didn't know much about shepherds, or what they might be warning people about – being attacked by roaming flocks of vicious wild sheep, perhaps?

Her thoughts kept straying back to the *Macbeth* cast list. There was one name Cat hadn't noticed in the *minor parts*. But Belle had . . .

The Second Messenger was Jack Thorne.

It was a small part for someone who – if Bianca was right – was a hot-shot acting type, but Belle guessed he'd been too late to audition for the major roles.

Not that she was particularly interested, of course!

But she was really looking forward to the first rehearsal . . .

CHAPTER SIX

Belle: The Antarctic Food Chain

Where was Cat?

The science lesson had started. Belle was sitting in her usual place with Holly next to her, but the stool on her other side was empty. In the last seat of the four, Nathan was also looking worried.

Mrs Salmon slapped her desk. 'I'm not waiting for latecomers. Turn to page twenty-three – "Food Chains and Food Webs".'

'Where is she?' Holly whispered.

Belle shrugged her shoulders. When she'd returned to her room after her run, she'd woken Cat up and they'd gone down to breakfast with Holly. When Cat disappeared from the dining room, Belle assumed she'd just run back upstairs for a forgotten book, but . . .

Of all the lessons to be late for, double science was the *worst*! Cat and Mrs Salmon – or The Fish, as Holly had christened her at the beginning of term – were *sworn enemies*. Belle knew that Cat had hoped that her record of late homework and detentions would ensure her a place in a lower set, with a more lenient teacher. But The Fish had seen through Cat's devious plan, and decided to keep her in the top set.

Where she could keep an eye on her.

If she actually turned up, that was!

'We're going to start with a film!' Mrs Salmon said, adjusting the projector. There was a comfortable murmur as the class settled down to watch.

A penguin darted out of the mouth of a killer whale and swam backwards through clear blue water.

Belle could hear Bianca and Mayu giggling in the row behind her.

'Erm, what's going on . . . ?' Mrs Salmon muttered as she leaned across to fiddle with the controls. A shoal of sardines was now reversing rapidly across her face.

Holly got up and walked across to the projector. She pressed a few buttons and the sardines began to swim forwards. There was a round of applause and she took a shy bow. 'My mum uses the same projector for school,' she whispered as she sat down.

Belle smiled, remembering how Mrs Devenish's job as a teacher had come in handy once before – helping Holly to convince Belle's father that the Garrick was the brainiest school in Britain.

Mrs Salmon's face was pinker than ever. 'Yes, well, as I was saying . . .' she blustered. Suddenly the classroom door banged open. Everyone looked up. *Bad timing*, Belle thought. *Cat is going to get the full force of The Fish's projector-rage.*

But it wasn't Cat.

It was Jack Thorne.

With those dangerous, defiant eyes that looked right into her secret soul! Belle looked down to hide her face, as if suddenly fascinated by the chipped wooden surface of the workbench.

Jack flashed Mrs Salmon a charming *silly-old-me* grin. 'Jack Thorne reporting for duty! Sorry I'm late. Went to the wrong room.' His voice was deep and surprisingly gentle-sounding.

'Just find an empty place and sit down quickly,' Mrs Salmon snapped.

Jack smiled and strolled into the room. *Directly towards Belle.* She felt as if she had a big red flashing light on top of her head. *An empty place!* Of course, he was heading for Cat's place, between her and Nathan. This was crazy, but *her hands were actually trembling*! She fixed what she hoped was a neutral kind of smile on her face and waited.

Jack walked right past her.

Belle couldn't help turning to see what he was doing.

Bianca was smiling and patting the empty stool next to her. Jack hooked his foot round the leg and sat down.

Bianca shuffled her stool closer to Jack's and leaned over – making sure her gleaming Arctic-fox blonde hair brushed his shoulder. Belle could almost see the scoreboard flickering behind her eyes: BIANCA HAYFORD – 1, BELLE MADISON – 0.

'*Belle Madison, eyes front please!*' Mrs Salmon shouted.

Belle whipped round. She wasn't used to being reprimanded in class. She took a deep breath. *Of course Jack was going to sit next to Bianca. She was the only person he knew.* Belle wasn't sure whether to be relieved or disappointed.

A few minutes later, she looked up from her work to find Nick Taggart loitering at her desk, supposedly on his way to sharpen his pencil. He casually slid his exercise book in front of her, open at the Antarctic food-chain diagram. Nick had customized his version. He'd given the killer whale the blonde bob and frosty blue eyes of Bianca Hayford. And with just a few clever strokes of his pen, the penguin had unmistakably become Jack Thorne, complete with striped T-shirt and jeans.

'Predator meets prey!' Nick mouthed, nodding towards the desk behind them, where Bianca was now helping Jack select a pen from her pencil case. 'He doesn't stand a chance!'

Belle couldn't help laughing.

'Belle Madison! What *has* got into you today?' Mrs Salmon scolded.

Suddenly the door opened again. This time it *was* Cat.

Belle glanced at her watch. Cat was almost twenty minutes late. This was not good. Serious misdemeanours in morning school could lead to students being banned from taking part in extra activities – like end-of-term plays, for example. Belle hoped Cat had a *very* good excuse

Come on, Cat! she willed her friend. *Abducted by aliens* might work. Or *sudden-onset memory-loss*.

There was a collective holding of breath as the whole class waited.

'Er, sorry – I, erm, overslept,' Cat mumbled.

Nathan sank his head into his hands. Holly gulped. *Overslept?* Belle thought. *How feeble is that?* And it wasn't even true! For once Cat *had* got up early.

'*Overslept?*' Belle quizzed as Cat slid into place next to her.

'Er, I ran back to the room to text Mum about getting the Lady Macbeth part, and then . . .' Cat whispered.

'And then?' Holly asked.

'Then I was practising a few lines – you know, in the mirror – and I just got a bit carried away—'

'*Miss Wickham!* If you ever come to my class so much as one second late again, you will be going straight to Mr Fortune's office. Do I make myself clear?'

'Crystal-clear, Mrs Salmon,' Cat replied sweetly.

CHAPTER SEVEN

Holly: The Special to Share

After the tensions of the science lesson, Mr Potter's art class following morning break was all peace and tranquillity. Soothing classical music was playing in the background (Beethoven's *Pastoral Symphony*, according to Belle and Lettie; Holly had no idea, but it sounded lovely, anyway) as they sketched portraits from photographs of famous people. Holly lost herself in cross-hatching Barack Obama's nostrils.

A group of the more artistically talented students – including Zak, and Gemma's best friend, Serena Quereshi – were gathered in one corner of the studio working with Mr Potter on designs for the costumes and scenery for *Macbeth*.

Holly glanced across at Cat. *I'd have a serious case of post-traumatic stress if Mrs Salmon had yelled at me like that in the science class*, she thought. But Cat didn't seem bothered. She was shading Marilyn Monroe's eyebrows with a dreamy look on her face. She was probably in Lady Macbeth mode, miles away in her Scottish castle, plotting murder and treason.

Cat, that was, not Marilyn Monroe.

After the lesson, Holly was walking to lunch with Belle and Cat when she heard someone call her name. She turned to see Ethan hurrying towards them.

She still wasn't used to the idea that she was actually *going out with Ethan.* Because of the half-term holiday, they'd not seen each other much since their first magical happy-after-ever kiss, although there'd been a lot of texting. She was still shy and uncertain, her ears in danger of overheating again. *What do you actually do with a boyfriend once you've got one?* OK, she wasn't *totally* clueless – she knew about kissing and stuff, but obviously that wasn't a full-time occupation.

Especially not at midday in front of Mrs Butterworth's desk.

'Hey, Holly, do you want to go for a pizza at Café Roma?' Ethan asked.

'Oh, er . . .' Holly could think of nothing she'd rather do, but she had been about to have lunch with her friends. How would they feel if she dumped them to go off with Ethan?

'Of course she does.' Cat gave Holly a little shove. 'See you later, Hols.'

'Have fun!' Belle waved.

Seems they don't mind too *much!* Holly thought happily.

Café Roma, on the other side of Kingsgrove Square, was a regular haunt for Garrick students. The owner, Luigi, greeted them warmly and argued about football with Ethan as he brought them their menus.

Then there was a moment of awkward silence.

But it was only a moment. Suddenly they were chatting – about dancing and acting and friends and football and singing and pizza . . .

They ordered the special. *To share.*

Holly started to relax. This was fun!

Then they talked about front crawl and backstroke. Not the most romantic of topics, Holly realized, but they were both keen swimmers. 'I'm going to enter the regional qualifiers again,' Ethan said, 'but I need to work on my breathing—'

'But your breathing's perfect,' Holly objected. Then she caught his eye and they both laughed. 'No, really, I love your breathing!' she teased. *I love your breathing* was one of the first things Ethan had ever said to Holly. He'd been talking about her swimming then too.

Ethan grinned. '*Don't kiss me – I'm alive!*' he quoted – the very first words Holly had said to him when

49

he'd literally knocked her off her feet in the courtyard.

'Don't!' Holly giggled. 'That's the most embarrassing thing I've ever said in my entire life!'

But suddenly it wasn't embarrassing any more. It was funny. And Holly realized that what she liked more than anything about Ethan was not the sea-green eyes, or the perfect square jaw; it was the way he made her feel special when they were together.

Then they talked about *Macbeth*. Ethan had got the part of Banquo he'd auditioned for. Holly wanted to know why he'd not gone for a bigger role – he was one of the school's most talented actors. Ethan looked serious when she asked.

'Well, I played the lead in *Othello* last year. But it all got too much. All the rehearsals, on top of football and swimming and regular lessons as well. I nearly lost the plot! In the end I had to go and have a word with Mr Fortune. He was great. He arranged it so I could drop some of my classes for the term and make them up later. But I don't want to go down that road again – and anyway . . . I want to have some time to spend with you too . . .' Ethan looked down, as if embarrassed about sounding too cheesy. But he did that fantastic smiling thing with the corners of his eyes, and Holly thought her heart would melt.

He could be as cheesy as he wanted!

A few moments later, Holly looked up from a fork-fight for the last olive on the plate to see Bianca and Mayu coming into the café. She couldn't help smiling at their expressions when they saw her with Ethan Unbelievably-cool-and-incredibly-popular Reed. Bianca looked as if she'd just swallowed a live tarantula.

'I hope you weren't planning on keeping it quiet,' Holly said a few minutes later, as she and Ethan hurried back across the square in the biting east wind.

'Keeping what quiet?' Ethan asked.

'You and me. Because now Bianca's eyeballed us, the whole school will know by tea time. She may even take out an advert in the national press!'

'Why would I want to keep it quiet?' Ethan laughed, putting his arm round her as a gust of wind threatened to blow her into the street.

Holly felt a stupid smile spreading across her face. *Is it possible to burst with happiness?* she wondered.

As they arrived back in the entrance hall, they were greeted by Ethan's best friend, Felix Baddeley, hobbling towards them on crutches, his dreadlocks bobbing frenetically.

Felix had broken his ankle in a football match before half-term. *The Ankle of Destiny*, Holly called it. If Ethan hadn't had to rush off to hospital with Felix, he wouldn't have arrived late at the gala showcase party, and he might never have rushed in with roses and apologized and kissed her . . .

'Watch out for The Chairminator!' Ethan shouted, grimacing as Felix narrowly avoided a head-on collision with Mrs Butterworth, who was skidding across the hall. 'He's going to be out of the football team all term,' Ethan sighed. 'And we haven't got another decent striker, so we're going to get thrashed in the Cup—'

'Holly!' Felix called as he drew near. 'Just the girl I was after.' He grinned, realizing what he'd said. 'Sorry, mate, not stepping on your toes or anything,' he added, winking at Ethan. 'I mean your band. Nobody's Angels. I saw you at the talent show. You were wicked! The deal is, I'm in a band too, and we've got this wedding reception gig coming up. We need some female vocals. Would you be interested?'

Holly felt a rush of Christmas-morning excitement. She was *extremely* interested.

And she was sure Cat and Belle would be too.

CHAPTER EIGHT

Cat: The Loathsome Worm-being

After shooing Ethan and Holly out on their lunch date, Cat and Belle sat down with their pasta and salad in the dining room.

Cat pulled her books out of her bag, pushed her plate to one side, and started scribbling frantically. She had to get this play review in by the end of the lunch break. Mr Grampian had taken a group of students in his advanced acting classes to the Barbican Centre on Saturday to see a new production of *Hamlet*, and had asked them all to write a short review. Cat loved the play – she'd spent the entire coach journey back to school discussing it with Duncan Gillespie; the production had given them both lots of ideas that could be adapted for *Macbeth* (not that Cat *knew* she had the Lady Macbeth part then, of course, but she didn't let a minor detail like that stop her!). It was so much fun! She pictured herself flying on a plane to New York to star in an award-winning Broadway production, poring over her scripts and deliberating over a difficult line with her director . . .

'. . . band rehearsal tonight . . .'

Cat was vaguely aware that Belle was saying something to her. 'Yeah, mmm,' she muttered back.

'I've booked a rehearsal room for six o'clock . . .'

'Mmm, OK . . .'

'Cat, can you hear me?!' Belle shouted, waving a hand in front of Cat's book.

Cat dragged herself back from her plane, midway across the Atlantic. 'Oh, sorry. What?'

'Band rehearsal tonight,' Belle repeated.

'Oh, no, I can't make it,' Cat groaned. 'The Fish has given me extra science homework. You heard her: *Next stop Mr Fortune's office!* So I can't skip it.'

Belle looked crestfallen. 'Maybe you could get up early tomorrow morning and do it?' she suggested.

Cat shuddered. 'Eu-urgh! You know I hate getting up early!'

'Well, you managed to get up to check the cast list at six a.m. this morning,' Belle replied in a tight voice.

Cat ground her teeth. She could feel rage rising up in her chest like bubbles in a can of Coke that's been shaken . . . and shaken . . . and is ready to *explode*! *It's all right for Belle,* she fumed to herself. *Top of every class . . . leaps out of bed at the crack of dawn, as fresh as a daisy . . . and—*

'. . . you just need to organize your time more efficiently,' Belle was saying.

'And *you*,' Cat snapped, unable to contain her annoyance any longer, 'just need to stop being so . . . *perfect* all the time and leave me alone!'

A hurt expression clouded Belle's face. Cat steeled herself against feeling sorry for her. *Belle shouldn't be such a . . . control freak—*

'Hey! I've got some amazing news . . .'

Cat and Belle both looked up to see Holly flying towards them, radiating Deep Joy as if she'd just won the lottery. On a rollover week. It must have been a good date.

Holly faltered as she reached the table. 'What's up with you two?'

'Er, nothing,' Cat muttered, knowing how much Holly hated arguments of any kind. 'What's this *amazing news* then?' she asked, feeling the seething bubbles subside as quickly as they had flared up.

Holly sat down. Belle grabbed the salad dressing out of the Elbow Hazard Zone just in time.

'Felix said—' Holly began.

'Felix?' Cat asked with a grin. 'We don't want to hear about Felix. We want to know about Ethan! *Details, girl, details!*'

To Cat's relief, Belle laughed. Cat hadn't *meant* to start a quarrel; her temper just had a life of its own sometimes.

'I'll tell you about that later,' Holly said shyly. 'But you know Felix has that really great band, The Undertow, with Mason Lee and Ben Stein . . . ?'

'Yeah . . . and . . . ?' Belle and Cat chorused in matching *where-are-you-going-with-this?* voices.

'Well, he's only asked if we want to do a gig with them. It's a big wedding reception. They have to do loads of dance music and old stuff as well as their own music. They want Nobody's Angels to join them!'

'Awesome!' Belle screamed, hugging Holly across the table.

'But' – Belle slumped back into her chair and gazed mournfully at Cat – 'we'd need extra band practice. I don't think Cat will have time . . .'

Now Holly was gazing at Cat too, adding her big brown starving-puppy eyes to Belle's big blue orphaned-kitten eyes. Cat felt terrible. She felt like the most loathsome worm-being in existence. She couldn't let Belle and Holly down. *Look at their little faces!* And it *would* be amazing to play a wedding gig.

'Who said I don't have time?' Cat heard herself saying. 'I'll *find* the time!'

Belle and Holly grinned and high-fived.

'And, Belle, I'm sorry I yelled at you earlier,' Cat went on. 'I don't really think you're perfect. Well, I do, of course. *Nice-perfect*, though, not *annoying-perfect*! It's just that I'm really tired and grumpy at the moment. I, erm . . . got up too early this morning,' she added, grinning. 'And then Mum was on the phone nagging me about my "career" again. I thought she'd be really pleased when I texted to say I got Lady Macbeth, but she was just banging on about doing professional auditions again. When's she going to get that I'm not interested in *Joseph and the Stupid Technicolor Dreamcoat?*'

'I'm sorry too.' Belle smiled. 'And I'll help with that science homework.'

'No, that's my job,' Nathan said as he and Nick stopped by the girls' table on their way out of the dining room. 'Let's meet after singing class. It'll only take half an hour.'

'Cheers, Nate,' Cat replied. 'If it wasn't for you I'd have been thrown out of Mrs Salmon's class ages ago. In fact . . . I don't know why I'm thanking you. *It's all your fault!*'

Nick laughed. 'Yeah, I thought The Fish was going

to feed you to the killer whales when you turned up late this morning!' he joked as they all walked out together.

'Me too!' Cat said, grimacing at the memory. 'Now, *to the library*! I've got ten minutes to finish this *Hamlet* review.'

She turned and trudged up the stairs. She felt exhausted just thinking about all the work that lay ahead of her.

'Ooh, watch out, it's Lady Macbeth!' Cat looked up to see Mayu and Bianca coming out of the library. 'Overslept this morning, did we?' Bianca sneered.

Cat was about to retaliate – but she just didn't have the time.

This is how bad it's got, she thought. *I don't even have time to argue with Bianca any more!*

CHAPTER NINE

Holly: Monsters of Rock and Top Scorers

'*And it's a* legendary *moment in rock music history!*' Felix proclaimed as he unlocked the rehearsal room the following Saturday afternoon. 'The first *ever* combined rehearsal of teenage rock legend, The Undertow, and the hottest new girl band in town, Nobody's Angels . . .'

'Just open the door, will you?' laughed Ben, the bass guitarist. 'We're getting old waiting around here for you.'

Felix pointed at his ankle, still in its plaster cast. 'Excuse *me*, I'm mobility-challenged here, you know!'

'*Mentally* challenged, more like,' quipped Mason, the drummer.

Holly exchanged smiles with Cat and Belle. After their initial excitement, they'd all been feeling a little nervous about the first practice with the boys' band: would they all get on OK? Would their musical styles clash horribly? And would the boys try to boss them around? *Although, with Cat's fiery temper and Belle's control-thing, the boys would be venturing into very hazardous waters if they attempted that!* Holly thought.

But she needn't have worried. Felix's laid-back jokey style soon put them all at their ease. And they knew Mason already, of course – he was in Year Eight and hung out with Nick, Zak and Frankie; he'd only recently joined The Undertow to replace their original drummer, a Year Eleven boy who'd left to join a world tour with one of London's top youth orchestras. That only left Ben Stein, a tall, gangly Year Ten boy in camouflage trousers and ripped Arctic Monkeys T-shirt. At first Holly found Ben's mean-and-moody scowl a little intimidating, but she soon relaxed when she heard him goofing around with the others.

Holly, Cat and Belle followed the boys into the rehearsal room. Mason adjusted the drum kit, while Ben plugged his bass guitar into the amplifier. Felix settled into a chair with his electric guitar and a microphone, the Ankle of Destiny propped up on his guitar case.

There was an ear-splitting squeal from the amp as Ben tuned up his bass.

Belle clapped her hands over her ears.

'OK, we get the message!' Cat laughed. 'You guys are Monsters of Rock!'

'Yeah, Deaf Monsters if you keep the levels up that high,' Belle commented, turning the dial down several notches.

Holly cringed. The boys were really going to *love* being told to keep the noise down! She waited for trouble to break out, but Felix just grinned and made a face. 'Girls! Such sensitive creatures!'

'What are we waiting for?' Cat yelled. She grabbed a microphone and started to sing Pink's *So What*. She really looked the part, Holly thought, in her black mini-skirt and biker boots and a tight purple top. She'd even added red lipstick and piled her hair into an Amy Winehouse-style beehive to complete the rock-chick look. Holly jumped up and joined her, improvising some dance steps, which Cat quickly followed. Belle picked up the lead vocal, her powerful voice resonating around the room. Soon the boys joined in and they finished the song with a rebel-rousing chorus.

For the next two hours, The Undertow and Nobody's Angels worked together, practising all the old-favourite dance-floor-fillers they'd been asked to perform at the wedding. They would also have a chance to play some of their original songs, Felix explained, when the oldsters left the reception and the younger guests stayed on for an evening party. The Undertow's sound was an original fusion of indie rock and reggae, which the girls loved.

They all got on brilliantly, and laughed and joked together as they worked. The girls even gave the boys the music for one of their own songs, the lively Latin American number, *Done Looking!*, which Lettie Atkins had written for them. Mason knew the song already, of course, because he was in the school orchestra that played the accompaniment at the talent competition, and the other two soon picked it up and added a quirky rock sound to the mambo beat.

'Wow, that was great!' they all agreed as they eventually sank to the floor, exhausted but elated by their efforts.

'Here's to The Under-Angels!' Holly laughed, leading a toast with her bottle of water. She'd completely forgotten her earlier doubts; now she couldn't wait for the next rehearsal.

'So where's the wedding?' Belle asked.

'Walthamstow,' Felix replied. 'North London. It's my sister, Carly, and her fiancé.'

Holly gave a big smile. 'Walthamstow's where I live!' Then she had what Belle would have called an Awesome Idea. She would invite Cat and Belle to stay at her house after the wedding reception. Mum had met them at the gala showcase, and would *love* having them all home for the night.

'See you next week!' Holly called. She followed Cat and Belle out of the rehearsal room and straight into a three-person pile-up in the doorway as they almost crashed into a boy who was careering down the corridor after a football.

With perfect timing, Belle stretched out an elegant Jimmy-Choo-sandalled foot and stopped the ball.

But the next moment her trademark poise and style suddenly disappeared. 'Ooh, er . . . ' she stammered. She tried placing her hand casually on her hip, slipped and stumbled to one side.

Whatever can be causing Belle to act so . . . well, like me? Holly wondered: *shy, clumsy, tongue-tied* – these were not the words that usually leaped to mind when describing Belle!

Oh, that *was why!*

The boy chasing the football was Jack 'Pirate Boy' Thorne.

'Er, is this a football?' Belle spluttered.

'I hope so!' Jack laughed. 'I've been kicking it around the football pitch for the last hour!'

She giggled and stared at it.

Cat's eyes were round with astonishment. *Yep,*

Holly thought. *Cat's definitely noticed Belle's major coolness-malfunction too.*

'Hi, I'm Holly,' she said, holding out her hand. 'This is Cat, and this is Belle.'

'Hey, good to meet you!' Jack gave a lopsided grin as he shook hands and leaned back against the wall in a leisurely slouch. 'Belle? As in Belle Madison?' he asked.

Oh, no! Holly was horrified. He's going to ask if her dad is Dirk Madison, the famous American film director, and Belle hates it when people bring up her celebrity parents.

But, 'You're the girl with the amazing voice, right?' Jack asked. 'I've heard about you . . .'

Oh, wow! This guy is good, Holly said to herself. Really good! If Belle hadn't been completely hearts-flowers smitten already, she would be now! Her greatest dream in life was to be recognized for her singing talents.

'Oh, er, erm, thanks,' Belle muttered as Jack continued to gaze at her, his hazel eyes blazing with admiration.

'So you're a keen football player then, Jack?' Cat asked — when it became obvious that the part of Belle's brain in charge of intelligent conversation hadn't kicked back in yet.

'Yeah, love it!' he said. 'I used to play a lot in Singapore.'

Holly suddenly remembered what Ethan had said about the Garrick team. 'You're not a striker by any chance, are you?' she asked. If Jack was good enough, perhaps he could take Felix's place . . .

Jack grinned mischievously. 'Top scorer last season!'

'Hey, Jack! You planning to stand around chatting up the babes or are you bringing that ball back some time today?' Nick and Zak had poked their heads in through the open window at the end of the corridor – where the ball must have bounced in from the playing field.

'I'm on it!' Jack shouted back, flicking the ball up with his toe and catching it. 'See you around!'

'See you!' Holly and Cat called.

'Yeah!' Belle mumbled, her face a shade of flamingo-pink.

Holly thought she saw Nick giving Belle a strange look. Maybe he'd noticed the signs of strange un-Belle-like activity too . . .

'Wow! Top scorer!' Cat laughed when Jack was barely out of earshot. 'And I think our Belle's his next goal, don't you, Hols?'

'Shh!' Holly hissed, shaking Cat's arm. 'He'll hear you.'

But when she glanced up, she realized that Jack hearing them might not be the biggest problem on their horizon.

Bianca Hayford was standing at the end of the corridor.

How long has she been lurking there? Holly wondered. *And has she spotted the sparks between Jack and Belle too?*

From the look that Bianca was aiming at Belle, Holly could stop wondering: Bianca had clearly seen *everything*.

It was a look as icy as the frozen wastelands of Antarctica. The look the penguin sees gleaming in the eye of the killer whale as it's about to become lunch.

It seemed that Belle had just made Bianca even more of an enemy than she already was.

CHAPTER TEN

Cat: Attack of the Designer Waifs

Later on Saturday afternoon Cat was alone in her room. She was due to meet Nathan in a few minutes to polish off another batch of science homework before going to a *Macbeth* rehearsal.

There was just one tiny, microscopic problem.

She couldn't find her *Macbeth* script; the one that she'd spent hours marking up with notes about how to deliver each line.

She looked around in despair. On Belle's side of the room, clothes were hanging neatly in the wardrobe, books were lined up in alphabetical order and the cushions were arranged symmetrically on the bed.

On Cat's side, a tsunami of clothes and shoes had washed up all over the bed. A volcano of books and papers had erupted across the desk

Va-a-a-lerieee . . . And now, somewhere in the chaos, her mobile phone was ringing!

She finally tracked the ringtone to a pile of laundry.

'Yes! What?' Cat answered, flopping down amongst the discarded clothes. '*Arggh!*' she screamed as she felt a furry body stir beneath her. Shreddie, deeply offended at being disturbed during his afternoon nap, stretched and stalked out of the door.

'Whatever's the matter, Catrin?' her mum asked.

'Nothing!' Cat replied.

Nothing? *Only that I've lost my* Macbeth *script, I've got a rehearsal in half an hour, a pile of science homework to do and my room's a natural disaster . . .*

'Everything's fine, Mum!' she said.

'Good,' her mum replied. 'Now, listen, love. They're re-casting for the chorus of *Oliver!* next week, and I've managed to get you on the audition list for Tuesday afternoon—'

'No!' Cat said flatly. It wasn't that she didn't like *Oliver!* It was a great musical. It just wasn't her style.

'No what?'

'No, I don't want to be in *Oliver!* And no, I can't go on Tuesday afternoon. I've got a *Macbeth* rehearsal.'

'Don't be silly, of course you do! Everyone who's *anyone* started out in *Oliver!*'

'I don't want to be *anyone*,' Cat insisted. '*I want to be Lady Macbeth!*'

'Yes, love, I know. But it's just a school play. This is West End. It could be your big break!'

'It's not *just a school play*!' Cat snapped. 'The Garrick Shakespeare production is a Big Deal!' She sighed. When was Mum going to get it? She didn't want West End. If she got into one of those shows, she'd have no time for *Macbeth* – or for Nobody's Angels. She might even have to leave the Garrick and have a private tutor. But *this* was where she wanted to be. Superstar High! The best place in the world to train as a serious actress . . .

'And anyway,' Cat said, trying a different tack, 'I'd be useless for *Oliver!* I don't exactly *look* like a half-starved orphan boy!'

'Oh, that's no problem!' Her mum laughed. 'We can strap those boobs down. And there *are* corsets, you know . . . '

'Thanks, Mum,' Cat said. 'That's really done wonders for my self-image. I do *not* need a corset!'

'So,' Mum continued, deaf to all objections, 'I'll be there at two thirty on Tuesday to pick you up. I've cleared it with Mr Fortune for you to miss class. What a *lovely* man he is. I'll be in the car, waiting in the drive. If you're not there, I'll start blaring the horn. And make sure you look like a *waif*!'

Cat had no choice.

Tuesday afternoon found her trailing down the

broad stone steps on her way out of Superstar High, looking vaguely waif-like in a pair of raggedy trousers and an oversized jacket she'd borrowed from the school costume store. Grumpily she yanked open the door of the people-carrier to find a smartly dressed Japanese woman in the passenger seat. 'Hop in the back with Mayu, love,' Mum told her.

Speechless with surprise, Cat slammed the door. What were Mayu and her mother doing in Mum's car? Reluctantly she climbed into the back seat.

'We're giving Mayu and Mrs Tanaka a lift to the TV studio in Covent Garden,' Mum explained. 'They were about to get a taxi – Mayu has a try-out for a skin cream commercial!' she added in an awed tone – as if Mayu had received a personal invitation from the Queen to perform a one-woman show at the Albert Hall!

Mrs Tanaka turned and smiled proudly at her daughter. 'How *nice* that you two girls are in the school play together,' she said sweetly.

As Mum threw the car around the busy London streets, trading insults with taxi drivers, Cat festered with silent rage. She didn't want to go to the audition, and she *certainly* didn't want to be trapped in a confined space with Mayu for the next twenty minutes. She just wanted to be back at Superstar High in Mr Grampian's drama class. Mayu, looking all cute and adorable in a Nesquik-pink jacket and shorts, was glaring out of the window, radiating resentment like a sugared almond dipped in sulphuric acid – she'd still not got over the humiliation of being Cat's understudy.

'You two are quiet back there,' Mrs Tanaka remarked.

'Nerves, I expect, bless them,' Mum said as she beeped furiously at a bus that had the audacity to try and *actually drive in the bus lane.*

Cat sighed. The only thing that made it even remotely bearable was that Mayu was hating it even more than *she* was.

But at least Mrs Tanaka had ensured that *their* appointment would be over in plenty of time to get back for the *Macbeth* rehearsal. Unlike Mum, who just murmured, 'We'll see . . .' Which everyone knows means *Don't bank on it.*

Finally they dropped off their passengers and arrived at the Galaxy Theatre, where Mum immediately whisked Cat into the ladies and swaddled her with tape under her waif-jacket to pull in her curves. *This must be what those Egyptian mummies felt like,* Cat thought. Then she smudged Cat's cheeks with black powder to give her that authentic *guttersnipe* look, and scraped her hair back under a ridiculous tweed cap.

Cat gritted her teeth, determined to get it over with as quickly as possible.

When they emerged into the foyer of the theatre, it was Waif Central. Skinny boys with big Pokémon-character eyes. Tiny girls with matchstick legs and designer-grunge rags. After what seemed like hours, an assistant called out Cat's name and ushered her onto the stage.

Cat didn't want to be in *Oliver!* and she was going to make sure that *Oliver!* didn't want her either.

She sang the first three verses of *Consider Yourself* completely out of tune.

She read out the short speech that she was asked to perform in the manner of a chirpy London street urchin in a broad Yorkshire accent.

'Next!' called the casting director, without even looking up.

Cat spent the journey back to the Garrick in stony silence while Mum lectured her on the error of her ways. 'I would have *jumped* at the chance of *Oliver!* when I was your age!' she began. Mum had done some acting in her younger days, even appearing (or rather not appearing, underneath a furry teddy-bear costume) as a walk-on Ewok in a *Star Wars* movie. But then she met Dad, had kids, and the rest was history.

'Shakespeare's all very well,' she continued, 'but he's not exactly *box office*, is he?'

As they pulled up to the Garrick, it was almost half past five. Cat raced along to the Redgrave. *Only half an hour late*, she thought as she burst into the theatre to find the rest of the cast sitting in a circle on the stage, doing a read-through of Act One. *Half an hour wasn't so bad!*

Unfortunately the director didn't agree. 'If you can't make it to rehearsals on time, Catrin, there are plenty of other students who would be only too happy to take your place!' he roared.

Mayu giggled and flashed him one of her dimple-power smiles.

'Sorry,' Cat stammered. 'I was unavoidably delayed – er . . . family problems.'

Well, it was true! Mum *was* family, and she was *definitely* causing problems . . .

'Oh yes, how *did* your audition for *Oliver!* go, Cat?' Mayu asked, sweet as syrup.

Duncan Gillespie, the student director, raised an eyebrow. Mr Sharpe looked like he was going to explode, but Duncan leaped to Cat's defence. 'Never mind, we didn't need you for the first few scenes anyway . . .' he said. Cat smiled at him gratefully.

Belle shuffled along and made room for Cat next to

her. 'Smudge,' she whispered behind her script, pointing at Cat's face.

Cat scrubbed at the black powder with a tissue, feeling – not for the first time lately – that her life was spiralling out of control.

CHAPTER ELEVEN

Belle: Belly-dancing and Sweet Music

Belle loved the Garrick library.

The old-fashioned desks each had their own little green lamp. Light streamed in through the tall windows at each end, illuminating motes of dust suspended in the still air.

She settled down with a book on the Tudors. It was Thursday lunch time, and she'd come straight from a history lesson. Their teacher, Miss Chase-Smythe – who looked like minor royalty herself, in pearls and a frilled blouse – had been telling them in her ultra-posh voice all about the Tudor kings and queens. As an American, Belle hadn't studied much English history before and she was fascinated: all that marrying and beheading and burning at the stake – it was so gory, yet so romantic . . .

Some time later, she looked up from reading about Henry VIII's six wives to see Jack Thorne strolling towards her, silhouetted against the window. She felt the familiar popcorn sensation in her stomach, but she was determined not to let his x-ray eyes phase her this time.

He smiled and was about to say something, when Bianca shot out from behind a shelf of Greek myths. 'Oh, Jack! I'm so-o-o glad you're here!' she gushed. 'I need a book but I can't reach it. That one, right up there!' She pointed – at random, as far as Belle could tell – at a book on the very top shelf.

'Are you sure this is the one you want?' Jack asked, grinning as he handed Bianca the book. '*Belly-dancing for Beginners*?'

'Oh, er, it's not for me!' Bianca spluttered. 'It's for . . . Lettie. She's got this thing about, er, *belly-dancing*, you know. Weird or what! Come on, let's go and get lunch.'

Yeah, right! Belle thought. Bianca had appointed herself as Jack's personal stalker ever since she'd seen him talking to Belle in the Football-in-Corridor Incident. She'd also taken to dressing even more fashionably than usual. She was now wearing a red Christian Dior suit with a velvet-trimmed tulip skirt, which – even to Belle's sophisticated tastes – was a *little* over the top for a Thursday afternoon library session. But Bianca was clearly a girl who was used to Getting What She Wanted.

And she wanted Jack!

And although Jack wasn't exactly leaping into her arms, he didn't seem to be objecting much either.

As she returned her attention to Anne Boleyn's beheading, Belle felt an odd hollow sensation under her ribs, like a swallowed yawn. Was it indigestion? Or could it be that she was actually *jealous* of Bianca?

She sighed. If she was jealous of Bianca, it could only be for one reason . . .

And it *wasn't* that Christian Dior suit!

Mr Garcia's Thursday afternoon advanced singing class was Belle's favourite lesson of the week. The only downside was that neither Cat nor Holly were there – they had advanced acting and dancing classes on Thursday afternoons instead. After a thorough warm-up of breathing exercises, scales and arpeggios, Mr Garcia told them to take a short break and then get into pairs. 'We're going to work on improving our phrasing today,' he boomed in his earthquake-rumble.

Belle leaned back in her chair, sipped her water and glanced around for Nick Taggart. She usually worked with Nick in singing classes, ever since they'd been top of the class on a harmony project together. No doubt he'd charge over to find her any second now, teasing her with one of his dumb jokes! But, to Belle's surprise, it was Jack who sat down next to her.

'So, could you bear working with the new guy?' he asked.

Belle's heart did a somersault. But before she could reply, Bianca zoomed in like a heat-seeking missile. She hovered behind Jack's chair, leaned over his shoulder and said – in a stage whisper that Belle was so-o-o meant to hear – 'Don't bother, Jack. Belle *always* works with Nick Taggart. They make *such sweet music* together – if you know what I mean!'

Belle was outraged. Bianca was obviously trying to make it sound as if Belle and Nick were dating or something – just to put Jack off. 'Don't be so *ridiculous*, Bianca,' she said quietly, her voice trembling with fury. 'Nick and I do not make *sweet music together*, as you call it – and we never have done!'

Belle looked up to see Nick Taggart standing right in front of her with an odd expression on his face. It was clear he'd heard the entire conversation. Suddenly she felt dreadful. *Poor Nick! He must think I'm trying to deny that we ever work together*, she fretted, *just so I can be partners with Jack. But that's not what I meant!*

Belle was torn. She would love to work with Jack. But Nick was her friend and she couldn't just drop him . . . *I must be crazy*, she thought. *I'm turning Jack* down because it might hurt Nick's feelings. Nick Taggart! The class clown who makes fun of me and winds me up every chance he gets!

But friends were friends . . .

Just as she was about to refuse Jack's offer, Nick suddenly spoke up irritably. 'Yeah, so Belle and I work together *sometimes*. But we're just *friends* – not sure you'd know the meaning of that word, Bianca – and I was just about to ask *Lettie* to be my partner anyway.'

Now Belle was *totally* confused! She was shocked by the anger in Nick's voice. And had he really been planning to work with Lettie all along? She couldn't help feeling a little disappointed that Nick didn't want to be her partner any more.

'Break over!' Mr Garcia shouted. 'In your pairs, now.'

Bianca grabbed Jack by the hand. Nick and a delighted-looking Lettie followed them over to where Mr Garcia was waiting with Frankie and Mayu and all the other happy couples.

'Not found a partner yet, Belle?' Mr Garcia asked her. 'Never mind, you can work with me today.'

The rest of the class passed in a blur. Belle couldn't help worrying about Nick. He'd sounded *furious*. Was he upset because he thought she'd been going to work with Jack? And would he even *believe* her if she tried to explain that she'd been about to *refuse* Jack's offer? Out of the corner of her eye she watched Nick laughing and chatting with Lettie. But as Belle knew only too well, he was a great comic actor. Maybe he was just hiding his injured pride. The thought of losing Nick as a friend was giving Belle a lump in her throat that wasn't helping her singing at all.

And then there was Jack! Watching him work with Bianca, poring over the sheet music of *Love Changes Everything* from *The Phantom of the Opera* and marking in the best breathing places, Belle felt that peculiar pain in her ribs again.

There was no doubting it now.

It was pure, one-hundred-per-cent-organic *jealousy*.

When the class was finally over, Belle drifted across the courtyard, scuffing through piles of fallen leaves. Usually Nick would have been in her face, making her laugh with his stupid pranks. But today he had mumbled a quick '*Hasta la vista*' and hurried off with Lettie. Belle smiled ruefully to herself: all those times she'd wished Nick would leave her alone, and now that he had, it felt terrible!

Belle was due at a *Macbeth* rehearsal in ten minutes. She'd been looking forward to it, but she was suddenly overcome with gloom. Normally she didn't mind being alone – but for the first time since she arrived at Superstar High, she was *lonely*. What she longed for, Belle realized, was a girls' night in with Holly and Cat. They'd be able to tell her what to do about Nick; they were so much better at all this complicated friendship stuff. It was all uncharted territory to Belle, who'd been educated by private tutors and coaches before coming to the Garrick.

Maybe she would even tell them how she felt about Jack! *Which is* what *exactly?* she asked herself. *OK*, she finally admitted, *I like him. I like him a lot!*

But Holly was so busy with her dance classes, and being *in luuuurve* with Ethan. And Cat was always rushing around in a frenzy these days . . . Would the three of them ever find time to just hang out and have fun like they used to?

Could their friendship survive the pressures of Superstar High?

CHAPTER TWELVE

Belle: March of the Zombie Robot

Belle arrived at the Redgrave Theatre and added her name to the sign-up sheet that Mr Sharpe put up on the stage door to keep track of attendance at rehearsals. Most of the other actors had signed in already.

But there was one name missing.

Cat was not there yet.

Where *was* she? This was the first costume call – for the wardrobe managers, Serena Quereshi and a Year Ten student called Lucy Cheng, to check whether anything needed altering – and the entire cast needed to be there. Mr Sharpe had been hopping mad when Cat turned up late after the *Oliver!* audition. She would be in a heap of trouble if it happened again today . . .

Belle pushed open the door to find Mayu and Bianca loitering on the other side. 'You're late!' Mayu told her.

'And why haven't you got your costume on yet?' Bianca asked. Belle noticed that she was sporting a spectacular black witch-goddess dress, woven with tiny serpents crafted from silver wire, while Mayu was in the long plain dress and white apron of a castle servant. 'Lucy and Serena want everyone on stage *in costume*,' Bianca whispered. 'Right now.'

'But where *is* my costume?' Belle asked, rattled by the prospect of being late, and still distracted with worries about Jack and Nick.

'Look in the main dressing room,' Bianca hissed. 'All the costumes are hanging up with name tags on them!'

'Thanks,' Belle muttered.

She soon found her costume. A cardboard tag, clearly bearing the name BELLE MADISON, was firmly attached.

She was a little surprised to find that it was a full suit of armour.

Complete with helmet.

She'd thought it was just knights who wore armour . . . But who was she to argue? *Macbeth* was set in the olden days, after all. In Scotland. Maybe messengers had to wear armour as they travelled around in those times – to protect them from highwaymen or wolves or something.

But getting into the armour was no easy task. The metal sections were heavy and cumbersome and they fitted together in some mysterious, intricate fashion. It was like a cross between a tank and a Rubik's cube. But Belle was not going to be beaten by *an article of clothing*, and finally – bruised, battered and dripping with sweat – *she was in!*

Now she just had to get to the stage. But the armour weighed a ton and the joints were so stiff she had to walk with her arms and legs sticking out like a zombie robot. She peered through the narrow eye-slit in the helmet. The other dressing rooms were all deserted. *Everyone else must already be in the theatre*, she thought. She lumbered along the corridor – *move right leg, clank; drag left leg, clatter* – somehow pulled herself up the stairs into the wings and, with a noise like an explosion in a cymbal factory . . .

. . . crashed onto the stage.

She paused, waiting for the clanging to stop reverberating in her ears.

There was silence. Then laughter. Loud, uproarious laughter.

Belle tugged off the helmet and looked around. There were all the other students, in medieval dresses, tunics and breeches. *No armour in sight! Not even a breastplate!* And there were the other Messengers – all wearing simple tunics and cloaks.

One of those Messengers was Jack. He was laughing at her.

Nick was working on something down on the sound-editing desk. He was laughing at her too.

'Belle Madison! What do you think you are doing?' Mr Sharpe yelled, bristling with rage. 'This is not a fancy dress party! Get off my stage now!'

Serena looked up from pinning the hem of Nathan's tunic. 'Belle, where did you get that costume?' she gasped.

'Do you need a tin-opener, dude?' Zak shouted from the back of the stage, where he was painting scenery with Frankie and Mason.

Every fibre of Belle's body screamed out 'RUN AWAY!' But, clad in several tons of steel, running wasn't an option.

Just when she thought she might die of humiliation, there was a commotion on the other side of the stage. Everyone turned to see Cat rush in, holding up the train of a black velvet cloak. Beneath it was a long blood-red dress with a low bodice that exposed acres of snowy-white cleavage, adorned with a magnificent necklace dripping with ruby-red stones. There was a stunned silence as everyone admired the effect. Even Mr Sharpe was speechless.

But not for long. 'I will not tolerate a Lady Macbeth who is constantly late!' he bellowed. 'You obviously don't realize how important this production is for the reputation of the entire school!'

'Tut, tut!' Mayu simpered, her dimples going into overdrive.

Duncan shook his head sadly. 'Yeah, sorry, Cat, but this is getting a bit much . . .'

'My sentiments precisely,' announced Mr Grampian. The head of the Drama Department had been sitting quietly at the back of the theatre, observing the rehearsal. 'I quite agree that a final warning would be appropriate at this juncture, Mr Sharpe.'

Mr Sharpe harrumphed irritably. Belle had the distinct impression that in his view, Cat had gone way past the final-warning stage some time ago.

Relieved that everyone's attention was now focused on Cat's dramatic arrival, Belle took the opportunity to slink – or rather clank – back to the dressing room.

As she wriggled out of the armour, she was kicking herself. Mentally, that is; actually kicking yourself in full armour would be a very dangerous move.

Why, oh, why hadn't she smelled a big fat rat when Bianca and Mayu informed her, oh-so-helpfully, where to find her costume?

No wonder they were laughing louder than anyone else when she appeared on stage looking like the Tin Man meets Frankenstein's Monster.

They'd set a trap – and she'd walked right into it!

CHAPTER THIRTEEN

Cat: Inner Peace and Fairy Juice

'*OH – MY – GOD!*' Belle groaned. 'That was so-o-o embarrassing!'

Cat grinned sympathetically as they sat down in front of the roaring fire in the common room after supper. *She* was used to putting her foot in it and making a spectacle of herself – it was all in a day's work! But poor Belle usually conducted herself in a cool and dignified manner. Being the school laughing-stock in a full suit of armour was not exactly in her comfort zone!

'Bianca and Mayu *told* me to look for the costume with my name on . . .' Belle muttered.

'Yep!' Cat laughed. 'Those two must have thought they'd hit the jackpot – Belle making a prize eejit of herself *and* Cat getting a humungous rollicking from Mr Sharpe. *Two for the price of one!*'

Cat was trying to make light of it to cheer Belle up, but in reality she was quite shaken by Mr Sharpe's outburst; the thought of letting down the entire school was *much* harder to laugh off than her usual blips and blunders. 'We'll *rise above it!*' she said bravely, reminding Belle of the Bianca-proof slogan they'd coined at the beginning of term. 'And don't worry – everyone will have forgotten about the armour-thing by tomorrow.'

'Do you really think so?'

'Yeah – no doubt I'll do another of my amazing *Cat-turns-up-late-again* or *Cat-forgets-her-homework* tricks, and give them something else to gossip about.' Cat laughed her sprightliest *am-I-bothered?* laugh, but she knew she'd just lost one of her nine lives. If Mr Grampian hadn't stepped in, she was sure Mr Sharpe would have thrown her out of the play then and there. He hadn't even given her a chance to explain that she was late because she'd run to ask Miss Candlemas if she could borrow the string of red glass beads she'd seen her wearing last week, for her Lady Macbeth costume.

Belle must have detected the wobble in her voice. 'Cat, I know things are getting a bit crazy. Are you OK?'

Cat grinned. 'Yes, of course!' Although deep down she wasn't so sure. She was so tired her bones ached. She felt as if she were running on a treadmill that was going faster and faster – and she couldn't find the switch to turn it off . . .

'Tell you what you need!' Belle said.

'A body-double? A time machine?'

Belle laughed and shook her head. '*Upekkha.*'

'*Up-a-what?*'

'*Upekkha* – it's a yoga thing – it means balance, inner peace. Come to my yoga class with me tomorrow morning . . .'

Cat wasn't *entirely* convinced yoga was going to solve her problems. She didn't need *inner peace*. She just needed to run faster or find the off-switch.

'*SOMEBODY HELP ME!*'

The fake scream was coming from Nick Taggart, who was racing into the common room with Nathan and Serena. A group of Year Ten students, including Ethan Reed and Lucy Cheng, followed. '*I'm a damsel in distress!*' Nick continued, waving his hands girlishly. '*Behold! Methinks a knight in shining armour approacheth!*' With that, he threw himself at Belle's feet. The others drew up armchairs around the cosy fireplace, laughing at Nick's performance.

Eek! Cat thought. The last thing Belle needed was Nick winding her up with his court jester act. But to her astonishment, Belle didn't seem annoyed with Nick at all. In fact, she was grinning at him as if he'd just made the wittiest joke in the history of comedy.

'I'll challenge you to a joust if you're not careful,' Belle quipped, suddenly looking a lot more cheerful.

'You *were* pretty funny, Belle!' Serena laughed as she pulled a cape from her bag and started sewing braid around the hem. 'But how did you get the armour? It was hidden away right at the back of the stores.'

Before Belle could reply, Holly, Gemma and Lettie arrived, excitedly discussing the meeting they'd just had with Miss Morgan and Miss LeClair to check the fitting of the new *pointe* shoes they'd all bought during the half-term holiday; the advanced ballet class would be starting their *en pointe* work very soon.

'Lucky Holly,' Gemma teased. 'Miss Morgan says she's got *perfect* feet!'

Ethan laughed and made room on the arm of his chair for Holly, who sat down with a shy smile and exchanged a little True Romance look with him. *Those two are so sweet together I'm getting a sugar-rush just looking at them!* Cat thought. If it was anyone other than Holly, it would be totally sick-making.

And now Nick and Lettie were sharing a bag of Maltesers, engrossed in a technical sound-editing conversation – but, Cat noticed, Nick had a daft, dreamy look on his face that had nothing to do with the choice of music for the banquet scene in *Macbeth*.

Then Jack poked his head into the common room, looking for a library book he'd mislaid. 'Oh, how's the belly-dancing going, Lettie?' he called over with a big grin. Lettie stared at him blankly.

What was that all about? Cat asked herself. Belle

blushed, and gazed at Jack as he did a quick book search before hurrying off to look in the dining room. Nick glanced at Belle, smiled, and then winked knowingly at Cat. He'd obviously seen her reaction too.

What was going on? Cat wondered. Were they putting something in the water at Superstar High? It was like the scene from *A Midsummer Night's Dream* where everyone wakes up with fairy juice on their eyelids and falls in love with the first person they see . . .

Cat was almost *relieved* when Bianca and Mayu came into the common room. At least *those* two could be relied upon to break up the love-a-thon with a bit of good old-fashioned, no-nonsense spite.

'Come on, Lettie,' Bianca called. 'We're going to get ice creams at Café Roma – and wait till you hear this: the most *hysterical* thing happened at the costume call today . . .'

Yep! Bianca is nothing if not predictable! Cat thought.

Lettie smiled awkwardly and got up to join Bianca and Mayu. 'What happened?' she asked.

'Ooh, can't tell you here.' Bianca smiled wickedly, looking straight at Belle. 'Sir Prance-a-lot might get upset and run me through with her sword!'

'So what *did* happen?' Holly asked after they'd left. Cat and Belle recounted the story of the Armour Fiasco and the Delayed Arrival of Lady Macbeth. They could both see the funny side of it now, and everyone was soon roaring with laughter.

'So that explains it!' Gemma said, still laughing. 'I *wondered* why Bianca and Mayu were fossicking about in the wardrobe storeroom this afternoon when I went to look for Serena. *Said* they were helping clear out some old costumes. I thought that seemed a bit too *useful* for those two!'

Gradually everyone started heading off to their rooms. Holly waved goodbye to Ethan, who left rather reluctantly to revise for a French test.

Cat stared into the embers of the fire and sighed. 'Time to tackle that history essay,' she murmured to nobody in particular. A miserable ache oozed through her body at the thought of an evening with Henry VIII and her laptop.

'You should take a night off,' Belle told her. 'You look shattered.'

Suddenly Holly jumped up. 'Ooh, Bianca's just given me a Great Idea!' she announced. 'Meet me in your room in half an hour.'

Cat and Belle exchanged bamboozled looks.

What Great Idea could Holly Devenish – the kind of girl who helps old ladies across the road and rescues stray hedgehogs – possibly have that had been inspired by *Bianca Hayford's* scheming brain?

CHAPTER FOURTEEN

Belle: Girls' Night In

'*Ta-da!*' Holly fanfared, throwing open the door and letting the contents of her overloaded arms tumble onto the coffee table. 'There's Chocolate Chip Cookie-dough, Very Berry Swirl and Rocky Road . . . courtesy of Café Roma!'

So that was Bianca's Great Idea!

Belle had to admit that for once Bianca was right. Whatever the question was, family-size tubs of Italian ice cream were definitely the answer! But how had Holly got permission to go off alone to Café Roma at this time? Year Eight students weren't allowed out of school unaccompanied after 6.30 p.m.

'I asked Ethan to run out and get it for me,' Holly explained. 'Year Tens can sign out until eight o'clock.'

'I don't know about you, Hols, but I'm in love with Ethan already!' Cat laughed, pulling the lid off the tub of Rocky Road.

'And for my next trick' – Holly whipped an envelope

out of her bag like a rabbit out of a hat – '*Mamma Mia! Mum posted me the DVD.*'

'Girls' night in!' Cat shouted, jumping on her bed and sweeping aside piles of clothes and books to make seating room.

'Way to go!' Holly was a genius, Belle thought. This was exactly what they all needed. 'Er, let me help you with that, Cat,' she added.

Cat's attempts to tidy up were just spreading the chaos around the room. Pairs of tights were now dangling from the curtain rail, and a Spanish dictionary was splayed across the dressing-table mirror.

'Is this that Macbeth script you were looking for?' Belle asked, holding up a sheaf of papers she'd excavated from under Cat's bed.

'My baby!' Cat cried, kissing the script. 'You've come back to me!' But suddenly her face fell. 'Eugh! I've just remembered: homework – I had a date with Henry the Eighth tonight . . . '

Holly grinned. 'Dump him! This is a girls-only zone!'

'And you can borrow all my Tudor notes tomorrow,' Belle offered.

Cat didn't need any more convincing.

Belle snuggled up among the cushions on Cat's bed, took her first mouthful of Very Berry Swirl and sighed contently. Cat was settling in next to her, with Shreddie purring on her lap, and Holly was starting up the DVD on the laptop. This is perfect, Belle thought. In fact, maybe it was the perfect moment to share her big secret. 'I have this kinda . . . secret . . .' she started hesitantly.

Holly pressed the Pause button. 'Ooh, I love secrets!'

'Er, you know that new boy, Jack Thorne . . . ' Belle went on.

'Mm-mm,' Cat mumbled through a recklessly large mouthful of Rocky Road.

'What do you think of him?' Belle asked, trying to sound casual.

Holly giggled. 'Not as much as you do!'

'Is that it? Your deep, dark secret?' Cat laughed. 'That you fancy Jack? I thought you were going to tell us something we didn't know!'

'You mean you could tell?' Belle asked, watching in horror as Cat and Holly both nodded, grinning. She squirmed with embarrassment; she'd been so sure she'd kept all her emotions safely under wraps. What if everyone knew? 'Oh, no, is it that obvious?' she stammered.

'Only to us,' Holly said reassuringly. 'With our finely honed powers of observation. Oh, and I'm sure Bianca suspects—'

'And Nick Taggart, of course . . .' Cat added.

'Oh yes, Nick,' Belle said. 'I thought I'd really hurt his feelings in Mr Garcia's class today – but then he was acting his usual goofball self in the common room, so I think we're OK again.' She sighed. She'd been so relieved when Nick started poking fun at her about the armour; he obviously wasn't mad at her. Maybe it'd been worth making a fool of herself after all, if that's what it took to get their friendship back on track.

Cat smiled. 'Don't worry about Nick,' she said. 'He's got other things on his mind—'

'Like Lettie Atkins,' Holly interrupted.

'*Argggh!* Brain-freeze!' Cat yelled, clapping her hand to her forehead.

Of course! Belle thought. *Now it's starting to make sense.* When Nick insisted that he wanted to work with Lettie in the singing class, he wasn't just covering up his injured pride. He really *did* want to work with Lettie. He was probably annoyed because Bianca was teasing him and Belle, not because he was heartbroken that Belle might want to work with Jack!

'So, do you think I stand a chance with Jack?' Belle blurted out.

'Hmm . . .' Cat murmured, scrunching up her forehead as if pondering a fiendishly difficult question. 'Is he likely to be interested in the most elegant, tall, blonde and gorgeous girl in the year? She's clever, funny, loyal, generous . . . What do you think, Hols?'

Holly grinned. 'It's a no-brainer! But,' she added seriously, 'he's going to have to have the operation first . . .'

'*Operation?*' Belle winced. 'What operation?'

Holly laughed. 'The one to have Bianca surgically removed from his side!'

Belle giggled and swatted her with a cushion. 'Come on, start the film. My ice cream's melting!'

Soon they were transported to a sunny Greek island and singing along to Abba's *I Have a Dream* . . .

Yes! Belle thought, a wave of confidence washing over her. *The three of us all have our dreams and our songs to sing, and together we really* can *cope with anything . . .*

CHAPTER FIFTEEN

Cat: Honeysuckle and Avocado Heaven

Cat was still singing *I Have a Dream* as she ran herself a bath the next morning.

Everything was going to be fine, she told herself. The girls' night in had been just what she needed. Now she was up bright and early, for a relaxing bath and a spot of history homework before breakfast. In fact she was so early she'd managed to nab the nicest of the three bathrooms on their floor – the one with the extra-deep tub.

Cat poured in a generous glug of Honeysuckle and Avocado Heaven and watched it bubble—

'Cat! Are you in there?' Belle was knocking at the door. 'Yoga time – come on!'

Cat groaned, suddenly remembering she'd agreed to join Belle at her yoga class, in search of Inner Peace and Perfectly Toned Muscles. She gazed at her beautiful bath. She could say no, but Belle was so ultra-organized and she was easily offended if you messed up her plans – and she was trying to help . . .

'OK! Coming!' Cat sighed, tying her dressing gown and taking a last longing look at the steaming, foaming water.

The yoga class was in one of the dance studios off the courtyard. Cat rolled out her borrowed mat next to Belle's. She'd had no idea so many people were up this early in the morning . . . being peaceful! She followed the instructor's directions through the warm-up of stretches and sun salutations. *'And now . . . into the child's pose . . .'* he chanted. Cat copied Belle, kneeling on the mat, leaning forward, head down. *'And breathe . . . and relax . . .'*

OK, this isn't too bad, Cat thought. *Quite calming really.* But Inner Peace was getting a bit boring now. There was only so much *breathing* you could do. She started to run though her Lady Macbeth lines in her head – that difficult opening monologue: *'What thou wouldst highly, that wouldst thou holily . . .'* She really needed to talk to Duncan about that line . . . but she still had the Henry VIII essay to do . . . and Mrs Salmon had given them *another* heap of food-chain homework . . . at least her *Hamlet* review was only slightly late . . . but she'd not done any practice on her steps for the Latin dance class this afternoon . . . or looked over her French vocabulary . . .

'*And calm . . . and breathe deep . . .*' the instructor went on.

Calm? Cat thought. *I haven't got* time *to be calm . . .*

She was back on that treadmill and now it was going faster than ever!

Suddenly she had the feeling that she'd forgotten something. Was there some homework she'd not handed in? Something was tugging at the edges of her memory . . .

Then it hit her: *she'd left the bath running!*

Cat rocketed up off the mat. Head spinning, she stumbled towards the door, ignoring Belle's call of 'Cat! What's wrong?'

Everything's wrong! Cat screamed silently as she bombed out of the studio, across the courtyard and into the entrance hall. Water would be cascading down the stairs like a Honeysuckle and Avocado-scented Niagara Falls. She imagined the beautiful moulded ceiling of the dining room beneath the bathroom collapsing under the weight of water. Students having an early breakfast would be buried under falling plasterwork . . .

She rushed past the dining room. *No despairing cries from the rubble!* Raced up the staircase. *No torrential waterfall!* Sprinted along the corridor. *No white-water rapids!*

Only Miss Candlemas – standing outside the

bathroom door in her batik-print dressing gown, with a mop in her hand and a thunderous look on her face.

'Aha! I was wondering who'd flooded the bathroom!' she stormed. 'The guilty party returns to the scene of the crime . . .'

'I'm really sorry,' Cat panted in a fragile voice.

'Yes, well, luckily Gemma discovered it before it got too bad,' Miss Candlemas said, her anger abating. 'We don't need to start building an ark just yet . . .'

'Cat! Cat! What's happened?' Belle was running along the corridor towards her.

Cat squared her shoulders and tried to arrange her face into a chirpy smile. *Panic over!* she intended to say. *What am I like? Can you believe I left the bath running?*

But it didn't work.

Not even close!

What actually came out of her mouth was a sob. And then another.

Then she felt Belle put her arm around her and lead her gently back to their room.

CHAPTER SIXTEEN

Holly: Finding the Off-switch

Meanwhile Holly was *thinking about* getting out of bed. She was planning to meet Ethan at the sports centre for fifty lengths of the pool before breakfast. *Just five more minutes*, she told herself.

She'd vaguely heard Gemma getting up to go for a bath earlier and then coming back giggling about someone leaving the taps running and flooding the place . . .

Holly stretched luxuriously. Her new room was almost identical to the one she used to share with Bianca, except the colour scheme was soft mauve and lilac instead of yellow and orange and the atmosphere was completely different. Gemma was trying to get dressed quietly so she didn't disturb her. Bianca would have been stamping around, blasting her hairdryer and accusing Holly of stealing her make-up by now. *Poor Lettie*, Holly thought. She'd seemed delighted to share a room with Bianca — they'd been friends since they'd played with their My Little

Ponies in reception class together – but even so, you kind of lost the will to live after a few weeks of Bianca . . .

One more minute. Holly was looking forward to seeing Ethan at the pool. And to going with him to the big bonfire party in Kingsgrove Park on Saturday. She was gradually getting used to the idea that Ethan was her *boyfriend*. In fact, bizarrely, Bianca and Mayu had done her a favour there: ever since they'd spotted her and Ethan together at Café Roma and broadcast the news to the entire school, their relationship had become common knowledge; now they were so totally last week's story, no one was very interested any more – like Posh and Becks.

CRASH! WAIL! SLAM!

Holly's snooze was interrupted by a disturbance outside her room. It sounded like a herd of mutant wildebeest stampeding along the corridor. *Not that she knew what mutant wildebeest sounded like, but . . .*

Then she recognized Belle's voice: '*Cat! What's happened?*'

Alarmed, Holly vaulted out of bed, long-jumped across the corridor and skidded through the door into Cat and Belle's room.

Her friends were sitting on Cat's bed. Belle had her arm around Cat, who was crying.

'What's happened?' Holly asked anxiously, sinking down on the bed next to them.

'I think the bath tub running over was the last straw,' Belle said gently.

'That . . . and Lady Macbeth and Mr Sharpe . . .' Cat sobbed. 'And Henry the Eighth and Mrs Salmon and killer whales and Latin dance and Mum and *Oliver!* and *Hamlet* and . . .'

'I know,' Holly murmured, rubbing Cat's back. 'It's too much.'

'. . . I just can't find the *off-switch*!' Cat wailed.

Holly wasn't entirely sure what Cat was talking about but she got the general idea. 'Maybe you can't do it all. Perhaps there's something you can give up—'

'I can't give anything up! That would be like . . . like . . . *giving up*!'

'Well, you could talk to one of the teachers,' Belle suggested. 'Someone you trust, like Mr Grampian. Maybe they can help—'

'And let them think I can't take the pace? *No way!*' Cat protested.

'But everyone needs a little help sometimes—' Holly said.

'Like who?' Cat snapped. 'You two don't have any trouble. You never turn up late or get detention. Even Bianca manages to keep it together, for goodness' sake

– she does loads as well, *and* she has time left over for playing tricks on people and running after Jack. And what about Ethan?' she added, on a roll now. 'He's playing Banquo, he's captain of the football team, a champion swimmer *and* he has time to be the perfect boyfriend. He's probably writing a one-man stage show of the Bible and developing a cure for cancer in his spare time . . .'

If only Cat knew, Holly thought, *what Ethan told me when we were sharing our special pizza in Café Roma. How he'd almost lost the plot last year when he took too much on. How Mr Fortune had helped . . .*

And that's when she had another Great Idea. Maybe it wasn't in the same league as last night's Ice-Cream Initiative, but it could just work . . .

'*Stay!*' she commanded, holding up her hands and backing slowly towards the door, as if training a pair of puppies. 'I'll be back in a minute!'

She turned and ran in the direction of the sports centre.

CHAPTER SEVENTEEN

Cat: Time Management for Dummies

After Holly had gone, Cat lay back on her bed. Her problems hadn't gone away but she was too worn out to worry about them any more.

Belle was plying her with cups of herbal tea and trying to Google 'nervous breakdown' on her laptop when she thought Cat wasn't looking.

Cat closed her eyes and escaped into a daydream. She was the tragic heroine in a Victorian novel, suffering in a sanatorium with one of those illnesses they used to have – *consumption* or *nervous vapours* or something. She coughed delicately into a lace handkerchief – *she would never see her true love again . . .*

Her eyes fluttered open and she saw . . . Ethan Reed.

'Oh, er, Ethan . . .' she mumbled, struggling to sit up. 'Sorry, I was miles away.'

Holly was hovering at Ethan's elbow. 'Ethan's got something to tell you, Cat!' she said carefully.

Now that she was officially a crazed, raving

psycho-maniac, Cat noticed, everyone was tiptoeing around as if she might jump out of the window with her knickers on her head if they said the wrong thing.

But what could Ethan possibly have to tell her? *He'd proposed to Holly and they wanted her to be their bridesmaid?*

Cat was intrigued enough to drag herself out of her tragic-deathbed scenario and listen. 'I'm all ears,' she said.

'Thing is,' Ethan mumbled, clearing his throat, 'I had *exactly* the same problem as you last year.'

'You left the bath taps running and flooded the bathroom with Honeysuckle and Avocado Heaven?'

Cat knew that making a joke when people were being serious was a bad habit, but she couldn't help it. She'd gone past *miserable* now and was veering towards *borderline hysterical*.

'Not *that* part.' Ethan laughed and sat down on a beanbag. 'Taking too much on and getting overwhelmed. Er, nobody else knows this – apart from Felix obviously – but he found me one morning, running round the football pitch in my swimming trunks, reciting lines from *Othello*, "*Reputation, reputation, reputation! Oh, I have lost my reputation!*"

'What happened?' Cat asked, wide-eyed, picturing the scene.

'Well, first I punched Felix on the nose—'

'Wow!' Cat giggled. She could see why Holly thought Ethan was so great. Not because he punched Felix on the nose – she liked Felix – but he was funny and sympathetic and . . . she had to admit, this really *was* helping.

'What did you do next? I don't suppose you just lay around on your bed, dying?' she asked forlornly.

'I went to see Mr Fortune and told him the whole story – except the bit about punching Felix, of course. He was really helpful, and let me drop some classes – and after that, everything was much better.'

'So,' Holly piped up, 'we thought maybe *you* could do the same.'

'Yeah, thanks, Holly!' Cat laughed. 'Maybe I can.'

Holly and Belle smiled at each other.

'Thanks, Ethan,' Cat said. Knowing that even someone as cool and popular as Ethan had buckled under the pressure made her feel a whole lot better. 'And Holly . . .' she went on.

'Yeah?'

'You didn't actually run all the way to the sports centre in your pyjamas, did you?'

Holly looked down. 'Oh yeah, I suppose I did.'

'You want to watch that, girl!' Cat said with a grin. 'People will think you're going crazy!'

Rather nervously, Cat spoke to Mrs Butterworth, who made an appointment for her to see Mr Fortune about a 'personal matter'. So, at lunch time, she found herself knocking on the heavy oak door of the principal's office. She couldn't help remembering the last time she'd been here – with Holly and Belle – all frantic with worry that Nobody's Angels would be disqualified from the talent competition. Mr Fortune had made everything come out right that time. She prayed he could work his Principal Magic again.

'Ah, Catrin!' Mr Fortune crinkled his forget-me-not blue eyes and rubbed his neat-but-rugged white stubble as she entered the book-lined room. 'You don't mind if Leslie – er, Mr Grampian joins our little chat, do you?'

Cat didn't mind at all. Mr Grampian, with his long white ponytail, hawk-like nose and shabby corduroy suit, was her favourite teacher and had always stuck up for her in the past.

'Now, what seems to be the problem?' Mr Fortune asked, placing his hands on the desk and lacing his fingers.

Cat explained the too-much-stuff-too-little-time issue as calmly as she could. 'I don't want to give anything up,' she concluded, '*but I just can't go on like this* . . .' The actress in her couldn't help cringing at how melodramatic that sounded, like something out of an *EastEnders* Christmas Special, but the two men were nodding understandingly.

'And what do you consider your top priority at the Garrick?' Mr Fortune asked.

'Acting,' Cat replied instantly. 'I want to be a classical actress. That's why *Macbeth* is so important to me.'

'I'm deeply gratified to hear you say that, Catrin,' Mr Grampian stated, smiling kindly. 'In all my years' teaching the dramatic arts, you are indubitably one of the most talented young actresses I have encountered . . .'

Cat stared at Mr Grampian, hardly able to believe her ears. She could barely resist the urge to jump across the desk and hug him. *Most talented young actress (one of)!*

'Well, now, let's see what we can do to lighten your workload . . .' Mr Fortune said, examining a copy of Cat's timetable. 'I think we could drop the advanced Latin dance, and one core singing lesson a week – just until *Macbeth* is done and dusted.'

OK, so it wasn't the complete cancellation of all science and maths lessons for the rest of eternity that

Cat had been secretly hoping for, but you couldn't have everything. 'Thank you!' she said happily.

Cat skipped out of the office. Now she understood what people meant when they said a weight had been lifted off their shoulders. She realized that she'd been walking around like the Hunchback of Notre Dame for the last few days. Now she was strutting along like a model on a catwalk.

Back at her room, she found Nathan with Belle and Holly. They all hugged her, and smiled with relief when she told them what she'd arranged with Mr Fortune.

'Er, I brought you this from the library,' Nathan said. 'Thought it might be useful.'

Cat glanced at the book he was handing her: *Time Management for Dummies*. 'Who are you calling a dummy?' she said, batting him with it.

'And we've tidied your things for you,' Belle said.

Cat noticed that her side of the room looked like an illustration from a 1950s *Guide to Good Housekeeping*. 'Thanks,' she said.

'Oh, and we had a word with Miss Candlemas,' Holly told her. 'She's OK about the bath thing . . .'

'Thanks,' she said.

At which point the housemistress put her head

round the door. 'Let me know if you're getting down in the dumps again, dear. Don't let things get on top of you . . .'

'Thanks,' she said, yet again.

Cat had never said so many thank-yous to so many people in one day! She was full of energy and on top of the world again. And she now had a couple of free hours to work on her Lady Macbeth lines and catch up on her homework instead of going to the Latin dance class. The play was only a few weeks away and there was still a lot of work ahead, but she had everything back under control again.

As long as I don't go to any more yoga classes, she thought.

CHAPTER EIGHTEEN

Holly: Stokissimo

The following Thursday afternoon Holly was in her favourite class – advanced ballet with Miss Morgan. Holly could see Cat's point: Miss Morgan could be really fierce at times – shrunken by old age, wearing a black leotard with her sparse white hair under a black band, she hopped around like a hyperactive magpie. And when she banged her stick on the floor, everyone jumped to attention.

But today Miss Morgan was in an unusually good mood. She complimented Holly, Gemma and Lettie on their demi-pointe exercises at the barre. '*Bellissima!*' she shouted, clapping her hands. 'Now we are ready to commence *pointe* work!'

Holly was so excited she could hardly breathe. She remembered her first lesson at Miss Toft's dance school when she was four years old, watching the older girls dancing *en pointe* – and dreaming that one day it would be her turn. Now that day was finally here! She slid her feet into the new pale-pink *pointe* shoes and crisscrossed the smooth satin ribbons round her ankles. How she loved those shoes!

The girls waddled awkwardly over to the barre, their shoes all thwacking on the wooden floor.

'*Pointe* work is not just about toes,' Miss Morgan began. 'Not just about feet. *Every* muscle must work. Every cell of the body. Pull up from the core. The abdomen. *Lo stomaco!*'

Holly pulled up. All that early morning swimming had paid off: her core muscles were super-strong.

'Feet in parallel. Rise up – slowly!' Miss Morgan instructed, marching along the line of girls.

Holly pushed up and felt her toes cram against the blocks. She resisted the temptation to wiggle them back, absorbed the pain, tensed her muscles and held the position. Miss Morgan looked her up and down, nodded slowly and then, with her stick, gently pushed her shoulders forward. Holly felt as if she were about to topple forward flat on the floor, but she stood firm. '*Bellissima*, Holly!' Miss Morgan shouted. 'And down! And up!'

Holly glowed with pleasure. She was actually *en pointe* at last – and it was *bellissima*!

When Miss Morgan finally told them to relax, Holly was exhausted. She glanced at the clock and couldn't believe they'd only been working for ten minutes –

rising onto full *pointe* in parallel, then turned out in first position, and finally *relevés*. Some of the girls had struggled to complete the exercises, but Holly had done so well she was even able to let go of the barre for short, exhilarating moments.

Her toes felt as if they'd been stamped on by an elephant; her calf muscles were in agony – but she had never felt happier. She'd taken another huge step towards her dream of being a true dancer!

The girls were sitting on the benches, removing their shoes and comparing notes on the state of their toes, when Miss Morgan announced that she had a big surprise for them. She opened the door to admit Mr Korsakoff and his class of male dancers, in their white T-shirts and black leggings. They had been working in the next-door studio.

'Next term,' Miss Morgan announced, 'the Dance Department will be staging a small but *magnifico* ballet recital – *Nutcracker Sweeties*.'

Holly turned and exchanged excited grins with Gemma and Lettie – and Zak, who was now sprawling on the bench next to them. She couldn't wait! Mum had taken her to see *Nutcracker Sweeties* – a jazzy, razzmatazz version of *The Nutcracker Suite* – for her birthday several years ago, and it was amazing! But it was Zak who spoke for all of them: '*Whoa!*' he shouted. '*Miss Morgan, dude! Stoked to the max!*'

Oops, Holly thought. *You don't call Miss Morgan 'dude'.*

But to her surprise, Miss Morgan laughed. 'Stoked indeed, young man. *Stokissimo!*' she replied, cackling at her own joke; the first joke Holly had ever heard her make.

The boys guffawed, but the girls all stared open-mouthed in amazement.

'Don't know what you girls are talking about,' Zak whispered. 'Fierce? Miss M's a total *pussycat!*'

'Try telling that to my toes,' Gemma groaned. 'They're killing me!'

After a quick change, Holly rushed off for band practice. She found Belle and Cat already setting up with Mason and Ben. 'I got the keys from Mrs Butterworth,' Belle explained. 'We're not wasting time waiting for Felix to show up!'

Cat laughed. 'Belle's been reading my copy of *Time Management for Dummies.*'

'Sounds like Belle probably *wrote* it!' Ben quipped.

Belle looked worried for a moment, then grinned when she realized he was only teasing.

Holly smiled as she adjusted the microphone. It was great to see Cat back to her old self, laughing her infectious, bubbly laugh. Her meeting with Mr Fortune last week had been a real turning point. She was full of life again.

'Ah, here comes Felix,' Ben said as they heard the *tap, tap, tap* of his crutches in the corridor.

Mason struck up a drum roll. 'At last,' he cried, with a crash of the bell cymbal as Felix appeared. 'The man we've all been waiting . . . and waiting . . . for!'

'OK,' he said. 'Sorry I'm late. Let's work through the list Carly gave me. We have to start with this really slow, schmaltzy song where the bride and groom get up and lead the dance – do you know *Eternal Flame* by The Bangles?'

'Of course,' Belle replied. 'I love that song!'

'I was hoping you'd say that' – Felix grinned at her – 'because we'd like you to sing lead vocals. There's no way I'd get those high notes . . .' And he launched into a warble, missing the notes by several light-years to prove the point.

'Sure, OK!' Belle replied, grimacing and putting her hands over her ears.

She said it as if it were no big deal, but Holly could tell from the sparkle in her lavender eyes that she was deliriously happy to be asked.

Stokissimo, in fact!

★

Two days later, Holly woke up early. She peeped out of the window. A cruel wind was stripping away the last few leaves clinging to the branches of the plane trees in Kingsgrove Square. The sky was saucepan-lid grey. It would be the perfect Saturday morning to climb back under the duvet, but she'd promised she'd watch Ethan lead the Garrick All-Stars out onto the football pitch in a crucial Cup match against their arch-rivals, the Westminster Wolves.

As she pulled on her thermal vest and a pair of dance tights under her jeans, Holly had yet another Great Idea. Jack Thorne was playing in the match – she had told Ethan about Pirate Boy being a *top scorer* and Ethan had given him a trial: he'd been so impressed he'd selected Jack for the team straight away. If Belle came along to watch the match, it would be a chance for her to meet Jack without Bianca buzzing around like a wasp at a picnic. Holly knew that Bianca liked to have a lie-in on Saturday mornings.

Holly knocked on Belle's door. Belle was awake, of course: she'd already been out for her morning run. She loved Holly's idea, and pulled on a thick cream cashmere poncho.

'Have fun!' Cat mumbled from under her duvet.

Holly and Belle stood with the other home spectators and Felix hobbled over to join them. They all cheered as Ethan led the Garrick All-Stars out in their red and white strip and the referee blew his whistle. The Westminster team were big and strong – several of their players looked like stand-ins for the Incredible Hulk – but the Garrick team were faster and more creative.

It was bitterly cold and Holly's feet were feeling frozen by the time they entered the last few minutes, with the score at one–nil to Westminster. When Ethan headed a long ball in past the keeper to equalize, the crowd roared. Holly thought her heart would burst with pride. But a moment later, the Garrick supporters were cheering again as Jack took the ball and sprinted the length of the pitch, weaving his way round three defenders. *Wow!* Holly thought. *Pirate Boy should be a dancer. That was like Billy Elliot meets Gene Kelly in* Singin' in the Rain. He lined up for the shot – and scored, just seconds before the referee blew the full-time whistle.

Jack punched the air and back-flipped into a celebration dance with the rest of the team. Then he and Ethan ran over to where Holly, Belle and Felix were standing for a round of high-fives. 'Respect!'

Felix grimaced. 'Looks like I might be out of a job!'

Ethan laughed. 'Hey, don't worry, we'll keep your place on the team!'

Still caught up in the victory, Jack scooped Belle up by the elbows and swung her round in a triumphant whirl. 'Thanks for coming to watch. Hey, I love this cape-thingy,' he said as he returned her to her feet. 'It's toasty-warm! I'm freezing. It's not like playing in Singapore – there's less risk of frostbite there for one thing!'

'It's a poncho,' Belle told him, blushing furiously.

'It must be our *lucky* cape-thingy!' Ethan said. 'We've never beaten Westminster before!'

'Come on. Let's go to the common room for hot chocolate,' Felix suggested. 'Can't have players keeling over with hypothermia!'

Holly sipped her hot chocolate and chatted with Belle, drowsy and contented in the warmth of the common room, as the boys regaled each other with blow-by-blow accounts of the match, each re-telling more heroic than the last. Eventually the group started to break up as everyone wandered off to get on with the rest of their day.

'See you at the bonfire party tonight!' Ethan called to Holly as he left.

'See you there, Belle?' Jack asked as he followed him towards the door.

'Sure!' Belle smiled, her face glowing with pure, undiluted rapture.

Which was certainly *not* the expression on *Bianca's* face as she entered the common room at that precise moment. She glanced from Jack to Belle and back to Jack again. *Yep, that look could definitely give you frostbite!* Holly thought.

'Ooh, bless,' Bianca sneered. 'The footballers and their WAGs. How *sweet*!' Her smile was as brittle and dangerous as a crack in the ice on a frozen lake.

'Since the wives and girlfriends are usually glamorous models or pop stars,' Jack said, winking at the girls, 'I'd take that as a compliment!'

'Oh, we will,' Holly said, although she was quite sure it hadn't been intended as one, 'won't we, Belle?'

But Belle just smiled a dreamy over-the-hills-and-far-away smile.

CHAPTER NINETEEN

Belle: The Washing-powder Plot

After lunch Belle went back to her room with Holly and Cat to help Cat practise her Lady Macbeth lines.

'*But screw your courage to the sticking place,*' Cat was reciting, '*And we'll not fail . . .*'

But, unusually for her, Belle was having trouble concentrating. Her head hadn't stopped spinning since Jack whirled her round at the soccer match. She could still feel the gentle grip of his hands on her arms.

And now there was the bonfire party!

She could still hear him saying, *See you there, Belle?*

See you there! That was *almost* a date!

Belle had dated before, of course. Whenever she stayed with her mother, Mom would magically produce an eligible boy. She had friends in every city in the world – at least, the fashionable ones – and many of these friends had sons, perfect for accompanying Belle to a film premiere in Cannes or the opening of a new restaurant in Milan. Some of the boys had been nice and she'd dated a few, but none of them had x-ray eyes like Jack Thorne.

'So what exactly is Bonfire Night?' Belle asked, as soon as Cat paused to scribble some notes on her script. 'We don't have it in America.'

'Well, there's a bonfire . . .' Holly said.

'I could probably have guessed that part,' Belle said, grinning.

'And fireworks . . .'

'Sounds great. What's it all about though?' Belle asked.

'The Gunpowder Plot!' Holly told her. 'It's meant to be on the fifth of November really, but the celebrations take place on any weekend around November. This guy called Guy Fawkes tried to blow up the Houses of Parliament in sixteen hundred and something . . .'

'Maybe it's just me, but that doesn't sound like much of a cause for celebration,' Belle pointed out.

'It's, er, complicated . . . They caught him, anyway . . .' Holly mumbled vaguely as she flopped down on a beanbag and opened a carton of orange juice.

'O-kay,' Belle said. She still wasn't much clearer, but a party was a party, and Jack had said, *See you there!* and that was all that mattered! 'So, let's get down to the important stuff. What's the dress code?'

'Well, you're standing outside in the cold, so it's

pretty much wellies and woollies' – Holly laughed – 'and a hat!'

'Wellies and woollies?' Belle asked. Were they speaking the same language here?

'You know, gumboots and baggy sweaters,' Cat mumbled, looking up from her notes, a pencil in her mouth.

'Sounds like a fashion nightmare!' Belle said. *How am I going to look cute, alluring and sophisticated in gumboots?* she wondered.

'What about that poncho you wore for the football match?' Holly suggested.

'Oh, yeah, my Armani cashmere,' Belle said, taking the cream poncho from its hanger.

Cat nodded. 'That would be perfect!'

'And you know how much Jack liked it,' Holly added. '*Toasty-warm* I think were his exact words.'

'*Toasty-warm!*' Cat snorted. 'What was going *on* at that football match? I thought you went to cheer the players on, not cuddle them!'

Belle laughed. 'I don't usually wear the same outfit twice in one day,' she mused, holding the poncho up in front of her. Now that Jack had admired it, it was her favourite garment in the entire universe. 'But I think I'll make an exception this time.'

'And it *is* your lucky cape-thingy. You *have* to wear

it – you want to be lucky in lu-u-u-rve, don't you?' Holly teased, raising her orange juice in a toast.

Belle watched in horror as Holly's elbow – which had been resting on the coffee table – slipped. The carton jerked sideways, spraying luminous orange liquid all over the front of the beautiful cream poncho.

'Oh, no, I'm so sorry!' Holly cried. 'Quick, let's run down to the laundry room and I'll wash it for you!' She grabbed the poncho and hared off down the corridor.

Belle jogged after her. She hoped Holly knew what she was doing. Did orange juice stain? She had no idea, but as she ran, she crossed her fingers and muttered fervently, *Please, please let it come out.* Now that she had set her heart on wearing that lucky poncho, nothing else would be quite the same.

By the time she caught up with Holly in the laundry room – a cavernous basement below the kitchens, which always smelled of hot irons and washing powder – Holly was in conversation with Miss Candlemas.

'Miss Candlemas says we can put it in the washing machine on the cold/delicates cycle,' Holly told Belle.

'When it's finished, stretch it out flat to dry and it'll be right as rain!' Miss Candlemas beamed at them, before reaching inside an industrial-sized tumble-dryer with a screwdriver. 'Boys! More trouble than they're worth!' she grumbled, her voice echoing from inside the drum.

Belle exchanged a confused shrug with Holly. 'What's the matter with boys?' she asked.

'Always leaving coins in their pockets!' the housemistress said, holding up a pound coin. 'I'm forever fishing them out. Never had this problem when I worked in a girls' school!'

Belle was singing as she skipped down the steps to the laundry room half an hour later: '*Greensleeves was all my joy . . .*' She'd just read in her history book that Henry VIII was thought to have composed *Greensleeves* for Anne Boleyn, and now she couldn't get the tune out of her head . . .

She pulled open the door of the washing machine and felt around inside for her poncho. '*Greensleeves was my delight . . . Greensleeves wa—*' Was this the wrong machine? She was sure it was this one, but she couldn't feel her poncho in there – only some little wadded thing stuck to the side. Was it an old abandoned sock or . . .

. . . or a tiny, miniature poncho?

It was stiff and matted – and the perfect size for a three-year-old.

Belle checked the dial on the machine. It was no longer pointing to COLD/DELICATES.

Someone had turned it to BOIL WASH.

Belle groaned as she turned the shrivelled garment over in her hands. Well, the orange stains had certainly gone – but so had any chance of her wearing her lucky poncho tonight, or ever again!

She knew it was childish to be upset over something so silly, but she felt tears sting her eyes as she climbed slowly back up the laundry-room steps.

By the time Belle met up with Holly and Cat in the common room a few hours later she'd totally recovered from the disappointment of the Shrunken Poncho. She'd borrowed the accompaniment to *Eternal Flame* on CD from the music library and had spent the rest of the afternoon practising her big song for the wedding gig. She was really pleased with how it was sounding. And when her singing was going well it always made her happy.

'And, anyway, I've picked out a gorgeous black rollneck sweater to wear instead,' she told Cat and Holly as they walked back upstairs after an early supper to get ready for the bonfire party.

'Well, I'm still baffled as to how a washing machine can switch *itself* to boil wash!' Cat commented.

'Don't!' Holly groaned. 'I feel terrible. I bet that poncho cost a fortune as well – it was Armani!'

'Don't worry,' Belle said. 'Someone gave it to my mom as a gift but she already had one the same. That's how I get half my wardrobe.'

Bianca, Mayu and Lettie were chatting on the landing at the top of the stairs.

Bianca turned to Belle, Holly and Cat with a big smile. 'So what are you guys all wearing to the party?' she asked casually.

Belle was surprised – to say the least – that Bianca was making polite conversation. In fact, she couldn't have been more astonished if she'd surfed down the banister singing *I'm a Little Teapot*!

Perhaps she's feeling guilty about the suit-of-armour trick, Belle thought. 'Well, I was planning to wear my cream poncho,' she replied as they all walked along the corridor towards their rooms, 'but it had, er, a bit of an accident.'

'Yeah, *I* was that accident!' Holly said, rolling her eyes at her own clumsiness. 'And it *would* have to be orange juice!'

Cat laughed. 'It looked as if someone had graffiti-tagged Belle's boob-zone!'

'Well, perhaps you could still squeeze into it if you went on a crash diet,' Bianca suggested.

'How did you know it shrank, Bianca?' Cat asked,

stopping so abruptly that Holly bumped into her. 'No one said anything about shrinking.'

'Oh, I just assumed . . .' Bianca blustered.

'You know – cashmere, it's *so* prone to shrinking,' Mayu piped up.

'Nobody mentioned *cashmere* either,' Belle added, no longer in any doubt as to the identity of the Phantom Poncho-boilers. One look at Cat and Holly told her they'd figured it out too.

Bianca treated them all to an extra-frosty glare before darting into her room, followed by a bemused-looking Lettie.

'How dare they!' Cat fumed.

'It doesn't matter!' It was almost time for the party and not even Bianca and Mayu and their Washing-powder Plot could spoil Belle's excitement.

CHAPTER TWENTY

Holly: Sparklers and Treacle Toffee

Pulling on her boots ready for the party, Holly was still feeling terrible about the Poncho Affair.

Why did she always have to be so clumsy?

And why did Bianca always have to be so mean?

Two of life's great unsolved mysteries! she thought as she wrapped her long pink and grey stripy scarf around her neck.

Suddenly she had a brainwave. She ran to Belle's room and asked her to give her the shrunken poncho. Then she hurried to Serena's room for help. Luckily Serena hadn't left for the party yet – she was still doing her make-up and chatting with Gemma. She immediately grasped the idea Holly spilled out to her and quickly cut out a Barbie-sized poncho from the matted fabric. Then she hemmed it with tiny blanket stitches to stop it fraying, and Holly secured a safety pin to the back.

'Look, we made you a brooch!' Holly cried breathlessly as she sprinted back into the room. She reached up and pinned it to Belle's jumper. 'Now you *can* wear your lucky cape-thingy, after all!'

'Thanks, Holly – it's awesome!' Belle cried, giving her a big hug.

'Wow! That's so cool!' Cat laughed. 'Could you shrink some of *my* clothes and make jewellery out of them for me too?'

Holly felt much better. Now she could go to the bonfire party with a clear conscience.

Holly linked arms with Cat and Belle and joined a group escorted by Mr Garcia to walk the short distance across the square to the bonfire party in Kingsgrove Park.

Belle looked fabulous in her designer jeans and black jumper with her hair in two long thick plaits like a blonde Pocahontas. Cat looked great too, of course, in her leather jacket over a short red wool dress, worn with thick black tights and biker boots, and her auburn hair spilling out from under her black wool cap. It was a cold night and Holly was glad of her fluffy grey cable-knit jumper.

Almost all the students from Superstar High were there, as well as several of the staff, who'd come along to make sure they were all safe – but the park was also open to the public, and was crowded with dads carrying small children on their shoulders and mums pushing toddlers in buggies. Holly closed her eyes and inhaled the magical Bonfire-Night smell: smoke, hot dogs, baked potatoes, toffee apples . . .

She spotted their friends and they hurried over to join Nathan, Gemma, Serena, Nick, Lettie, Zak, Frankie and Mason, their faces all glowing orange in the blaze of the fire.

A few moments later, Ethan arrived, with Ben Stein, pushing Felix in a wheelchair. Ethan was grinning. 'We borrowed it from the St John Ambulance people. They took pity on a poor invalid!'

The large group of friends chatted, stamping their feet and blowing on their hands to keep warm. 'Whose idea was it to have a fireworks party in November?' Gemma asked. 'In Australia we wouldn't pick the coldest time of year for a cookout!'

'Nor in Mexico,' Nathan agreed. 'Carnival in the cold? *No gracias!*'

Holly grinned. She couldn't see Nathan Super-shy Almeida as a fiesta-animal, whatever the weather!

'Suggestion for you, mate!' Nick yelled at the Guy on the bonfire. 'Next time you want to blow up Parliament, try August!'

Holly laughed, and took the hot dog that Ethan offered her. She glanced at Belle, who was anxiously scanning the crowds for Jack.

'There he is now,' Cat whispered. 'With his shadow as usual.'

Jack was hurrying towards them; Bianca minced along behind him, her high heels sinking into the mud, followed by Mayu. Belle smiled and looked down at her feet.

'Hey, Belle!' Jack called, working his way through the group to stand next to her. 'How's it going?'

Bianca elbowed in next to Jack and thrust a lit sparkler into his hand. 'I'll write your name and you write mine,' she simpered, starting to emblazon *Jack* on the night sky.

'That reminds me . . .' He passed his sparkler straight to Belle, then reached into his coat pocket and pulled out several packs. 'The sparklers are on me!' he said, handing them round. Everyone cheered and jostled to light them from the tip of Belle's sparkler. Soon the darkness was etched with a mass of glowing white spirals.

'Lettie and I are going to get some drinks,' Nick announced as the last of the sparklers fizzled out. 'Anyone want anything?'

Jack turned to Belle. 'Let's go and give them a hand.'

Holly watched Belle's face – which was already glowing from the cold and the bonfire flames – light up even more as she set off with Jack towards the drinks tent, leaving Bianca scowling at her cold, dead sparkler.

Mason, Frankie and Zak had started goofing around, sword-fighting with candyfloss sticks. Ben was pushing Felix – who was now sporting a PENNY FOR THE GUY sign – in the wheelchair, spinning it like a BMX stunt-bike. A few minutes later, Jack and Belle pushed their way back through the crowd with a tray of hot chocolates. They were talking nonstop.

The lucky poncho must be working! Holly thought happily. 'The fireworks are about to start,' she said, handing round a bag of home-made treacle toffees her mum had sent specially for Bonfire Night.

'Mmggh!' said Cat, and Nathan and Gemma and Nick and Lettie, all nodding as their molars fused together.

'Mmggh!' said Belle and Jack, grinning at each other.

'Mmggh!' said Ethan, smiling at Holly with his sea-green eyes.

'No, thank you,' said Bianca grumpily. 'Some of us don't want to wreck our teeth!' Then she turned to Mayu. 'Come on, let's get out of here – fireworks are so-o-o boring!'

Holly felt Ethan take her hand. She squeezed back, then slipped her hand inside his glove and felt the warmth of his palm against her own. The booms and bangs of the fireworks reverberated from the walls of the stately London buildings all around the park. Colours exploded in the night sky and flickered across the faces of her friends, all staring upwards, captivated by the display.

Her heart swelled in celebration.

Life at Superstar High couldn't be better.

CHAPTER TWENTY-ONE

Belle: Nothing to Declare

The following Monday afternoon Belle was coming to the end of her piano practice. She always booked the five-o'clock slot on Mondays and Wednesdays in the corner practice room, which housed her favourite piano – a lovely old Steinway.

She started to play Chopin's *Nocturne in E-flat major*, and was so absorbed in the romantic melody that it was several minutes before she registered that someone was watching her. Lettie Atkins – who usually booked the six-o'clock slot for her cello practice – must have arrived early.

But when Belle turned round, she was astonished to find not Lettie but Jack standing in the doorway.

Her stomach leaped.

'Beautiful,' Jack murmured, strolling into the room, hands in pockets.

'Oh . . . er . . . thanks . . .' Belle mumbled, flustered by the compliment.

'You play beautifully,' he added.

Of course, he meant the music! Belle realized. This was real life – not some soppy love-story film; he was hardly going to just march in and tell her she was beautiful! 'I love Chopin.' She smiled. 'Do you play?'

'Badly!' he said, grinning. He reached across and picked out the first few notes of *Greensleeves.* 'Er, hope you don't mind me barging in . . .'

'No, of course not!'

'I was, er . . . well, hoping to catch you . . .'

Belle looked up into those clear hazel eyes, trying to hold his gaze. She was getting that x-ray feeling again. She suddenly remembered what it reminded her of: walking through the Nothing to Declare channel at the airport. When the customs officers looked at you, you couldn't help *feeling* guilty even though you *knew* you weren't – as if just maybe you *had* accidentally slipped a few endangered reptiles into your suitcase at the last minute . . .

Except that now all she was trying to smuggle through was a racing heart and a bungee-jumping stomach.

It had been so much easier at the bonfire party, with all the hustle and bustle of the crowds; they'd chatted and laughed like old friends all evening. But now she felt awkward again.

'Have you ever been to the Tower of London?' Jack asked.

Belle shook her head, confused by this turn in the conversation. 'Er, no, why?'

'Me neither. I was thinking of going to have a look round on Saturday.'

'Great idea! I bet it's so-o-o interesting,' Belle said, forgetting her emotional-smuggling worries in her enthusiasm. 'It's where the Tudor kings and queens kept their prisoners locked up. Where Henry the Eighth had two of his wives beheaded.'

Jack grinned. 'Yeah, I could tell you were really into the Tudors in history class. And you were reading that book in the library.'

'It's amazing,' Belle agreed. 'Did you know that Lady Jane Grey was executed in the Tower when she was only sixteen? She was Queen for nine days.'

'So that's why I wondered if you, er, well, might like to come with me . . .'

There was a silence. Belle gazed at him in disbelief. Now it was Jack's turn to look away, unnerved by her stare. Did he really just ask her to go with him to the Tower of London?

'You mean, like, on a *date* . . . ?' Belle said slowly, gripping the sides of the piano stool. She felt dumb asking, but she needed to be sure she wasn't imagining things.

'Yeah! Kind of a *weird* date, I know,' Jack said, 'but I

heard they have a small ice rink in the grounds, so we could maybe go skating when we've had enough torture and execution.'

'That sounds perfect!' Belle was so happy she could hardly stop herself from bursting into song. She started gathering her music, trying to keep the big smile on her face under control.

Suddenly she heard a knock at the open door. 'Oh, hi, Lettie,' she gabbled, stuffing the music into her bag. 'I'm just on my way out. See you Saturday!' she called over her shoulder to Jack.

Belle floated on her own personal pink fluffy marshmallow-cloud all the way back to her room. Jack had asked her to go on a date. Even better, Jack had asked her to go on *the perfect date*. The Tower of London! Somewhere she'd been longing to visit. And then ice-skating. How did he *know* she loved skating?

Maybe Jack really could read her mind.

'Guess what!' she screamed, throwing open the door of her room, where Holly was helping Cat practise her *Macbeth* lines.

'Er, Justin Timberlake's asked you to sing on his next album?' Cat wondered.

'The English National Opera want you to sing Madame Butterfly?' Holly suggested.

Belle was far too impatient for any more guessing. 'Jack asked me on a date!'

'*Woo-hoo!*' Holly and Cat screamed as they leaped up and hugged her.

'The Tower of London!' Cat giggled, when Belle had filled them in on the details. 'He certainly knows how to show a girl a good time!'

'Now, I wonder what I'll wear . . .' Belle mused, opening her wardrobe and contemplating the neatly hanging garments.

Cat grinned. 'Tricky! What *does* one wear to make a stylish transition from Tudor prison to ice rink?'

'Well, whatever you pick, don't let me within a mile of it,' Holly joked. 'I'll only tip something all over it!'

One thing is certain, Belle thought happily. *I'll definitely be wearing my lucky poncho brooch!*

CHAPTER TWENTY-TWO

Belle: Shepherds' Warning

Two days later Belle was humming *Eternal Flame* – the mega-romantic opening song for the Walthamstow wedding gig – as she strolled across the courtyard to her afternoon piano practice. The wedding was only ten days away now, and Nobody's Angels and The Undertow had all been putting in as much rehearsal time as they could. Belle was looking forward to her next big chance to sing in public, and to spending the night at Holly's house – and, of course, now she had her date with Jack on Saturday to look forward to as well. All in all, Belle was in a blissful Snow-White-singing-with-baby-birds-in-a-sunny-wood-land-glade kind of mood as she floated down the corridor.

She immediately noticed that the door of the corner practice room was standing open. *Strange!* she thought. It was usually locked when she got there.

Then Belle recognized the arm of the person standing in the doorway – or rather the sleeve the arm was wearing. It was Jack – in his favourite blue and black striped T-shirt. She felt a ripple of excitement. Maybe he'd found out that she practised at this time and come to see her again. She ducked into a corner and quickly smoothed down her hair and applied a touch of lip gloss.

Suddenly she heard voices: Jack was talking to someone in the room.

'We'll have a few moments to talk in private here . . .' he was saying gently.

Who could it be? Belle tiptoed along the corridor and stopped outside the practice-room door, which was now firmly closed. She felt a little sneaky but it wasn't *really* spying, was it? There was a glass pane in the top of the door, after all. It wasn't the place to pick if you wanted privacy. Anyone who happened to be passing could just look in.

Which she did.

And immediately wished she hadn't.

Jack was in there with another girl!

And whatever they were doing, it wasn't talking!

And it wasn't piano practice either.

He was holding her tight, stroking her blonde hair. She had her head buried in his shoulder.

Belle gasped. She couldn't bear to watch but she couldn't look away either.

The girl glanced up mid-nuzzle and caught her eye.

Belle turned and ran. Piano practice was cancelled for today – maybe for ever.

The girl was Bianca Hayford.

Belle tore across the courtyard, past the Redgrave Theatre, and only when she reached the dark sports field did she slow to a miserable trudge.

Why was Jack doing this? she puzzled. He'd asked her on a date – yet now he was *snogging* Bianca! *OK, I didn't actually see them kissing, but it was pretty obvious what they were up to*, she fumed, her despair gradually turning to rage. Just when she'd started to think that that rebellious look in his eyes was charming and gorgeous, he'd proved himself to be a *total creep*.

This must be what the shepherds were trying to warn me about with the red sky the other day, she thought. *Not killer sheep but a two-timing boy! A wolf in sheep's clothing!* But she'd been too dumb to pay attention.

Jack was worse than Henry VIII. No wonder he wanted to go to the Tower of London. All that cheating and torturing and beheading would be right up his street. Well, there was no way she was going to go out with him now, she vowed, now on her third lap of the football pitch. She never even wanted to *see* him again

– not even for long enough to *tell* him she didn't want to see him again.

In fact, she would leave him a note!

Belle had been too distraught to notice the fine drizzle before, but now, as she headed straight for Mrs Butterworth's desk, she felt damp and shivery. She borrowed a pen and notepad, and scribbled a short note:

> *Dear Jack,*
> *Thank you for the offer of the Tower of London on Saturday. On second thoughts, I think it would be better if I don't come with you.*
> *Belle*

She folded the note and placed it in Jack's pigeon hole, then wandered in a daze to the common room, where Holly and Cat were sitting with Gemma and Nathan, toasting marshmallows on the open fire.

'Belle, where've you been?' Holly gasped, making room for her to sit down. 'You're soaking!'

'You look as if you've seen a ghost,' Cat added. 'What happened to your piano practice?'

Belle didn't trust herself to say anything without bursting into tears, so she smiled weakly and stared into the flames.

Just then, Jack entered the common room and came towards them. 'Hi, Belle!' He smiled at her. 'No piano practice today?'

Belle ignored him. *Talk about rubbing it in!* Well, if he thought she was going to speak to him, he was very much mistaken . . .

'I don't think Belle's feeling very well,' Holly explained. 'She got caught in the rain.'

'You'd better change out of those wet things,' Jack said in a concerned voice. 'You'll get a chill . . .'

Like you'd care! Belle thought. How could he act as if nothing had happened? He obviously thought she didn't know about his secret love-tryst with Bianca in the practice room. And he probably hadn't checked his pigeon hole yet so he hadn't seen her note.

Belle risked a quick glance at Jack's face through her curtain of dripping hair. He was looking at her with a confused, hurt expression. *Well, tough!* What did he expect if he was going to get all smoochy with Bianca?

'Yes, I *am* starting to feel sick,' Belle said through clenched teeth. 'I'm going to bed.' She mustered her last shreds of dignity and stalked out of the room with her head held high.

She would never, ever trust Jack Thorne again.

CHAPTER TWENTY-THREE

Holly: Tumble-dryers and Broken Hearts

What on earth had happened to Belle? Holly wondered as she and Cat ran after their friend. She wasn't the kind of girl to even leave her room without perfectly straightened hair and a co-ordinated designer outfit. But she'd lurched into the common room with mascara running down her face and mud spattered over her boots.

Belle threw herself down on her bed and, with the help of a cup of camomile tea and a hot-water bottle, eventually sobbed out the story of Jack's Treachery.

'The stinking slimebeast!' Cat shouted. 'How dare he? And with Bianca of all people! The boy's insane, as well as a two-timing sleazebag!'

'Maybe things weren't how they looked?' Holly suggested, unable to believe that Jack could be so out-and-out monstrous as to cheat on Belle only two days after asking her on a date. 'Perhaps there's some other explanation?'

Belle snorted into her tea. 'I know what I saw!'

'Hols, just because *you're* going out with one of

the few decent boys on the planet, don't try and make excuses for that *scumball*!' Cat stormed. 'Some other explanation? Let's see . . . Oh yes, maybe Bianca asked him to check her wisdom teeth for her – *with his tongue?*'

'*Aaarghh!*' Belle wailed.

Holly knew better than to try to defend Jack further. The case against him did look pretty conclusive, she had to admit. But she couldn't help wondering. Bianca would do *anything* to get what she wanted. And she would do *anything* to get one up on Belle. Conning Jack into kissing her, just when she knew Belle would be there to witness the event, would tick *both* those boxes.

But how could you possibly *trick* a boy into kissing you?

Then again, Bianca wasn't playing Hecate, Goddess of Witchcraft, for nothing!

The next morning, as Holly swam up and down the pool with Ethan, she was still pondering the Belle, Jack and Bianca situation. But she didn't come up with any answers.

Jack seemed like such a *genuine* guy, in spite of his Pirate Boy looks. Surely he couldn't have been *faking* how much he liked Belle – Holly had seen the way he looked at her – at the football match and at the bonfire party.

The last lesson of the morning was history. As Holly sat down between Cat and Belle near the back of the class, Jack turned round in his seat and glanced uncertainly at Belle. She ignored him. She was wearing a glazed, rigid look, but as they unpacked their books, she returned Holly's smile bravely.

As usual, Miss Chase-Smythe was talking like the Queen or an old-fashioned newsreader. 'In the Tudor period,' she began, switching on the projector, 'traitors would be imprisoned, tortured and even executed, here in the Tarv-Londen . . .'

The Tarv-Londen? Where was that? Holly wondered, squinting at the slide on the screen. It looked just like – oh, yes, it *was* . . . the Tower of London.

Uh-oh! she thought, instantly turning to check Belle's reaction. Her smile had faded. Now a silent tear was rolling down her cheek.

Perhaps Miss Candlemas was right, and boys really were more trouble than they were worth. Holly gave Belle's hand a little squeeze under the desk.

It wasn't just tumble-dryers they broke. It was hearts too.

CHAPTER TWENTY-FOUR

Cat: Mini-Molls and Giant Peaches

The following Tuesday morning Cat was snoozing away her last few seconds, visualizing exactly how she would take the dagger from Macbeth's hands at the end of the murder scene—

DRRIIINNNNGGGG! DRRIIINNNNGGG!

Cat high-jumped off her bed.

She hated Belle's alarm clock more than she had ever hated anything in her life – and that *included* pickled gherkins!

They'd devised a system whereby Belle set the alarm to go off again ten minutes after she went out for her yoga class or run at 6 a.m. The clever part was that she positioned it by the door, so that Cat had to get out of bed to turn it off.

Painful as it was, the system worked. Cat was getting so organized, she'd soon be graduating from *Time Management for Dummies* to *Time Management for Experts*. And Mrs Salmon hadn't found anything to yell at her about for ages!

DRRIIINNNNGGGG!

Va-a-a-lerieee!

Cat dropped the alarm clock and grabbed her mobile phone. Her heart was hammering. No one called at this time unless it was an emergency!

'Hello,' she gasped.

DRIINNNGG!

'Oh good, you're up, dear,' Mum said.

'What's wrong? Has something happened to Fiona?' Cat panted, imagining her little sister in hospital – or worse.

'Nothing's wrong. Whatever is that noise?'

'Alarm clock,' Cat said, turning it off.

'I've got some *wonderful* news for you!' Mum gushed.

Cat sighed, slumping down on the edge of the bed. If it wasn't a 999-situation, she dreaded to think why Mum was calling her with a dawn alert.

'You remember Seth Martinez?' Mum asked. 'No? Well, he's an old friend from my *Star Wars* days, and he's a casting agent now, and he's just given me the tip-off that they're casting for a new production of *Bugsy Malone* . . .'

Cat stared out of the window at the rain. She had a horrible feeling she knew where this was going.

'. . . and wait till you hear this!' Mum crowed.

'They're auditioning for Tallulah – by invitation only! Your clever mother has only managed to *wangle you an invitation* – and it's this afternoon!'

'Mum, I've got a *Macbeth* rehearsal at five. It's a full run-through. If I'm late this time, I'll be thrown out!'

'Oh, *Macbeth, Schmacbeth!*' Mum breezed. 'I'll have you back in plenty of time. This is big-time, Cat, a career-maker. You could be the next Tallulah!'

Cat wanted to be many things, but *the next Tallulah* – a gangster's moll in a kids' musical about black-market custard pies – was definitely *not* one of them.

But there was no arguing with Mum; she was like quicksand – the more you struggled, the faster you sank.

After lunch Cat called at Mrs Butterworth's desk to sign out for the afternoon. 'Oh yes' – Mrs B smiled, scooting out from her office – 'your mum phoned to let us know. Good luck, dear – break a leg!'

'Auditioning for West End shows, Catrin?' Mr Fortune remarked as he passed on his way to his office. 'I'm not entirely sure that's a good idea with all your other commitments.'

'You try telling my mum that,' Cat muttered grimly.

'Ah, yes, your mother – a force to be reckoned with!' he said with a trace of a grin. He'd only met Mum once, when Cat came for interview, but she'd clearly made an impression.

Cat heard the horn starting to blare outside. 'You could say that,' she replied, smiling weakly.

Cat timed the journey. With Mum's rally-driver technique of 'nipping' into bus lanes and jumping amber lights along Piccadilly, it took exactly half an hour through the lashing rain. 'Promise me we'll leave by quarter past four at the latest,' Cat pleaded, 'so I won't be late for the rehearsal.'

'Yes, yes, dear,' Mum replied vaguely as she did a high-speed U-turn across three lanes of traffic and parked on a double yellow line. 'Now, I've got a lovely costume for you in the back of the car.'

Cat followed her mother into the theatre. They found Seth Martinez in the brightly lit foyer, swigging from a bucket-sized cappuccino and barking orders to a fleet of assistants. A mountain of a man, wearing a suntan the shade of a ginger biscuit and a white linen suit, he air-kissed a spot two feet above Mum's head. 'Terri, Terri, Terri, great to see ya,' he drawled. 'This *Bugsy*'s gonna fly, baby. We're going to Broadway with this!'

Cat thought he was kind of smarmy, but he *was* Mum's friend so she smiled politely. Mum looked as if she would implode with excitement.

Cat made her way across the foyer, which was swarming with girls dressed up as 1920s nightclub singers, and signed in with one of the assistants at a makeshift desk, trying not to panic about the long list of names ahead of her own, before taking Mum's costume bag and setting off for the ladies to get changed.

She pulled the apricot chiffon dress out of the bag. Mum was right. It *was* lovely.

Lovely for someone six foot tall with the figure of a drainpipe.

Who didn't have red hair.

Cat stuffed the dress back in the bag. Mum had been playing the audition song on the way in the car. Cat actually quite liked it. She would stand up and sing it, just to keep Mum happy, but there was *no way* she was going to look like a giant peach while she was doing it.

She trailed back out into the foyer, which was still full of mini-molls sending texts, drinking bottled water and flicking their feather boas.

'I'm not wearing that dress. End of story,' Cat stated as she sat down.

Mum wrinkled her nose at Cat's short black dress

and leather jacket. 'We'll see about that. Oh, and Seth says it's going to be at least an hour before they can see you.'

Cat groaned. She looked at her watch. It was now 2.45. If she was seen in one hour, and it took fifteen minutes to belt through *My Name Is Tallulah* and answer a few questions, they'd be out of there by four o'clock. That should be OK. *Just!* She pulled out her *Macbeth* script and tried to focus.

An hour passed. Cat checked her watch for the millionth time. They were still in the foyer and only a few names had been called. There had been a flurry of excitement when one of the Tallulahs fainted on stage and was stretchered out. As a result, the casting panel were now behind schedule, the assistant explained, and there was very little chance that Cat would be seen before 4.15.

Cat felt as if she were standing on the edge of a cliff, with the ground starting to crumble away beneath her feet. *She was going to be dashed to pieces on the rocks far below!* If she was late for the *Macbeth* rehearsal, Mr Sharpe would definitely throw her off the production. Mayu would gleefully take over her role and Cat would lose her chance to play Lady Macbeth in her first ever Garrick Shakespeare production – and to wow all the important theatrical agents and reviewers in the audience with her acting skills.

Macbeth was the first step towards her most-talented-young-actress big dream and she couldn't let it slip away.

I need a backup plan, and I need it fast! she thought.

She took out her mobile phone and started writing a text message.

CHAPTER TWENTY-FIVE

Holly: Improvise!

Meanwhile, Holly was in a core jazz dance class, working on sequences of turns, kicks and jumps inspired by dance numbers from the musical *Chicago*.

'. . . *and take a break!*' Miss LeClair shouted, halfway through the lesson. Holly sank down onto the bench, then leaped up as something buzzed underneath her like a giant bumblebee. She was sitting on her sweatshirt, and her mobile phone was in the pocket. Students weren't allowed to use phones in class, but Holly couldn't resist a quick peek to see who was texting her.

URGENT — POSS NT BACK 4 MACB. NEED U GO 2 REDGRAVE @ 5 & B ME 4 FEW MINS, CAT X

Holly was worried. This sounded like trouble.

'Excuse me, Miss LeClair,' she called, hopping . . . '

She ran into the nearest bathroom and dialled Cat's number. 'What's up?'

'I'm stuck here,' Cat groaned. 'If I'm not back by five, can you go and sign in for me and shut yourself in my dressing room. Just make a lot of noise so it sounds like I'm getting ready. Lady Macbeth isn't on stage until near the end of Act One – I'll be back by then—'

'But what if you're *not* back?' Holly asked. 'There's no way I'm going on stage or anything!'

'I *will* be, I promise. *Please, Hols.* If Mr Sharpe suspects I'm even a second late, my days as Lady Macbeth will be over.'

Holly really didn't want to see that happen to her friend. 'Well . . . OK then,' she agreed reluctantly.

The class ended at four thirty. Holly couldn't tell Belle about Cat's message in the changing room in case she was overheard, but as soon as they emerged into the courtyard, she pulled Belle into a corner behind a large shrub and hurriedly explained the dilemma. As she was doing so, another text appeared on her phone: *Still here! Do it plse!*

'Sign in for her?' Belle gasped. 'It's a bit risky. If Mr Sharpe finds out, Cat'll be in even *more* trouble than if she just showed up late.'

Holly nodded. Belle had a point. 'Perhaps Cat could just phone Mr Sharpe and explain the problem . . .' she suggested.

But Belle shook her head. 'No! I saw Mr Sharpe's

reaction last time she was late. Explaining won't do her any good!'

'So we'll just have to go through with this sign-in-and-pretend-to-be-Cat scheme then,' Holly said, trying her best to sound upbeat. 'I'm sure she'll be back in a few minutes anyway.'

'I guess so,' Belle agreed. 'We can't let her be thrown out of the play.'

Holly smiled at her. She knew how much Belle hated breaking the rules, but neither of them wanted to let Cat down. '*All for one!*' she proclaimed, in her best *Three Musketeers* voice.

'*And one for all!*' Belle rallied, with a swashbuckling flourish as they stepped out from behind the bush, nearly crashing into Nick and Lettie, who were hurrying past on their way to the Redgrave.

'Whoa! You two been at the blue Smarties again?' Nick joked.

Holly smiled weakly. *I have a bad feeling about this*, she thought.

At the theatre, Belle signed in on the line marked BELLE MADISON: CASTLE MESSENGER while Holly scrawled something vaguely like Cat's signature next to CATRIN WICKHAM: LADY M. Then they ducked into Cat's dressing room – luckily, playing the female lead, Cat had her own private room. Holly slammed the door and leaned back against it.

'Now what?' Belle asked.

'You go and change into your Messenger costume,' Holly whispered. 'I'll stay here and clatter about a bit until you get back.'

Belle slipped out of the door. 'See you later, *Cat*!' she yelled over her shoulder.

Holly tried Cat's mobile number to see how much longer she would be, but it went straight to voicemail. 'Help!' she squeaked to it before hanging up. She rattled coat hangers along the rail for a few minutes, then pressed her ear to the door, just as Belle opened it and slipped in.

'They're starting in a few minutes,' she whispered, wide-eyed with panic. 'Duncan wants everyone who's in Act One to go to the wings. Have you heard from Cat yet?'

Holly grimaced. 'No!'

Belle opened the door a crack and peeped out. Holly held her breath as she heard Mayu's little-girl voice. 'Is something wrong with Cat?' she simpered. 'Duncan's looking for her. If there's a problem, I don't mind standing in—'

'Nope, no problem at all,' Belle replied breezily. 'She's just having a few issues with her costume. *How are you getting on in there, Cat?'* she shouted as she slammed the door shut. 'It's starting to get messy out there,' she whispered urgently, turning back to Holly. 'What are we going to do?'

'We could set off the fire alarm,' Holly suggested.

Belle shook her head. 'Won't work! As soon as we get to the assembly point they'd count us and find Cat missing.'

'Oh, no,' Holly groaned, clutching her head in her hands. '*Think!'*

'What about flooding the toilets?' Belle said.

'It'd take too long—'

'I've got it!' Belle exclaimed, jumping up and down on the spot. 'I'll ask Nick to help – he could pretend there's a problem with the sound system. It could buy us some time . . .'

'Genius!' Holly grinned. 'I'll keep trying Cat's mobile.'

'*See you in the wings in a moment, Cat!'* Belle yelled as she ran out of the dressing room.

'*All cast for Act One on stage immediately,'* the tannoy blared.

A few moments later, the air was torn apart by a deafening electronic screech. '*Arggh!'* Holly yelped, clapping her hands over her ears. By the sound of it, Nick had agreed to Belle's plan.

A few moments later, Belle reappeared, grinning.

'OK, Nick's on board. Now we just have to wait for Ca— *Arggh!*' She screamed as the sound system produced another high-pitched squeal, followed by a series of booms, a clap of thunder and a swirl of bagpipes.

Still Cat didn't arrive or answer her phone.

The chaotic noises finally stopped. Holly and Belle looked at each other bleakly. They were running out of ideas. And time.

Then there was a knock at the door. Holly's heart leaped into her mouth.

'*Cat, Belle, hurry up!*' Nathan shouted. 'Mr Sharpe's given up on the sound system and he's going to start Act One now!' He sounded desperate. He obviously had no idea what was going on, but there was no time to explain.

'We'll be there in a minute!' Belle called.

Holly and Belle both jumped as Holly's phone rang. 'Cat, where are you?' she hissed, switching to speaker-phone so that Belle could hear. 'Please tell us you're back!'

'I'm next in line to audition . . .'

'This is crazy!' Belle groaned. 'We can't stall any longer!'

'You'll have to go on stage and pretend to be me,' Cat said.

'No-o-o,' Holly whimpered. 'I can't!'

'Belle can't do it – she's a Messenger and we're in the same scene together. You're my only chance, Hols—'

'Cat, have you completely lost your mind?' Belle snapped. 'Do you think people won't notice? Holly's got a completely different accent, she's about a foot shorter, she's black and you're white . . .'

'. . . and I can't even act . . .' Holly added sorrow-fully.

'Improvise! You could wrap my big cloak round you, wear high heels, pretend you've got a cold. And you've helped me practise so much, you know all the lines!'

'I know all the words to *Thriller* – it doesn't mean I'm Michael Jackson!' Holly snorted.

'Look, I've got to go,' Cat said. 'You'll be *brilliant*, Hols.'

Holly stared at the phone in dismay. Cat had hung up.

Belle laughed. 'That's the *craziest* plan I've ever heard!'

'Yeah, I know!' Holly sighed, rolling her eyes. 'It's totally gaga! But,' she added slowly, 'I haven't got a better one . . .'

'Me neither,' Belle agreed.

'How did we let Cat talk us into this?' Holly asked. Belle shrugged her shoulders. *'All for one!'*

'And all for a one-way ticket to Mr Fortune's office if we're not careful!' Holly said. 'Come on, we'd better get started on my disguise if we're going to have *any* chance of pulling this off . . .'

CHAPTER TWENTY-SIX

Cat: Jodie Foster's Attitude

Cat felt like a despicable slug as she hung up the phone. She knew she'd bulldozed Holly into something she really didn't want to do. But she was fighting for her theatrical life here. *There was no other option.*

The assistant called the next name. The Tallulah-wannabe next to Cat exchanged excited fingers-crossed gestures with her mother, and teetered through the door in her sequinned dress and silver heels, swinging her hips and working her feather boa for all she was worth.

Cat was now at the front of the queue, standing at the theatre door. 'Nearly there,' Mum whispered. 'Puff your hair up, dear. And put my shoes on,' she said, bending to take off her stilettos. 'You've got to have heels!'

'I don't want heels, Mum.'

'Of course you do. And stop sulking! You're *Tallulah*, a nightclub singer, remember. Now, when you get in there, *flirt* with the casting panel, *enchant* them . . .'

Something about the concept of *flirting* with Seth Martinez was the final straw. Suddenly Cat had an out-of-body experience. She was looking down at herself, waiting around for hours for the chance to *enchant* a casting director into giving her a *ludicrous* role that she didn't even *want*, while her chance of playing one of the very finest Shakespearean characters was hanging by a thread.

What had she been thinking? No one was going to be fooled by Holly-in-a-cloak for a second!

She would lose her part in the play. And worst of all, her hare-brained plan was going to land Holly and Belle in a whole swamp of trouble too.

There *was* another option!

'*I'm not doing this!*' Cat shouted, flinging Mum's shoes onto the floor. '*It's all wrong!*'

'Cat, please, calm down,' her mum said soothingly.

'I don't want to play flipping stupid, flirting Tallulah—'

'But Tallulah's a lovely part—'

'Well, if you think it's so great, *you* go in and audition. *I'm out of here!*' Cat stormed.

'You could be the next Jodie Foster!'

'I don't want to be Jodie Foster. I want to be . . . *Catrin Wickham!*'

'*And right now "Catrin Wickham" is going to stay here and stop making an exhibition of herself!*' Mum bellowed, drawing herself up to her full four-foot-three and stamping her foot.

'No, Catrin Wickham is going back to the Garrick. Which is where she belongs – playing a *real* part in a *proper* play!'

'Well, I bet Jodie Foster never gave *her* mother this kind of attitude!' Mum wailed, looking to the other mothers in the foyer for support. There was an embarrassed silence.

'Goodbye,' Cat said firmly, marching towards the exit.

'*We'll see Catrin Wickham now, please . . .*' called the assistant.

Oh, no you won't! Cat thought as she ran into the street and hailed a taxi.

As the taxi pulled away, she noticed that Mum's car had been clamped. She felt sorry about that, but at least it meant her mum wouldn't be able to give chase through the streets of London.

'To the Garrick School of the Performing Arts, please,' Cat panted. '*It's an emergency!*'

CHAPTER TWENTY-SEVEN

Holly: Some Kind of Medieval Bag Lady

In the Redgrave Holly was preparing for the biggest acting challenge of her life. Playing Lady Macbeth would be bad enough, but playing Catrin Wickham playing Lady Macbeth was in super-advanced *don't-try-this-at-home* territory.

And Holly was the first to admit that classical acting was not her strong point. She could dance, of course. And she could sing. She could even dance and sing at the same time. In fact, she would make a perfect Tallulah!

If only I could swap places with Cat right now! she thought.

'Arms up,' Belle ordered. 'Quickly!'

Belle had taken charge of Operation Fake Lady Macbeth and had somehow managed to convince herself they could actually make it work. Holly wasn't so sure, but she did as she was told and slid into the long red dress. It was several sizes too large and pooled around her feet.

'We need to cover every inch of your skin,' Belle

muttered as she rummaged among the costumes on the rail. 'A long tunic . . . and gloves. Put these on.'

Obediently Holly piled on the layers.

'And you need to be taller,' Belle said, running back from her dressing room with the strappy sandals she'd removed when she put on her Messenger-costume boots. 'Wear these – they've got high heels.'

Holly's hands were trembling so much she could hardly buckle the straps. The sandals were far too big and she had to do them up extra tight to keep them on.

'And this . . . ' Belle handed her a thick black cloak, complete with hood.

Holly pulled the hood up around her face. She was so nervous she thought she might be sick. 'Remind me of my lines again?'

'First you read that long letter from Macbeth that starts, *They met me in the day of success . . . blah blah*,' Belle said, 'and then I come in and give you the message that King Duncan's on his way. Here, you need more *up front* to look like Cat. Use these!'

'No, not my Lady Macbeth lines, my *cover story*!' Holly took the wadded tissues Belle was offering and stuffed them into her sports bra for an instant boob-boost. 'About why I'm dressed like' – she looked at herself in the mirror – 'some kind of medieval bag lady . . .'

'You've had an allergic reaction to a new skin-cream. The school nurse told you to keep your skin covered at all times,' Belle recited.

Holly groaned. This was the best story they could come up with at such short notice.

'Repeat it back to me in Cat's voice,' Belle commanded.

'I've had an allergic skin reaction . . .' Holly said. Her Irish accent was beyond bad. It was awful.

Belle cringed. 'OK, and remember, it's affected your sinuses as well. You can't talk properly.'

'*Lady M to the stage this instant!*' the tannoy announcer said, sounding extremely bad-tempered.

'OK, this is it,' Belle stated. '*No turning back!*'

Holly swallowed. *She was petrified!* 'I can't even walk in these shoes,' she muttered as she tottered to the door. 'It's worse than being *en pointe* . . . Belle – are you *laughing at me?*'

'Sorry!' Belle snorted. 'I know this isn't funny, but you look . . .'

'Idiotic? Clinically insane? I *had* noticed!' Holly growled, opening the door – and bumping into Jack, who was hurrying along the passageway, dressed in his Messenger costume.

'Ooops, sorry,' he said. 'Er, who is that under there anyway?'

'It's Cat,' Holly said, pulling the hood down over her face.

'Hey, Cat!' Jack laughed. 'Why all the extra clothes?'

'I've had an allergic skin reaction . . .' Holly mumbled in an accent somewhere between Darth Vader and an Irish leprechaun.

'Come on, *Cat*!' Belle snapped, taking Holly by the arm. 'You're needed on stage. We haven't got time to stand around nattering to random people!'

Even through her panic and her black hood, Holly couldn't help noticing Jack's hurt look as Belle referred to him as a *random person*.

Standing in the wings, Holly felt like a prisoner in the Tower of London about to be led out to the chopping block. Scene Four was ending and the stage hands were preparing to roll on the castle interior scenery for Scene Five, which opened with a twenty-nine-line monologue by Lady Macbeth.

Holly's internal organs were turning to jelly – not the nice kind but the horrible transparent kind that you find inside a pork pie – as she stepped out onto the stage.

She caught sight of Mr Sharpe in the front row, his glasses glinting menacingly. *He's going to go* ballistic *when he finds out*, she thought.

'And cue Lady M,' said Duncan Gillespie, tapping her on the shoulder.

This is it! Holly could just about make out a scroll lying on a table centre stage and teetered towards it, keeping the cloak pulled tightly around her. *That must be the letter I'm meant to read.* She could hardly see anything from under the hood, but she could hear people grumbling suspiciously all around the theatre. *Here goes nothing!* She picked up the scroll, took a deep breath and opened her mouth to speak. But her tongue felt as if it had been coated in sand.

There was a silence.

'*They met me in the day of success . . .*' the prompter read out.

'They—' Holly rasped.

THUD! CRASH! ARGGGHHH!

Some kind of commotion was coming from the wings.

'*Oh my God, Jack's dead!*' Bianca screamed.

'He's not dead! Looks like he's passed out,' Duncan Gillespie replied calmly.

Holly stood there, fixed to the spot, as Mr Sharpe vaulted onto stage and ran through to the wings, yelling, '*Call the nurse!*' Then she crept offstage and tried to peep through the mass of people crouched around Jack, who had now been placed in the recovery position.

'Where am I?' he murmured. 'The lights . . . the heat . . . dizzy . . . spinning . . . '

By the time the school nurse, Miss Patel, ran in a few moments later, he was sitting up, sipping from a glass of water. She shooed Duncan Gillespie and Mr Sharpe away. 'Give the boy some space. It's far too hot under these stage lights! I'm surprised you've not had more students passing out.'

'I'm so sorry,' Jack groaned. 'I'll be fine in a moment. The show must go on . . . '

Mr Sharpe clapped his hands. 'OK, people, we'll take a thirty-minute break to cool down!'

Holly couldn't believe her luck! Surely Cat – the real Lady Macbeth – would be back in half an hour.

'*Cursed! We're cursed!*'

Holly spun round to see Duncan standing behind her, holding his head in his hands.

'Someone must have said the *M-word* in the theatre today. That's why we've had all these problems – first the sound system and now people collapsing.'

'That's just a ridiculous superstition!' Mr Sharpe said. 'It doesn't matter how many times we say *Macb*—'

'*No-o-o, don't say it!*' Duncan wailed. 'I've got to walk three times round the theatre to undo the curse,' he called as he ran towards the door.

Holly blushed. *It was me*, she realized. *I said the*

M-word in the dressing room. She felt terrible. It was *her* fault that Jack had fainted. And even worse, she thought guiltily, she'd been busy congratulating herself on her brilliant luck when the poor boy could be *really ill*. She looked around and found Belle huddled at the back of the wings, her face pale and anxious. 'It was me. *I* said the M-word,' Belle mumbled miserably. 'Jack Thorne is a two-timing creep, but I don't want anything *bad* to happen to him . . .'

Holly smiled weakly. 'Snap!' she said.

'You boys! Take Jack out for some fresh air,' Miss Patel shouted.

Holly shrank back into the shadows with Belle as Jack staggered towards the stage door, supported by Nick and Nathan. As he passed, he turned and looked at Holly, and – to her utter amazement – he winked.

A slow, deliberate wink.

That's when Holly realized: *The curse of the M-word didn't have anything to do with it!* Jack had seen right through the cloak *and* the allergic reaction. He'd known she wasn't Cat all along, and he'd faked the 'faint' to cause a delay.

Jack Stinking-slimebeast Thorne had just saved the day!

CHAPTER TWENTY-EIGHT

Cat: Emotionally Unstable Psycho-chicks

Cat thrust some money at the taxi driver and raced through the school, her heart pumping as if it would burst. She *had* to get to the Redgrave Theatre – even though she *dreaded* what she would find when she got there. There was *no way* Holly could have got through the opening speech without someone noticing that she was . . . well, that she was Holly.

Cat was expecting to find Mr Sharpe and Duncan Gillespie waiting to frogmarch her to Mr Fortune's office.

She was expecting to find Belle and Holly vowing never to speak to her again.

She wouldn't even have been surprised to find a police SWAT team waiting to haul her off to prison in handcuffs.

The one thing Cat *wasn't* expecting as she peeped in through the stage door was . . . *nothing.* Where was the wailing and the yelling and the gnashing of teeth?

Where was Mayu, dancing a victory jig in her Lady Macbeth costume?

All was quiet!

Luke Morgan, alias Macbeth, emerged from his dressing room, sipping from a can of Coke. 'You been out for some fresh air?' he called to Cat as he spotted her coming through the door. 'Good idea – you look a bit hot.'

Fresh air? Cat wondered. *In the middle of a rehearsal?* She tiptoed along the corridor – past the Three Witches buying packets of Monster Munch from the vending machine – and pushed open the door of her dressing room.

'*Caaaaaat!*' Holly screamed, leaping up to hug her – although it was a hug that bordered on grievous bodily harm, as she gripped Cat's shoulders and shook her.

'What took you so long?' Belle gasped, pulling Cat further into the room. 'It's been a nightmare here . . .'

'I'm so sorry . . . I couldn't get away . . .' Cat stammered. 'But what's happening?'

'The rehearsal got postponed by half an hour' – Holly laughed – 'thanks to Jack Thorne and his Fabulous Fainting Fit—'

'Holly thinks Jack fainted deliberately to help us,' Belle interrupted, 'but I don't believe it!'

'Belle thinks it was just *coincidence* that he passed out

186

at the precise second I was about to start the speech and make a total twit of myself . . .'

Cat felt as if she might faint herself. The raw panic that had propelled her back to the Redgrave began to seep away. Relief was kicking in. She sank down into a chair. She had no idea what Belle and Holly were talking about, but somehow *she'd got away with it* – even if she *had* lost another of her nine lives.

Then she looked at Holly, still wearing the black cloak with the hood pulled up, and couldn't help laughing.

'I think it's time for Lady M to get an *extreme make-over!*' Belle giggled, and they both helped Holly out of her motley collection of ill-fitting garments. Cat put on the red dress, black velvet cloak and ruby necklace.

'So, how did you get on as Tallulah?' Holly asked, looking like her usual self again in jeans and T-shirt.

Cat squinted into the mirror and applied her Lady Macbeth black eyeliner. 'Er, I didn't. I had an attack of artistic temperament and stormed out.' She laughed, but was suddenly sideswiped by a major guilt-trip. Although Mum would be furious, Cat knew she'd be worried about her too. She pulled out her phone and sent a quick text to say she'd arrived safely back at school – but couldn't *quite* bring herself to add an apology. She *wasn't* sorry she'd left; she knew that saving her part in *Macbeth* was the right thing to do.

'I'm going to find Jack and thank him,' Holly was saying. 'I *know* he helped us on purpose – even if Belle thinks I'm imagining it!'

'I'll come with you,' Cat said, finishing her make-up. There were a few minutes to spare before the rehearsal re-started and she was dying to get to the bottom of this weird fainting story.

'I think I'll hang on here,' Belle said. 'I can't face Jack right now – even if he did help us out for some reason.'

Cat and Holly found him sitting in the large dressing room he shared with the other boys playing minor parts in the play. Unfortunately Bianca was there too, mopping his brow with a cold flannel, a pious Florence Nightingale expression on her face.

Cat was about to leave, but Holly suddenly piped up, 'Oh, Bianca, Mr Sharpe's looking for you. He wants a word with all the Witches about their timing or something.'

Wow, that was impressive, Cat thought. *Holly* can *act when she wants to!*

Bianca sighed. 'I suppose I'd better go. They'll only

mess it up if I'm not there!' She blew a kiss to Jack and flounced out.

'Thank you,' Holly said to Jack after Bianca had gone, 'for the fainting thing.'

'No problem!' Jack said with a grin. 'I guessed something had happened to Cat. No offence, Holly, but you didn't look or sound *anything* like her. Or like Lady M for that matter . . . So where were you, Cat?'

'Er, long story.' Cat laughed. 'I'll tell you when we've got a couple of hours to spare!' She was trying her best to dislike Jack on Belle's behalf, but he was, she realized, very, very charming. And those dangerous hazel eyes were gorgeous. What a shame he was such a sneaking cheat-monster! It just went to show that you could never tell with boys . . . 'Anyway, thanks again. You're the *man of the moment*, Jack!' she added.

'I wish Belle thought so,' Jack sighed. 'I just don't get it. One minute we were going on a date, the next she can't even bear to look at me.'

Cat couldn't believe the *nerve* of the boy. What did he expect? '*Hel-lo – Earth calling!*' she snorted. 'Do you think it might just be something to do with the *luurvve-thing* you've got going with Bianca? Most girls find two-timing a bit of a turn-off, you know!'

'The *what*-thing?' Jack spluttered. 'I don't have *any* kind of thing going with Bianca!'

'Oh, so Belle just *imagined* that cosy little snog-scene, did she?' Cat fumed.

'What *snog-scene*?' Jack demanded, looking utterly baffled.

'You know, in the practice room?' Holly prompted. 'Last Wednesday?'

Jack frowned in thought and then clapped his hand to his forehead. 'Oh, *that*!' he exclaimed, eyes widening as the truth dawned.

'Hah! Now it all comes back to him!' Cat scoffed. *What a weasel this boy is!*

'It wasn't a *snog-scene*!' Jack protested indignantly. 'Bianca asked me to meet her there. Her little dog, Foo-Foo, had just died and she was in bits about it. I was just letting her cry on my shoulder, that's all. She's been really helpful – showing me the ropes and stuff since I got here . . .'

Cat gulped. She turned to see Holly's reaction to this revelation and almost laughed out loud. Holly was as wide-eyed as a baby owl, her mouth agape in a perfect O of astonishment. She caught Cat's eye and they both grinned at each other. Jack was obviously telling the truth. Maybe he wasn't such a slimebeast after all!

'What did—?' Jack started to ask, but he was interrupted by Nathan rushing into the dressing room.

'Oh, there you are, Cat!' he cried. 'There's a rumour flying around that you've got some hideous skin disease. Mayu thinks it's her lucky day!'

'Sorry to disappoint Mayu, but it's all better now.' Cat grinned. 'It was just one of those stress-related things, you know.'

'Stress-related? You can say that again!' Holly muttered.

'Come on, guys,' Nathan said anxiously. 'Rehearsal's starting again. Mr Sharpe's going to hit the roof if anything else goes wrong.'

Cat hurried off to the wings, where Belle was already waiting. She was *bursting* to tell her the great news, but it would have to wait. There were too many people around. And anyway, right now she was Lady Macbeth again – and she had a murder to organize.

Later that evening the three friends gathered in Cat and Belle's room. Cat's ear was feeling bruised from a ten-minute phone-lecture from her mum about her *disappointing behaviour* – which had apparently been *ungrateful, rude, disrespectful, stubborn, hot-headed and childish* . . . Cat had tried to explain, but Mum wouldn't let her get a word in.

It had been a long, complicated sort of day, and now they were flopped on the beds and beanbags like a collection of rag dolls. 'So, what's this *big news* you two have been hinting at all through supper?' Belle asked.

'Well . . . when we spoke to Jack at the rehearsal—' Holly began.

'Turns out he *wasn't* kissing Bianca when you saw them together in the practice room!' Cat butted in, too impatient for Holly's feature-length version. 'He was just *comforting* her because her dog had died.'

'What? Are you sure?' Belle gasped.

'One million per cent,' Holly confirmed.

'*He wasn't . . . she didn't . . . how could . . . ?*' Belle was so surprised her words jolted out in fragments.

Holly and Cat nodded.

For a moment Belle's face was illuminated by a huge smile of relief, but then she groaned and threw herself back on her bed.

'What's wrong?' Cat asked. 'Get yourself over to his room right now and tell him he *can* take you to the Tower of London after all!'

'I can't,' Belle mumbled from under the cushion she was holding over her face. 'I feel like such a *dope!*'

'It's obvious when you think about it. I bet Bianca set the whole thing up so Belle would see them and get the wrong idea,' Holly said. 'I've never even heard her *mention* a dog before!'

'And what kind of a name is Foo-Foo, anyway?' Cat snorted.

'I've really blown it, haven't I?' Belle sniffed. 'Jack won't want to know me now that I've freaked out over *nothing*. He'll think I'm some kind of emotionally unstable psycho-chick!'

'Hey, he's friends with Bianca,' Cat joked. 'I think he *likes* emotionally unstable psycho-chicks!'

Belle whimpered and pulled the duvet over her head. 'I need to sleep on this,' she sighed.

Cat suddenly felt extraordinarily tired herself. She was lying on her bed and it was very, very comfortable. 'Thanks again for saving me today, both of you. I owe you,' she said drowsily.

Holly grinned. 'Yeah, you do. Big time!'

But Cat hardly heard her.

She was drifting off to sleep . . .

CHAPTER TWENTY-NINE

Belle: The Show Must Go On

The following Saturday was the day of the Walthamstow wedding gig.

The girls all decided to wear black for the performance: Cat selected her 1960s mini-dress, Holly a halter top and shorts over footless tights, and Belle, her little black velvet dress from last year's Chanel collection. First thing on Saturday morning, Cat had the idea of adding piles of fake-diamond jewellery for extra glamour, and they rushed off to Oxford Street for a shopping spree in Claire's Accessories. It wasn't exactly Cartier, but Belle couldn't believe that you could buy sparkly things so cheaply – and they looked *almost* like the real thing. Then they piled into Belle and Cat's room, turned the *James Bond* theme tune CD up to jet-engine volume, and spent a blissful hour transforming themselves into superstars.

'Dazzling!' Belle proclaimed as they admired the end result in the mirror. She smiled, starting to feel the familiar tingle of excitement shot through with nervousness that always preceded a performance.

Belle's emotions had been in turmoil ever since she'd discovered that she'd got totally the wrong idea over the dead-dog-comforting-in-practice-room scenario. Yes, she was ecstatically happy that Jack hadn't been snogging Bianca. It was such a relief to know that he hadn't really been doing a Henry VIII on her. But at the same time she was so embarrassed about having made such a stupid mistake that there was no way she could ever bring herself to talk to him again. She was just so mad at herself for messing up her chance to go out with the first boy she'd ever known who gave her that special stomach-fluttering-butterflies feeling . . .

So, girl, she told herself, you're just going to have to get over it and move on. She wasn't going to let her Jack-angst spoil the wedding gig. Nothing could come between Belle and her one true love – the thrill of standing on stage singing in front of an audience. Not even a boy with x-ray eyes.

When they were finally ready, they packed their overnight bags – Holly had arranged permission for them all to stay at her house for the night – and signed out at Mrs Butterworth's desk before setting off in a taxi with Ben and Mason. The boys had obviously not invested quite as much time in their appearance, being dressed, as usual, in black T-shirts and torn jeans.

The reception was in a grand old church hall. It was already teeming with guests in festive mood. Belle soon spotted the bride, Carly, looking like a fairy-tale princess in white silk and lace. She embraced them all and showed them where to set up.

'Stop fussing with the band, Carly! The photographer wants you!' someone shouted.

'That's Greg, my husband!' Carly nodded towards a tall young man with a goatee beard. 'He thinks he's the boss. He'll soon learn, won't he, girls?' she joked.

'Er, Carly, where's Felix?' Holly asked. They'd been expecting him to travel directly from the wedding service with the rest of his family and meet them at the reception.

'Oh, you know what he's like – always late! He said he was popping out to get something he needed for the gig . . .'

Belle felt a cold trickle of anxiety. Where was Felix? They were due to start soon. Everyone else was being all laid-back and go-with-the-flow about it, but she couldn't help worrying; she wanted the gig to be perfect!

Ben tried Felix on his mobile phone, but there was no reply.

Half an hour later, there was still no sign of him. The speeches were over and the wedding guests were beginning to glance expectantly at the stage.

Carly tried Felix's number again, but he still wasn't answering. 'I'll throttle my dear little brother when I see him,' she growled. 'Sorry, guys. We'll just have to start without him,' she said. 'We'll miss our honeymoon if we wait any longer!'

Belle nodded. She was singing lead vocals on the first song anyway, and although it wasn't ideal, she could manage without the support of Felix playing the melody on guitar. Her stomach churning, Belle stepped to the front of the stage, took the microphone and glanced back at the rest of the band. Holly and Cat smiled in encouragement, Ben gave a thumbs-up sign and Mason counted them in.

Belle began to sing. She was in paradise: on stage, microphone in hand, singing her heart out! This was where she was *meant* to be!

Carly and Greg moved onto the dance floor to a round of applause and began to dance. Belle could see the love shining in their eyes and drew on that feeling as she sang, her voice swelling, becoming even stronger and purer. Cat and Holly's harmonies were perfect, and she hardly noticed the missing guitar. After a few moments, others joined the bride and groom, and soon the room was full of couples swaying back and forth – some more than others; there'd been a lot of champagne drunk during the speeches.

As the last note ended, the room erupted with applause. Belle smiled and bowed, thrilled by the whistles and cheers of the enthusiastic audience. She looked round at Cat and Holly, who grinned at her, both radiant with the joy of singing. Mason and Ben were beaming triumphantly too. Belle turned back to the hall to see Carly and Greg in the middle of the dance floor, still smiling up at her and clapping.

Then Belle glanced up at the sound of the door at the back of the hall crashing open. It was Felix! He hobbled in on his crutches, through the throng of guests towards the stage – followed by a man carrying a large chair.

Belle couldn't believe what she was seeing. *Felix went out to get a chair?* But the church hall was full of chairs! They'd already put one out for him . . .

But when Felix and the chair were lifted onto the stage, Belle realized it was no ordinary chair. It was a large, black swivel chair with wheels and a footrest for his ankle. Felix scooted across the stage, did a couple of spins, grabbed the microphone and began to sing the opening lines of the next song on the play-list: *Livin' La Vida Loca* . . .

The crowd cheered and laughed. They seemed to think Felix's late arrival was all part of the act. Belle could only join in as she fell into step with Cat and Holly, clicking her fingers and dancing as they sang their harmonies.

Within seconds the party was jumping! Old aunties in floral dresses were bopping with little boys in page-boy suits; flower girls were dancing around in their long party dresses . . . and at the end of every song the guests went wild and shouted for more.

'I've not had this much fun since the karaoke party!' Belle shouted to Holly and Cat over the noise of the applause. The karaoke was the first time they'd sung together, before they'd even formed Nobody's Angels.

'Me neither!' Holy and Cat chorused back, both glowing with exhilaration.

When they took a break, there was a flurry of hugs and high-fives. 'What's with the chair, man?' Ben asked Felix when they finally sat down with their drinks.

'Wicked, eh?' Felix grinned. 'I got the idea from Mrs Butterworth. I hate not being able to move around the stage. I borrowed it from Uncle Mattie's furniture shop down the road.'

The band took their places on stage for their second set – this time performing their own material, including Nobody's Angels' song, *Done Looking!* The vibrant mambo number went down so well, they played it twice more during the evening. There was more dancing and applause until, finally, the best man took the microphone and thanked them all, rather drunkenly, for making the party rock.

Belle was on a high . . .

And she'd hardly thought about Jack once all day!

CHAPTER THIRTY

Holly: Cheese Toasties and Angelina Ballerina

Holly was still buzzing with excitement as they stood chatting with the boys, waiting for their taxi at the end of the gig.

And when a friend of Felix's father came over and asked if both The Undertow and Nobody's Angels would perform at his company's Christmas party, she thought she would swoon with joy! The company was a well-known advertising agency with trendy offices in Docklands. *Wow!* Holly thought. *How cool would* that *be!*

The boys clearly thought so too. They high-fived and agreed immediately.

Cat jumped up and down, clapping her hands and shouting, '*Yippee!*'

But Holly hesitated. The *Macbeth* production was only a week away and Cat really had to focus on that a hundred per cent now. Would she have time for another gig?

Cat stopped jumping and looked serious for a moment, as if she'd read Holly's thoughts. Then, 'It's

OK,' she said, suddenly grinning. 'The party gig's going to be a week after *Macbeth* – right at the end of term, just before we all go home for the Christmas holiday – and if we can just do the songs we did tonight . . .'

'Yeah, we'll be ladies of leisure by then!' Belle laughed with relief. 'As long as we start rehearsing again the day after *Macbeth*, we'll have plenty of time!'

Holly nodded, her excitement flooding back.

'There's one condition, though!' Belle added, grinning. 'Cat and Felix both have to promise to be *on time*. No West End auditions. No more last-minute furniture-shopping. After two nail-biters this week, my nervous system can't *take* any more!'

'*DEAL!*' they all shouted.

Holly spent the short taxi ride home pointing out the local landmarks in the orange glare of the streetlamps. 'My old school!' she exclaimed. 'The park . . . the shops . . . Miss Toft's dance school . . . my street . . .' It was so much fun to show her friends her own special corner of the world. She knew it was a very ordinary north London kind of a corner, but it was *her* corner, all the same.

It was after eleven o'clock when they pulled up in front of the familiar small red-brick house; warm golden light spilled cosily from the bay windows on each side of the front door. Mum threw open the door and Holly dropped her bag and gave her a huge hug. It was *so* good to be home again!

'Don't you all look fabulous? Aren't you freezing? Are you hungry?' Mum bombarded them with questions as she welcomed them in. She had only met Cat and Belle once, at the party after the gala showcase, but she treated them as if she'd known them all their lives.

'Where's Steve?' Holly asked, once they were settled comfortably round the kitchen table.

Mum smiled as she cleared away a pile of school books she'd been marking. 'Good old Boiler Repair Man has put on his cape and flown off to rescue an old lady with an exploding combi,' she told her.

'My stepdad's a gas-fitter,' Holly explained, in response to Belle's puzzled look. 'A combi's a type of boiler.'

Mum bustled around making hot chocolate and cheese toasties. She joined in the laughter as the girls recounted their latest escapades at school, including Holly's attempt to impersonate Cat as Lady Macbeth. Belle even told the sorry tale of Jack Thorne, Bianca Hayford and little Foo-Foo.

'Oh, yes, the lovely Bianca!' Mum said. 'Holly's told me all about her. There was a girl at my school like that when I was your age. Her name was Felicity Pritchard – a right cow, she was!'

There was a pitter-patter on the stairs. Holly ran to scoop her little brother, Will, up in her arms, all warm and sleepy, in his Thomas the Tank Engine pyjamas. She carried him upstairs and put him back to bed, snuggling her face into his neck – suddenly realizing how much she missed her family when she was away at Superstar High.

Only a few minutes later, the girls were ready for bed themselves.

When Holly opened the door, she saw her bedroom as if for the first time. It was very, very pink, with a border of ballet shoes and ribbons. The walls were plastered with old posters of Kylie Minogue, Beyoncé and Darcey Bussell, and one was covered with dance certificates and photos from her competitions and shows. Fluffy toy animals were piled on the bed. Two extra beds had been made up on air mattresses on the floor – one of them with an old Angelina Ballerina duvet cover she'd not seen for years.

'Sorry, my room's a bit . . . babyish,' Holly said. 'It looks like a five-year-old just moved out!'

Cat laughed. 'It's brilliant, Hols. Bagsy I get the Angelina bed!' She jumped onto the pink duvet printed with little mice in tutus.

'It's perfect,' Belle sighed. 'I wish I had a room like this!' She placed her Louis Vuitton overnight bag on the other airbed and started unpacking, arranging her toiletries on a shelf and laying her neatly folded clothes out for the morning.

Cat caught Holly's eye and laughed. She pulled her pyjamas out of her rucksack and threw them on. 'I'm so tired, I'm not even going to take my make-up off.'

'Yeah, let's live dangerously!' Holly agreed, crawling under her duvet in her pants and T-shirt.

'Sorry, I can't live that dangerously,' Belle said, sitting cross-legged on her bed, holding up a small mirror and delicately wiping her face with cotton wool dipped in cleanser from her selection of matching Clinique bottles.

'Hurry up!' Cat groaned, throwing her Angelina Ballerina pillow at Belle. 'Turn the light out, Hols!'

'Hey, I can't see what I'm doing!' Belle protested. But then she laughed and got into bed. 'If I have spots in the morning, I'll be holding you two personally responsible. Goodnight.'

'G'nigh . . .' Cat murmured.

Holly snuggled down happily in her bed. *Her own bed in her own room!*

'Goodnight,' she said, yawning.

It was a perfect end to a perfect day.

CHAPTER THIRTY-ONE

Holly: The Tragic Tale of Little Foo-Foo

By Monday lunch time, Holly was completely fed up with Bianca Hayford.

Before, Bianca had merely been velcroed to Jack's side; now she seemed to have applied the hot-glue gun and bonded herself permanently in place.

She passed notes to Jack all through the science lesson.

In art, Bianca smudged Madonna's teeth, and was only brought back from the brink of emotional collapse by sitting next to Jack and copying his Nelson Mandela.

In English, when Jack mentioned that his favourite book was *Nineteen Eighty-Four*, Bianca told him that it just happened to be *her* favourite too, and insisted they should write their book review together.

Jack smiled and nodded in response to Bianca's attention-seeking tactics, but he seemed preoccupied, Holly thought, and he kept glancing uncertainly at Belle.

Holly could see that Belle was trying to *rise above it* – but it was clear from the deep frown lines between her eyebrows that she was beginning to *sink beneath it.*

At lunch, Cat grabbed a sandwich and headed off to a *Macbeth* meeting and Belle disappeared to the music library. Holly queued at the baked potato counter in the dining room, mulling over the problem. *It was so frustrating!* Holly was sure Jack and Belle were made for each other, but it was starting to look as if they were doomed *never* to get together. It wasn't Jack's fault – he *had* tried to talk to Belle several times, but she was so embarrassed about the whole affair, she just mumbled excuses and scuttled away whenever he came near. And then, before he had a chance to try again, Bianca would ambush him. Holly didn't blame Jack for being friendly with Bianca either; she *was* the first person he'd met at Superstar High, and he was probably being extra kind to her right now because he thought she was devastated by the death of her little dog.

But, Holly thought, *surely Jack will feel differently if he finds out that Bianca has never even* owned *a dog.*

Holly wasn't *naturally* a suspicious person. But she was convinced that little Foo-Foo was an entirely *mythical beast,* invented by Bianca to dupe Jack into The Kiss and put an end to his romance with Belle.

Bianca didn't even *like* animals – she wouldn't let poor Shreddie near her!

But, without *proof* that Bianca was lying, Holly

couldn't say anything to Jack. She had to just stand by and watch Bianca dig her claws deeper into him, while Belle missed out on her chance of the perfect date!

But as she scanned the dining room for a place to sit, she spied Lettie Atkins at a table by herself and a Great Idea flashed into Holly's mind. Lettie had been friends with Bianca *for ever*. Surely she would know if Bianca had a little canine companion.

Holly sat down next to Lettie. 'Does the name Foo-Foo mean anything to you?' she asked, getting straight to the point with a line she'd picked up from an episode of *The Bill*.

Lettie looked up with a bemused expression, but before she could answer, Bianca, Jack and Mayu joined them – and Bianca immediately started telling them all about what she was planning to wear to the party after *Macbeth* on Saturday night, which totally put paid to Holly's investigations.

The afternoon's singing class with Mr Garcia was just as bad. Or rather, the class was fine, but Bianca continued to cling to Jack's side – like an FBI bodyguard prepared to leap out and take a bullet for him at any moment. And as they left the class, Bianca foiled Holly's second attempt to interrogate Lettie by dragging her (and Jack, of course) off to the library on some supposedly urgent book-returning errand.

Later, Holly was in her room, flicking through a new dancewear catalogue and chatting with Gemma about the thrilling prospect of the *Nutcracker Sweeties* production next term. They were both wearing their *pointe* shoes under thick socks; following Miss Morgan's advice to wear them as slippers to soften the glue and help shape them to their feet.

'I feel like a penguin in wellies in these!' Gemma said as she hobbled across the room.

Holly giggled, and then jumped up as she heard the door across the corridor banging shut. Lettie must be setting off for her six-o'clock piano practice.

At last – a chance to speak to her alone!

But when Holly peeped out, Lettie was disappearing down the corridor, hand-in-hand with Nick Taggart. *'Piano practice' seems to be taking on a whole new meaning these days*, she thought. She was about to go and share this latest snippet of gossip with Cat and Belle . . .

. . . but then she had a radical idea.

She would confront Bianca directly.

Before she could change her mind, Holly knocked on Bianca's door and marched – or rather *waddled* – in. Her stomach knotted with anxiety as she entered the room she had once shared with Bianca.

'What do *you* want?' Bianca snapped, barely looking

212

up from writing a text message. 'Not your room any more, in case you'd forgotten.'

OK, here goes, Holly told herself. 'Bianca, your dog . . .'

'Foo-Foo? What about him?'

'It's just that I didn't even know you *had* a dog . . .'

'Yeah, well, *newsflash* for you,' Bianca said sarcastically. 'I don't tell *you* all my personal secrets!'

'Er, a dog's not exactly a *personal secret*,' Holly pointed out. 'How did Foo-Foo die?'

Bianca stared at her hands for a long moment, as if mustering the strength to talk about it. Then she took a deep breath. 'Well, if you must know,' she gulped, 'it was c-c-can—' And with that her face crumpled and she burst into tears, unable to finish the terrible word.

'Cancer?' Holly whispered.

Bianca nodded. 'The vet tried everything,' she sniffed, 'but they couldn't save him, and Mum said it was better for him not to suffer, and . . . and . . . and . . .' Tears were flowing down her face now.

Holly felt dreadful for doubting her. Surely even Bianca couldn't just produce tears like turning on a tap – unless she happened to have a pile of chopped onions stashed under her pillow. And *no one* would lie about something as serious as cancer, would they? Holly realized, with a terrible pang of guilt, that

Bianca must have been telling the truth about Foo-Foo all along.

She sat down on the edge of the bed and tried to put her arm round Bianca's heaving shoulders, but Bianca shrugged her away.

'I'm so sorry, I – I didn't mean to upset you . . .' Holly stammered.

'Well, you've brought on one of my headaches,' Bianca complained, kneading her temples.

'Would you like some water?' Holly offered. 'I could ask Miss Candlemas for some paracetamol.'

'Are you trying to kill me now? You *know* I'm allergic to paracetamol!'

'Sorry, I forgot,' Holly muttered, backing out of the door. Bianca was allergic to so many things, it was hard to keep track. But one thing Holly hadn't forgotten from her time as Bianca's room-mate – it was not a good idea to stick around when Bianca had a headache.

Holly fled straight to Cat and Belle's room and told them what had just happened. 'So I was wrong,' she said. 'Little Foo-Foo really *did* die!'

'I still don't buy it,' Cat insisted, folding her arms resolutely.

Holly shook her head. 'If you'd seen her, you'd believe it.'

'OK, I believe *you*,' Cat conceded. 'But it doesn't change the fact that she made the most of it by snuggling up to Jack, just where she knew Belle was going to see them. If anything happened to my dog, Duffy, I'd be on the next train home, not weeping in the arms of the nearest gorgeous boy.'

'And you're sure it wasn't just another of Bianca's acts?' Belle asked suspiciously.

'Sure!' Holly replied.

No one could be *that* good an actress . . .

Could they?

CHAPTER THIRTY-TWO

Cat: Cappuccino and the Meaning of Life

At last it was Saturday, the Big Day – the day of the *Macbeth* performance.

The final dress rehearsal had gone smoothly. No one forgot their lines or missed their cue. The music and sound-effects, scenery and costumes were perfect.

Duncan Gillespie hugged them all. 'The curse has finally lifted!' He laughed. 'As long as no one says the M-word again!'

Even Mr Sharpe was smiling as he gathered everyone on stage – actors, stage crew, wardrobe and props managers, lighting and sound engineers – for a final team talk. 'If William Shakespeare were here today . . . '

'He'd be a very smelly four-hundred-year-old corpse,' Nick whispered. Cat suppressed a giggle: this was *serious*.

'He'd be *proud*,' Mr Sharpe continued, the light on his glasses more a kindly twinkle than a blinding flash today. 'Well done, everyone!'

'Indubitably,' Mr Grampian added. 'An auspicious beginning to a momentous occasion . . .'

'And remember, the Shakespeare production is one of the most important events in our entire calendar,' Mr Sharpe reminded them. 'The reputation of the Garrick is in *your* hands tonight . . .'

So, Cat thought, *no pressure then!*

After checking that her costumes were ready for the evening's performance, she wandered across the courtyard with Nathan. Distant shouts drifted over from a football match on the sports field. Holly would be there watching Ethan play. Belle had gone to help Serena print out the *Macbeth* programmes. The sun was shining in a pale blue winter sky, but Cat was uneasy. Of course she was nervous about tonight, but it was more than that. A strange sensation was gnawing at her stomach.

'Café Roma for lunch?' Nathan suggested.

Cat knew that the gnawing feeling was definitely not hunger – she was far too nervous to eat – but a coffee would be perfect . . .

'What's wrong?' Nathan asked, when they'd been sitting at a corner table in the warm café for several minutes. 'You've been staring into that cappuccino as if it holds the key to the Meaning of Life!'

'Oh, sorry, Nate,' Cat murmured. She'd finally identified the gnawing feeling. 'I feel ashamed of myself,' she said quietly.

Nathan's eyes widened behind his glasses.

'It's OK.' Cat smiled at his shocked expression. 'I've not stolen the Crown Jewels or anything!'

'You've not been putting rude comments about Mrs Salmon on RateMyTeachers dot com, have you?' Nathan joked.

Cat grinned. 'Ooh! Don't put ideas into my head!' Then she was solemn again. 'Thing is, I've really upset my mum . . .'

Nate nodded, sipped his coffee and waited for her to continue.

'We've hardly spoken to each other since I stormed out of the *Bugsy Malone* audition,' Cat sighed. 'I texted her about the play tonight, and she hasn't even replied. She must be so angry she doesn't want to come. I *thought* I didn't care, but I do. Mum's always been there to support me before – I just *wish* she could see how important it is to me to be a serious actress . . .'

'Have you got your phone with you now?' Nathan asked.

'Yeah, of course,' Cat said, 'but I checked a minute ago. There's no message.'

'Phone your mother,' Nathan said. 'Just speak to her, Cat.'

'But . . . I can't!' Cat moaned. 'I feel so *guilty* – and we'd probably end up just yelling at each other again . . . '

Nathan stirred his coffee. 'Don't leave it too late,' he said quietly. 'My mother died in a car crash when I was eight years old. There are many things I wish I'd said . . .'

Cat swallowed her mouthful of coffee. The hot liquid burned her throat. 'Oh, Nathan, I'm so sorry,' she said, reaching out to touch his hand. 'I had no idea.' No wonder he was so convincing when he played the part of Macduff finding out that his family had been killed – *he was drawing on his own experience.* Tears were pricking at her eyes.

Nathan smiled bravely. 'It's OK. It was a long time ago.'

Cat felt *terrible.* There she was, whingeing on about some pathetic little quarrel with her mum, when Nathan didn't even *have* a mother any more – somehow it put everything into perspective. 'You're right, Nate,' she said, suddenly making up her mind. 'I need to get over myself and make the call!' She took her phone out of her pocket and dialled home. Her sister, Fiona, answered.

'Is Mum there, Fi?' Cat asked.

'Yeah, she's just coming. She's been really miserable,' Fiona whispered. 'Says you're pushing her out of your life . . .'

Now Cat felt even worse!

'Yes?' Mum's voice sounded unusually stiff. 'Catrin?'

'Mum,' Cat said, swallowing hard, 'I'm sorry. I didn't mean to push you away. I just . . . need to do some things my own way.'

There was a silence. For an awful moment Cat thought her mum had hung up. But then she heard a little sniffle. 'I'm sorry too, dear. I know I've been bossy — it's just I want *so much* for you . . .'

'I know,' Cat gulped. 'So will you come and see me in *Macbeth* tonight?'

'I was worried you didn't really *want* me to come—'

'Of course I want you to come,' Cat replied. 'This is *huge* for me. There'll be agents and critics in the audience and everything. I couldn't do it without *you* there!'

Mum's voice sounded a whole lot brighter as she replied, 'Of course I'll be there, darling!'

Cat hung up and smiled at Nathan as they got up from their table to leave. 'Thanks, Nate. I can't tell you how much better I feel now!' She hugged him warmly. 'You're a truly special friend, you know,' she whispered.

Nathan grinned and wiped a tear from her eye. 'You too,' he mumbled.

'Uh-oh!' Cat said as she turned to see Bianca and Mayu standing in the doorway, mouths hanging open. 'I think we've just provided next week's school gossip!

'Hello, girls! Table for two free in the corner now!' she chirped as she and Nathan squeezed past on their way out.

For once Bianca and Mayu were speechless.

Cat threw back her head and laughed, feeling the delicate winter sun warm her face. She was on top of the world again. 'Race you back to school!' she shouted over her shoulder to Nathan, setting off across the square.

She leaped up the steps three at a time, neck and neck with him. As they bolted into the entrance hall, Cat spotted Holly and Belle sitting on the big leather sofa.

'End-of-term reports,' Holly called, waving an envelope. 'It's only a week until the Christmas holidays!'

Cat said goodbye to Nathan, took her report from her pigeon hole and joined the other two on the sofa. 'Your report OK?' she asked Holly.

'Yeah, fine,' Holly replied. 'Miss Morgan's given me some really nice comments.'

'And I bet Belle's is the usual Picture of Perfection?'

Belle looked down modestly, but Holly grinned. 'Of course – A-stars all over the place!'

Cat opened her report quickly to get it over with. '*A mixed bag*, I think you'd call it!' Her school subjects included some Bs and Cs, with only one A, for English, and a rather embarrassing D for science. But Mr Grampian had written almost an entire page of praise for her work in acting classes and *Macbeth*.

And, in the end, as far as Cat was concerned, that was all that mattered!

That, and the fact she had a show to do tonight.

She was more nervous than she'd ever been about anything in her life.

But she couldn't wait!

CHAPTER THIRTY-THREE

Holly: Lavender Oil, Raspberry Ripple and Polos

Holly settled into the seat next to Gemma. The Redgrave Theatre was rapidly filling up with smartly dressed people – all anticipating a fabulous performance of . . . *The Scottish Play*. No one would dare even *think* the M-word in the theatre tonight!

A small party of butterflies was having a little sympathy-flutter in her stomach. What if Cat or Ethan or Nathan forgot their lines, or Belle missed her cue? What if Lettie's music didn't play or Nick's sound-effects squawked? What if one of Serena and Lucy's costumes fell apart and left an actor standing in their underwear? *So many things could go wrong!* But *nothing* must go wrong. This was a big chance for her friends – especially Cat – to shine and show their Star Quality in front of all these important people. It was almost more nerve-racking than being up on stage herself.

It'll be my chance next term, Holly thought excitedly. She was determined to win a part in the Dance Department's *Nutcracker Sweeties*.

Then Gemma nudged her elbow as they heard a woman's voice behind them. 'I hope Bianca has remembered her lavender oil. She gets so stressed out before a big performance, poor lamb . . .'

'That must be Bianca's mother!' Gemma whispered.

Holly nodded. 'No one but her mother could call Bianca a *poor lamb*.'

She couldn't resist turning to look. She saw a statuesque woman in a severe black and white tailored dress, with the same platinum-blonde hair and ice-blue eyes as Bianca, sitting next to a short, round man in a pinstripe suit. *He must be Bianca's father, head of the Hayford baby-food empire*, Holly realized.

On impulse, she smiled and introduced herself.

'Pleased to meet you,' Mrs Hayford replied, not looking *terribly* pleased.

'I've seen some of the rehearsals. Bianca is brilliant as Hecate,' Holly persisted.

Bianca's mother thawed a little. 'Thank you. Yes, Bianca is an *exceptionally* talented actress . . .'

Holly suddenly remembered how upset Bianca had been about little Foo-Foo. Losing a pet must be awful for the whole family. She felt she *had* to say something. 'I'm so sorry about Bianca's little dog,' she said. 'Poor Foo-Foo—'

'*Dog?*' Mrs Hayford wrinkled her nose in disgust, as

if Holly had suggested that Bianca owned a colony of dung beetles or a pet tarantula. 'Bianca's never had a *dog*! In fact, she's hated dogs ever since . . .'

'. . . she was nipped by a rogue shih-tzu when she was five,' Mr Hayford finished for her.

'In a very delicate place,' Bianca's mother added, pursing her lips. 'She couldn't sit down for weeks.'

'Oh, dear,' Holly murmured. 'I must have been thinking of someone else.' She turned away to hide the giggles that were threatening to erupt, and refused to meet Gemma's eye. Gemma had obviously heard the conversation and was also quivering with suppressed laughter. But for Holly, Bianca's unfortunate encounter with the shih-tzu wasn't the only thing that was plastering a huge grin across her face – it was the realization that Bianca had invented the entire Foo-Foo's-gone-to-the-Great-Poodle-Parlour-in-the-Sky story after all – just as she had first suspected.

Bianca had tricked Jack.

And she'd tricked Holly into feeling guilty for doubting her.

Mrs Hayford was right – Bianca was an *exceptionally* talented actress!

The lights went down and spine-chilling cello music filled the theatre. Soon Holly was totally swept up in the dark, menacing mood of the play. It opened with the three witches in a thunderstorm, plotting their fateful encounter with Macbeth, '*When shall we three meet again . . .*' and the action was soon hurtling towards the crucial scene where Macbeth and Lady Macbeth murder King Duncan in his sleep.

Everything went perfectly. Ethan was gorgeous and noble as Banquo, even *after* he was murdered and appeared as a ghost. Belle delivered her Messenger lines beautifully. Nathan was great as Macduff. But it was Cat who really stole the show, stunning in her red and black outfit – ruthless, determined and very, very dangerous. Holly was overjoyed, and proud of all of them!

At the end of Act Three, the curtain went down for the intermission. There was a moment's silence as the audience returned from the murky world of witches and ghosts to the reality of queuing for drinks and ice creams.

But Holly was a girl with a mission more pressing even than a tub of raspberry ripple. The information she'd gleaned from Bianca's parents was too important to keep to herself for a second longer! She stole down the steps and out through the fire exit, taking a short cut to the dressing rooms at the back of the stage. She found Belle in the room she shared with the other girls playing minor parts, adjusting a lace on her tunic.

'Quick, Belle,' Holly whispered. 'Come with me to Cat's room. I've got something to tell you, and Cat won't want to miss it!'

Frowning with curiosity, Belle followed Holly along the passage. Holly knocked and entered to find Cat changing costumes, ready for the sleepwalking scene. 'What's up?' she asked as she popped her head out of the top of a long white nightgown.

'OK, news just in,' Holly announced. 'I've spoken to Bianca's parents. *Foo-Foo didn't die!*'

'You mean . . . they saved him?' Belle asked, her eyes wide with surprise. 'Like, from a coma or something?'

'*No-o-o.* I mean Foo-Foo didn't *die* because he never even *existed* in the first place. Bianca made the whole thing up. She tricked Jack.'

Cat and Belle both stared at Holly in amazement. 'Are you sure?' Belle gasped.

She nodded. 'Absolutely!'

Cat laughed. 'Wow! Amazing! Bianca is an even better actress than we thought.'

'Not as good as you though! You were brilliant, Cat!' Holly said, suddenly remembering that Cat was in the middle of a vitally important play and still had a scene to do. 'Now we'll leave you in peace and talk later . . .'

She dragged Belle out of Cat's dressing room into

the corridor. 'Belle, now we know Bianca was tricking Jack, why don't you go and talk to him?' she suggested.

'Er, well, maybe . . . I'll think about it . . .' Belle's voice trailed off.

Holly looked up and saw Jack buying mints at the vending machine. She turned to give Belle an encouraging no-time-like-the-present smile. They were even dressed in identical Messenger costumes. This was obviously the perfect romantic moment.

But Belle had disappeared!

This is ridiculous! Holly thought. She was going to have to tell Jack about Bianca's trickery or these two were never going to make it to the Tower of London! But then she hesitated. Would telling Jack be the right thing to do? She had a high-speed debate with her conscience. If someone she thought was a good friend had deceived her, would she want to know about it? *Yes, she would!* But was she interfering? *Yes, she was!* But if Belle and Cat hadn't interfered in *her* love life, she might never have got together with Ethan . . .

Holly reached a decision just as Jack looked up. 'Jack,' she said, 'can I talk to you for a moment?'

'Sure.' He grinned, slouching against the machine and offering her a Polo.

Holly went over and checked for eavesdroppers before speaking very quietly, 'Bianca was lying to you about the dog . . .' she began, and quickly recounted the whole story.

Jack stared at her in silence throughout. 'I can't believe it!' he said, rubbing his forehead.

'I'm sorry. I wouldn't have told you if I wasn't certain,' Holly explained.

'No, I mean I just can't get my head round it! I knew Bianca had a bit of a thing about Belle. But I thought it was just, you know, friendly rivalry.'

'Yeah, like Harry Potter had a friendly rivalry with Voldemort!' Holly laughed grimly.

'But I never realized Bianca could stoop so low. She's been lying to me all along to get my sympathy!'

'So maybe you could try talking to Belle again?' Holly coaxed.

Jack kicked the base of the vending machine in exasperation. 'Chance would be a fine thing! She's acting as if I've got rabies or something. I can't get near her.'

Holly nodded. That was certainly true! But she was sure that if she could just bypass Belle's force-field of embarrassment and get them alone in the same room together for five minutes, everything would work out . . .

Suddenly she came to another decision. *Now I've*

started down this matchmaker route, I may as well go the whole hog, she thought. 'Meet us in Cat's dressing room straight after the play,' she whispered.

Jack shrugged. 'OK, but don't hold your breath. Belle will probably climb out the window when she sees me.'

My work here is done! Holly thought as she slipped back into the theatre and found her seat, accepting the slightly melted ice cream that Gemma offered her.

The house lights dimmed and the Witches' sinister theme music struck up again.

Holly smiled happily.

There was no window in Cat's dressing room!

CHAPTER THIRTY-FOUR

Cat: The Best Feeling in the World

Cat took a deep breath and stepped out on stage again.

She *was* Lady Macbeth.

She stumbled across the stage in her ghostly white nightgown, trying to wash away the blood of King Duncan. *But the blood kept coming back.* She could tell from that special, magical theatre-silence that the audience was spellbound. Everyone could *see* the blood – a red spotlight playing across her hands – just as Lady Macbeth could see it in her tormented hallucination. '*Here's the smell of the blood still . . .*'

After her scene, Cat waited in the wings for the play to end, in a limbo of suspended elation. As the final curtain fell, she could hear the swell of applause. The curtain rose and everyone ran onstage to take their bows. Finally it was her turn. Catching Luke's eye, she jogged out to join him centre stage, took his hand, walked forward and . . .

. . . the applause grew louder and louder as they

raised their hands and bowed. Louder still, with cheers and whistles, and then there was movement. *It was a standing ovation.*

Suddenly Mr Sharpe and Mr Fortune were standing on either side of her, placing bouquets in her arms.

Hardly able to breathe, Cat scanned the rows of smiling faces. Mum had promised to come, but Cat hadn't been able to spot her in the audience yet. She could see Holly and Gemma . . . And then she saw her. Mum was standing on her chair to see over the crowd, clapping and cheering. And there was Fiona, waving from her wheelchair in the aisle, and Dad and Danny and Kieran too.

They had all come to see her!

Cat was overflowing with joy and pride. The hard work, the nerves, *the treadmill* – it was all worth it for this moment! She knew she had given the performance of her life and that she was one step nearer to her dream of becoming a superstar.

A serious, classical Shakespearean superstar, of course!

This was the best feeling in the world!

When Cat arrived back at her dressing room, Holly and Belle were already waiting to scoop her up in a celebratory group hug.

There was a knock at the door.

'Oh, hello,' Cat panted, a little surprised to see Jack. 'Come in and join the celebrations!'

Jack stepped hesitantly into the room, the door swinging shut behind him. Belle stood there, frozen to the spot, a *bedazzled* look on her face.

Suddenly Cat felt her elbow being grabbed. 'Come on, Cat,' Holly said. 'We've got to go. I just remembered that really important . . . er, important *thing* we've got to do . . .'

'N-no, don't go,' Belle stammered.

'Oh yes, *that* really important thing . . .' Cat grinned, suddenly catching onto Holly's cunning plan. 'Yep, off we go . . .'

As she pulled open the door, Bianca almost fell into the room on top of her – she must have been crouching outside with her eye pressed to the keyhole.

'*Jack!*' Bianca called, in a voice like a rapier dipped in honey, as she jostled past Cat and Holly. 'Whatever are you doing in *here*? My parents are dying to meet you . . .'

'Er, no thanks,' Jack replied, without even turning to look at her. 'I'm busy right now.'

'Come on, Ja-a-a-ck – I thought we were best friends . . .' Bianca wheedled.

'Yeah, so did I,' Jack replied coldly. 'Shut the door on your way out, would you, Bianca?'

Cat was flabbergasted. Jack usually obeyed Bianca's every wish! Bianca was obviously just as shocked. She stepped back to join them in the corridor, shutting the door as if in a trance.

'You told him?' Cat whispered.

Holly nodded.

'What *precisely* did you tell him?' Bianca demanded.

'Oh, just something interesting your parents said. About Foo-Foo,' Holly replied innocently.

'*You . . . you . . . you . . .*' Bianca spluttered, her face contorting with rage at being caught out in her lies. Cat hadn't seen anything so scary since the New Zealand rugby team doing the haka.

'Ah, there you are, Cat!' came a cheery voice.

Cat turned to see her mum click–clacking towards her in her high heels, as bright as a budgie in an extravagant blue and orange silk dress. 'You were *tremendous*, darling. *Everyone's* talking about how *fabulous* you were!' she crowed, her eyes swimming with tears of pride. 'Ooh, give us a hug,' she said, enveloping Cat in her arms and squeezing her tight. 'My little star!'

'Little?' Cat laughed, resting her chin on the top of Mum's red curls. Out of the corner of her eye she noticed Bianca turn on her heel and march off down the corridor.

'I'm sorry, darling,' Mum gulped. 'I was being a pushy old dragon – I can see that now. This is where you belong. I'm so proud of you.'

'No, *I'm* sorry, Mum, for . . . well, being a stroppy cow,' Cat told her, holding back tears. It felt so good to be back on the same side again.

'Now, come on, let's get to the after-show party,' Mum said. 'I've left Fiona with Dad and the boys. I couldn't get her chair down the steps. Heaven knows where they'll end up! You know your dad couldn't find his way out of a paper bag . . .'

'You go on ahead, Mum. I'll catch you up.' Cat pointed at her Lady Macbeth white nightgown. 'It's not a pyjama party. I'll have to change.' She turned to Holly and grinned. 'And I think my dressing room's going to be occupied for a few minutes.'

CHAPTER THIRTY-FIVE

Belle: The Time of Our Lives

Trapped!

Jack was standing in front of the door and there was no window. Belle stared at the floor, tempted to start tunnelling with her bare hands.

She had avoided being alone with Jack since the awful moment she'd seen him with Bianca in the practice room. Belle knew she'd treated him appallingly. She'd jumped to conclusions and assumed the worst about him, and then ignored him for weeks. She'd behaved like a neurotic little drama-queen. And now she didn't know what to say for herself. On a scale of embarrassment from one to ten, this was one hundred!

But unless she wanted to end her days imprisoned in this dressing room, she was going to have to make a move. The quickest way out, she decided, would be to mutter an apology and then make a dash for the door.

'I'm really sorry . . .' Belle muttered.

'I'm really sorry . . .' Jack said at exactly the same moment.

They both stopped and laughed awkwardly.

Belle looked up. Jack was leaning against the door, hands in pockets, smiling at her. His clear hazel eyes were searing deep into her soul, but she forced herself to meet his gaze and hold it. Somehow she couldn't help smiling too.

Jack stepped forward, and as if hypnotized, Belle took a step forward too. And another.

'Am I forgiven?' Jack asked softly.

'It was all my fault,' Belle said.

'Would you still like to go to the Tower of London?'

'And ice-skating!' Belle nodded. 'Yes, please.' Was she dreaming? she wondered. After all this time, it was so easy to talk to each other . . . Why had she waited so long?

'Tomorrow afternoon?' Jack said, smiling.

'Tomorrow afternoon!' Belle agreed.

They both took another step forward. The air between them fizzed and crackled like static electricity. They were standing very close together now, eyes still locked.

And then, somehow, they were kissing.

Belle closed her eyes. She felt as if she were dissolving from the inside out. It was like sparklers and bonfires and singing and ice-skating all rolled into one.

Suddenly she became aware of a commotion, and jumped away from Jack just as the door crashed open to admit a boisterous crowd: Nick, Lettie, Nathan, Holly, Cat, Ethan, Luke, Lucy, Serena – all the friends who'd been involved in *Macbeth*, including some of the audience, like Felix, Zak and Gemma.

Belle felt her face burning and her mouth seemed stuck in a huge slice-of-watermelon grin. Everyone must know exactly what she and Jack had been doing, as surely as if she had SNOG-FEST tattooed across her forehead. She braced herself for comments, but to her surprise, no one teased her. They were all too busy high-fiving and hugging and congratulating each other on the resounding success of the play.

Belle turned to the mirror and picked up a brush, as if intent on tidying her hair. She studied her reflection. Her face was a little pink, but otherwise fairly well under control.

Nick came over and stood next to her. 'You really *nailed* that First Messenger part,' he said, grinning into the mirror. 'The way you delivered that line, *The king comes here tonight!* Genius! And some critics might argue with me here,' he continued, in pompous, theatre-critic tones, 'but *I* think leaving the suit of armour off was a good call. Controversial, perhaps, but there you go!'

Belle laughed. 'Glad you liked it! Your music was amazing, Lettie' she added as their friend came and joined them.

Nick beamed proudly. 'It was, wasn't it?' He draped his arm across Lettie's shoulders and she gazed up at him with her serious brown eyes.

Suddenly Ethan was rapping on a Coke can for attention. 'Let's hear it for Cat, the greatest Lady Macbeth you ever saw!' he cried.

Everyone cheered enthusiastically.

Somehow Cat had managed to change out of her nightgown into her party dress behind the costume rail. She cleared her throat. 'Ahem! I need to say some thank-yous. Firstly to some boys – apparently they can be useful *sometimes* . . . So, Ethan Reed for *time-management therapy*, Nathan Almeida for *family therapy*, and Jack Thorne for fainting at exactly the right moment. But my biggest thank-you goes to Holly – the greatest Lady Macbeth you *never* saw!'

There was laughter, and befuddled looks from those who knew nothing of Holly's narrow escape in the rehearsal. But everyone cheered anyway. Holly bowed and tucked her braids behind her ears. Ethan gave her a hug.

'Come on!' Nick shouted. 'It's *p-a-a-a-r-ty time*! In the dining room!'

As people started to leave, Belle felt someone squeeze her hand.

'See you at the party,' Jack whispered. 'And *tomorrow*, of course.' He turned and winked, before following Ethan out of the door.

Soon only Cat and Holly were left in the dressing room with Belle. 'So?' Cat demanded. 'Spill!'

Belle grinned, still a little dazed. 'It must be a world record.' She laughed. 'We got to kiss and make up *before* we even went on a first date! Thank you,' she added. 'Both of you. Even though that was a *terrible* bit of acting – *Just remembered that important thing we have to do!*'

'You're welcome!' Holly and Cat chorused.

'How can I ever repay you?' Belle wondered.

'Well, for a start,' Cat told her as they left the theatre, 'by not setting your alarm clock tomorrow morning. Being a leading lady, a time-management expert *and* a matchmaker is exhausting. I'm looking forward to a big fat lie-in.'

'Sorry . . .' Holly sighed, shaking her head. 'We've got band practice tomorrow morning with The Undertow boys. We've got that Christmas party gig coming up, remember?'

Belle grinned. 'It's OK, Cat. That's meant to start at nine thirty. Translated into Felix-Baddeley-time, that'll be more like ten. And it'll have to be over by midday – some of us have *dates* to go on!'

Cat laughed. 'The life of a superstar! It's just work, work, work . . .'

Arm in arm, Belle, Cat and Holly crossed the courtyard and stepped into the entrance hall. Loud dance music and a hubbub of chatter were spilling out from the dining room on the other side of the hall. Through the open doors Belle glimpsed Cat's family waving and beckoning them to join the party.

Then Belle noticed three figures sitting on the girls' favourite leather sofa in the hall. She nudged the other two and they all looked across to see Mr Grampian, Mr Garcia and Miss Morgan deep in conversation over their cups of coffee.

'*Next term . . . really spectacular . . . involving all three departments . . .*' Mr Garcia was saying. It was hard *not* to overhear his booming voice, even if you weren't eavesdropping shamelessly. Which Belle was, of course.

'Don't you think you're being a little ambitious, Enrico?' Miss Morgan warned. 'The Dance Department has *Nutcracker Sweeties* coming up as well . . .'

'Ah, but my dear Drusilla, where would we be in

this world without ambition?' Mr Grampian asked dramatically.

Belle looked at Cat and Holly and they all smiled. 'Something really *big* next term?' Belle said.

Holly nodded. 'I can't wait to find out what it is!'

'And be a part of it,' Cat whispered.

'All of us!' Belle agreed. She could hardly contain her excitement.

And then she noticed the magnificent Christmas tree that had appeared next to the grand staircase. It was festooned with gold and red tinsel and baubles and sparkled with hundreds of fairy lights. She suddenly realized that there were only a few more days until the Christmas holidays. Cat and Holly would be going home to their families, and Belle . . . Well, for once she was really looking forward to the holiday: Mum had promised to take the whole three weeks off work and they were going to stay in a ski chalet in Chamonix, and then perhaps do some shopping together in Paris . . .

She wondered where Jack would be for Christmas. Well, she would have plenty of time to ask him tomorrow. *She couldn't wait!*

'Stop wobbling it, Joyce, for goodness' sake!' Mrs Butterworth cried, scooting out from behind the tree and bellowing at Miss Candlemas, who was clutching the base of a very tall ladder.

'I am not *wobbling* it, Norma!' Miss Candlemas snapped back. 'I told you we should have done this *before* we decorated.'

Ignoring her, Mrs B craned her neck and peered upwards. 'Left a bit – no, *left!*' she yelled.

Belle looked up to see Mr Fortune balanced on the highest rung of the ladder, attaching an enormous gold star to the top of the tree.

She glanced at Cat and Holly, who were also gazing up at the star, the flickering tree lights reflected in their shining eyes.

'Having a good time at the party, girls?' Mr Fortune called down.

'*We're having the time of our lives!*' Cat called back.

Belle's heart skipped a beat as she caught sight of Jack, smiling at her from the dining-room doorway.

Cat was right. It *was* the time of their lives.

And the party was just getting started!

★★★★★★★★★★★★★★★★★★★★★★★★★★★★★★★★★★★★★★★

TURN OVER FOR TOP TIPS ON BEING A SUPERSTAR

★★★★★★★★★★★★★★★★★★★★★★★★★★★★★★★★★★★★★★★

TEN TIPS FOR STAYING ON TOP!

How *you* can manage your life
to become – and stay – a superstar . . .

★ Life as a superstar is often jam-packed – practice, rehearsals, classes. It's always useful to make a list of things you need to get done, put them in order of importance and work through them. It will feel really good when you get to the end of the list and everythings ticked off!

★ Try and remember that however busy you are, you have to make some time to relax. No superstar can keep going all day, every day. Take a tip from Belle and try a bit of yoga before bed, or chill out and listen to music – whatever works for you.

★ If it really feels like everything is getting on top of you and things are too much, make sure you talk to somebody you can trust. Whether it's a teacher, parent or friend, it helps to have someone to listen and help you work it out.

★ When things seem stressful, try not to take it out on anybody else. Good friends are really important. If you feel you're about to snap, take a deep breath and count to ten before you speak!

★ Try and make the most of the time you do have. Unless you've definitely set an hour aside for a chill-out session, use it wisely. You could listen to a song you need to learn while you're in the bath, for example, or maybe do some homework while you're not needed in rehearsals – there are ways to fit things in.

★ Sleep is important for every superstar, especially a busy one! If you need to wake up early to get something done, then make sure you go to bed early to catch up on sleep – no superstar looks great with bags under their eyes!

★ Learn how to say no! You can't agree to everything – you just don't have time! If you've been asked to do something you really don't want to do or don't have time for, then don't agree to it just to keep everybody happy. If you explain politely, they're sure to understand.

★ When you're busy, it can be easy to let things slip so that they're not up to your usual high standards. Remember that even though you're busy, everything still needs to be done to superstar standard! So take the time you need to do things properly.

★ There are times when things will seem too tough. It's important to stay calm. Do what any good superstar would do – put your head up, your shoulders back, take a deep breath and smile!

★ When you're struggling with your workload, try to remember that every superstar has gone through the rigorous training and endless practice. The route to stardom is hard work! You will make it – just believe in yourself and persevere!

Bindi Babes
by **Narinder Dhami**

Meet the coolest chicks on the block . . .

These girls have been through tough times, but now that
they've got their perfect world sorted, the one fashion
accessory they don't need is an interfering live-in auntie
trying to cramp their style.

Bring on the collective power of the Bindi Babes! Nothing
in life, not even their formidable auntie-ji, can stop these
sisters . . . can it?

'A fresh voice and fun characters that girls will love'
Jacqueline Wilson

ISBN: 978 0 440 86512 4

The Lady Grace Mysteries:
Assassin
by Grace Cavendish

MURDER AT COURT!

One suitor dead with a knife in his back, and another
under suspicion . . . Can Lady Grace, Queen Elizabeth's
favourite Maid of Honour, solve the mystery and bring
order back to the Queen's Court?

Open up the daybooke of Lady Grace for a tale of daggers,
death and a very daring girl . . .

'A gripping historical thriller'
Sunday Times

ISBN: 978 1 862 30376 8

Best Friends
by Jacqueline Wilson

Alice is my best friend.
I don't know what I'd do without her.

Gemma and Alice have been best friends since they were
born. It never seems to matter that Gemma loves football
while Alice prefers drawing or that Gemma never stops
talking while Alice is more likely to be listening.
They share everything.

Then one day Gemma finds out that there's something
Alice isn't sharing. A secret. And when Gemma discovers
what it is, she isn't sure if she and Alice can stay Best
Friends Forever . . .

ISBN: 978 0 440 86851 4

Witch Baby and Me
by Debi Gliori

My life is in ruins.

Here's why:
★ I have a baby sister called Daisy. She's not a baby baby, she's a witch baby.
★ Only I know this (that she's a witch baby). Everyone else thinks she's sweet and adorable.
★ Daisy's summonded up an invisible dog called Way Woof to be her pet. People can smell him but they can't see him – so they think the smell is me.

But the worst of all is:
★ Mum and Dad have decided that we're moving house. To the far, far North of Scotland. Which means I'll never see my friends again!

'I can't recommend this story highly enough for lovers of magic, humour or even books.
A wicked triumph'
Eoin Colfer

ISBN: 978 0 552 55676 7